Iain Philpott

About the Author

LISA JEWELL is in her thirties and was born and raised in north London, where she lives with her husband and their daughter, Amelie May. She worked as a secretary before redundancy, a bet, and a book deal took her away from all that. She is the author of four other bestsellers: *Ralph's Party, Thirtynothing, One-Hit Wonder,* and *A Friend of the Family.*

Vince and Joy

LISA JEWELL

HARPER

NEW YORK • LONDON • TORONTO • SYDNEY

HARPER

A hardcover edition of this book was published in Great Britain in 2005 by Penguin Books, a division of the Penguin Group.

HarperCollins books may be purchased for educational, business, or sales promotional use. For information please write: Special Markets Department, HarperCollins Publishers, 10 East 53rd Street, New York, NY 10022.

First Harper paperback published 2006.

Library of Congress Cataloging-in-Publication Data

Jewell, Lisa
    Vince and Joy: a novel / Lisa Jewell.
       p.   cm.
    ISBN-10: 0-06-113746-4
    ISBN-13: 978-0-06-113746-4
      1. First loves—Fiction. 2. Man-woman—Fiction.
3. Reunions—Fiction. 4. England—Fiction. I. Title.

PR6060.E95V46 2006
823'.914—dc22   2006041202

06 07 08 09 10 RRD 10 9 8 7 6 5 4 3 2 1

For Jascha and Amelie, my happy ending.

Acknowledgements

Thank you, as ever, to Judith and Sarah. My books would all be unfinished and unpublished if you two didn't have a hand in the early stages. Please don't ever emigrate, die or go blind.

Thanks to Siobhán, who really had her work cut out for her trying to smooth out my wayward timelines. Thank you for ensuring that everyone was gestating, menstruating, marrying, divorcing and ageing at roughly the appropriate times. No one deserves to be pregnant for twelve months.

Thanks to Oh Paxton for the beautiful cover, to Rob for the brilliant words and to Louise for being the Best Editor in the World™. Thanks also to Mel, without whom there would, literally, have been no book. And lastly thank you to Amelie, whose presence in my life has transformed me into a lean, mean, disciplined writing machine who can now throw out 5,000 words before lunchtime. Thank you for being such a good little girl and for all those afternoon naps when I managed to squeeze out another 1,000 words. You are my angel.

Either marriage is a destiny, I believe, or there is no
sense in it at all, it's a piece of humbug.
Max Frisch

If it is your time, love will track you down like a
cruise missile.
Lynda Barry

Al & Emma's Kitchen, Saturday,
19 September 2003, 12.35 a.m.

Vince glanced around the table at his friends. They were all roughly the same age as him – thirty-five, thirty-six. This conversation, or one very like it, was probably going on around a thousand London dinner tables at this very moment. But this was special because it was one they hadn't shared for so long and because it was being brought out, like the best china, for a very special guest. For him.

This was the first group gathering since he and Jess had split up, and everyone seemed extra-sparkly, like guests at a pretend TV dinner party. He'd seen them do it before, with new girlfriends and old friends, who arrived suddenly from overseas, out of the blue, like characters in a soap opera.

They wanted him to know that he was still one of them, whatever his status. Look, they were saying, you've got fantastic friends and life is going to be just great. And in showing themselves to him afresh, they were reairing their shared history. Remember when, they said. Remember that time in Amsterdam – Simon's stag night, remember – on the ferry on the way back and Simon projectile-vomited all over the food counter. And remember that weekend in Cornwall; remember Al standing on that rock in the middle of the sea at five in the morning fucked out of his brain on speed and how that wave

I

crashed over him and we all thought he was dead. Remember that?

The conversation turned to a time before Vince had known half these people, to a time they shared at university before he'd come into their lives. Stories of snakebite and acid and STDs. Stories of grim fridges and disastrous casseroles, of sleepwalking and incontinence.

He rested his chin on his clasped hands and absorbed the atmosphere while he listened to his friends reminisce. The clock on the microwave said 12.38 a.m. He'd usually be home by now, he mused, paying the baby-sitter, looking in on Lara. Instead he was still here. Nowhere to go; no one to get back to. He was a married man who wasn't married, a father who didn't live with his child. He was all wrong. Everything in his life felt upended, unbalanced. But here in the genial, familiar warmth of Al and Emma's kitchen, red wine and whisky basking in his bloodstream, the world was righted once more.

The conversation regressed further. They were talking about schooldays now, days before even the oldest of the friends had known each other. They were talking about crazes and crushes and snogging – then Natalie asked an open question.

'So,' she said, smiling mischievously over her fingertips, 'how old was everyone when they lost their virginity? And who to? You first, Al.'

Al groaned, but went on to tell everyone that it was to a girl called Karen on a school trip to Paris when he was sixteen years old. They'd had sex in the bottom bed of the hostel bunks, while his friend Joe farted audibly, odorously and deliberately overhead.

Emma lost hers when she was seventeen, to a married man

who promised he'd leave his wife for her, then never contacted her again.

Natalie was more traditional, losing her virginity at the age of fourteen to a guy called Darren who looked like Steve Norman from Spandau Ballet. It was all over in thirty seconds and he cried when she didn't bleed because he thought it meant she wasn't really a virgin.

Steve had lost his at fifteen at his parents' B & B, to an Austrian guest who lured him into her bedroom while he was on his way to the toilet in the middle of the night. She was forty-five with the worst stretchmarks you could possibly imagine and a scar from her ribcage to her groin from some kind of life-saving surgery. She grabbed his (at the time) long hair so hard while she rode him that she actually pulled a clump of it out. Afterwards, she waved it in the air like a trophy.

Claire shocked everyone by announcing that she'd lost it to her seventeen-year-old cousin on a Hoseasons boating holiday when she was only thirteen. They had sex under a bush on the banks of the Coventry Canal while their parents got drunk and shouted at each other inside the boat. Claire found out five years later that her older sister had lost her virginity to the same cousin and that he ended up being gay and living with a seventy-year-old man.

Tom lost his at sixteen in the back of a transit van being driven by his friend who'd just taken two tabs of acid and thought that they were a pair of giant writhing lizards. He'd pulled over to the side of the road, grabbed handfuls of grass out of the verge and thrown them all over the newly consummated couple because he thought maybe the lizards were hungry. Tom couldn't remember the name of the girl.

And then it was Vince's turn. His friends turned and smiled at him encouragingly.

'Go on, Mr Mellon,' said Al, rubbing his hands together, 'hit us with it. What kind of depraved, repellent, deviant experience did you have?'

Vince smiled and half-toyed with the idea of lying, just to gratify his friends, but then he looked at Natalie's soft face, glowing in the candlelight, one arm draped lovingly around her drunken husband, and decided he'd tell the truth.

'The night I lost my virginity,' he began, 'was the most brilliant night of my life.'

There was a second's silence broken by Tom. 'Oh, give over,' he said. 'No one enjoys losing their virginity.'

'But I did,' said Vince, simply. 'It was perfect. Just – perfect.'

The group fell silent as they absorbed this unconventional statement. The men looked slightly disappointed, while the women around the table looked at him enquiringly.

'Go on, then,' said Claire. 'Tell us. Who was it?'

'It was a girl I met in Norfolk. When I was nineteen. Her name was Joy.'

July 1986
Late Bloomers

One

Vince threw his bag on to the bottom level of the stale-smelling bunks, pulled apart the papery curtains painted with ugly brushstroke daisies, and saw her for the first time.

She sat in a deck chair, her knees brought up to her chin, holding a magazine in her right hand while she picked absent-mindedly at black-painted toenails with the other. Her hair was dark brown and to her jaw, with a slight curl that kicked it across her cheeks like wood shavings. She wore all black – a sleeveless vest, oversized army surplus shorts, a frayed canvas ribbon in her hair.

'Vince – give me a hand with the gas, mate.' Chris popped his head around the cream melamine door and winked at him.

'Yeah. In a minute.' Vince turned back to the window and lifted the curtain again.

She was turning a page and rearranging her neat limbs. She fiddled with a small silver cross on a leather thong that hung around her neck and curled her toes around the frame of the deck chair.

Bang, bang, bang.

A hairy fist thumping at the window disturbed his reverie.

'Come on, mate.' Chris's face loomed into view.

'Yeah. OK.' Vince let the curtain drop, and straightened up.

Shit.

There was a beautiful girl. In the caravan next door. Where for the previous four years there had been three boys, two Staffordshire bull terriers and a couple called Geoff and Diane from Lincolnshire. He stared at his reflection for a minute in the mirror above the gas fire in the living area. He was thrown. He hadn't factored the possibility of a beautiful girl into the prospect of two-weeks-on-a-caravan-site-in-Hunstanton. There'd never been a beautiful girl here before. Just an ugly girl. An ugly girl called Carol with an even uglier mate called Theresa who threw poorly phrased insults at him, then tried to get off with the sinewy guys who strode across the moving platforms of the Waltzers on Hunstanton pier, pretending to fancy ugly girls as they spun them masochistically in painted cups.

When Vince first came to Hunstanton with Chris and his mum, there'd been other kids of his age to hang out with. They'd gang together and mooch around the fairground, even went to a nightclub once. But as the years passed, they stopped coming. They stayed at home to hang out with their mates or their girlfriends, or they went on holiday with friends to places you needed a passport to get to. Even ugly Carol and Theresa seemed to have something better to do with their summer this year, evidenced by the drawn curtains of their caravan across the way.

Outside, Vince could hear Chris making friendly conversation with the mysterious girl. Fearing that he was missing out on something or, worse still, that Chris was embarrassing him in some way, he pulled his hands through his James Dean hair, ran a fingertip across the angry red scars beneath his jaw line and headed outside.

'Just outside London,' Chris was saying, 'Enfield. What about you?'

'Colchester,' she said, sliding the silver cross back and forth across the leather thong. 'You know, in Essex?'

'Aye,' said Chris, 'I know Colchester. Oh, look who it is.' He turned to look at Vince. 'Vince,' he said, 'come and meet our new neighbour. This is Joy.'

She was even more beautiful close up. Her skin was alabaster white, but there was something about her features that suggested something far-flung. Her nose was small and chiselled, and her cheekbones were set high in her face, but it was her eyes that held clues to the uncommon. Compact and wide-set, flat-lidded and framed with dense, dark lashes — the eyes of a painted china doll.

'Hi,' he said, smiling his new, stiff smile.

'Hiya,' she said, resting her magazine on her lap and sitting on her hands.

He noticed her eyes stray to the scars on his jaw, and turned his hands into fists to stop them wandering protectively towards his face.

'So,' she said, 'are you two mates?'

Vince looked at Chris in mock horror. 'God, no,' he said, 'Chris is my stepdad.'

'Really? How come?'

'Well, he married my mum.' He and Chris exchanged a look and laughed.

'Oh, right. Of course. Just you look kind of the same age.'

'Yeah – everyone says that. Chris is ten years older than me, though. He's twenty-nine. I'm nearly nineteen.'

'Right,' she said, looking from one to the other, almost as if doubting their story. 'And where's your wife? Your mum?'

'She's at the Spar,' said Chris, hauling the gas canister out of the little wooden cupboard and blowing some cobwebs off it. 'Getting us some tea. Should be back in a minute. Oh, talk of the devil, here she is.'

Kirsty's green Mini pulled up alongside the caravan and came to a halt with a crunch of gravel under rubber.

'Give us a hand, you two,' she said, heading for the boot.

Chris instantly dropped the canister and went to his wife's assistance. Vince nodded at Joy and rubbed at his scars.

'God, is that your mum?' said Joy.

'Uh-huh.'

'She's gorgeous.'

Vince turned, expecting to see Beatrice Dalle or someone standing there, but, no, it was just his mother.

'How old is she? She doesn't look old enough to have a son your age.'

'Thirty-seven, I think. Thirty-eight. Something like that.'

'Bloody hell. She's younger than my mum was when she *had* me.'

They both stared at Vince's mum for a while, and Vince tried to think of something to say. This was officially the longest dialogue he'd ever exchanged with a girl who wasn't either in his class or going out with one of his mates, and the conversation felt like a flighty shuttle-cock he was trying to keep in the air with the force of his will alone. He wanted to ask her something inter-esting. Something about music maybe, or her intriguing slanted eyes. Or what a beautiful girl like her was doing on a shitty caravan site like this. A dozen potential con-versational openers formed in his head and were dis-counted in a nano-second – too personal, too naff, too boring, too much.

The silence drew out like a held breath.

Vince looked from Joy to his mum's car and back again while he tried to think of the next thing to say. 'You staying long?' he managed eventually, with a rush of blood to his head.

'Another fortnight,' she said, 'worse luck.'

'What happened to Geoff and Diane?'

'Who?'

'The people who own your caravan.'

'No idea,' she said. 'Mum and Dad are renting it off someone or other.' She pulled her hands out from under her and turned them upwards in a gesture of ignorance. She obviously didn't care about Geoff or Diane, or whose caravan she was staying in. He was officially the most boring man in the world.

'Right,' he said as silence descended again. Joy rustled the pages of her magazine and Vince felt a deep blush developing in his chest area.

'So,' he said, his hand rising subconsciously to his scars again, 'I'll see you around then?'

'Yeah,' she said, 'I guess you will.'

Her eyes were already dropping to her magazine. He'd

lost her. But then, mused Vince, as he took a cache of carrier bags from his mother and mounted the stairs to the caravan, he'd never really had her. Of course he hadn't. He was Vincent Mellon. Or Melonhead, as he'd been known at school. He'd been stupid to think that some operation, some bit of surgery, was going to change that. He couldn't talk to girls when he was ugly, and he couldn't talk to girls now he was supposedly 'good-looking' either.

When he came out two minutes later, the deck chair was empty and the girl called Joy was nowhere to be seen.

Vincent Mellon had been born with an underbite. It hadn't really shown up until he was a few years old, but from that point on he'd resembled a very small, hairless bulldog. As he got older it transpired that Vince didn't just have an underbite – he didn't have a small but charming imperfection that added character to his face – but that his bottom jaw protruded so far ahead of his upper jaw that he couldn't actually chew properly. Anything that required being fed into the oral orifice and bitten through – a doner kebab, for example, or a custard cream – was out of bounds. Things needed to be cut up and transferred into the very back of his mouth, bit by bit, with a fork or spoon. Not only that, but because of the misalignment of his upper and lower teeth two of his molars had started to erode as well, and eventually anything chewier than a tender piece of chicken had become virtually impossible to deal with.

Vince's underbite, in other words, was not just an aesthetic blight and a total embarrassment; it was also a significant physical disability. Which was why after years of treatment and check-ups, the NHS had finally paid for him to have corrective surgery last year. Too late to save his schooldays from being a complete washout, or to do anything about that fact that he was still a virgin at the age of nearly nineteen, but just in time, he supposed, to give him a chance in hell of getting a girl to French kiss him before his twenty-first birthday.

No girl had wanted to kiss him with the underbite. No girl had even wanted to *talk* to him with an underbite, unless they really had to. And by the time he'd had surgery, he'd left school, hence severing the only contact he ever had with girls.

The surgery itself had been a nightmare: months of agony, of mouth braces, pureed food and painkillers. He'd made a recluse of himself, unable to face the world looking like Jaws and feeling like a cripple.

'Oh, my goodness,' his mum had squeaked when the final braces were removed two months ago. 'Oh, my God, look at you. *Look at you.* Oh, heavens – you look so . . . *handsome.*'

Vince had stared at his new reflection in the mirror and tried to make sense of what he was looking at. He saw hazel eyes in shadowy sockets and he saw the soft wide boxer's nose he'd inherited from his dead father. And just below the nose he saw a whole load of new stuff: a strong, solid jaw, a full shapely mouth with lips that met and a good-shaped chin. He'd pulled his lips apart and stared in awe at his teeth as the upstairs set finally made the acquaintance of their downstairs neighbours. Then he'd turned his head slightly to view his new profile. His lips had an almost regal curl to them and his nose now formed the peak of his facial contours, instead of his lower jaw. He no longer looked like a bulldog. He looked like . . . like . . .

'You look just like your dad,' his mum had said, finally peeling her hand away from her mouth. 'Just like him. It's . . . uncanny. It's like, like . . .' Then she'd started crying.

Vince's dad, Max, had died on his motorbike when Kirsty was eight and a half months pregnant with Vince. Vince had seen his dad only in photos, a big, strong, long-haired man in jeans and leather who seemed so far removed from him in every way that he'd never even considered the possibility that he might look like him.

He'd tried to bring Max's face to his mind in the consulting room that day, tried to mentally superimpose it over his own. But he couldn't. All he could see was a tall, skinny bloke in a black polo neck with a face that didn't quite look familiar, an image he would never be able to reconcile with that of his macho, moustachioed dead father.

Vince had vowed that he wouldn't go to Hunstanton again after he left school. Last summer was the last time, he'd promised himself. He was booked in for surgery this time last year; had envisaged that come the following summer he'd be far too busy having sex to come back here with his mum and Chris. But it hadn't quite worked out like that. His social life, if anything, had diminished since the surgery as he'd lost touch with his school friends. And here he was, five days off his nineteenth birthday and stuck on a bunk bed in a damp old caravan with his mum, her husband and a chemical toilet. Still, on the bright side, he'd just bought himself a Sony Discman and five new CDs, the sun was shining and there was a beautiful girl next door. A really, really beautiful girl.

All he had to do now was miraculously turn into an interesting, sexy, vibrant and irresistible man whom said beautiful girl might have even the slightest interest in talking to and this experience might turn out OK after all.

Two

'Shit,' said Joy, dashing back into the caravan and fanning her face with her magazine, 'shit, shit, shit, shit, shit.'

She slammed the door closed behind her and leaned against it breathlessly, taking a moment to catch her breath before heading for the mirror.

'Shit,' she said again, examining her pasty face with disgust and wiping away kohl smears from under her eyes with the back of her index finger. She lifted her arms and stared in horror at the dark hairs growing obliviously from her armpits. She lowered her head and took a little sniff. Gross. She hoped he hadn't noticed. She'd kept her arms glued to her side throughout the whole painful encounter, acutely aware of the fact that she hadn't bothered to put on any deodorant this morning.

She thought back to their awkward conversation and felt a slug-like trail of dread slither down her spine.

'Shit,' she hissed to herself. '*Shit.*'

That bloke. Vince. God. Gorgeous. Just gorgeous. Just the best-looking bloke she'd ever seen in her life. Tall and cool and handsome. Handsome in an old-fashioned way – strong jaw, mellow eyes, beat-up-looking. And those scars. Joy loved scars. *Smouldering*, that's what he was. Like James Dean, like Humphrey Bogart, like Marlon Brando.

And Joy had blown it, hadn't been able to think of anything to say. Apart from that stupid question about why his stepfather was his stepfather. He must have thought she was a cretin.

She moved from the bathroom to the living area at the front of the caravan and peered gingerly between the lurid orange curtains that smelled of dust and other people. The mother was locking up her little green Mini. Joy watched her with interest. Trim and petite in tight cotton shorts, a pink sun top and plimsolls, she looked about twenty-five years old. Her hair was a dyed ash blonde, cut into a neat helmet around her fine-featured face, and she wore a pair of Raybans on a string around her neck. Joy had never before seen a mother as girlish and unbroken as her. She looked light-hearted and care-free. She didn't look capable of having borne a child as tall and broodingly masculine as her son. She didn't look capable of having borne *any* child. Her hips were too narrow; her step too light.

The door of the next-door caravan opened and the stepfather emerged. He looked like B. A. Robertson, without the chin. His hair was dark and shiny, curling around his collar and over his ears, with a small fringe swept across his forehead. He wore a chambray shirt tucked into tight jeans only a shade or two darker than the shirt, and a heavy-buckled belt. Joy saw a hint of tattoo on his dark-haired arms and a rough stubbled chin that looked as if you could strike matches off it. He was tall and broad and macho. Lots of women probably fancied him, she pondered, thought he was a real *hunk*. Not Joy's type, though. Too hairy, too obvious, too old.

She watched the mother and the stepfather interacting with interest. They were still new to each other – you could tell that from the way they touched each other and circled each other. They were in love. It explained the mother's girlish gait.

Joy was fascinated by other people's families, always had been, ever since she was a child. She'd loved watching the other kids meeting their parents at the school gates at the end of the day, wanted to see what other people's mothers were wearing, what cars they drove, how they greeted their children. She compared hairstyles and nail polish and heel size. Even now she didn't really feel like she knew someone until she'd met their parents. And even now, at nearly eighteen years old, she still compared other people's parents to her own.

She looked up again as the front door opposite opened and Vince emerged. She studied him minutely now that she wasn't being taken unawares. He looked as if he slept with French girls and smoked American cigarettes, as if he could win a fight and write a poem all in the same afternoon.

Joy ran a fingertip down the bare underside of her arm and felt goosebumps erupt across her flesh like a field of detonating mines. Then she heard the familiar rumble of her father's car as it bounced its way over the pockmarked gravel and mountainous speed humps towards their caravan. She sighed and let the curtain fall.

'Hello, love.' Joy could hear her mother wheezing lugubriously from the other end of the caravan.

'Hi, Mum.'

'And what time did you eventually emerge?' her father said, following spryly behind.

Emerge, thought Joy, with annoyance. She hated the way her father said that. *Emerge.*

She shrugged at him and fiddled with her crucifix.

'People next door,' he said, resting some musty-smelling packages on the dining table and indicating the next-door caravan with a jerk of his silvery head.

'Yes,' said her mother, leaning against the kitchen counter while she drew some breath, a light but insistent sweat trickling from her hairline and disappearing into her heavy brows. 'Have you seen? Can't quite work out what they are though — a family or what.'

'Ugly bunch,' said her father, unfurling a parcel of old newspaper and string, and pulling out something made of brass that looked like yet another coal scuttle. 'You missed an excellent morning's antiquing,' he held the brass thing to the light and smiled at it with satisfaction. 'Lots of super little shops up at Burnham Market. And we had a marvellous pub lunch.'

'Have you eaten, love?' said her mum, finally having regained enough puff to make it to the other end of the caravan and collapse in a lump on the seat opposite Joy. She was wearing one of the tight dresses she always insisted on wearing in the summer, constructed of a heavy cotton with a belted waist and cap sleeves that ate into the thick flesh of her upper arms and restricted her movements. As if her rheumatism, her asthma and the five stones of excess weight she carried with her weren't restrictive enough.

Joy glanced down at her mother's poor ruined legs, at the red shins marbled with bluish spider veins and the angry ankles that spilled from her Sunday supplement shoes like pie crusts. Poor Mum. Summer was a nightmare for her. The heat, the pollution and the need to expose the ungainly, unloved body she was happy to keep under wraps the rest of the year.

And then she looked at her father, cool and slim in his crisp white polo shirt and beige slacks, seemingly designed for the hot weather. It was almost as if he was taunting his wife with his ability to remain unravaged by time and the elements.

They'd had her late in life – her mother, Barbara, had been forty; her father, Alan, forty-two.

'So, what are your plans for the afternoon?' said her father.

Joy sighed. *Plans.* There it was – another of his special words designed purely to irritate her. What plans did he possibly think she might have stranded here in a dingy caravan on the outskirts of Hunstanton? She shrugged, and scratched her upper arm.

She had no idea where they'd found this godforsaken, manky old sardine can. Even in comparison to some of the other eyesores on this site this one was shockingly ugly. The interior was brown and unappealing, with knobbly nylon stretch covers on everything, and why her parents had thought for a second that bringing her to this sad, mildewy box on the very edge of the brash north Norfolk coast to spend two weeks cocooned away with a pair of twittering geriatric parents was going to help heal the still-raw wounds of the past few months was a mystery to her. In all honesty, she suspected it was a mystery to them, too. But they were still sensitive, still desperate to remain 'upbeat' no matter what. They would, she knew, enjoy this holiday by hook or by crook, however uncomfortable or unappealing they found their surroundings. There would be no negativity in this family, no moaning, no complaining. And she'd comply because it was all her fault, because after everything she'd put her parents through the least she could do was smile and pretend to be having a good time.

And as she peeled back the orange curtain again and saw the shadowy movements of the intriguing family next door she thought to herself that with any luck she might not even have to pretend.

Three

The Nelson's Arms was heaving with sunburned, shell-suited couples, and the beer garden was full of their children clambering around a multicoloured climbing frame and sliding down the enormous red tongue of a large plastic clown's head.

Chris put a round of drinks down on the table and sat down.

'Cheers,' he said, holding his pint out to Kirsty's white wine and Vince's Guinness. 'Here's to the summer and to a cracking holiday.'

'Hear! Hear!' said Kirsty.

'And here's to our Vincent finally offloading his sodding cherry. With any luck.'

'Chris!'

'Well, what was the point of going though all that pain and suffering if you're not going to make the most of it? You haven't got for ever, you know. You're nearly nineteen, it's summer and you're surrounded by gorgeous women. Go for it!'

Vince looked around the pub in mock disgust, at the married couples and lardy teenage girls wearing cheap Chelsea Girl tops and stonewashed denim jeans. He threw Chris a withering look. 'Gorgeous women?' he said. '*Where?*'

'Oh, the night's yet young. It's not even six o'clock yet. You never know who might turn up.'

'Chris, mate, this isn't St Tropez. Gorgeous women are not attracted by the bright lights of Hunstanton Pier.'

'Oh, I don't know,' he said, picking up his pint and winking at Kirsty. 'What about that lass next door?'

Vince felt himself flush, and buried his face in his Guinness. 'What lass?'

'You know what lass. That pale, winsome thing in the crucifix and all the black clobber on. You know.'

'What – that girl from Geoff and Diane's caravan?'

'Aye, that's the one. She looks right up your street. Looks like she'll be into that depressing stuff you like. And she had a nice pair of legs on her, too. Did you see her, K? Little Miss Goth.' Chris turned to his wife. She shook her head and laughed.

Vince tutted, and raised his eyebrows at Chris. Vince was going through his Goth phase when Kirsty had first met Chris five years ago, and Chris couldn't accept that he'd moved on and that nowadays he was more of a . . . well, he didn't really know what he was any more but, in Chris's mind, Vince would for ever be a Goth.

'Well, whatever, she was a cracker, and she looked like she was up for the job.'

'Oh, Chris, leave him alone,' Kirsty chastised affectionately.

'Yeah, Chris – leave me alone,' said Vince. But he was feigning indignation because the truth was that he didn't really mind Chris ribbing him. It was the nature of their relationship and had been ever since Chris had first come into his life, when Vince was fourteen years old.

*

Kirsty had had other boyfriends before Chris. She'd worked for years as a receptionist at the Belling Factory at Ponders End where the men outnumbered the women by twenty to one. She called it the Ponders End Knocking Shop, but, even though she was chased round the office day after day by men in suits and wedding rings, Kirsty preferred men who worked with their hands, so it was the guys from the shop floor that she ended up dating.

Vince had known that Chris was going to be something serious before he even met him. Mum had gone on about him for ages, on and on about this new guy from Sheffield.

'Oh, that bloke I was telling you about, Chris, the one from Sheffield, well, he went to see *Omen 3* last week – said it was crap.'

'Oh, you know that Chris from Sheffield, he's got a new car – Golf GTI. Bright green it is, with spoilers and alloy wheels.'

'That Chris from Sheffield – he's got a mate who used to be a plumber. Said he'd ask him to pop round and sort out the boiler.'

She'd talk about his girlfriend as well. 'Chris's girlfriend's had her hair done brown, apparently. Weird thing to do, go brown.'

'Chris's girlfriend's mum's down from Sheffield – I think it's getting to him a bit. She sounds like a right old battleaxe.'

'Looks like things are getting a bit tense between Chris and his girlfriend.'

By the time the girlfriend with the brown hair and the battleaxe mum had been dispatched and Chris was finally available, it felt as if Vince had been hearing about him for years and had known him for ever.

He wasn't sure that they were going to get on at first. Chris liked soft rock and getting greasy under cars. His hair was just that bit too long; his trousers too tight. Vince, as a pale, melancholic teenage loner with an enormous chin and a taste for locking himself in his bedroom and listening to suicidal music, could not have been more different. But he'd warmed to Chris quickly. He liked the way Chris treated his mum with respect, phoned her when he said he would, always saw her home to her door, introduced her to his friends and family, never let her down. And he liked the way he made the effort to get on with Vince without ever trying too hard. He didn't try to ingratiate himself. He respected Vince's space and privacy. If he came upon Vince watching TV in the living room, for example, he'd pick up a paper and read it, only lowering it to address Vince once the adverts were running.

Chris was one of those guys who got everything right. He was a perfect judge of character and mood, and always timed everything to perfection.

Including proposing to his mum.

Chris had been seeing Kirsty for six months and, just as Vince had begun thinking how great it would be to have Chris around for the long haul, how much it would make everything right if Chris were to propose to his mother and marry her and hang out with them full-time, Kirsty came home one night wearing an engagement ring.

They'd married at Wood Green register office six months later and had a big party afterwards at a pub in

Enfield. Chris had played a set with his dodgy Status Quo-style band and Vince had been best man, and when he'd given his speech and told everyone how unexpectedly pleased he was to have a new man in his life, and how happy Chris had made not only his mother but also the whole family and how proud he was to call Chris his stepfather, Chris had actually burst into tears in front of the entire wedding party.

Chris was a rock during Vince's surgery – he'd been there during the dark moments, pureed food for him, kept him light and focused on the positive. And now, even though they were chalk and cheese in nearly every respect, even though they'd never have become close under any other circumstances, Chris had become the greatest ally he'd ever had.

'Don't look now,' Chris muttered secretively into his pint, 'but guess who's just walked in.' His eyes floated over Vince's shoulders to the front door of the pub.

Vince turned discreetly to have a look. And there she was. Joy. She looked less wild and dishevelled than earlier – her hair was combed straight into a middle parting, and she was wearing a crisp white collarless man's shirt over a pair of grey leggings with chunky DM shoes. She had very good posture, Vince couldn't help but notice, carried herself as if she had no bone, only muscle.

Following behind her were two rather old people – a fat uncomfortable-looking woman in a too-tight denim dress and enormous sunglasses, and a svelte man with a marked tan wearing a shirt, slacks and blazer. They looked all wrong in their surroundings, as if they'd got lost on their way back from a day trip to Stratford-on-Avon. Vince felt a small swell of surprise when he noticed Joy turning to address one of them and realized that they were probably her parents.

He turned away abruptly and found Chris and his mother staring at him with half-smiles.

'What?'

'That's the one,' said Chris, tapping the side of his nose. 'Mark my words, that girl is the One.'

'Oh, shut up will you.'

'No, I'm serious. Look at her. She's got your name written all over her. Here – I'm going to invite them over for a drink,' he rose from his chair.

'What? No!' said Vince, grabbing Chris's wrist and pulling him back.

Chris gently unfurled his fingers and stood up. 'Don't be so soft, Vincent. It'll be fine. Trust me.' Then he was gone.

'Oh, God.' Vince clasped his hands together and prayed hard that they'd say no, but he knew they wouldn't. That was the problem with Chris – he was impossible to resist.

Sure enough, a few seconds later he was scraping his chair around the table, making room for other chairs to be added as Joy and her parents hovered awkwardly in his peripheral vision. He turned and smiled at Joy. Joy smiled back at him, and he snapped his head back. Introductions were made, and Joy slipped her slight frame on to the chair next to him. Vince stared studiedly into his pint and tried to control his blush.

'Well,' said Chris, clapping his hands together, 'what brings you to sunny Hunstanton?'

27

'Ah,' said Alan, the father, 'just a break with routine. You know.'

'A break from routine, eh?' chuckled Chris. 'Well, you came to the right place for that. Nothing routine about Hunstanton, is there?' He turned to Kirsty and Vince, and chuckled again.

Vince looked at Joy's parents, stiff and embarrassed on the other side of the table, Barbara clutching a warm-looking orange juice in a wine glass, Alan sipping masterfully from a pint of stout.

The mother had a strange moon-like face, baggy eyes of an indiscriminate shade, a slightly beaky nose and an overly ruddy complexion. She smiled benignly as Alan and Chris conversed, taking the occasional controlled sip from her glass. There was a small slick of sweat on her upper lip. She didn't look as if she'd ever been pretty in her life.

The father had the look of a man who'd persuaded himself a long time ago that he was a catch and wasn't about to let go of this misguided notion. His features were neat and symmetrical, but were slightly too small for his head, as if someone had forced them all into the middle of his face in order to make room for something that had never materialized. There was something colonial about him, like he'd spent time living in hot climes, being attended to by natives and watching cricket under parasols. It was blatant that he felt he'd done the wretched Barbara a favour by marrying her – it oozed from his body language and his offhand manner.

The conversation rolled on, Chris doing the hard work of steering it, Mum doing her best to inject some levity into it, Alan tolerating it and Barbara, Vince and Joy maintaining an embarrassed silence.

'So,' said Alan, 'you're regular visitors to Hunstanton, then, are you?'

'Aye,' said Chris, 'this is our fourth summer up here.'

'And you like it, do you?'

'Love it. It's not grand or anything, but there's just something about it. And there are some fantastic beaches.'

'Yes, I've heard about the beaches. That was one of the main attractions, to be frank. The rolling sand dunes, the bracing, briny sea air, the pine forests.'

'Aye, that's right, Alan. I've seen a lot of beaches in my time, but the beaches here – well, you can hardly see the horizon, it's that far away. Not often in life you can get that much clear space between yourself and the edge of the world. Humbling . . .'

'Yeees,' murmured Alan, dreamily.

'Sounds lovely,' said Barbara, as the conversation began to trickle away.

'Mmmmm,' said Kirsty, smiling stiffly.

'So!' said Chris, breaking through the rapidly descending silence like a brick through a window, 'Joy. What kind of a girl are you, then?'

'Sorry?' She looked at him in bemusement.

'Tell us about yourself. What do you do? What do you like?'

Joy laughed. 'Erm, well, I've just finished my A levels.'

'In what?'

'Art, Drama and English.'

'Oh, right, you're the creative type, then?'

'Yeah, sort of.'

'So's our Vincent. He's the creative type, too. Aren't you, Vince?'

Vince shrugged and made a strange gurgling noise that he'd never made before in his life.

'Yeah – he paints, draws, makes things. And you should have seen the creative things he used to do with his hair and a can of his mum's hairspray when he was a kid.' Chris laughed out loud and Alan looked at Vince as if he'd only just noticed he was there.

'Are you off to university, then?' Kirsty asked Joy, galloping to the rescue.

Joy squirmed a little in her seat. 'Well, I was supposed to be. I had a place at Bristol. But I, er . . . had to defer. Hopefully I can take up my place next year.'

'Oh,' said Kirsty, nodding encouragingly, 'right.'

'Yes,' said Joy.

'Mmm,' murmured Barbara, apparently apropos of nothing.

Vince took a deep breath and tried to control his growing sense of anxiety. This was a fucking nightmare. Never in the whole history of the universe had six people had less in common with each other. Even Chris with all his puppyish gregariousness could do nothing to salvage a decent conversation from this motley mix of people.

'So, you two poor buggers, stuck here with your parents at your age.' Chris looked from Joy to Vince and back again. 'Not exactly two weeks in Tenerife with your mates, is it? I reckon you might have more fun if you made a break for it.'

'Eh?' said Vince.

'Yeah – do a runner. Scarper. Get lost. Go and have some fun doing ... doing ... well, whatever it is that overgrown teenagers do when they've managed to escape from their bloody parents.'

Vince felt a surge of excitement rising in his chest. As heavy-handed as Chris's proposal might have been, the idea of getting away from this hideous situation, walking out of the door, getting some fresh air and feeling the evening sun on his skin was too good to resist. But Alan had other ideas.

'Oh, well,' he said, 'that's a very nice idea, er, Chris, but actually Barbara, Joy and I have dinner plans for tonight.' He smiled tightly and folded his arms across his chest, obviously a man who was used to his word being final, obviously a man who'd never before encountered anyone as persistent as Chris.

'Oh, come on now, Alan. Would you have wanted to go out for dinner with your parents when you were a young whippersnapper of a lad? You and Barbara go and have a nice romantic dinner, just the two of you. Or, better still, why don't you join my wife and me? There's some smashing fast-food places up on the seafront. Do you like burgers, Alan?' He eyed Alan with a determined twinkle.

'We're not really fast-food people, Chris, to be frank. Greasy food doesn't really agree with my constitution.'

'Well, then – how about a nice curry?'

'Oh, well. I like a curry, yes I do. But Barbara can't really eat spicy food. It bloats her. And to be frank, I rather think we were hoping for a *quiet* night this evening. You know – a *family* night. No offence.'

'None taken, Alan. None taken. But, tell you what, how about the young 'uns head off for the evening, you and Barbara go and have your quiet evening somewhere and me and the wife grab a curry, and we can try to get together later this week for a big night out. When you're feeling less . . . *quiet*? Eh? How about that, then?'

'Well. I don't know.' Alan looked across at his daughter in desperation, 'Joy, er . . . what do *you* think?'

'I think that's a really good idea. I wasn't hungry anyway. What do you think, Vince?' She turned and glanced at Vince.

'God – well, yeah. Why not? It's nice out. We could go down to the seafront.'

'Cool. Right. Let's go, then.' She stood up and picked up her bag.

'What – now?'

'Yeah. Come on.'

'Cool. OK. Right.'

Two minutes later Vince was leaving the Nelson's Arms and walking into a warm and balmy evening of complete and utter mystery with the most beautiful woman he'd ever been alone with in his life.

They stood on the pavement outside the pub, next to a large weather-beaten sign that said, 'Welcome to Seavue Holiday Home Park.' It creaked a little as a gentle, salty breeze passed over them.

'Christ. What a nightmare!' said Joy.

Vince laughed. 'I'm really sorry about that, in there. Chris can be a bit . . . overwhelming sometimes.'

'God, don't be sorry! It's *him* I feel sorry for. Him and your mum. They're stuck with them now.'

'Oh, don't worry about Chris. He'll find a way of getting rid of them when he gets fed up. He's clever like that.'

There was a small dog tied up outside the pub, white with brown patches and disproportionately short legs. Its owner had left it with some water in a Tupperware box. The dog looked up at them appealingly, and they both crouched down in unison to say hello. He strained enthusiastically at his lead to greet them.

'Hello,' said Joy, scratching his neck.

'You're a friendly little bugger, aren't you?' said Vince, rubbing the dog's haunches.

The little dog contorted itself in raptures, and Vince looked up to see Joy smiling at him.

'I like people who like dogs,' she said.

'Do you?'

'Uh-huh. Never trust a man who doesn't like dogs, that's my motto.'

'Right,' said Vince, dropping his gaze. He stared at Joy's hand where it rested on the dog's ruff. It was long and thin with raised blue veins that flowed from her wrist to her knuckles like icy tributaries. She wore a silver ring on her index finger, in the shape of a furled dragon. A thought landed in his head as he stared at the ring, one so overwhelming that he had to clench his jaw tightly to stop him speaking it out loud.

Do you believe in love at first sight?

'So,' he said, getting to his feet, blood rushing to his head, 'we've been granted our freedom. What shall we do with it?'

Joy gave the little dog one last pat and stood up. Her knees clicked audibly as she straightened her legs. 'Well,' she said, 'you're Mr Hunstanton – you decide.'

'Right.' Vince surveyed the road from left to right. He had no idea what to suggest. He'd never had to decide what to do in Hunstanton before. He always just did what his mum and Chris were doing. What would a girl like Joy want to do, anyway? he wondered. She looked like she read Russian novels and listened to difficult music. She probably spoke fluent French and knew how to eat oysters. He mentally scrabbled through all the possible options, trying to find something, *anything*, with even the slightest whiff of culture or class about it.

'There's a cinema down at the seafront,' he said eventually. 'We could see what's showing?'

'Tell you what,' said Joy, 'let's just go and find a nice pub and get pissed, shall we?'

Vince turned and smiled at her with relief. And then they started walking.

Four

Joy hadn't had a boyfriend for almost two years. She hadn't felt a hand in her hand, lips against her skin, hair against her cheek. The only men she'd had any contact with since she was sixteen years old were teachers, doctors and counsellors. She couldn't remember what men smelled like. She was sure the professionals she'd dealt with these past months had wives who thought they smelled delicious, who loved nothing more than to breathe in their heady, unique scent, but all she remembered of the whole experience was words — no smells, no noises, no feelings — just endless words.

Her last contact with a real man hadn't even been with a real man. It had been with Kieran Saunders, an acne-stricken seventeen-year-old from Dagenham she'd met at a bus stop when she was fourteen. He'd strolled past, in a fringed leather jacket, stringy legs in black denim and oversized feet in enormous DMs. He'd done a double take when he saw Joy sitting there in her school uniform. She'd watched him wander up the road away from her, turning back every now and then to glance at her, before suddenly doubling back, plonking himself down and offering her a cigarette.

Joy's first impression of Kieran was that he smelled — of cigarette smoke and clothes that had dried forgotten in the washing machine. And she'd been mesmerized by one pimple in particular, a red one on the underside of his jaw with the ripest-looking yellow head she'd ever seen. She had agreed to give him her phone number mainly because she was too polite to say no and too slow off the mark to give him a false one.

He'd arrived at her house to pick her up for their first date the following week. He stood on her doorstep in leather and denim, fuchsia Crazy-Color combed through the peroxide of his cockatiel hair and a large bunch of matching chrysanthemums in his scuffed hands.

He told her he loved her after their third date and bought her an engagement ring from Elizabeth Duke six months later. It was gold with three small sapphires and two tiny rubies embedded in the band. She'd worn it because she didn't want to hurt his feelings.

'How come you never tell me that you love me?' he'd asked one evening. 'You do love me, don't you?'

She'd looked into his big, tender eyes, felt every shred of his nervous and unadulterated love for her and realized that there was only one thing she could possibly say to him.

'Yes,' she'd said, smiling and taking his hand. 'Yes, of course I do.'

It hadn't even occurred to her that she could say no.

They had spent hours on his single bed kissing and caressing. Joy didn't enjoy the feeling of his slick tongue inside her mouth or his bitten-down fingernails on her flesh. As their fumblings progressed from over clothes to under clothes and from under clothes to inside clothes, Joy enjoyed it less and less. But she never denied him anything. She even let him guide her hand into his trousers one wet afternoon, and on to his clammy testicles. Once there she had no idea what to do next, and Kieran was too shell-shocked to find himself with Joy's hand on his balls to push things any further, so she'd cupped them with as much enthusiasm as she could muster until she'd felt it was polite to remove her hand and place it somewhere less personal.

Joy didn't permit Kieran's fumblings because she felt sorry for him. It wasn't an act of charity. Nor did she permit them because she was intimidated in any way. And she didn't permit it because she felt she should be grateful, either. She permitted it, purely and simply, because she didn't believe she had the right not to. If she'd said no to Kieran at any point, she would in effect have been suggesting that she was better than him. And although anyone looking at Joy and Kieran objectively would have seen in a flash that she was way out of his league, although her parents were openly nauseated by the well-intentioned but unsavoury Kieran and the thought of him laying a finger on their beautiful, delicate girl, Joy just didn't see it that way. She wasn't anything special, so she had no right to deny other people the things they really wanted.

Luckily for Joy, Kieran never asked her for her virginity. He'd treasured Joy's virginity almost as much as Joy had been baffled by it; had held her hand in his while his eyes welled up with tears when she told him that she'd never had sex with anyone. As far as Kieran was concerned, Joy's virginity was such a precious jewel that no one in the world, least of all him, should be allowed to take it away.

They'd split up after two years when Joy had got to

the end of her tether with the incessant hours of unful-
filling canoodling on Kieran's single bed and had realized that ending the relationship was the only way to
make it stop. He'd cried so much that snot had bub-
bled out of his nose, but been otherwise dignified.
He'd brought her yellow flowers and a nylon bear on
her birthday a week later, then she'd never seen him
again.

On her first day in the sixth form, Miranda, one of
the school bullies, took a sudden shine to her. She plied
Joy with cigarettes and spliffs and little blue pills until
one autumn evening, two months into their new 'friendship', sitting on the banks of the M25, watching the setting sun and halfway through a bottle of Wild Turkey,
Miranda had suddenly pinioned Joy to the grass and stuck
her tongue down her throat.

Joy allowed Miranda to explore the inside of her mouth
and the contours of her teeth, to her heart's content. She
even allowed Miranda to pull up her T-shirt and lick her
nipples, but as neither of them really had any idea what
happened next in an encounter of this kind it never really
went any further. The friendship had fizzled out when
Miranda met a proper grown-up lesbian at half term who
taught her how to do things properly and since then Joy
had remained completely untouched.

Joy didn't really understand the concepts of sex or
desire. She'd never in her almost eighteen years met
anyone with whom she could contemplate having sex;
never felt her loins stir or tingle. The idea of being pen-
etrated felt alien to her, like swallowing a hardboiled egg
whole, or threading a piece of string through her head,

from ear to ear. She'd had crushes on pop stars and actors, and she'd had crushes on the unattainable boys from the grammar school down the road, but she'd never, ever felt pure carnal desire in her life.

Up until now.

She watched Vince walking back towards her, across the pub, clutching two pints of lager. She liked his hair, thick and light brown, curling naturally into a soft quiff at the front, military short at the back and sides. He was wearing a black Fred Perry tucked into black gabardine peg-fronted trousers. His neck was heavy and smooth, and his shoulders were wide and strong. His big, handsome hands made the pint glasses look insubstantial. He was the man she wanted to lose her virginity to. From nought to sixty. Just like that.

'So,' she said, breathing him in as he sat down next to her, 'tell me about the scars.' And that was the other thing about this Vince person – he made her feel as if she could say anything she wanted.

He smiled and touched them. 'Aah,' he said, 'the scars. Do you really want to know?'

'Uh-huh,' she nodded.

'OK. Well, I had some surgery. A year ago. I had some bone taken out of my jaw, pins put in, that sort of thing.'

'What – really? How come?'

Vince shrugged. 'To de-ugly me,' he said.

Joy laughed. 'What do you mean, "de-ugly"?'

'I mean, I was weird-looking. I had an underbite, like this ...' – he pushed his lower jaw out a little to show her – 'and it was affecting my eating and my teeth and everything, so I had corrective surgery. That's where they went in to get to the bone.' He pointed at the scars.

Joy winced. 'Did it hurt?'

'God, yeah. It was fucking agony. I couldn't eat properly for months after – lost loads of weight. I was under ten stone by the time they took the braces off. Looked like a skeleton. It was like hell, you know, couldn't talk, couldn't swallow, couldn't move my jaw. All I did for a year was take painkillers and listen to music. It was a total nightmare.'

'God, you poor thing. Is it OK now?'

'Yeah. Well, sort of. It still aches a bit, still feels stiff when I wake up in the morning, and yawning and stuff can be quite uncomfortable.'

'And did you . . . were you . . . I mean how ugly *were* you, exactly?'

'Well, the kids at school seemed to think I was pretty hideous. Melonhead, they called me.'

'Melonhead? Why Melonhead?'

'That's my name. My surname. Well – the "melon" bit, anyway.'

'Your surname is Melon?'

'Uh-huh. With two *l*s.'

'No way.'

'Yeah. Mellon. Could have been worse. I could have been a girl with enormous tits.'

'I think it's a beautiful name.'

'Do you?'

'Yes. It's pretty.'

'Hmm. I never thought of it like that before. I even thought about changing it after Chris and mum got married – changing it to Chris's surname.'

'Which is?'

'Jebb.'

'Oh, no.' She frowned and shook her head. 'Mellon's much nicer.'

'You reckon?'

'Oh, God, yeah. I'll swap with you, if you like.'

'Why? What's yours?'

'Downer. Nice, eh?'

'Oh. It's not so bad. Especially with your first name. They kind of cancel each other out.'

Joy smiled. 'I guess so,' she said. 'But the therapists had a field day with it.'

'Therapists?'

'Yes. Therapists.' Joy breathed in. She wanted to tell him. She wanted him to know her. 'I suppose it's only fair for you to know that you're sitting in a pub with a nutter.'

'Yeah, right.'

'No, seriously. I spent four weeks in hospital earlier this year. I had a nervous breakdown.' She stopped and smiled tightly, waiting for his reaction, knowing already that he would understand.

And then she told him everything – all the things she'd vowed never to tell anyone because they were so sordid and so seedy. She told him about the day she'd got back from school and found her father sitting on a chair in the kitchen with his trousers around his ankles and Toni Moran from across the road sitting astride his lap and how Toni Moran had carried on pumping up and down obliviously for a full five strokes after she'd walked in, while her father stared at her in mute horror over her shoulder.

She told him about how her father had given her £500 in crisp £10 notes not to tell her mother and how she'd spent it all on clothes from Kensington Market which she'd taken back the following weekend because she'd felt so guilty and how she'd then hidden the £500 in a shoebox in the bottom of her wardrobe and how for weeks afterwards she'd had to watch her mother kow-towing to her father, cooking his dinner, polishing his shoes, rubbing his feet on the sofa at night, in the full knowledge that he was still conducting his affair with Toni Moran. She told him how much she'd wanted to tell her mother but hadn't dared, too scared of the reper-cussions which she could only imagine would impact harder on her mother than on her father, and how she'd learned to recognize the smell of Toni Moran on her father when he came home from the golf course or a committee meeting.

She told him about the awful sense of complicity that her father had tried to foster between the two of them, as if the duplicity was some great adventure they were sharing and how instead of getting easier it had become harder and harder to keep the secret locked away inside.

It had all come to a head while she was going through the stress of university interviews, dragging a twenty-pound A1 portfolio around the country in the middle of an unseasonal heatwave, sitting outside offices with a dozen other candidates, knowing that they were all better than her, wondering why the hell she was even bothering.

She began to get this unsettling, panicky feeling all the time, as if her body was nothing to do with her.

She'd forget how to walk, sometimes, how to make her legs move. And other times she'd forget how to breathe properly and her heart would stop, then start racing, then stop again. She spent so much time focusing inside herself, existing inside a strange, tinny little bubble of self-obsession, that she became absent-minded and distracted to an almost comical extent. She left things everywhere she went, forgot entire conversations, and failed to turn up for prearranged appointments. But she didn't know how close she was to falling apart until one spring afternoon when she turned up for an interview at Chelsea School of Art – without her portfolio. She didn't realize she'd left the portfolio at home until the interview panel had asked to see it, at which point she burst into tears and ran from the room. She got on the wrong train at Fenchurch Street and ended up in Norwich. She didn't have enough cash on her to buy a ticket back to London, so her mother had driven all the way from Colchester and brought her home.

The following morning the postman delivered not one but three letters of rejection from her top three choices of university, and Joy decided that it would be better for everyone if she wasn't around. This revelation cleared her head for the first time in a month, and it was with an amazing sense of clarity that she sat cross-legged on her bed and ingested twenty-three paracetamols and a third of a bottle of peach schnapps.

Her mother found her half an hour later and rushed her to Colchester General, where they pumped out her stomach with salty water until she felt like a wrung-out flannel.

In retrospect, Joy knew that she hadn't really intended to kill herself. She'd known her mother would find her; she'd known she hadn't taken enough. She just wanted to go home and forget that it had ever happened. But everyone involved took it very seriously – seriously enough to do something about it. She was admitted to a psychiatric ward the next day.

The day after that she received a letter from Bristol University offering her a place on their Graphic Design BA degree course. Her mother wrote back on her behalf to explain why she wouldn't be able to take it up.

She couldn't really remember much about the next few weeks. It was a blur of pills and questions. Somewhere along the line she must have told someone about her father and Toni Moran because by the time she finally came home, four weeks later, her father was a in a state of high contrition and everything felt different. Hence this holiday. Hence the atmosphere of forced geniality that hung over everything they said and did.

It was Alan who'd put Joy in hospital. Alan owed them. And Alan was paying the price.

When the pub closed at eleven-thirty, they instinctively turned in the opposite direction to the Nelson's and the Seavue Holiday Home Park, and headed towards the seafront instead. 'Word Up' blasted from the open windows of a spartan nightclub over an arcade on the promenade. They crossed the road and passed the open doors of the club. Hard-faced girls in sunbleached denim stood outside, smoking full-strength Marlboros and drinking half-pints of cider. Burly boys in nylon bomber jackets drank beer from plastic cups and sneered at each other.

They wandered across the soft, manicured grass of the seafront promenade, past the neat pavilion and towards a bench facing out towards the sea. A few shadowy sea-gulls circled overhead, their angry cries merging with the ghostly din of Cameo still echoing from the club. The beach was completely empty.

They sat down in unison and breathed in the fresh sea air, and as the brine hit Joy's lungs she felt herself swell up with happiness. She'd drunk too much and life had taken on a golden, blankety feeling she'd never thought possible. For the first time in her life Joy felt . . . *normal.*

She was no longer daunted by Vince's good looks and brooding aura. Vince wasn't what he appeared. He wasn't cool and moody. He wasn't intellectual or hard. He wasn't intimidating.

He was interesting and kind and funny.

He was human and generous and thoughtful.

He was awkward and a misfit.

He'd missed out on great big chunks of his youth.

He was just like her.

Joy had never met anyone just like her before. She'd spent her life trying to bend herself to fit to other people's shapes. For years she'd contorted herself into tricky positions, like those people who could fold themselves into boxes, but walking out of the Nelson's that evening with Vince had felt like stretching her legs after a long journey, like rolling her head on her shoulders after too much studying. She didn't have to pretend to be cool, pretend to be clever, pretend to be interested, pretend to be aroused, pretend to be anything. It was a relief.

'I think you're great,' she said, bringing her knees up to her chest and turning to smile at Vince.

He started, and a shy smile spread across his face. 'Me?' he said. 'Really?'

'Yes. You. Really.'

She pulled his hand off his lap and, without even a moment's hesitation or awkwardness, brought it up to her lips and kissed it.

'I think you're great, too,' he said. He smiled again, picked up her hand and brought it to his lips and, as his mouth connected with her flesh, Joy's whole body tingled like a sneeze.

And then they both laughed, reached for each other's faces and kissed to the distant sound of teenage Hunstanton girls singing along to 'Venus' by Bananarama.

Five

Vince was awoken the next morning by the sound of wood pigeons cooing from the trees.

He wiped away the thick condensation that covered the letterbox-shaped window, and as the view came into focus he considered the mist fogging the corresponding window of the next-door caravan. Was it the sweet, tangy morning breath of Joy Downer? Was it the visual accumulation of her night's dreams, thoughts and movements, every droplet a moment's sleep? Was she there now, on the other side of the brown aluminium siding, murmuring gently in her sleep, one leg outside the covers maybe, bent slightly at the knee? Or maybe she was just waking up, rubbing her eyes, stretching her arms, tousling her silky hair with bunched-up fists?

He brought his own fist to the window to wipe away the new layer of condensation he'd created, and as he did so the curtain opposite shot open, a meaty hand cleared the opaque mist from the window and a large, greasy face appeared, squinting into the morning sunshine.

Barbara.

Vince pulled his curtain closed and let his head fall upon his pillow, shuddering gently at the terrifying image left lingering in his mind's eye.

He got out of bed and wandered through to the living

area. Chris was eating freshly baked bread spread with thick peaks of peanut butter, and Kirsty was still in her dressing gown, suggesting that Chris had been up first to do the breakfast run. There was a fresh pot of tea on the side, and Vince poured himself a mug and sat down. Half the curtains at the far end of the caravan were still closed against a dazzling sun that cast a dank orange light through the interior, highlighting the clouds of smoke from Kirsty's cigarette. Radio 1 was on, some overexcited DJ shouting about the wonderful weather and introducing 'Living Doll' by Cliff Richard and the Young Ones.

'Bread?' said Chris, reaching for the bread knife.

'Nah,' said Vince, eyeing the crusty loaf and finding it strangely unappealing.

'Lovesick?'

'Eh?'

'Lovesick,' Chris repeated, nodding at Kirsty.

Vince tipped a teaspoon of sugar into his mug and grunted.

'So, what time did you two crawl back last night, then?'

'I dunno. One, two, something like that.'

Chris laughed. 'One or two, my arse! *Three-thirty* – that's what time it was. What the hell did you two find to do in Hunstanton until three-thirty in the bloody morning? Or shouldn't I ask?'

'We just talked – that's all.'

'Aaaah,' said Chris, gouging another large knifeload of peanut butter from the jar and flopping it on to a slice of bread. 'Talking, eh? That's the ticket – best way into a girl's drawers, that. Up all night talking – you're halfway there, mate.'

Vince watched Chris's peanut butter merging with the oily yellow butter already pasted on to his bread and felt his stomach wriggle. 'It's not like that,' he muttered.

'Course it's like that.'

'It's not. Honest. Joy's — she's not that kind of girl. We're just friends, that's all.'

Chris shook his head and laughed wryly.

Vince caught the vibration of a look being thrown across the table from Kirsty to Chris. Chris closed his mouth against his next comment and dropped his gaze. 'Good,' he said. 'Friends. That's grand, that is.'

A moment passed in silence, save for the hysterical babble of the Radio 1 Roadshow and the crackle of Kirsty's tabloid as she peeled apart the pages.

'So,' began Chris, 'your new "friend". D'you think she'd like to come to the beach with us today?'

'I don't know,' snapped Vince, beginning to lose patience. All he wanted to do was sit here and ruminate on the exquisite perfection of last night. He didn't want to have to reconcile it with the reality of his circumstances. He didn't want to consider the practicalities of his parents and her parents and the banality of making plans and arrangements. He just wanted to drift around in this state of rapture until he somehow floated his way back into her company again. Was that too much to ask?

'I'll ask her, if you want,' said Chris.

'Oh, for fuck's sake — just drop it, will you?'

'Oh, come on, Vince. Don't be like that. Don't you want to see her in a bikini?' He threw him a raised eyebrow and Vince cracked a smile. 'Leave it to me. I'll sort it.'

*

Great, thought Vince a couple of hours later, as he peered into the rear view mirror of his mum's Mini.

A poker-straight Alan sat behind the steering wheel of his shiny Jaguar, negotiating the treacherous speed humps of the dirt track to the beach with strange, diagonal swooping motions. Next to him, barely visible above the dashboard, sat the overly radiant Barbara, mopping at her brow with a handkerchief and wearing some kind of hat. And there, in the back, pinioned against the door by the sheer volume of an oversized picnic hamper, sat Joy.

She had one elbow on the hamper and the other on the window frame, and stared pensively at the windswept landscape as the breeze swept her hair away from her face. Every time Alan performed one of his peculiar swervy negotiations of a speed bump, she gripped the window frame and grimaced slightly.

Chris's plan had backfired somewhat. In the process of inviting Joy to join them at the beach, he'd inadvertently asked her parents, too.

Stupid bastard.

Holmes Beach was part of a nature reserve encompassing acres of fragrant, shady pine forests, endless tide-stippled beaches and undulating sand dunes. A ruddy man in a balsawood hut charged them 50p per car to take the ginger-dust road down to the beach. Every half a mile or so, Chris got out of the car, swung open a gate and gestured Alan's car through after theirs with an exaggerated flourish and a bow.

The sky stretched endlessly overhead, sapphire blue and studded with tiny thumbprint clouds. Salty sweat gathered in sticky pools between Vince's thighs on the green vinyl seats of the Mini. He took a swig from a warm can of Coke and watched Chris's thumb massaging the back of his mum's slender, suntanned neck.

And then an image came to mind, an image of he and Joy on the seafront last night, of Joy's lean fingers threaded through his hair, her breasts pressed up against his chest, her leg wrapped round his thigh. He remembered the alien, thrilling feeling of his tongue as it made its way around hers and how quickly it had felt normal. But most of all he remembered how passionate Joy had been, the little pants and whimpers that escaped from between her lips, the hardness of her mouth against his, the clash of teeth that neither of them acknowledged. She'd set the pace, guided his hand on to her bare breasts under her shirt, pressed her hand against his groin through the gabardine of his trousers, pushed herself closer and closer to him.

They'd kissed like that for nearly three hours.

People had passed them, thrown comments at them – 'Oy-oy,' 'Go on, my son.' But they'd remained oblivious, tied up together in a knot of frenzied passion.

When they'd finally pulled apart and decided to get back to the caravan site Vince had felt engorged with blood from head to toe – every last bit of him felt taut, swollen and ready to burst. As they walked back to the Seavue, hand in hand and slowly detumescing, he'd considered his first experience of sexual contact and decided that those three hours on a bench with Joy Downer at the age of nearly nineteen had more than compensated for everything he'd missed before. And as he said good night to her outside the door of her caravan and felt her hands running up and down his bare skin underneath his T-shirt, he'd decided that this was it. This was the girl he was going to lose his virginity to.

The car park for the beach was full, and they found themselves stranded a hundred yards from the path to the beach. Alan pulled up beside them, rolled down his window and gestured ahead.

'Just dropping the ladies off first, with the food. Back in a tick.'

'Good idea.' Chris and Kirsty waved him on his way, smiling widely until his car was far enough away to allow their faces to drop.

'I really don't like that man,' said Kirsty, unclipping her seat belt and shuddering slightly. 'He gives me the willies. I'll bet you anything he hits that Barbara. Probably goes to prostitutes, too,' she added as an afterthought.

'Blimey,' said Chris, 'and you've based all that on half an hour of conversation, have you?'

'Yes,' she said, defiantly, squinting into the distance at Alan's car. 'It's just the way he looks at me. And the way he talks to his wife. He's just creepy, that's all.'

They emptied the Mini's boot of beach towels, sun cream, carrier bags full of crisps and Tupperware boxes of varying sizes and shapes, and walked towards the path where Joy and Barbara waited in the sun with their ludicrous hamper.

They waited for Alan to catch up with them, then set off towards the beach in a strange convoy of oversized picnic equipment, mismatched beach towels and incongruous people. Vince quickened his pace to meet up with

Joy halfway down the wooden slatted path. She was wearing her black combat shorts again, with a khaki cheesecloth shirt that looked like it had originally belonged to a man. Her hair was tied in a messy pony-tail on top of her head. She looked as if she was on her way to scrape monkey faeces off tree trunks in Borneo.

'What are you listening to?' he said, gesturing to the Walkman peeping out of her shirt pocket.

'Oh – just stuff,' she said. 'A compilation.' She smiled at him and tucked her earpieces into her pocket.

'Sorry about this,' he said, sliding his sweaty hands into the pockets of his shorts.

'What?'

'This whole, you know – Chris dragging you all out to the beach. I told you he could be persuasive.'

'Don't worry about it,' she said lightly. 'Dad was going on about coming to this beach anyway. And besides – we get to spend the day together.'

Vince glanced down at her to check she'd really just said that and felt pleasure rise through him when he realized that she had. 'Cool,' he said, 'positive thinking. I like it.'

They wandered for a while, searching for the perfect dune that Chris had claimed as his own last summer.

Up and down sand dunes they wandered, the midday sun beating down on their heads, the dune grass tickling at their calves, until finally they found a dune that both Alan and Chris agreed was acceptable.

They laid out hairy blankets and lurid velour beach towels. Alan and Barbara spent ten minutes constructing a yellow-and-green-checked windbreak, completely missing the point of settling in a sand dune, then they all began the slightly uncomfortable process of disrobing in front of total strangers.

Chris pulled off his T-shirt with all the confidence of a hairy-chested, twenty-nine-year-old man with a full set of weights in his garage and thirty sunbed sessions under his belt. Kirsty wriggled self-consciously out of her shorts and halterneck, uncovering a tiny black bikini held together between the breasts with a fake Gucci 'G' in gold that caught the sun with her every movement.

Alan pretended not to watch her undressing and held his stomach in so tightly that his ribcage looked as if it might come bursting through his speckled skin. Every time he removed an item of clothing he folded it into a precise square and packed it tightly into a plastic bag. His legs, Vince noticed, were devoid of any kind of hair from mid calf down, and he wore a pair of navy polyester shorts with an elasticated waist.

Barbara clambered awkwardly out of her tight cotton dress to reveal what looked at first glance like yet another tight cotton dress, but was actually a rather bulky, full-figured swimsuit, which could only be described as a bathing costume. The legs of the bathing costume ended a quarter of the way down her thighs in an elasticated bunch, forcing her curdled flesh into florets.

Vince turned to glance at Joy. She had gone as far as removing her DM shoes and unbuttoning her cheese-cloth shirt to reveal a grey singlet, but didn't appear to have any intention of removing any further garments.

Alan scooped off his leather sandals and laid them side by side on the sand. 'Come on, love,' he said, glancing at his daughter, 'strip off. You can't sit there all day looking like a prisoner of war.'

'Yes, I can.'

'Oh, for goodness sake,' he muttered, 'beautiful day, sun's out, having a lovely holiday, sitting there like a nun in all your clothes. I really don't understand you. It's not as if you've got anything anyone would want to see.'

'Oh, Alan,' said Barbara, 'leave her alone. She can keep her clothes on if she wants.'

'Yes, well, you would say that, wouldn't you?'

'Alan,' she chastised ineffectually.

'Yes, yes,' he muttered, 'mustn't say anything to upset our precious daughter. I know – *I know.*' He started ranting quietly to himself under his breath while he squirted sun cream down the full length of his arms and began rubbing it in vigorously.

'Here,' he said, throwing the bottle at Barbara, who'd just managed with some difficulty to settle herself into a sitting position, 'do my back, will you?'

Kirsty shot Chris a look as a sour atmosphere descended upon the dune.

Joy watched her mother patiently rubbing cream into Alan's freckled shoulders with a look of barely disguised disgust, then got to her feet. 'I'm going for a walk.' She threw Vince a look. 'You coming?'

'Yeah. Sure.' He leaped to his feet.

'Make sure you're back in an hour for lunch,' said Alan, tapping his watch.

'I'm not hungry.'

'Well, make sure you're back anyway, for politeness sake, if for nothing else. Honestly,' he murmured under his breath, 'why does it all have to be such a bloody *per-formance*? One o'clock. Sharp. Back here,' he said, tapping his watch at her.

'Yes,' she hissed, 'whatever.' And then they clambered over the small hillock at the foot of the dune and headed for the beach.

'Sorry about that,' said Joy, adjusting her ponytail.

'Is he always like that?'

'No, not always. Just when he forgets to pretend that he's nice. Which is most of the time.'

As they climbed over the top of the last dune, the beach appeared before them, like a foreign country. It stretched out for miles in every direction, with families scattered across its vast expanse like dropped coins. Sandy-tailed dogs ran in lunatic circles across the hard, damp sand, mad with disbelief at how much space they had to play in. Small children sat with splayed legs and plastic buckets, constructing castles and cars out of the malleable sand. Further out the paper-flat beach turned to silvery saltwater wrinkles, like glass eels. The sea was nothing more a thin navy line in the very furthest distance.

'Mmm,' said Joy, breathing in deeply and wrapping her arms around her chest.

Out of the cauldrons of the dunes, the temperature was at least five degrees cooler and there was a refreshing breeze.

They surveyed the awesome view for a moment, then started walking.

'So,' said Joy, 'what's it like having cool parents?'

Vince smiled. 'I don't know,' he said. 'It's good, I suppose.'

'You're so lucky, you know?'

'Yeah, I guess so. I mean, they're not perfect or anything, but –'

'I used to think I was adopted,' she cut in.

'Really?'

'Yeah. I could never quite believe that my parents were really my parents. And it's not just that I don't look like them. It's just ... I don't feel like we're from the same *tribe* – do you know what I mean? It's like, you and Chris and your mum – even though you're all completely different, there's this unity about you, as if you all came from the same place originally. I don't know, maybe it's because I wasn't born in England ...'

'You weren't?'

'No, I was born in Singapore.'

Vince looked at her in surprise. 'Really?'

'Uh-huh. My dad used to work for Jaguar. He was a sales director for the biggest showroom in Singapore. He and my mum were out there for about ten years. They came back when I was a few weeks old.'

'It's funny, you know. I thought the first time I saw you that you looked kind of exotic.'

'Exotic?' she scoffed.

'Yeah. It's the eyes,' he said, framing them with his fingers. 'Kind of oriental-looking.'

Joy laughed, looking pleased. 'Do you think?'

'Yes. Definitely. They're stunning.'

She put a hand up to touch her eyes, and for a moment they stared at each other.

'Maybe you *were* adopted,' he countered. 'Maybe that would explain the eyes?'

She smiled, and pushed some hair out of her eyes. 'Nah,' she said, 'I've seen my birth certificate. It's there in black and white. I am the spawn of Alan and Barbara Downer. It's official. Worse luck.'

Vince shrugged. 'Maybe it was something in the water,' he said.

'So, what about you? Do you look like your dad? I mean, do you know what he looked like?'

'Yeah. I've seen pictures. A couple of pictures anyway. He and my mum hadn't known each other that long when he died. They weren't married or anything.'

'And do you look like him?'

'Apparently, yeah. Especially since all this,' he indicated his scars. 'I can't see it myself – he was a bit of a rocker, you know. Long hair, 'tache, denim waistcoat. Not much like me when it comes to style.'

'Seriously?' she laughed.

'Yeah. My mum likes macho men. I sometimes wonder –' he began, then stopped.

'Go on.'

'I sometimes wonder what it would have been like for me if he'd been around when I was growing up. I sometimes think it might have been hard, you know? Maybe he'd have been disappointed in me, thought I was bit soft, a bit of a girl. I'm just not into all that "man" stuff – motorbikes, football – maybe he'd have had a problem with that.'

'Well,' said Joy, 'you might not have a 'tache and a motorbike, but you're certainly not girlie.'

'No?'

'No – you're incredibly manly.'

Vince laughed. 'Stop taking the piss,' he said.

'I'm not taking the piss,' she laughed. 'You are.'

Vince threw her a sceptical look.

'Come on,' she said, 'you must realize?'

'Realize what?'

'That you're a total hunk.'

'Er . . . *no.*'

'What, you mean to say that no one's ever told you before?'

'Like who?'

'Like *girlfriends.*'

'Well,' Vince shrugged, ran his fingers through his hair, shrugged again. 'I haven't had any girlfriends.' There. He'd said it.

'What, really?'

'Well, not proper girlfriends, you know. I mean, I've had friends who were girls, but I've never . . . I've never actually been out with anyone. Properly. It was just, all the girls I used to know just didn't see me in that way. I was just, *Melonhead*, you know? And then I've been pretty much out of circulation this past year. And . . . *shit*. I can't believe I'm telling you this. Do you think I'm a loser?'

'No. Of course I don't. I haven't exactly been around myself.'

'No?'

'No. I've only had one boyfriend. Kieran. He was three years older than me. But it was nothing serious. Well,' she laughed, 'apart from the fact that he gave me an engagement ring.'

'You were *engaged*?' An image of this older, engagement-ring-bearing man flashed through Vince's mind. He looked like Bryan Ferry.

She laughed again. 'No, I was *fourteen*, for God's sake. It was just a laugh. And besides, I was never in love with him.'

'You weren't?'

'No. He was a sweet bloke, but it wasn't as if we were going to get married or anything. It was just a phase, you know, getting stuff out of the way.'

Aaah, thought Vince, there it was. The mystical *stuff*. The stuff that meant that Joy had 'done it'. The stuff that meant that she'd caressed, undressed, seduced, had and been had.

'I've never really been in love,' she continued, 'never really been one of those girls, you know, those sitting-by-the-phone girls. Those *normal* girls.'

And she laughed again. But Vince wasn't listening. He was too busy pondering the myriad carnal possibilities conjured up by the word 'stuff'. The positions, the emotions, the emissions. Handjobs, blowjobs, missionary, doggy, oral sex, anal sex, girl on top, boy on top, from behind, spoons, frigging, licking, sucking, fucking – each one an alien, terrifying, *thrilling* concept.

Vince knew what these things *looked* like. Of course he did. He'd read the magazines, watched the videos, seen his mates fumbling in corners with dishevelled girls with their skirts ruched up to their waists. He'd seen these things, this *stuff*, just not felt it.

But Joy had.

Of course she had.

Everyone had.

Everyone except priests and nuns and freaks like him.

'Do you want to go and hide somewhere for a while?'

Joy was smiling up at him, using a hand as a visor to shield her eyes from the sun.

'Hide?'

'Yeah. You know. Somewhere private.'

He smiled. 'Like where?'

'Like one of those dunes,' she said as she indicated behind them with a jerk of her head.

'Yeah,' he said, 'OK.'

They chatted as they made their way back the way they'd come, and as they chatted and walked Vince felt himself changing, as if he was leaving a whole part of his life behind him, as if his real life was finally about to start.

He was walking along a beach with a girl who was just beautiful enough to make him feel like a character in a film, but not so beautiful that he couldn't think straight. A beautiful girl whose breasts he'd caressed, who he'd kissed for three hours, who wasn't a virgin, who thought he was handsome and hunky and great. A beautiful girl who'd never met 'Melonhead', who saw him only as he was now. And he was walking along a beach, barefoot, bare-chested, in the sunshine, just chatting in an easy, intimate manner with this beautiful girl as if it were the most ordinary thing in the world. And that, in itself, was the most extraordinary thing of all. How normal it felt, how right.

And Vince knew with the cool confidence of a grown man that, once they'd found themselves somewhere 'to hide' and stretched themselves out on the sand, they'd kiss again. He knew he'd touch her breasts again; her tongue would reach for his tongue, this beautiful girl. He also knew that his hand would cradle the back of her neck and the soles of his feet would caress the silky skin of her shins and that he could handle all of this, take it in his stride. Because he'd waited so long for this, thought about it for so many years, watched it happening to everyone he knew and now it was happening to him and he was nineteen and he was a man and she was a woman and it was his turn at last and he was ready.

He was ready for it all.

Five minutes later Joy put her hand into his trunks and gently, tentatively passed the palm of her hand over his shaft.

Two seconds after that he came all over her hand.

Six

The following day Vince awoke resolved to redeem himself. It didn't matter how much Joy had soothed him and reassured him that it didn't matter, that it happened to everyone, that it was no big deal, he just couldn't live with himself. It wasn't even that he was embarrassed about it – he was just disappointed.

A beautiful girl had been about to administer him a handjob and he'd blown it, completely. He had to prove to himself that he was capable of receiving a handjob without shooting his load like fourteen-year-old boy.

Chris was doing the washing up in a pair of pink Marigolds and singing along to 'Dancing on the Ceiling' by Lionel Richie when he surfaced from his bedroom.

'Morning.'

'Morning.'

'Where's Mum?'

'Gone to the butcher's. We're having a barbie tonight. Is that OK?'

'Yeah,' he murmured, 'cool.'

'You seeing the lovely Joy again today?'

Vince flopped on to the sofa and sighed. 'Dunno,' he shrugged. 'Maybe.'

Chris looked at him with concern. 'You all right, mate?'

'Yeah, I'm fine.'

'You sure?'

'Yeah. Totally.'

'Everything going all right with you and Joy? Yeah?'

'Fine. Great.' He picked up yesterday's *Daily Mirror* and flicked through it mindlessly for a while, but he couldn't concentrate. He was completely preoccupied with what had happened at the beach yesterday. He glanced across at Chris, who was now headbanging along to 'Addicted to Love' and playing air drums against the dishwater with a plastic brush.

Had it ever happened to him, he wondered, to macho Chris? He glanced at him again and licked his dry lips tentatively.

'You know . . .' he began tentatively. 'You know . . .'

'What's that, mate?'

'You know . . . you know . . . like, *wanking*?'

Chris laughed and pulled off his Marigolds. 'I certainly do, young Vincent.'

'Yeah, well, you know when a *girl* does it to you?'

'Ooh, yeah.'

'Well, you know how, like, when you're not expecting something, you know, does it ever . . . have you ever . . . ? *God!*' He thumped his thighs in exasperation.

'Here, Vince, take a deep breath.' Chris sat down next to him, clutching a tea towel. 'Now, take your time. Tell me what's on your mind. OK?'

Vince breathed in deeply, and flashed Chris an apologetic smile.

'Joy went for my dick yesterday.'

Chris's eyebrows shot into his hairline and a smile spread across his face. 'Oh, she did, did she?'

'Yeah. At the beach. And I wasn't expecting it. And . . . and . . .'

'You spunked your pants?'

Vince breathed out. 'Yeah. Like, two seconds later. And she said it was cool and everything, but now I'm just . . . *I don't know*. She's so experienced and everything, and I feel like such a loser.'

'Oh, Vincent, Vincent, Vincent.' Chris rubbed his back affectionately. 'It happens to everyone.'

'Does it?'

'Yeah, course it does.'

'Has it ever happened to you?'

'Of course it's fucking happened to me! Not for a while, I hasten to add. But when I was your age – yeah. Definitely. More than once. It's just, like, your body is this tightly wound coil, right, you're a man, your whole reason for being is to get your sauce up a woman's crack and knock her up – yeah?'

Vince nodded.

'And so when you get near a woman, the sun's out, you've got the horn, you're bound to get a bit . . . *ahead* of yourself. It's only natural.'

'But what can I do to make sure it doesn't happen again?'

Chris shrugged. 'There are no guarantees it won't, especially with you being a bit . . . *overripe* as it were. Best thing you can do is learn to feel relaxed with her. You know. Hang out with her. Get to know her. Build up to it slowly.'

'Yeah, yeah. You're right.'

'And remember she's just a girl, yeah? Go and see her now. Remind yourself. Just a girl. Just a human being. Sooner you see her, the more relaxed you'll feel. Get back on that horse, eh?' He nudged him gently in the ribs and got to his feet.

'Yeah,' said Vince, feeling fired with renewed confidence. 'Yeah. Thanks, mate.'

'No problem.' He sauntered away towards the draining board, clutching his tea towel. 'So,' he said, picking up a wet mug and twirling it idly around his fist. 'Just went for it, did she? Just, you know, *in there*, job in hand, no invitation?'

Vince nodded. 'Uh-huh.'

He nodded sagely and looked impressed. 'What a girl,' he said, and chuckled happily under his breath.

Vince did everything at double speed that morning in his rush to get over to Joy's. He threw the soap over his body in the shower, barely giving it time to lather. He jumped into his boxers and trousers, feet first. He gulped down his tea so fast he choked on it, and he checked his reflection for a total of ten seconds, a twentieth of his usual time.

Alan answered the door when Vince rapped on it impatiently ten minutes later.

'Oh. Good morning, Vincent.'

'Morning, Alan. Mr . . . er . . . Downer. Is Joy around? Please?'

'Hmm, I'm not sure if she's emerged yet. *Joy,*' he called over his shoulder, '*are you alive?*' Vince heard a muffled grunt coming from one of the bedroom doors. '*Visitor for you.* Come in. Come in,' he gestured to Vince, unenthusiastically.

He left Vince standing in the kitchen and sauntered

back to the dining table where he picked up the *Telegraph* and started rustling through it, ostentatiously. Two seconds later, the bathroom door opened and Barbara appeared looking terrifying in a pink quilted dressing gown and a see-through shower cap. She clutched at her gown with her hand when she saw Vince standing there. 'Oh, Vincent. You gave me a fright.'

And then the bedroom door opened and Joy appeared. A smile spread across her face when she saw him.

'Morning.' She scratched at her bed hair.

'Morning,' he grinned. 'Fancy a walk?'

She beamed at him. 'Give me ten minutes. No – give me five.' She reached up on to her tiptoes, kissed him gently on the lips and disappeared back into her girl-fragrant bedroom.

They walked towards the seafront, their arms looped round each other, and wandered around the tacky part of town for over an hour, never once loosening their grip on each other. Vince thought back to the hundreds, *thousands* of entwined couples he'd walked past in his life, clamped together at the hips. He thought back to those blokes he'd glanced at enviously, wondering what the hell it felt like for a girl to want to be seen out in public with you, *conjoined* that way. And now he was one of those guys and it didn't feel strange at all. It didn't even feel that exciting.

It just felt right.

They bought doughnuts that glittered in the sunshine, and wiped the sugar dust from each other's cheeks.

They spun round creaking carousels of postcards and

laughed at the tragic donkeys and municipal buildings photographed in lurid 1970s Technicolor. Joy bought a postcard of the seafront to send to her friend in San Diego, purely because of one poor man, unwittingly captured on film all those years ago, wearing orange tartan flares and stack-heeled shoes.

As the sun soared overhead the funfair came to life with the cloying scent of boiling sugar and axle grease. They meandered through its maze of coconut stalls and hooplas, past stacks of ugly nylon bears, oversized plastic dolls, see-through bags packed with pink sugar clouds and long ropes of pastel-coloured marshmallow, hanging like sugar cables. They smiled at small children riding on slow-moving carousels, their faces rigid with excitement.

At lunchtime they wandered back to the caravan site and ate salad in deck chairs with Kirsty and Chris. They lazed the afternoon away there in the sun, padding barefoot in and out of the caravan every now and then to get cold drinks from the fridge. Chris listened to the football on a crackling transistor and Kirsty painted her toenails electric blue, her toes separated by a pink foam knuckleduster.

At five o'clock the ice-cream van arrived and the silence was broken by the sound of thirty children screaming at their mothers for money and clambering all over each other to reach the vendor's hatch. Vince got them all Screwballs and Chris brought out the Monopoly. The four of them sat cross-legged on a hair blanket and threw dice for pieces, while they ate their ice cream. Joy was the top hat, Vince was the iron, Chris was the car and Kirsty was the Scottie dog because she always was.

Nobody had won by six-thirty and nobody cared.

Barbara and Alan returned from wherever they'd been all day just before seven, clutching brown paper bags and both wearing hats. Alan threw a disapproving glance at Joy as he wandered towards them and saw her hand clasping Vince's bare thigh.

There then followed a brief altercation, as Alan tried to persuade Joy to join them inside for a 'discussion re our dining plans'.

'But I'm not hungry,' she said. 'I've been eating all day.'

'Honestly,' he muttered, clenching and unclenching his fists, 'I thought this was supposed to be a *family* holiday. Barbara? Wasn't this supposed to be a family holiday? Wasn't that the whole bloody *point*?'

Joy tutted loudly and Alan's face turned puce. 'We're only here for your sake, you know that, don't you?' he snapped.

'Alan . . .' chided Barbara.

'Well, really – I'm just telling it as it is . . .'

'Yes, but Alan, we agreed –'

'Yes, yes, yes,' he sighed, angrily. Barbara smiled apologetically, and guided Alan gently back to their caravan by the elbow.

The four of them looked at each other. Chris gurned childishly at Joy and she smiled. 'Sorry,' she said, sheepishly.

'Have you noticed,' Vince said to Joy, 'how much time we seem to spend apologizing for our parents.'

'What do you mean?' said Chris in mock indignation. 'What the fuck have you got to apologize about *me* for? I'm totally fucking perfect, I am.'

'Yeah. Right,' harrumphed Vince, then Chris set about him in one of his affectionate but slightly overwhelming play fights, wrestling him on to his back and pummelling him around the ears.

Joy watched them in wry amusement. 'You know that sort of behaviour means you're gay, don't you?' she said, nonchalantly running a strand of her hair back and forth across her top lip.

Kirsty let out a loud hoot of laughter and slapped her thighs in delight.

'Eh?' said Chris and Vince in unison.

'Uh-huh. Latent homosexuality manifested in a strong desire for physical contact with a member of the same sex.'

Vince didn't take offence; just felt a frisson of delight that he had a girlfriend who could a) use long words and b) take the piss out of Chris. Chris on the other hand looked appalled. 'Fuck off,' he scoffed.

'Oh, no,' Vince teased, 'you've really done it now. Questioned the sexuality of a Northern male.'

'Too right,' said Chris, smoothing down his hair. 'There in't no poofs north of Watford, I'll have you know. They only get bred down South.'

'Oh, like John Inman and Larry Grayson, you mean? Oh, and Russell Harty, too, while we're at it.' Joy shrugged her eyebrow at him, and Chris threw Vince a look of mock exasperation.

'And I thought she was such a nice girl,' he said. 'Well, the competition's off. You can keep her. She's all yours.'

And then it was Vince's turn to give Chris a good pummelling, while Kirsty and Joy burst into laughter so loud that a flock of wood pigeons took sudden flight from an overhanging tree, like a groundsheet being shaken free of crumbs.

Chris pointed the trigger at the coals and squeezed. A fine mist of violet droplets fell over the embers, igniting a wall of amber flame, and Chris prodded at an annihilated sausage, easing it gently on to its side.

'Come on,' he wheedled, 'one last sausage. Who's up for it?'

Everyone declined politely and rubbed their swollen bellies.

The lazy drunken afternoon had drifted seamlessly into a lazy drunken barbecue. Chris had managed to persuade a reluctant Alan and Barbara to join them in their barbecue, as well as another unsuspecting couple who'd happened to wander past as proceedings were kicking off. The floor was littered with greasy paper plates, greying bones and leathery potato skins, and Alan was opening yet another bottle of Beaujolais. He was turning slightly pink around the edges and his voice was getting louder with every glass of wine.

'So,' he said, swinging himself round to address Kirsty, who sat on a blanket with her legs folded beneath her, '*Kirsty*.' He said her name so loudly that she jumped slightly. 'It hardly seems possible that a young slip of a thing like you could have mothered this hulking great lad —' he gestured at Vince. 'Do they start early where you come from?'

'*Alan*,' hissed Barbara.

'What?' he snapped. 'Can't a man give a woman a compliment any more? I suppose it's *sexist*, is it?'

'Oh, Alan . . .'

'It's OK,' soothed Kirsty. 'I'm not bothered. I was seventeen when I had Vince.' She turned to Alan and smiled. 'Not that young, really.'

'Well,' Alan boomed, a smile spreading across his face, 'I must say that you're very well preserved, my dear. You don't look a day over thirty.'

'Thank you,' smiled Kirsty, handling the compliment like a true professional. 'It's having a toy boy.' She winked at Chris. 'Keeps me young.'

Alan chortled. 'Oh, yes, yes, yes. I can see that it would. All that blood pumping through your system, eh?' He winked. 'Nothing better for the skin than a healthy sex life.'

'*ALAN!*'

'Oh, for God's sake, *what*?! I'm just stating fact. It's well known that an active sex life keeps you young. Isn't that right, Kirsty?'

'Absolutely right, Alan,' Kirsty agreed gamely.

'And it's an excellent form of aerobic exercise, too. Or so it would appear.' He cast an appreciative eye up and down Kirsty's trim, toned legs. 'Not an extra ounce on you. Like a young girl.'

Kirsty laughed politely, but an uncomfortable silence was descending elsewhere.

'Nice to see,' he continued, obliviously, 'a woman on the cusp of middle age, taking such good care of herself. Very nice to see.' He smiled at her, revealing burgundy-tinged teeth.

'Right,' announced Joy, grabbing Vince's hand and hoisting him to his feet, 'we're going for a walk.'

The adults turned and looked at them in surprise.

'Yup,' said Vince, getting obediently to his feet, 'off for a walk.'

Before anyone had a chance to protest, they strode into the caravan, picked up Joy's bag and a couple of beers, bade a forceful good night to everyone and walked as fast as they could away from the tragic sound of drunken middle-aged revelry.

Seven

'My father is the most heinous creature known to mankind.' Joy took an angry gulp from a can of Heineken. 'God. Your poor mother. How totally embarrassing.'

'Oh, Mum can handle herself,' he said, squeezing her hand reassuringly. 'She's had plenty of practice at that kind of thing.'

'That's not the point. It's just, you know, in front of Mum, in front of me, in front of Chris – it's . . . it's *psychotic*,' she shuddered. 'You know, as if your mum would be interested in *him*. When she's so pretty and she's got Chris and everything. But he's so fucking vain that he really thinks he's in with a chance. You know. As if if he really switches on the charm, she's just going to fall *swooning* into his arms . . . *Aargh!*' she cried out in frustration, letting herself flop backward against the grass.

They'd wandered away from town, out towards the country lanes and found themselves in a small moonlight-dappled field. Vince glanced down at the prostrate and angry Joy, and smiled.

'Do you know what I like best about you?' he said.

'No,' she said grumpily. 'What?'

'Everything.'

She let out a loud snort of laughter.

'Do you know what I like best about *you*?' she said.

'No. Tell me.'

'This,' she said. And she grabbed him by the shoulders, pulled him down on top of her and stuck her tongue in his mouth.

Vince's head began to swim.

Their kisses were becoming more and more passionate, and Joy's hands had started roaming wildly around his body, pulling at the fabric of his T-shirt. It dawned on him eventually that she was actually trying to pull his T-shirt off, so he adjusted his pose while she yanked it roughly over his shoulder blades and flung it to one side.

Joy's sudden and unprompted passion was so overwhelming that it left Vince in the strange position of feeling pleasantly disengaged from the proceedings, as if he were sitting in the branches of a tree overhead, watching, munching on an apple, maybe.

Objectives, he thought, as her thigh passed over his shaft, I need objectives here. He concentrated on the rhythm of his tongue in her mouth for a while, trying to build up a twirly, swirly massaging motion. And then he decided. *Breasts*. Breasts would be his next objective. He tugged at the buttons on her shirt, feeling the little pearly discs slipping around underneath his fingertips. Fuck the buttons, he thought, fuck them. He concentrated on getting the loose-fitting shirt off over her head. He'd worry about the bra once that had been accomplished. But he didn't need to worry about the bra because, the moment the shirt was off, Joy's hand crept round her back and unclasped it, and now it was slithering around between them, untethered, like something alien and nonsensical. He pulled at it and it fell to one side, and now here they were, a man and a woman, top-less. Together. They embraced again, and Vince felt his bare flesh against her bare breasts, and at that point he lost all objectivity and went completely fucking mental as all the blood that wasn't supporting his astonishing hard-on rushed to his head.

Joy whimpered and gasped into his ear as they rubbed against each other, but then she took his hand from her breast and he thought, here we go, we're slowing it down now, too fast, too fast, back off, but even as he was thinking it she was leading his hand elsewhere, down below her waist, towards the loose waistband of her shorts, slowly past her soft abdomen, and then, like an electric shock, he felt it – Joy's pubic hair.

His ears started to buzz with excitement.

She brought his hand down further until it cupped her entirely, and suddenly he was on the threshold of a whole new world.

'Are you sure?' he whispered urgently in her ear.

'Mmmmmm.' He felt her nodding vigorously against his shoulder.

And as he started to make the acquaintance of this whole new world, to feel gingerly and cautiously around the folds and mounds and floppy bits, to absorb the textures and wonder what he should do next, Joy moved the game along again. She was fiddling with the buttons on his 501s, pulling apart the denim, her hand in his trousers, in his shorts, and now here they were, topless, inside each other's trousers, in the moonlight, miles from anyone. Vince tried to concentrate on the myriad things he was supposed to be doing, the kissing of the mouth, the caressing of the breast, the feeling of the whole new world, the hand in his own trousers, grasping him like a warm, soft kiss.

Just as Vince was thinking that things had gone as far as they could possibly go, that this was what they were doing, *all* they were doing, she was tugging at his jeans, tugging at his shorts, tugging them down his thighs, and it seemed as if she was trying to undress him, undress him completely so that he'd be naked, and he had no idea if it was what she wanted or not, but he didn't want to be the only one naked, the only one vulnerable, so he moved his attention to removing her shorts, her knickers, and then they were completely bollock-arsed-naked and they were rolling around on the grass together, *completely naked.*

And this, Vince couldn't help feeling, was the exact point at which he needed to start asking questions.

'Urhm,' he murmured, trying, with some difficulty, to detach his mouth from hers, 'erhm, hold on, hold on, hold on.'

'What?' She pulled away from him, her hair streaked across her face, her lips swollen and red in the moonlight.

'Well, what, what are we doing exactly?'

'I don't know,' she said breathlessly.

'I mean, are we ... ?'

'I don't know,' she said again.

'Because I need to know, because ...'

'I'm on the pill,' she said.

'Right,' he said.

'For PMT.'

'What?'

'I'm on the pill for my PMT. Not for ... I'm still a virgin.'

'You are? But I thought ...'

'What?'

'Nothing. You're a virgin,' he said.

'Uh-huh. Are *you*?'

'Er, yeah. I am.'

'And do you ... do you want to?'

'With you?' he said.

She nodded.

'God. Yes. Please. Do you?'

She nodded again. 'I really do. Really, really do ...'

'Are you sure?'

'Yes. Are you?'

'Yes.' Vince gulped. 'Oh, Jesus.'

Eight

They walked back across dry, shorn fields and dark, empty country roads. Joy felt raw and used between her thighs, like she'd been riding a very big horse all day. Her face was taut with dried saliva, and her mouth was sore and felt twice its normal size. Vince had his arm round her shoulders, and she had her arm round his waist.

Her knees had given way when she'd first tried to stand upright a few minutes ago. Gone like jelly. Collapsed to her knees in hysterical giggles. Vince had pulled her back to her feet, wrapped her in his arms and kissed her again.

She'd done it. They'd done it. Done everything in fact. They'd both wanted to try everything, everything they'd never done before. They'd done it in every possible position; from behind, her on top of him, even up against a tree. They'd given each other oral sex, too. Joy had never thought for a moment that she'd want to put a man's penis in her mouth, but the minute Vince suggested it, enthusiastically, as if it was a new flavour of ice cream, nothing could have stopped her. She hadn't had an orgasm – it was too uncomfortable for that – but doing it, having sex, losing her virginity to this strong, handsome man who made her feel so comfortable and so self-assured, had been the most exciting experience of her life.

'Can we do that again tomorrow?' she said, squeezing his waist.

'Yeah,' said Vince, 'why not? And how about the day after?'

'Definitely. Of course, we'll have to do it on Tuesday because it's your birthday.'

'Of course. I have to get my birthday shag. It's a tradition.'

She laughed. 'And then – after this, after Hunstanton – can we do it in Colchester?'

'Uh-huh. And Enfield.'

'Oh, yes – Enfield. I've always wanted to do it in Enfield.'

'I think we should just do it for ever. You know, just keep on doing it, indefinitely. Everywhere. Travel the world, just doing it. Nonstop.'

She nodded and squeezed his waist again. He suddenly stopped and turned her towards him and looked at her really intensely for a moment.

'You know that was the best thing that ever happened to me, don't you?'

She smiled. 'Me, too.'

'And you know that, God, I've wondered for so long if it would happen, how it would happen, when it would happen, who it would be with. Years and years of just, you know, *imagining*, and nothing that went through my mind came close to that. Really. Nothing.'

'Me neither.'

'And, when I said that I thought I was falling in love with you, back there, I wasn't just saying that because – you know – because of what was happening, because I thought it was what you'd want to hear. I said it because . . . I am. Completely.'

Joy smiled. All those years, all the pain, Kieran,

80

Miranda, Toni Moran, the overdose, the hospital, losing her place at Bristol, all those years of *existing* without *being* – all of it faded away into meaninglessness. She'd started to leave that girl behind the minute she first set eyes on Vince three days earlier, but standing here, in the Norfolk countryside, her hands in his, hearing him tell her that he loved her, the rawness of her lost virginity still ringing between her legs, she could almost see that girl fading away into a small smudge on the horizon.

'Are you really?'

'Totally. I mean it.'

And then Joy told him that she loved him, too. And for the first time in her life, she meant it.

Everything was quiet and still when they got back to the Seavue. The blankets, the paper plates, the screwed-up bits of kitchen roll had all been cleared away. The barbecue still gave off a feeble glow of warmth. All the lights were off in Joy's caravan. The flickering cathode glow of a black-and-white TV lit the interior of Vince's.

They kissed and said good night in whispers, and Joy took off her shoes and held them in her hand while she mounted the steps to her caravan.

'See you tomorrow,' she whispered, kissing the palm of her hand. 'Sleep tight.'

'You, too,' he whispered back. 'And thank you.'

She blew her kiss at him, grinned, then disappeared from view.

There was a strange atmosphere inside his caravan – Vince picked up on it the minute he walked in.

The TV was on, but neither Chris nor Kirsty was actually watching it. They were sitting facing each other across the dining table, Chris clutching an empty mug, Kirsty stubbing out a cigarette into a full ashtray. Kirsty had a stiff look about her, as if she was trying to hold something back. They'd obviously been deep in serious conversation.

'Everything all right?' he said, reaching for a glass from a shelf in the kitchen.

'Yeah. Fine.'

'How come you're both still up?'

'Night went on a bit late.'

'Yeah?'

'Yeah – couldn't get rid of the bastards.' Chris laughed without sounding relaxed.

Vince filled his glass with water from the tap and sat down next to his parents. 'Why are you two being so weird?'

'Weird?'

'Yeah – cagey. What's been going on?'

'It's nothing, love,' said Kirsty. 'Just – everyone got a bit *pissed* tonight. A bit carried away. We had some bad behaviour. That's all.'

'What sort of bad behaviour?'

'Oh, nothing really. Nothing we couldn't handle. Anyway, how was *your* evening?' she smiled, and squeezed his hand.

'Excellent,' he said. 'Great.'

'Where d'you go?'

'Oh, just down into town.' He blushed.

'You know you've got grass in your hair, don't you?' said Chris, grinning at him.

82

Vince slapped at his hair and dislodged a clump of dead grass on to the Formica surface of the table. 'Oh,' he said, staring at it.

'Oh,' Chris laughed.

'Yeah, well,' said Vince, unable to prevent a big shit-eating grin from consuming half of his face.

Chris slapped him on the back and laughed. 'So, did you manage to control yourself this time? Keep your load in the bay?'

'Chris!' He glanced at his mother in embarrassed horror.

'Oh, come on, mate. You know I tell your mum everything.'

Kirsty smirked. 'Could have done without knowing that particular nugget, though, I have to say.'

'So – it was cool, was it?' Chris baited him for more detail.

'Very cool,' smiled Vince, suddenly wanting them both to know, wanting to share with them the incredible fact of his lost virginity. 'Very cool indeed.'

'Yeah?'

'*Yeah.*'

'And am I reading between the lines correctly here, young Vincent?'

'I don't know what you're talking about.'

'You've bloody done it, haven't you? You and that lass? You've done it?!'

Vince grinned, and shrugged. 'Might have.'

'Oh, you fucking beauty!' Chris grabbed Vince's shoulders and gave him a big back-slapping bear hug. 'You beautiful fucking bastard!'

'Oh, Chris, honestly,' chided Kirsty affectionately. 'Anyone would think he'd just conquered Everest the fuss you're making.'

'There are parallels, my lovely wife. The boy's nineteen in two days. It was a challenge and he rose to it, God love 'im!'

'Well, I hate to take the romance out of it, love, but I hope you used, you know, *precautions*.'

'She's on the pill,' he said happily.

'Yes, but it's not just about contraception these days, is it? What about AIDS?'

Vince smiled. 'She's a virgin,' he beamed. 'Was. A virgin. Like me. We were both brand-new.'

'Aah,' said Chris, folding his arms across his chest and beaming proudly. 'Late bloomers. Isn't that sweet?'

And Vince smiled to himself because it was. It was fantastic, in fact. He'd always presumed that if he ever managed to lose his virginity it would be to some faceless woman in fancy lingerie who'd done it with a couple of dozen other men, who knew tricks and would teach him everything she knew. He'd always imagined it would be an exciting if slightly embarrassing rite of passage, an X-rated hurdle to be crossed before he could pursue other goals, such as love and relationships.

Sex with a virgin, if he'd ever considered it, would, by its very nature, have been a clumsy, unprofessional affair; a pair of monkeys trying to change a tyre, two learner drivers taking a Learjet out for a spin – the blind leading the blind.

But it hadn't been like that in the slightest. It was more akin to visiting the Taj Mahal with someone who'd never seen it before; someone who didn't yabber on about how to avoid the relentless pedlars at the entrance, who didn't tell you exactly where to sit to get the best view and how much better it had looked when they saw it in the late afternoon, but someone who arrived at the wrong time, got fleeced at the entrance, waited in the wrong queue, then stood next to you in silent awe as you both caught sight of it together for the very first time.

At some nonspecific time that night, Vince was awoken briefly by the sound of a car engine starting up and the dazzling arc of headlights passing his window.

When he woke up the following morning, Joy's caravan was empty, her parents' car was gone and there was an envelope on the doorstep addressed to him.

Inside was a slightly soggy note in blue ink made illegible by the unforecast rain that had fallen in a single, fast-moving shower that morning, and it didn't matter how hard Vince stared at it and what angle he studied it at, he could decipher only four words —

'I feel so ashamed.'

'What?' said Emma. 'That was all it said?'

'Well, that was all I could actually read. The rest of it was just blobs and blurs. I could make out the odd word. The odd "the" or "because", but nothing to make any sense of.'

'Shit,' said Claire, 'that's awful. What do you think it might have said?'

Vince shrugged. 'No idea,' he smiled, embarrassed. 'I supposed she'd just had second thoughts, you know. Decided that throwing herself at me in the middle of a field wasn't something she was particularly proud of. Whatever, she obviously couldn't face me. So that was that.'

'But that's so tragic. Your first love and it was all over in less than a week.'

'I know. What can you do?'

'God,' mused Natalie, 'I wonder what happened to her?'

'I saw her,' he said, 'about seven years later.'

'Really! What was she doing?'

'Well,' Vince smiled, 'that's a very interesting question.'

September 1993
Lost Cat

Nine

Magda pulled the thermometer from under Vince's tongue and held it up to the light.

'Hmm . . .' she said, angling it slightly towards her, 'no temperature. Is it possible you might just have a *cold*?'

'Give that here.' Vince snatched the thermometer from Magda's hand, squinted at the silvery sliver of mercury and handed it back with a grunt.

'Well,' he said, 'I *feel* fluey.'

'Well, if you *feel* fluey, then I suggest you stay at home. But I'm not calling your office. You can do that.' Magda pulled herself off Vince's bed and ruffled his hair. 'OK – I'm out of here.' She flicked her shiny black hair over her shoulder and jangled the keys to her branch of Warehouse in her hand.

Vince glanced at the unseemly hour displayed on his radio alarm.

'Staff training,' she said, by way of explanation.

Vince pouted. 'But I'm ill,' he said. 'Can't you stay and tend to me?'

'No, I can't! I've got staff to train. Clothes to sell. Money to make. Cheer up, though. You can spend all day watching daytime TV, you lucky bastard. And you can always ask Jeff to come in and mop your brow for you if you're desperate.'

She leaned over him and dropped a lipsticky kiss on to his forehead. 'Will you live?'

'I guess so.'

'Do you want me to come round later?'

'Yes, please.'

She smiled at him, blew him a kiss and pulled the bedroom door closed behind her.

Vince listened to her leaving and turned to look out of his bedroom window. Some of the trees in the distance were starting to go bald, the sky had that watery, nondescript look of a season in flux and he had a cold.

Summer was well and truly over.

He wandered into the kitchen where Jeff was ironing a white shirt in his underpants. 'Thought you were supposed to be ill,' he muttered, his eyes yo-yoing between the breakfast news and the sleeve of his shirt.

'I am,' said Vince, sniffing loudly for dramatic effect. 'Just getting some toast.' He pulled a loaf of Mother's Pride out of the fridge. 'I'm thinking about finishing with Magda.' He hadn't expected to say that. He hadn't even really thought it until that precise moment.

'Right,' said Jeff, turning his shirt upside down. 'Why?'

Vince shrugged and took a tub of St Ivel Gold out of the fridge. 'Just, you know, where do we go from here? Five months. What? Move in together? *Get married?*'

'Yeah, right,' said Jeff.

'And she's such a sweet girl, you know. I mean, *you* know what she's like.'

'Sweet,' said Jeff, 'sweet girl.'

'So, what do you think? Do you think I should? Do you –'

'Sshhhh . . .' Jeff shoved the palm of his hand in Vince's face and pointed at a man in a loud suit on the TV. 'Markets.'

'Sheesh,' said Vince, 'I don't know why you bother. It's not as if there's any money in them. It's not –'

'Christ, will you shut up, Vincent.'

Vince tutted, scraped butter as noisily as he could across his toast and sat down heavily at the breakfast table. He was sure that Jeff used to be a laugh. They'd met as flatmates in another place in Lewisham a year ago and had got on so well that when they'd got fed up sharing a draughty, poky house with three annoying girls from South Africa they'd decided to bail out and get a place together.

They'd found this place in *Loot* – it wasn't exactly luxurious, but it had enough classy features like bare floorboards, high ceilings and intricate plasterwork to make them feel as if they were living the sophisticated London dream. The kitchen was rickety and unfitted, but it had a huge sash window at one end overlooking Blackstock Road, an enormous old range and a battered farmhouse-style work surface. It was a cool flat. And Jeff was a cool guy. Way too cool. Cool to the point of a cold shower. Vince used to like the fact that Jeff was cool, but that was when Jeff was only cool with other people – now he was cool with Vince, too, and it was like sharing a flat with a slow-moving glacier.

Vince sat and munched on his toast while Jeff glided from room to room getting ready for work, emerging fifteen minutes later in a sharp navy double-breasted suit, crisp white shirt, buffed black Chelsea boots and subtle patterned tie, reeking of Christian Dior and swinging his briefcase as if he was actually looking forward to going to work.

'You don't fancy giving the place a once-over with the Hoover, do you, mate? Since you're at home all day.'

'What am I – your wife?'

'Only asking. Right. I'll see you later. Don't wait up.' And then he left, leaving Vince feeling very much like a wife – and a neglected one, at that.

Four hours later, Jeff was back. His tie was loose and hanging round his neck like a noose. His breath smelled of pubs and his eyes had a red tinge to them.

'What's going on?' said Vince, eyeing him up in the hallway.

'Fucking cunts,' said Jeff by way of reply. He dropped his briefcase on the floor and ripped his tie off.

'What?'

'Fucking cunts,' he said again. 'Made me redundant. Wasn't even allowed to finish the day. Had to leave there and then. Jesus.'

'You're joking?'

'Do I look like I'm joking?'

'No,' said Vince, 'not really.'

'Fucking cutbacks. Last in, first out. Jesus Christ.' He grabbed a handful of his hair and slumped over the kitchen table. 'What am I going to do?'

'Get another job?'

'Yeah, *right*,' he thundered, 'because if Janssen Higham are making people redundant then there are bound to be *loads* of other jobs going spare in the City, aren't there? Because the other banks are just desperate to pick Janssen's shitty leftovers out of the gutter, aren't they?'

Vince shrugged. The way the City worked was a complete mystery to him.

'No,' sighed Jeff, 'it's over. The bubble's burst. The

dream's over. *Reality bites, man . . . reality bites.'*

Vince bit his cheek and tried not to laugh. Jeff always behaved as if he thought he was being filmed.

'So,' Vince propelled Jeff's original question back at him, 'what are you going to do?'

'I don't know,' said Jeff, letting his head flop backwards. 'I really don't fucking know.' He sniffed loudly and slapped the palms of his hands on to his thighs. 'Right now I just want to get arseholed. You well enough to make it to the pub?'

Vince weighed up the benefits of lounging around the house in his dressing gown watching daytime TV and eating toast against the rare and hedonistic pleasure of a solid midweek afternoon's drinking, and went to his bedroom to get dressed.

It took Jeff two further days and a hell of a lot of drinking to decide what to do about his future. He pondered various business ventures – up-market sandwich deliveries, up-market tie shops, up-market party planners – but when his parents told him they'd rented a luxury five-bedroomed villa in Estepona for the whole winter and invited him along to 'clear his head' and 'consider his options' he'd made his mind up immediately. He put his redundancy payment into a high-interest bank account, packed his tennis racket, his sunglasses and his swimming trunks, and headed for the Costa del Sol with barely a backward glance. His future could wait until next year.

Vince, in the meantime, needed a new flatmate.

Ten

Cassandra McAfee was quite patently mad. It was obvious from the moment she stepped through the door, half an hour late, back to front, and apologizing to Ted from the flat across the hallway for barging in on him in the middle of his dinner. She spun round as Vince opened the door and grimaced at him. Her legs were twisted round each other like coiled rope, and she was doing some strange kind of dance.

'Ooh – toilet – please. I'm totally bursting.'

Vince pointed numbly in the direction of the bathroom. 'Second door down.'

She dropped her bag at his feet, sprinted past him, with her knees still locked together, and flung herself bodily through the bathroom door. She was still buttoning her jeans when she emerged a minute later. 'Sorry about that,' she said as she flashed him a smile. 'Cassandra. Cass.' She gave him her hand. He shook it, gingerly.

'Vince.'

'Vince,' she repeated. 'Nice flat.' She put her hands in her pockets and looked around. She was tall and rangy, with swimmer's shoulders and curly honey-blonde hair tied on top of her head like a bobble hat. She had clear skin with a pink glow to it and full lips that wrinkled up with all the extra skin in them. But it was her clothes that got in the way of Vince being able to fancy her –

patchwork denim flares, Day-Glo trainers, a heavy hand-knitted cardigan in moss green with a red collar and blue patch pockets, and a multicoloured velvet scarf with sequins on it tied loosely round her neck.

She looked like she'd been covered in Superglue and rolled through Camden Market.

'Wow,' she said, staring up at the big, high ceilings and the intricate plasterwork in the corners, 'this is really lovely. And there's so much space. Which is just as well because I've got *tons* of shit.' She smiled as she said this, as if it were a *good* thing.

'Oh,' she said, as he pushed open the door to Jeff's spartan, minimalist bedroom a minute later, 'what a sad-looking room. How could anyone live like this? A room like this needs *colour*. And *drama*. It needs . . . *soul*.' She stood dramatically in the middle of the room, her arms spread messianically. She paused for a moment, her mouth still slightly ajar as if waiting for inspiration. 'Can I paint it?'

'Er, sure. Yeah. I'm pretty sure we're allowed to re-decorate.'

'Crushed raspberry,' she said, resolutely, folding her arms. 'A really rich, succulent crushed raspberry. So rich you'd want to *lick* it off the walls. Mmm.'

'Mmm,' he said, 'sounds great.'

Vince still had another two people booked to come to see Jeff's room tomorrow night, and he wasn't entirely convinced about this mad patchouli-scented woman with her heinous knitwear and crushed raspberry walls, but she appeared to have arrived here with every conviction that the viewing was a mere formality and everyone else he'd seen that evening had been marginally less palatable than her and she could move in pretty much immediately, and she seemed harmless enough so he'd acquiesced and had already made a mental note to himself to cancel tomorrow's viewings. It just seemed so much *easier*.

'Have you remembered about Madeleine?' she said over a glass of wine in the kitchen.

'Er, no,' he said, squinting as he tried to recall every detail of their conversation. 'Who's Madeleine?'

'She's my cat. I told you about her on the phone. You said it was cool. Remember?'

'Ah – yes. Your cat.'

'Well, she's more than a cat, actually. She's my best friend. We've got this . . . *connection*.' She tapped her temples and lit the little roll-up she'd just made for herself. 'I had this friend once. A spiritualist. She told me that Madeleine was a *monk* in a former life. In the twelfth century. Somewhere up north, apparently. On an island. But not just any old monk – a much-revered monk. A *famous* monk.'

Vince threw her a sceptical look.

'I know that sounds mad. I thought she was mad. But it turns out that it's true.'

He threw her another sceptical look.

'No, seriously, it is. She wakes up every morning at sunrise and chants. Like this,' she closed her eyes and proceeded to make a bizarre humming noise. 'And always to the west. *Always to the west.*'

Vince laughed. She looked so serious, he couldn't help himself. She smiled at him and exhaled a fan of smoke. 'Yeah,' she said, 'I know. I'm a fruit. But you'll get used to me. Honest. And you will *love* Madeleine. Trust me. She will add a new dimension to your life. Everyone who meets her says so.'

Cass moved in four days later. She arrived in a camper van driven by a white guy with ginger dreads and a goatee beard twisted into a knot. The van was so full that every single window was obscured. Her possessions spilled out of the damp van in tumbledown boxes, tied into bundles and wrapped in blankets, looking more like things to be *removed* from a property than brought into one.

The living room slowly filled up with plants during the course of the day. More and more plants were plucked from the back of the van and deposited in various locations throughout the room. Ferns, Swiss cheeses, wandering Jews, huge, aged-looking plants boasting cascades of new shoots that hung from them like tumbling children. They came in mismatched pots, some cracked, some split in two by huge overgrown roots. They settled on windowsills, on mantelpieces, on shelves, on the coffee table, and they brought with them the damp, earthy tang of outdoors.

Finally, when it seemed that there was no longer an empty surface or corner left anywhere in the flat, Cass and her ginger friend appeared on the doorstep, proudly holding aloft a wickerwork cat box. 'Here she is!' beamed Cass. 'Queen Madeleine herself.' She opened the gate on the box and the animal emerged. 'Welcome to your new home, Madeleine.'

She was large and extremely fluffy, with thick tufts of strawberry blonde fur tinged milky coffee around the edges. Her face was flat, as if she'd run into a wall, and her eyes were the colour of Lucozade. She shook the stiffness out of her legs and proceeded to wander very slowly around the flat, sniffing things, turning at every sound, peering around corners and behind furniture. Her thick-piled paws clicked prettily against the wooden floors.

'There you go, girl,' said Cass. 'What do you think, eh? Do you like it?'

She turned at the sound of Cass's voice and proceeded to wrap herself affectionately around her crouched legs, as if she were trying to bind her up in invisible string.

'And this is your new flatmate,' she said, indicating Vince.

The cat moved towards Vince, rubbed her big body against his calves and mewed loudly.

'There,' said Cass, folding her arms across her chest in satisfaction, 'she likes the flat and she likes you. Everything's going to be just perfect.'

Vince looked down at the huge swathe of strawberry blonde fur left spread across the legs of his favourite black trousers and hoped to God she was right.

Eleven

Baby Bethany Belle is about to take her very first steps! Smile at her determination as her lifelike little fingers grip yours and she totters bravely on her tippy-tippy toes! In her favourite pink romper suit with its true mother-of-pearl buttons, this fearless little mite is ready to take on the world!

Vince took a pen and ran a line through the word 'grip', changing it to 'grasp', then reread the text. He sighed and ran another line through the words 'lifelike little', changing them to 'tiny lifelike'. His gaze strayed from the paper in front of him to the view of Tottenham Hale Tube station through the window, and he had one of his occasional yet overwhelming reality checks: Vince had the silliest job in the world.

He was perfectly prepared to admit that. You couldn't work in the marketing department of Coalford Swann Collectibles without being able to admit that to yourself. No one who worked here took it seriously. Coalford Swann was a family-run business based in Essex, which had been producing treacly porcelain monstrosities such as Bethany Belle for forty years. As well as legions of tiny pink-cheeked little children in hand-stitched clothing, they also made reproduction Victorian dolls with spooky faces, a small range of terrifyingly lifelike newborn babies complete with swollen eyelids and umbilical stumps, and a whole cutesy miniature town by the name of Blissville which was designed to be collected tiny building by tiny building and displayed in a faux-mahogany shelving system, which came free with orders over £100.

Coalford Swann advertised in the flimsier of the Sunday colour supplements, but still saw itself as very much at the higher end of the 'modern collectibles' market. And, indeed, Vince couldn't deny that the products themselves were beautifully and thoughtfully made, full of detail and lovingly rendered. When you saw the dolls in close-up, when you looked at the tiny glass eyes, the hand-stitched silk dresses, the weeny leather buckle-up shoes and touched the soft, silky hair, you could only agree that they were worth every penny of the £59.99 they were being sold for, but for all the quality and craftsmanship there was nothing that could take away from the fact that they were truly disgusting in every single way.

Every week a large parcel would arrive, slathered in 'Fragile' stickers and addressed to Vince's boss, a twenty-eight-year-old by the name of Melanie. Every Monday morning Melanie would call a department meeting and the four of them would come into her office to find a new Coalford Swann creation sitting proudly on her desk. And every Monday morning the four of them would almost wet themselves laughing for at least five minutes.

It was Vince's job to create the copy that accompanied each new product in the advertisements that went out weekly. It was widely recognized that, of all the silly jobs in this department, Vince had by far the silliest, and the rest of the team never failed to be impressed by the saccharine literary depths to which he was able to plunge with just his Biro and a blank sheet of paper.

Vince still wasn't sure how he'd ended up in this job. He'd taken a diploma in Media Studies after his year out, done some work experience at an advertising agency for six months after leaving college and had somehow ended up in their copywriting department. He'd left the agency with absolutely no idea what he wanted to do with the rest of his life, and given that his six-month stint of copywriting was the solitary rose in the experiential desert of his CV, he'd somehow been forced on to that path and here he was, three years later, advertising copywriter for the tackiest company in the world.

Every few weeks he'd have a mini-crisis, think to himself, what am I contributing to humankind, to the future, to my own sense of self-worth? He'd toy with notions of working for charities, joining the VSO, writing a novel, becoming a care worker, but then he'd have a couple of laughs at work and the thoughts would recede into his subconscious like sun-dazzled moles creeping back into their holes.

He was experiencing one of these mini-crises this afternoon as he toiled over little Bethany Belle and her pink romper suit, but work wasn't the only thing on his mind today. His love life was bothering him, too. There'd been a scene the night before, with Magda. She'd obviously picked up on his restlessness and growing ambivalence because, after a solid bout of Magda-initiated sex (a sure sign that she was feeling insecure – she never usually bothered), she'd curled up towards him in bed and stroked his arm in a manner that suggested less a desire to stroke his arm and more an intention to broach an awkward topic of conversation.

'Vince?' she'd said.

'Yes.'

'How do you feel about me?'

'What?!' he laughed, groaning inwardly.

'You know – how do you feel about *me*? About *us*?'

'Well,' he said, stroking her arm, 'I think you're great – you know that.'

'No, but – *really*. Properly. You know. I mean, do you . . . *love* me?'

Oh, God. What could he say? He could lie. He could say yes. He'd done it before. But that was generally *before* sex. Not after sex. Not with a long-term girlfriend. This was different. Magda was different.

When a stunningly beautiful girl who most men would pay good money to spend just one night with, a girl with firm, olive breasts and buttocks like rose petals, snuggles up next to you after forty minutes of selfless, enthusiastic sex, wraps one long, smooth Mediterranean leg around you, looks up at you with enormous cocoapowder eyes and asks you if you love them, what sort of man was he not to punch the air and yell, '*Yes, yes, yes!*'? When a wonderful girl who's picked up your drycleaning for you, who's put up with your mates, who's reminded you about your mother's birthday, who's given you at least fifty brilliant blowjobs, asks you if you love them, how the hell do you say no?

He fiddled with a strand of her hair while he pondered his next move and smiled wanly, desperately, at her. She stared back at him, accusingly, and Vince felt her body tensing up beneath him.

'Right,' she said, sitting bolt upright and clutching the duvet defensively to her breasts.

'Magda . . .'

'No. Vince. It's fine.'

'But . . .'

'Look, at least you didn't lie to me.'

'But Magda, it's not that I don't —'

'Vince — just leave it. You'll only make it worse.'

'I mean, I don't even really know what love is.'

'Oh, *God* . . .'

'I'm sorry,' he said, grabbing her forearm ineffectually. 'There must be something wrong with me.'

'Oh, *God*!' Magda let her head fall on to her chest and smoothed her hair back wretchedly. '*Men!* Fucking men. You're all so . . . *pathetic.*'

'No, really,' he persisted, 'maybe there *is* something wrong with me. Maybe I'm . . . *dysfunctional*. You know. I mean, I feel as if I *should* love you. Maybe I even *do* love you. Maybe I'm just too fucked up to even know how I really feel. Maybe not having a father around when I was younger . . .'

'Look. Vince. Will you just *shut up.*'

'Shhhh . . .' Vince put a finger to his lips and indicated Cass's room with his eyes.

'I will *not* shush,' she said, snatching the rest of the duvet away from him and covering herself further. 'And I will not listen to your bullshit theories about why you don't love me . . .'

And then, of course, she started crying.

They talked for an hour. They got nowhere.

By the time Vince woke up the next morning he was convinced that it was over. That they'd split up. But Magda awoke with other ideas.

'I think we should spend some time apart,' she sniffed. 'I need some space.'

'Fine,' he nodded, 'I agree.'

'Don't call me,' she said.

'I won't,' he said.

'I'll call you when I'm ready.'

'Good,' he said. 'That's good.'

She'd kissed him meaningfully on the mouth as she left, and stopped once at the bedroom door to throw him a look of intense sadness.

And that was that. For the time being, at least.

Vince sighed. He always did this, he realized, left difficult situations dangling in the air, like maggots wriggling on fishing lines, hoping that if he left it dangling for long enough some nice big fish might just leap through the air and swallow it up. Awful thing to do really, as he had no intention of resuming their relationship. None whatsoever. He knew that with a shocking clarity. But he felt more comfortable in this place where he hadn't 'dumped' her and he wasn't a bastard and she wasn't bitching about him to her friends and crying into a wine bottle and losing weight. He liked the indefiniteness of it all. And although he knew that the situation couldn't remain like this for ever, that this trial separation was finite, he was hoping that things would sort of peter out rather than come to an abrupt end with tears and heart-breaks and the like, that things would just sort of *cease to be*.

He was, he fully accepted, an emotional turnip.

An emotional turnip with a stupid job.

Surely, he thought, life wasn't supposed to be this trifling and insubstantial.

Surely he was supposed to feel more than this.

He sighed again, and turned to stare at Bethany Belle, trying and failing to find the right words to describe her dimpled cheeks.

Twelve

Cass was crouched in next-door's front garden making kissy-kissy noises in the dark when Vince got home on Monday night.

'Cass?' he said, doing a double take.

'Vince!' She leapt to her feet. 'Thank God. You're home.'

'What?' he said. 'what's the matter?'

'It's Madeleine. She's gone missing. She went out last night and I haven't seen her since. Can you help me look for her?'

'Er ... yeah, sure,' said Vince, 'let me just, er, dump my stuff.' He indicated his off-licence carrier and work clothes.

'Bollocks,' he muttered to himself as he mounted the stairs to the front door and pulled his keys from his jacket pocket. The last thing he felt like doing was creeping around Finsbury Park in the dark with Cass, looking for her blessed cat.

'Thought you had a fucking *connection*,' he hissed to himself as he made his way up to the flat. 'Can't you send the fucking cat a telepathic fucking *message* or something?'

Cass was peering through the letterbox of Number 50 when Vince went back outside a few minutes later.

'What are you doing?' he said, coming up behind her with a torch.

'Look,' she said, pointing at the foot of the door. 'Flap. She might have wandered in here by accident and got trapped.'

'Hasn't she got a tag?'

'No,' snapped Cass, 'of course she hasn't. It's really dangerous to put a collar on a cat.'

'It is?'

'Yes. They can get strangulated. She's got a chip.'

'A chip?'

'Yeah – they're these new things, like a little microchip, size of a grain of rice. It's injected into her neck and all her ID's stored on it so if she gets lost or hurt the vet can just zap her with a gun thingy and bring up all her details on a computer.'

'Cool,' said Vince, 'but how will someone know who she belongs to unless they take her to the vet?'

Cass looked at him as if she were just about to tell him he was being stupid, but then changed her mind. 'I don't know,' she muttered, turning back to the letterbox.

'Has she done this before?' Vince swung his torch back and forth across the base of the privet hedge outside Number 50.

'No. Well, sort of. I mean she goes out and I don't know what she gets up to, but she'll always come back at least once during the night or day. It's not like her to be out for so long without coming back. I'm worried she might have got lost. Lost her bearings. Maybe she was trying to find her way back to the old flat. Maybe I let her out too soon. God, I can't bear it . . .'

They searched the full length of Finsbury Park Road, Wilberforce Road and even Blackstock Road that evening.

By the time they got back to the flat it was nearly nine o'clock, and Vince was so cold he could no longer feel his inner thighs.

Cass eyed the kitchen table when they walked back in and clocked the four-pack of Stellas and the Blockbuster video. 'Oh,' she said, 'shit. I'm sorry. I've spoiled your night. I didn't think.'

'Don't worry about it,' said Vince, lowering himself on to the Victorian-school-style radiator and feeling his thighs and buttocks thawing as he did.

'No. Really. I feel terrible. You must think I'm so selfish.'

'Well, yes, but that's all part of your unique charm.'

She smiled wanly at him. 'Let me make it up to you,' she said. 'Let me do you a reading.'

'Oh, God . . .' Cass had been yabbering on about giving him a tarot reading since the day she'd moved in.

'Oh, come on,' she persisted, 'I'm worried about you. Your life's in limbo. You're looking thin . . .'

'Thin?'

'Yes. Drawn.'

'That's all those fucking chickpeas you keep feeding me. I need meat, not a tarot reading.' As a strict vegan, Cass was stridently opposed to any form of ready-made meal and every night she commandeered the kitchen, cooking enormous pungent curries of chickpeas, lentils and strange root vegetables, which she foisted upon Vince like a Jewish mother. As a consequence Vince had been enjoying the most prolific and luxurious bowel movements of his life and had lost two pounds in weight.

'OK. How about I order us a curry. With meat in it. Just for you. On me. A nice chicken tikka, maybe . . .'

'Or a vindaloo.'

'Or a vindaloo. And then let me read your cards. Please?'

'Oh, go on, then.'

'Cool!' She pulled open the drawer in the kitchen table and pulled out a handful of takeaway menus.

'So,' she said while they waited for their delivery, 'what's happening with you and Magda?'

'I can't tell you that,' said Vince indignantly.

'Why not?' Cass looked affronted.

'Because that's cheating.'

'Cheating?'

'Yeah. Wheedling information out of me about my private life before you read my cards.'

Cass tutted and raised her eyebrows. 'That's *not* how it works. I'm not a fucking fortune-teller.'

'So how does it work, then?'

'The cards look at your current situation and help you deal with it. They give you *guidance*. And it'll help me read the cards if you let me know how things are. So,' she tried again, 'how's it going with Magda?'

'It's all right,' he said. 'We're talking. Just about.'

'And this "trial separation" – how long is it going to last?' She pulled plates out of cupboards and cutlery out of drawers as she talked.

He shrugged. 'I dunno,' he said. 'It's kind of informal. I think she wants me to do something dramatic. Tell her I love her. Propose or something.'

'Sheesh,' she said, tearing off two sheets of kitchen roll, 'that girl's got it bad.'

'What do you mean?'

'Well, you wouldn't catch me hanging around waiting for some guy to make up his mind whether or not he loved me. Christ. You either do or you don't. There's no middle ground in my world.'

After they'd eaten, Cass passed a block of slippery cards to Vince and pulled her left knee up to her chin, 'Now, I want you to really think about your current circumstances, your past experiences and your hopes and desires for the future while you shuffle the cards. Take your time. Really focus on what it is you want to know. Speak to the cards. Ask the cards questions.'

'OK,' he said, handling the cards gingerly, 'no problem.' Fragments of his life zipped through his thoughts like a slide show as he shuffled through the waxy cards. Bethany Belle's tiny fingers. Magda's silky thighs. A man he'd sat next to on the Tube that morning who smelled of raw onions. His little brother's third birthday party that weekend. Nothing of any consequence. No big questions. Because sometimes knowing what question to ask was harder than knowing the answer.

'OK,' said Cass, taking the cards back from him and starting to arrange them face down in small groups on the kitchen table, 'let's see what's going on in Vince Land.'

She turned cards over slowly and circumspectly, tapping her teeth with her fingernails and taking delicate puffs on a roll-up as she did. 'Hmmmm,' she said, drawing her other knee up towards her chin, 'this is interesting.

See this card, it suggests a kind of blockage, an obstacle. It's like you're *stuck* in the past. Like sinking mud. And this card here symbolizes regret, or unfinished business. Does that suggest anything to you?'

He shrugged, and gave it some thought. 'Well, I guess I always kind of wished I'd done a fourth A level. I wanted to. I wanted to take History of Art, but my tutors reckoned I wouldn't be able to deal with the workload, wanted me to concentrate on my three main choices, and I know it wouldn't have made much difference in the long run, that extra A level, but I don't know, I've always just felt that —'

'No no no,' snapped Cass, 'not piddling, poncing A levels, for fuck's sake. I'm talking about real stuff. Big shit. You know. Love. What about love? I'm getting a strong sense that this is a romantic regret. I mean, how many serious girlfriends have you had in your life?'

'Well, there's Magda,' he counted her off on his thumb, 'and then there was Helen before her for a few months . . .'

'And what went wrong with Helen?'

'Well, nothing went *wrong*. We just split up.'

'Why?'

'I dunno. It just wasn't working out.'

'Men.' Cass raised her eyebrows and rubbed out her roll-up in the ashtray, angrily. 'For God's sake, why are you all so useless at discussing your emotions?'

'I'm not being useless,' he countered. 'I just really don't know why we split up.' And it was true. He didn't. He'd met her, they'd gone out, they'd gone out again, they'd carried on going out, then, five months later, for whatever reason, they'd stopped going out. Something to do with him not 'opening up to her' he seemed to recall. He hadn't understood it at the time and he didn't understand it now. To open up to someone would suggest that there was something inside you weren't showing someone; it would suggest a tightly sealed clam or a locked box with something hidden deep inside. But that simply wasn't the case. He was nice to her, they did nice things together, they laughed, they had nice sex, they went away for a week to Cornwall and had a very nice time in a B & B in Port Isaac and didn't argue once. Everything about his five months with Helen had been perfectly nice, but it still, apparently, wasn't enough.

'She must have said *something*? Given you some kind of reason?'

'She said she wanted me to open up to her. Fuck knows what that meant.'

'Hmmm. Yes. I can see that. You are a bit . . . unforthcoming.'

'With what?! I've got nothing to hide.'

'Yes, but you look like you do. You look . . . *mysterious*.'

'*Mysterious?*'

'Uh-huh. The scars, the brooding brow, the overcoat. You look like you're full of secrets and angst.'

'*Me?*'

'Yeah, you. Quite fancied you the first time I came to see the flat.'

'You did?'

'Uh-huh. But then I realized you were just –' She clamped her mouth shut. 'Nothing.'

'What?'

'*Nothing.*'

'Jesus, Cass. You can't just start saying something like that, then stop. You realized I was just what?'

Cass sighed, and brought her knees back up to her chin – she was one of those bendy girls who always had to sit in strange positions, whether it was cross-legged, on counters, on the floor, in foetal scrunches. 'Just . . . a *bloke*. You know.'

'No, I don't know. Just a bloke. What does that mean? Is that a *bad* thing?'

'No. Not a bad thing, as such. But just – maybe a bit of a letdown when you look so . . . *dangerous*.'

'I look dangerous?'

'Yes. But you're not. You're safe. And safe is nice; safe is good. Safe is really, really lovely. But I can see that some girls might feel a bit *short-changed* if they thought they were getting a challenge.'

Vince shook his head in disbelief. 'Jesus. So that's all girls want, is it? Challenges? And danger?'

'Yeah. Well, some girls do. Not all girls. Some girls like suckers.'

'Christ. Now you're saying I'm a sucker?!'

'No. Not at all. But you're soft. And you're reliable. You could be taken for a sucker by the wrong girl.'

'Well, it's not happened to me yet.' Vince folded his arms angrily and defensively.

'Good,' said Cass, sounding thoroughly unconvinced. 'I'm glad. So, back to your romantic history. Who was there before Helen?'

Vince sighed. 'Well, there was Kelly – that was a couple of weeks – then there was Lizzie for a few months, and before that there was Jayne for a year – she went back to Australia. And that's it really.'

'And what about at school? Who was your first girl-friend?'

'I didn't have a girlfriend at school.'

'Oh, come on. You must have!'

'No. I was too ugly to have a girlfriend. I didn't lose my virginity until I was nineteen,' he boasted.

'No way!' Cass sat upright with undisguised delight.

'Yeah. Well, three days before my nineteenth birthday, actually.'

'Shit – you *were* a slow starter. And who was that to?'

'What?'

'Your virginity – who did you lose it to? Was it your first love?'

'No. It was just a girl.'

'What girl?'

'A girl I met on holiday.'

'What was her name?'

'Joy. Joy Downer.'

'So you remember her surname, then? It can't have been that casual. No one remembers the surnames of casual shags.'

'Well – it was kind of intense but brief, let's put it like that.'

'A holiday romance?'

'Yeah. That kind of thing. We fell in love, we had sex, then she left me a Dear John letter and did a moonlight flit.'

'Ow,' said Cass, flinching slightly. 'Nasty. Why did she dump you?'

Vince shrugged. 'I dunno,' he said. 'The letter got rained on. It was all streaky.'

'So how do you know it was a Dear John?'

'Because the only words on it that were legible were "I feel so ashamed." The same night we'd had sex. What else could that have meant?'

'Have you still got it?'

'What – the letter?'

'Yes. The streaky old letter. Is it here?' Cass bristled with excitement.

'Erm – yeah, actually. I think it is.' Vince had a pathological nostalgia for paper and was incapable of throwing away anything with handwriting on it. Consequently he had a cardboard box at the bottom of his wardrobe filled with five years' worth of birthday cards, party invitations and letters. He even kept Post-It notes with tedious little messages on them about remembering to leave money for the milkman and apologies for eating the Singapore noodles he'd left in the fridge. So it was inevitable that Joy's crispy little note would be somewhere in his room.

'Ooh – find it, will you? I want to see it.'

'What for?'

'I'm going to read it.'

'But I told you, it's illegible.'

'No, I mean read its energy.'

'Oh, God.' He raised his eyebrows at the ceiling.

'Oh, come on, Vincent. Humour me. Look – your cards are telling you to look at your past for regrets and blockages, and you're telling me that there was this girl you fell in love with who mysteriously disappeared and left you a soggy note. I think this calls for further investigation. I think you should get that note!'

Vince sighed, but slouched to his bedroom and pulled the box out of his wardrobe. He had a vague notion that the note was probably somewhere in the vicinity of his dissertation notes and finally found it buried between the pages of a notebook he'd used for his first week at college, next to a photocopied sheet of induction notes and a yellow-with-age till receipt from Safeway dated 23–09–87.

'Wow,' said Cass, feeling the note gently between her fingertips, 'this letter is just loaded with energy.' She laid it gently on the tabletop and smoothed it out. 'It's so heavy with vibes she needn't have bothered writing a word.'

'Look, Cass . . .' – he reached out to take the letter from her – 'can't we just go back to the tarot thing?'

'Yes, but not yet.' She clutched the letter towards her. 'There's sadness in this letter – tears.'

'Cass . . .' he reached feebly for the letter again, but she leaped from her chair and strode to the other side of the kitchen.

'Vincent, will you just let me do this. This is important.' She held the letter up again and closed her eyes. 'Tears, angry, sad tears. You know something?' She lowered the letter and faced him. 'I don't think this is a Dear John letter at all. I think there's much more to it than that. What happened that night, the night she left?'

'Oh, God,' said Vince gloomily, 'nothing much. We spent the day with my mum and Chris, we had a barbecue with her parents, then we went off and had sex in a field.'

'And how was it?'

'Cass!'

'No, I mean, was it a positive experience?'

'Yes, thanks for asking.'

'And afterwards, what were her last words to you?'

'I dunno. It's so long ago. Just something about see you tomorrow, I suppose.'

'And?'

'And what?'

'Well, did she say she'd enjoyed it?'

'What – the sex?'

'Yes.'

'Probably. I can't remember.'

'And then what?'

'Well, we just sort of kissed and hugged.'

'And?'

'Oh, God, Cass.' He glanced at his watch. It was a quarter to twelve. 'Can we stop this now? It's getting really late. I want to go to bed.'

'No, no, no,' she said, bounding towards him. 'No. Don't go to bed. I need to know more about this girl. What was she like? Was she pretty?'

'Yes, she was very pretty. She was very nice, very sexy and very pretty, and losing my virginity to her was the best thing that ever happened to me. Now – can I go to bed?'

'A-ha! Finally, we're getting somewhere. So, you have this perfect night with this perfect woman who then disappears overnight, and you never see her again and you never find out why. I would say that that is the root of all your woes. You've been left in limbo by this girl – for whatever mysterious reasons – and you've not been able to move on since. You're stranded in this perfect moment that nothing else will ever live up to. God, it's so tragic. You've got to find this woman!'

'What!'

'Seriously. You've got to find her and talk to her and find out why she left.'

'Cass,' Vince said, getting to his feet and running his fingers through his hair, 'I appreciate your enthusiasm and everything, I really do, but it's nearly midnight, this is a totally stupid conversation and I'm going to bed.'

'No! We've got to make a plan! We've got to find Joy Downer! We've got to – *Madeleine!*' They both turned at the familiar sound of the cat flap creaking open. '*Madeleine!* You're home!' Cass suddenly dropped the note she'd been waving in the air and flew towards the back door, scooping up an indifferent-looking Madeleine and holding her aloft. 'Oh, God, where've you been, you bad girl? We've been so worried about you.' – Vince raised an eyebrow at his unfounded inclusion in this statement of concern – 'We've looked all over Finsbury Park for you. Oh, you smell all funny. You smell of . . .' She stuck her nose into the cat's profuse fur and took a deep sniff. 'Urgh – *Obsession*. God, I hate Obsession. I used to have a flatmate who didn't wash her bed sheets – just squirted them every now and then with Obsession. Ever since I've just – urgh. You stink, Madam Madeleine. Stink, stink, stink. I can't believe you've been sitting in someone else's house all cosy and warm, getting cuddles off some *stinky perfumed woman* while we trawled the streets for you in the freezing cold . . . Honestly!' She put the cat down on the floor and went straight to the cupboard where she kept her food. 'You're a bad girl. A very, very bad girl. Now, how d'you fancy a nice bowl of tuna flakes . . . ?'

Vince retrieved the rain-spattered little note from the middle of the kitchen table and quietly slunk out of the kitchen, making his escape while the irrepressible Cass's attention was focused elsewhere.

He felt totally drained as he slipped under his duvet a few minutes later. If only that ridiculous cat hadn't gone missing he'd have been able to redeem a truly crap day by watching a video, downing a couple of beers and having an early night. As it was he felt like his ego had been pulled through a mangle, bottom first. Not only had he suddenly been made to realize that he was a total dullard and a source of great disappointment to every woman he'd ever met, but also he'd been forced to revive memories he'd really rather have left loitering in the past. Memories of having his heart ripped out of his chest and put back in upside down. Humiliating memories of giving his entire self to another person for the first time in his life and having it returned to him the next morning, like a shirt that didn't fit.

As he lay in bed, torturing himself with negative thoughts, his door slowly opened and a shaft of light fell across his duvet. There was then a gentle thud and crackle of cotton as something landed on his bed, followed by a loud and contented purr that rippled through the darkness like aural bubbles. And even though Vince didn't share Cass's enthusiasm for the creature, in his current state of emotional delicacy he couldn't help but take comfort from the fact that tonight, for the very first time, Madeleine had chosen to favour *him* with her nocturnal presence.

Thirteen

Vince was heading home for Kyle's third birthday party that afternoon and, as ever, had left it until the last minute to get his present. It didn't seem possible that it had been three years since Kyle was born. It felt like yesterday. Kyle's arrival into the world on 9 September 1990 had been one of the most incredible days of Vince's life. Chris had phoned him at six-thirty in the morning to tell him that Kirsty was six centimetres dilated and that if he wanted to get a hot-off-the-press viewing of his little brother or sister he should get to the hospital immediately. He'd been in a state of a shock for a few moments, not entirely sure what it meant to be six centimetres dilated, but presuming that it meant that some hole or other was readying itself for a head to come through it. And then the adrenalin had kicked in and he'd suddenly realized what was happening. He was minutes away from no longer being an only child.

It was just gone eight o'clock when he was told that his mother was in surgery, that the baby had been in distress so they'd taken her in for an emergency Caesarean. He'd waited outside the operating theatre pacing back and forth in a wholly clichéd manner until Chris had emerged ten minutes later, dressed head to toe in green scrubs and cradling a white bundle in his arms that looked way too small to be a baby.

'It's a boy,' he'd said, wiping away a tear from the corner of his eye. 'It's a lovely little boy. Look.'

And Vince had peered down into a small opening at the top of the blanket bundle and seen a pair of enormous blinking eyes, a squishy nose and a squiggle of damp dark hair and had thought that his little brother was the most beautiful thing he'd ever seen in his life.

And now Kirsty was pregnant again. The baby was due in January and Vince wasn't quite sure how he felt about it. What if it was a girl? He didn't understand girls of his own age, let alone tiny ones that came up only to his knee. What did little girls want to do in the back garden on a sunny afternoon – did they want to be spun round till they were nearly sick? He doubted it. They'd probably want to play tea parties. He looked at his watch and realized that he was in danger of being late and, although he was late for 90 per cent of his appointments, Kyle's birthday party was not going to be one of them, so he picked up the first lump of brightly coloured plastic his eye fell upon and ferried it briskly towards the till.

Chris was piling ice into the kitchen sink and burying cans of Budweiser into it when Vince came through the back door at two o'clock.

'Where is he?'

'He's just had his nap. Kirsty's getting him up. He'll be down in a sec.'

'Fuck,' he said staring at a pile of brightly wrapped gifts on the kitchen table. 'Wrapping paper. Have you got any?'

'Over there.' Chris wiped his hands off on a tea towel and indicated a carrier bag hanging off the back of the pantry door.

'Excellent.' He pulled out a roll of paper with balloons printed on it. 'Sellotape?'

'That's in there, too. And scissors.'

'Cool.' He sat down at the kitchen table and set to work wrapping Kyle's present, rapidly and very badly.

'So,' said Chris, pulling the ring pulls off two cans of lager and placing one on the table next to Vince, 'what's new with you?'

'Not a lot.'

'How's the beautiful Magda?' Chris had a real thing about Magda; had described her as 'fucking spectacular' the first time he met her.

'Hmph,' Vince muttered.

'Trouble in paradise, is there?' He pulled out a chair and sat himself down.

'Yeah – well, we're not together at the moment. It's a kind of break thing. A trial separation.'

'What the fuck d'you wanna go and do that for?'

'Oh, God – I dunno. It's complicated.'

'Bloody fuck. You need your head fixing, you do.' He tutted and knocked back a glug of lager.

'Yeah, well, things aren't always as simple as they appear, you know? Just because she's gorgeous, doesn't make being with her any easier.'

'Yeah, but she's not just gorgeous, is she? That's the whole point. She's the full bloody works, a total cracker in every department.'

'Yes, I know,' he muttered, trying to break off a strip

of Sellotape with his teeth. 'I can't explain why it's not working out, OK? It just isn't. End of story.'

'OK, OK. Fair enough. You got anyone else lined up?'

'No, I haven't. Look, it's not over with Magda – just on hold, that's all.'

'God, I don't know. You young 'uns – you don't half make your lives complicated these days.'

'I don't think it's got anything to do with my age. I think it's just me.' His voice grew smaller as he said this, and Chris's body language changed subtly as he left the bonhomie behind, hearing the need for counselling in Vince's tone.

'What d'you mean, it's you?'

'I mean . . . hold that down for me, will you?' He indicated the edge of the wrapping paper. Chris placed his thumb on it. 'I mean, I think there's something wrong with me.'

Chris furrowed his brow at him and threw him a look of bafflement.

'It's just . . . I was talking to Cass about stuff on Monday, and you know she's a bit . . . you know, *spooky*. Into astrology and all that shit. And she did a tarot reading for me and she reckons I've got a problem with relationships because nothing lives up to . . .' He paused as he tried and failed to find a more convoluted way of putting it. '*Joy.*'

'Joy? I don't get you.'

'Remember that girl in Hunstanton. You know?'

'Oh, aye. *Joy.* The little Gothy lass who popped your cherry. Oh, I remember her all right. But what's she got to do with anything?'

'Well, you know . . .' He battled for a moment with another piece of Sellotape, which folded against itself. He screwed it into a blob and threw it down in exasperation. Sellotape and heart-to-hearts didn't go. 'She was my, you know . . .'

'What, mate?'

'She was my first love, kind of thing.' He blushed a little and peeled more tape off the roll.

Chris looked at him in surprise. 'Was she?'

'Yeah. It was kind of intense, but yeah, we were, you know, *in love.*'

'Fuck me, I didn't see that one. You didn't tell me. I thought she was just getting it out of the way for you, you know, a means to an end.'

'No,' Vince shook his head, 'it was more than that. It was the real thing.'

'Blimey — that was quick work.'

'Yeah, I know. Like I said, it was intense. And I've tried not to think about it too much over the years, but now Cass has put it in my head and I can't get it out and I just feel like, you know, if she hadn't disappeared, if we'd stayed in touch and gone out together properly, we'd probably have ended up getting married or something.'

'Whoah!'

'Or maybe not married necessarily, but we'd definitely have been together for a while because, Joy, she really *got* me. D'you know what I mean?'

'No. Explain.'

'Fuck, I dunno. It's like, like she was a female version of me. We just understood each other. And ever since, it's like no other woman *gets* me like she did. And I *definitely* don't understand them. I just can't communicate with them the way I could with her. Being with her, it was so easy. And I know it was only a few days, but it felt like we'd known each other for ever.'

'So if you felt that strongly about her, why didn't you swap addresses or something?'

'Well, because she disappeared, didn't she? We didn't have a chance.'

'Oh, yeah, that's right.' Chris stroked his chin, 'I forgot about all that. Bloody hell, that bloke, her dad, remember him?'

'Alan.'

'Yeah. Alan. That's right. Fuck, he was a slimy piece of shit.'

'Yeah.'

'I broke his nose.'

'What?!'

'Yeah. Whap!' he thumped his fist into the palm of his hand and laughed.

'You broke his nose?! When?'

'Shit – I forgot you didn't know anything about all this, did you.'

'Er, no.'

'Yeah. Your mum didn't want you to know.'

'Where was I?'

'You'd gone off with whatsername. Remember? That night we had the barbie and you two stropped off into the sunset. And – oh yeah! That was the night, wasn't it? The night you two, you know . . .'

'No, no, no. I don't understand. What do you mean, you broke his nose?'

'I mean, I smacked him one in the face and his nose went splat.'

'Yes, but why?' The top of Vince's head felt as if it was going to burst open with the enormity of this bizarre revelation. But he was going to have to wait for his answer, as just then there was a clatter of tiny limbs hurtling down the hallway and ten seconds later there was a small overexcited little boy on his lap, telling him that Mum had made cakes in the shapes of clowns (his favourite thing) and wanting to know what was inside the big parcel on the kitchen table and was it for him.

Thirty people of various shapes and sizes, from new-born babies to elderly relatives, arrived over the next half an hour, and the house was swallowed up with noise and activity. Vince threw himself into the afternoon's activities, helping Kyle unwrap his presents – each of which was forgotten the instant it was opened in favour of the next one on the pile – arranging fairy cakes and Marmite sandwiches on plates, getting drinks for the grown-ups and entertaining the other children.

He disappeared to the pub later that afternoon with Chris and Chris's 'best Southern mate' Charlie, then came back to help his mum clear up and get a totally exhausted Kyle off to bed, so it wasn't until nearly eight o'clock that night that he finally got a chance to ask Chris about breaking Alan's nose.

'I suppose it doesn't matter any more,' said Kirsty, after chastising Chris for spilling the beans. 'It was such a long time ago.'

'What?' said Vince. 'Will you just tell me.'

Kirsty sighed and passed her hand absent-mindedly

over her bump. 'That night, we were all really hammered. Remember? And that Alan, he'd been getting really flirty.'

'Yeah – I remember that,' said Vince, 'Joy was really pissed off with him about it.'

'Yeah, well, about an hour after you two left I went inside to go to the toilet, and he followed me in. He was waiting outside the toilet door when I came out.' She took a deep breath. 'And he made a pass at me.'

'A pass!' scoffed Chris. 'He grabbed her tits and stuck his hand down her shorts.'

'Chris!'

'Well,' he said, 'Vince isn't a kid any more. There's no point in playing it down. That bastard sexually assaulted you. Let's not pussyfoot around.'

'Oh, my God,' said Vince, not quite able to believe what he was hearing, while simultaneously feeling entirely unsurprised. 'Christ – what happened?'

Kirsty opened her mouth to reply, but Chris got in first.

'He actually had her pinned up against the door – imagine that? A tiny little thing like your mum? I heard K shouting and I came in and there was actual *slobber* on her cheeks where he'd been licking her fucking face. I just lost it. Frogmarched him out of that caravan and threw him on the ground.'

'He kicked him in the gut,' Kirsty interjected, her cheeks flushing slightly.

'Yeah – I kicked him in the gut, but the bastard still came back for more. Stood up and called me an "oik"!' he laughed. 'And then he said something unspeakable about your mother, so I just flattened his nose into his face. He backed off the minute he saw blood. Started talking about the coppers and taking me to court. I just said, "go on, then, report me. Actually, I'll come with you. I've got a serious case of *sexual assault* to report." That shut him up. Then that Barbara drove him off to the local emergency ward and that was the last we saw of them.'

'But . . . but . . .' Vince tried to find words to form questions while pennies dropped in his head like winnings from a fruit machine. 'I remember you two were being really weird when I got back that night – and I asked you what was going on. Why didn't you tell me? I mean, that must be why she left. *That's* why she was ashamed. I don't understand why you didn't tell me.'

'Fuck,' Chris said, as he flung an arm round his shoulder, 'I wanted to tell you what happened, but your mum wouldn't let me – she thought you'd be too upset.'

'Christ, you could see how upset I was. I can't believe you thought that would make it any worse.'

'Vince, I'm not being funny or anything, but you didn't tell us how upset you were. I mean, you were a bit quiet and everything, but, to be honest, I just thought maybe you were relieved – you know, that you'd got it out of the way with a really nice girl, but didn't have to take it any further 'cos she buggered off. I didn't know you were in *love* with her. You never said.'

'Yeah, well, I was. And all these years I thought she'd fucked off because she was ashamed of what happened between us and now it turns out she was ashamed of her dad and if I'd known I could have . . . I would have . . .' He stalled for a moment as he tried to think what exactly he would have done if he'd known the real reason for Joy's midnight flit. 'I dunno what I'd have done, but at least I wouldn't have felt like it was my fault she went.'

But was there anything else he could have done? Any other path he could have pursued? And what was it that stopped him? He thought back to those few weeks of summer after the Downers had left Hunstanton, remembered mooching about, feeling bewildered, hurt and vaguely guilty. He remembered trying to talk to Chris about it, but feeling for once as if he couldn't confide his true feelings to him and mumbling something stupid and macho about how it was probably just as well it hadn't worked out with Joy because he was starting college in the autumn and how there'd be loads of women there to take his mind off her, and Chris had patted him on the back and said, 'That's right, look to the future. There's no point harking back to things that didn't work out.'

And that's exactly what he'd done. He'd thrown himself into college life with gusto, relishing being in a new environment with people who knew nothing about him. He'd arrived as the person Joy had seen him as – a charismatic hunk, a sexually experienced man of the world. All the girls had gone mad for him – he was one of the most popular blokes there. And he hadn't really thought about Joy again since. Not properly – only in a passing, wistful way, the occasional twinge of discomfort in the pit of his belly when he thought of her making her parents take her home because she was so embarrassed about having had sex with him. Until Cass had brought her back into focus on Monday night.

And now he couldn't stop thinking about her. It was

like he was suddenly obsessed with her. Everywhere he went at the moment he was subconsciously looking out for her – on the Tube, in pubs and bars, even on the streets of Finsbury Park. He had this fantasy of bumping into her somewhere, maybe in Soho, of casually drifting into a pub together, buying her a drink and talking the night away. They'd realize immediately that they still had feelings for each other, then they'd go back to his flat or her flat and have sex – more than once.

Of course he knew that the chances of this happening were slim to remote – she could be living in New Zealand or Paris or Barnsley; she might be married or even dead. But he just had this strange, tingly feeling (he couldn't think of a better way of putting it) that if he just kept his eyes peeled then he might draw her towards him with his positive energy.

Patently, he'd been living with Cass for far too long.

And now this new information – confirmation that she hadn't done a runner because she wished she hadn't slept with him, the possibility that she'd wanted to see him again, that she might have been waiting for his call, fretting, *crying* even. Maybe when she thought about Vince she thought of him as the One That Got Away. Or maybe she thought of him as That Bastard Shit Who Robbed Me of My Virginity Then Never Called. But more likely she'd probably just thought that Vince had been so outraged by what her father had done to his mother that he'd refused to have anything more to do with her and didn't blame him in the slightest for not getting in touch.

Whatever the truth of the matter, the bottom line was that fate had fucked up and Vince couldn't rest until he'd seen her again. And it wasn't enough just to wait for fate to throw her back into his path; he had to do something more proactive.

'I'm going to find her,' he said, crunching his empty lager can in his fist with the force of his resolve.

'What?!' spluttered Chris.

'Yeah. I'm going to find Joy. Track her down.'

'And how exactly are you planning on doing that?'

'Christ, I dunno. It can't be that hard, can it? She's got an unusual name. I'll think of something.'

He looked from Chris to his mother, both of whom were looking at him with a mixture of pity and bewilderment.

'Vince, mate,' Chris said as he grabbed Vince's knee under the table, 'I'm not being funny or anything, but what's the point? Eh? It's much harder walking backwards, you know – you can't see where you're going and you bump into things. Keep moving on, that's my attitude.'

'Yes,' said Vince, 'I hear what you're saying. But what if you were walking down the street and you suddenly realized you'd dropped a really expensive watch on the pavement half a mile back? You'd walk back to get it, wouldn't you?'

Chris shrugged, 'I suppose.'

'Well, Joy's that expensive watch, and I only just realized I dropped her.'

Chris smiled, and squeezed his knee. 'Well, in that case you'd better start running before some thieving bastard picks her up and pawns her for a fiver.'

And then he winked, and Vince knew that he understood.

Fourteen

Joy ripped the plastic casing off her tuna mayonnaise sandwich and opened up the *Evening Standard* at the flat-share section.

She'd persuaded herself six months ago that she could afford to pay £85 a week for a high-ceilinged studio flat in a Gothic Victorian mansion in Hammersmith; that it was worth it for the luxury of living alone. But then she'd split up with Ally three months ago and, without the long, lazy Sundays in bed with the papers and the cosy nights drinking wine together in front of the TV, coming home alone to an empty flat every night had lost its appeal. And when her cashcard had been swallowed by a machine at Oxford Circus last night when she tried to withdraw £10, she knew it was time for the beautiful, overpriced studio flat to go. It was time to find a flat share.

She picked up a blue felt-tip and started circling ads that caught her eye.

Two girls, a garden and a cat in Chiswick.

Five young professionals with a 'luxury' spare room in Battersea.

Two guys in Highbury who liked smokers.

She was sitting in the smoky staff room of ColourPro Reprographics, a massive print shop and art suppliers near Carnaby Street. There were tea rings on the Formica-topped tables, and the sprinkled remnants of somebody else's sandwich. Behind her Mark and Big Lee, two man mountains of unloved flesh in ColourPro T-shirts and clammy-looking trainers, were eating individual Domino's pizzas and slurping Coke out of enormous paper cups. An empty paper cup whistled past her ear and hit the wastepaper bin under the sink with a thud. Big Lee got to his feet and punched the air triumphantly.

'Yes-*sah*!' he said, high-fiving Mark inelegantly.

Joy sighed and looked at the clock. It was twelve-twenty. She still had another forty minutes of her lunch hour left, and no one to share it with. She glanced through the tiny barred window over the sink and saw fat droplets of rain splashing the dimpled glass. Another dull day in W1. Another long lunch hour killing time. Rachel, her only real friend at ColourPro, had left the previous week to work in the art department of a glossy travel magazine. It had dawned on her when she got into work on Monday morning that she didn't really like anyone else here, and now she felt like the new girl all over again.

She'd been at ColourPro for nearly a year. She'd only taken the job in the first place because it had been misleadingly advertised in the *Guardian* Media section to appeal to graduates with art degrees. In reality it was a cattle market for slightly geeky technical types who liked the smell of chemicals and drinking pints of cloudy ale after work. All thirty-two members of staff were obliged to wear the standard-issue ColourPro T-shirt, and the owners operated all sorts of 'crazy' motivational schemes such as paintballing days and bungee jumping. But despite all their best efforts to promote a 'one big happy

ColourPro family' environment, the staff turnover was remarkably fast, and Joy now found herself in the strange position of being one of the longest-serving members of staff. If she wasn't careful, she mused, she'd end up being promoted.

She flicked idly through the paper as she pondered her stagnant and uninspiring existence, and found herself looking at the personal ads at the back. Lonely Londoners, she thought, perusing them unthinkingly, look at them all. Dozens, *hundreds*, of them. Black, white, short, tall, young, old, gay, straight, north, south, east and west. All alone. All prepared to go to the effort and embarrassment of placing an advert in a public place to break the stalemate. She could see why, in a way. It was soul-destroying out there, even if you were a reasonably attractive young woman with fairly good social skills. But imagine being 'Curvy brunette, 5' 1", 56 years old, true romantic looking for soul mate.' Or 'Shy lesbian, 43, looking for friends for fun and socializing. Peckham area.'

Joy had been single for three months, since Ally had been made redundant by his company and decided to spend his pay-off on a round-the-world trip. Without her. Since he'd gone she'd been on two dates with men who'd never called again, been stood up outside the Swiss Centre on a Wednesday night by a man she hadn't even fancied in the first place and snogged a guy at a party who'd just taken five Es and was snogging everyone he happened upon, male or female, in the name of peace and love.

There were loads of blokes here at ColourPro, but most of them were disgusting, and the ones that weren't disgusting were gone and on to the next job before she had a chance to do anything about it. The only men who paid her any attention these days were the plimsolled foreigners handing out cards for language schools at Tottenham Court Road, lonely Africans who drove her home in minicabs and most recently, on Saturday night, a gone-to-seed man in cheap shoes called Ronald, who didn't seem to have noticed that he wasn't handsome any more. She'd started to feel invisible, as if she was sliding off a giant radar she'd only just realized existed. It was a strange and depressing sensation.

She sighed and turned the page. And suddenly her eye was caught by one of the adverts in the second column:

Handsome male, 29, likes: Thai food, empty beaches, extravagant picnics and *Twin Peaks*. Loves: London, life. Lives: SW8. Favourite park: Battersea. Looking for a beautiful girl to cook for and share with.

When she came to ponder it in years to come, as she frequently would, she would be unable to remember exactly what it was about the ad that appealed to her so greatly. Maybe it was the hint of sunshine in the picnics and the beaches, on a dreary September afternoon. Maybe it was the promise of good food and pampering. Maybe it was the suggestion that London and life were concepts worthy of love. Or maybe she was just incredibly shallow and had been reeled in by the word 'handsome'. But for whatever reason, for one unrepeatable moment in time, the advert had flashed acid neon out of the pallid paper, twinkling with multicoloured fairy lights and dancing Catherine wheels. Joy felt a shiver of anticipation running down her spine as she gently traced the outline of the ad with her blue felt-tip, and slowly refolded the paper.

'Want anything from the shops?' she said, turning to Mark and Big Lee.

They both looked up at her as if she'd just offered them her toenail clippings.

'Er, no thanks. We're all right.'

'OK.'

She took the paper and a handful of 10p pieces to the phone booth on the corner of Carnaby Street and Great Marlborough Street and made arrangements to view three flats that evening: one in Highbury, one in Tufnell Park and one in Finsbury Park. And then she went back to work and spent the rest of the afternoon mentally composing a letter to Mr Thai-Food-and-Twin-Peaks, little knowing as she did how much of an impact she was to make on her destiny that day, in more ways than one.

Fifteen

'Oh, Joy,' Barbara said, peering uncertainly through the windscreen at the street scene in front of her, 'I'm not sure I like this area very much. It's not like Hammersmith.'

Joy knew Finsbury Park fairly well, had been here to go bowling, for the Fleadh, but she'd never before been about to move into a flat here and was now seeing it through very different eyes. There were no appealing shops, no recognizable supermarkets, coffee shops, clothes shops, newsagents'. No WH Smiths, no Boots, no Marks & Spencer – none of the usual bedrocks of a British high street. Just scruffy off-licences, pungent fast-food outlets, late-night groceries displaying piles of withered peppers and black bananas, and makeshift boutiques selling knock-off sportswear and leopard-print miniskirts. Joy couldn't argue with her mother. Finsbury Park was undoubtedly very different to Hammersmith.

The flat was on the ground floor of a chunky Victorian house on Wilberforce Road, a quiet side turning parallel with Blackstock Road.

Julia, her new flatmate, was there to let them in. She was a big girl, Julia, in every respect. Five foot eight, a size sixteen at the very least and stupidly overendowed on the bosom front. She was wearing a loose T-shirt when she greeted them at the door, and her enormous waist-level breasts roamed unfettered beneath the flimsy fabric like two baby hippos. On her feet she wore shocking pink angora socks and in her hand she held a smouldering mauve Sobranie. Her thick copper hair had patently been on recent and very intimate terms with her pillow, and was scrunched up into a kind of bird's nest at the back.

'Joy, darling, welcome.' She transferred her mauve cigarette to her other hand and enveloped Joy in a soft, smoky, bedsheety embrace. 'And this must be mum. Mum – welcome.' She leaned into a startled Barbara and kissed her firmly on both cheeks. 'Apologies for my ungodly appearance. A bit of a heavy session last night. Now, let me get you both a nice strong cup of coffee.' She led them through the hallway, through the living room, which was littered with empty wine bottles and dirty glasses, and into the kitchen, which showed all the signs of a raucous dinner party. A pot of something brown and meaty-looking sat on the hob, and a little table was scattered with bowls of crisp crumbs and congealed dips. On a copy of last week's *Sunday Times* magazine sat a packet of Rizlas, a ripped-up Tube ticket and an ashtray full of multicoloured Sobranie stubs and squished-down spliff butts.

'Yes,' said Julia, tipping damp mounds of coffee grounds out of a cafetière and into a precariously full pedal bin, 'had a few friends over last night. All got a bit messy. Couldn't get rid of them until the early hours. Hence the ungodly mess.' She rinsed the cafetière and began spooning fresh grounds into it from a tin. Joy glanced at her mother, who was doing her best to look as if she often found herself in kitchens full of dirty dishes and drug paraphernalia on a Saturday afternoon.

'Well,' she said a minute later, as she unlocked the boot of her car, 'she seems like a character.'

'She wasn't quite so ... haphazard when I came to see the flat,' said Joy. 'She was wearing a trouser suit. And the flat wasn't such a mess. I think she must have tidied it specially for the viewings.'

'Well, I think she seems like fun. I think you'll have fun with her.'

'Do you really?'

'Yes. I do. She seems the sort to get you out of yourself. You know. Could do with losing a pound or two, though.'

'Mum!'

'Well, it's true. All that lovely thick hair and such a pretty face. Seems a shame for her to be so big. And at her age.'

Mum, despite having been overweight all her adult life, had always had a tendency to come down very hard on other overweight women. It was as if she saw her own situation as hopeless and felt that it was up to other big women to fight the good fight on her behalf.

Two cups of incredibly strong coffee and the sound of Julia singing loudly in the shower greeted them on their return. Joy showed Mum round the flat, showed her her lovely bedroom with its wooden floorboards and stripped-pine double bed, showed her the cute little back garden with its table and chairs and still-flowering rose-bushes. And then Joy filed back and forth between Mum's car and the flat for the next hour, unloading her pos-sessions while Mum, with the lung capacity of a baby mouse and the muscle tone of a gnat, set about the clearing away and washing up instead.

Julia was in raptures when she emerged into a clean and tidy flat an hour later, and called Barbara a 'beautiful angel'. Barbara blushed and looked thrilled, and Joy realized that it was probably the first time in her life she'd been called either. At four o'clock Julia, now clothed and coiffed, decreed that it was time for sundowners.

'Come on, Barbara,' she said, flourishing a huge wine glass, 'you will be having a glass of wine, won't you? You deserve one after all your hard work.'

'Oh, no, thank you, Julia,' she said, waving it away, 'I'm not really a drinker. And besides, I've got to get back. I won't be able to drive if I have a drink.'

'Well, stay the night, then. The sofa folds out into a bed.'

'Oh, I don't know . . .'

'We can go out for pasta – there's a fab place in Stokie, on Church Street. Great atmosphere and all the waiters look like Sylvester Stallone.'

Barbara started to smile. And then she started to laugh. 'Oh, Julia, that sounds lovely, it really does. But I can't. My husband's expecting me back.'

Joy had a sudden thought then, an image of her stiff, awkward mother laughing in a cosy Italian restaurant, slurping spaghetti, drinking red wine and being flirted with by handsome waiters. 'Oh, go on, Mum,' she urged. 'Dad won't mind. Call him.'

'Yes,' said Julia, pulling the cordless phone off its base and waving it at Barbara, 'go on. Tell him Joy's scary new flatmate won't let you go.'

Barbara looked from Joy to Julia and back again, a naughty twinkle in her eye that Joy had never seen before, like a Tiffany lamp in the corner of a dark room. 'Oh, all right, then,' she said, taking the phone from Julia's outstretched hand and looking at it like it might make a sudden lunge for her throat. 'How do I work this thing?'

Julia got her a line and Barbara pressed in her home number, smiling nervously, her eyes swivelling from Julia to Joy and back again.

'Oh, hello, Alan, it's me. I'm at Joy's new place. Yes, yes, it's all gone very well. Yes, it's very nice. Finsbury Park. Further north. That's right. Anyway, the thing is it's got quite late now and the girls are planning a nice Italian meal. Locally. And they've asked me if I'd like to come along. And I was thinking I might . . . yes . . . yes . . . I see . . .' Her head dropped slightly and she started talking more quietly. 'No. I understand. No. That's fine. Right. Right. I'll see you soon, then.' She glanced at her watch. 'About six o'clock. Maybe a bit sooner. All right, love. I'll see you then. Bye.'

She pulled the phone from her ear and smiled wanly. Julia took it from her and switched it off.

'Looks like I'm needed at home,' she said, still smiling that watery smile.

'Why?' said Joy.

'Oh, you know your father. He's not very good with his own company.'

'Oh, for God's sake,' muttered Joy.

'I know,' said Barbara, 'I know. But maybe another time, eh? Plan it in advance. Give your father some warning. You know.' She pulled her handbag on to her

142

lap and readied herself to stand up. 'But thank you for inviting me. It was a lovely thought. Really lovely.' She hugged her handbag to her soft chest and threw them both a tight smile.

Joy and Julia saw her to her car and watched her drive away, her headlights cutting holes through the late-afternoon gloom, a dry rectangle stencilled on to the wet road where her car had been parked.

'What a shame,' said Julia, turning back towards the house. 'It would have been lovely if she'd stayed.'

Yes, thought Joy, sadly, it would have been. It would also have been unprecedented. Barbara never did anything independently of her husband. She had no friends that hadn't been Alan's friends first, no hobbies, no pastimes. She shared his opinions on everything from politics to Sue Lawley's new haircut, and was an appendage in every sense of the word. Joy had occasionally seen small sparks of another Barbara inside the nylon dresses and cowed demeanour over the years. She'd seen her giggly after a glass of sherry on Christmas morning or flushed with pleasure at the news of a birth or an engagement. She'd seen her jump to her feet and punch the air with delight when Bjorn Borg (whom she decreed 'gorgeous') won the finals at Wimbledon. And she'd seen pictures of Barbara in her youth, lumpy-kneed in belted tweed mini-dresses, shiny-faced in unflattering Alice bands, puddingy in printed cotton dirndl skirts and helmet hair. She'd never been slim, she'd never been pretty, but maybe once upon a time she'd been charming, delightful, playful, a flirt. Maybe she'd been out dancing, cycling, to coffee shops and ice-cream parlours. Maybe she'd had suitors, young men vying for her attention. Maybe she'd even slept with some of them.

What had her father done to her, she wondered? How had he managed to make such a limp cushion of her? Had it been a slow process, pulling her spirit out of her, bit by bit, like feathers from a pillow. Or had something happened, a one-off, long-ago event?

She followed Julia back towards the flat and shivered as the cool, damp air made itself felt through her thin clothes. She drank a glass of wine with Julia and took a second into the bath with her. On closer inspection she noticed that the grout between the mint green tiles that rimmed the bath was mouldy. There was a three-dimensional limescale flume from the overflow to the plughole, and Julia's soap clung to the edge of the bath, green, lumpy and swollen, like a pat of rancid butter. A damp smell emanating from the clammy shower curtain took the edge off her strawberry bubbles and, as she lay in the hot bath sipping chilled wine, Joy tried not to think about the fact that her new flat wasn't perfect and that her new flatmate had low standards of domestic hygiene.

She tried not to think about her lovely little shower room in Hammersmith, with its pristine white tiles, used by her and only her. She tried not to think about Saturday nights gone by, Saturday nights spent eating takeaways and drinking wine on her very own sofa with a man who loved her. And she tried not to think about the wretched humiliation of standing outside the Swiss Centre for three-quarters of an hour waiting for a not-particularly-attractive man who evidently couldn't stomach the prospect of spending even one night with her, just to be polite. She tried not to think about the fact that all her friends in London had moved on, moved out and moved away, and that her social life had slowly whittled itself down to the size of a pea. And while she was at it, Joy tried not to think about her mother, driving sadly away in her ugly little car, back to her ugly little husband, sitting waiting for her in their ugly little house. She tried not to think about the night they could have been having and the conversations they could have had, and she tried not to feel guilty about not trying harder to persuade her mother to stay the night.

Instead she focused on the future.

She could take a bottle of bleach and a scrubbing brush to this bathroom tomorrow. She could make herself at home here. She could phone her mother tomorrow, make a proper plan for her to come and stay, arrange things for them to do, think about questions she'd like to ask her about her father and their vile marriage and all the mysterious empty spaces in their lives. She could make more of an effort with her remaining colleagues and maybe even track down some of her old friends from Bristol to kick-start her social life. And then her thoughts turned to a letter currently folded neatly in three and slotted between the pages of *London Fields* in one of her many unpacked boxes. A letter written on two sheets of thin lined paper with a fine-nibbed fountain pen in midnight-blue ink. A letter she'd read so many times since it had arrived on her Hammersmith doormat ten days ago that she'd almost committed it to memory. It was postmarked SW8 and was from man called George who liked big dogs, cooking, Catherine Deneuve, Cheech and Chong, Bill Hicks and Julian Barnes, and claimed not be the type of man to usually place a personal advert in a classified paper. A man who'd thoroughly enjoyed Joy's 'charming' letter and wanted to meet up with her, as soon as possible. He'd included his phone number – two phone numbers, in fact. One belonged to the 'comfortable but somewhat unruly' flat in a Stockwell mansion block where he lived alone and the other belonged to the 'sterile and soul-destroyingly corporate' office space he occupied in a firm of chartered accountants in deepest Mitcham. So far Joy had picked up the phone on at least ten occasions, even called the number of his flat during the day once, knowing that he'd be out at work, and listened to a warm, well-spoken, almost plummy voice tell her that he wasn't at home right now. But that was as far as she'd taken it. She didn't know quite what it was she was waiting for. But she would call him. Definitely. Tomorrow.

And at this thought she felt herself feel suddenly more positive about everything. She would sort out everything tomorrow – her mother, her job, this bathroom, her love life, her social life, all of it. Her life wasn't such a disaster, she decided, just at a juncture, that was all, at a turning point. Everything would work out in the end, she knew that.

Everything would be peaches and cream.

Sixteen

Joy looked at her watch: 12.55 p.m. Early as usual. It didn't matter how hard Joy tried to be fashionably late, she always got everywhere early. But under the circumstances it was probably a good thing.

She was standing outside a Thai restaurant on James Street, just behind Selfridges, waiting for the mysterious George to show up. She'd finally phoned him last week; they'd talked for half an hour and arranged a date. She'd suggested Sunday lunch, had thought it sounded unthreatening and gave them both some leeway to bail out if it turned out to be a disaster. He'd sounded nice. Very posh, but nice. He described himself as having a 'mop' of hair, glasses and a 'rather unimpressive physique' – 'but I've been told I have a lovely face,' he added when Joy had been unable to think of anything to say in reply. She'd described herself as small, mousy and kind of pointy. She hadn't seen any point in talking herself up after George's charming self-deprecation. He'd said she sounded absolutely delightful and that actually, he had a 'particular fondness for pointy women'. He'd suggested this place as he'd never been here before but had read good things about it and now here she was, on a sunny October Sunday, in her least sexually provocative clothes, about to embark on her first blind date.

George's description of himself had done nothing to

properly define her mental image of him and consequently every man who passed suddenly presented himself as a possibility. Maybe George wasn't wearing his glasses today. Maybe he wasn't quite as puny as he'd suggested. And what exactly *was* a 'mop' of hair, anyway? She had no idea if he was tall or short, or what colour the mop was, and he'd given no indication of the style of clothing she should except him to appear in. She could reasonably expect that as an accountant he wouldn't be a fashion plate, but his interests suggested a man with a grasp of the alternative, a certain lack of convention.

And in spite of his less-than-promising self-description on the phone, Joy was still clinging to the very first word of his advert: *handsome*. Would an ugly man ever describe himself as handsome? It was highly unlikely. No – he would be unassumingly handsome, she mused, floppy-haired, cute, lambswool-jumpered maybe? A sort of English teacher type, maybe. Boyish. Bookish. *Cute*.

A boyish, bookish, cute man in glasses appeared in the distance, and Joy caught her breath. The closer he got, the more boyishly, bookishly cute he became. By the time he was within touching distance, Joy had stopped breathing entirely and was primed and ready for him to make his approach. He walked straight past her, without even casting a glance in her direction.

Joy exhaled and reassured herself that this *wasn't* a stupid thing to be doing. Replying to an advert in a classified paper and arranging to meet a strange man on a Sunday afternoon was adventurous, and unusual and . . . and . . . *proactive*. She set her chin in resolve and hoped for the best.

And then she saw a man scuttling towards her intently and all her resolve dissipated into a puddle of disappointment.

Not her type. Not in any way, nor in any detail, from his slightly elderly-looking Barbour jacket, to his Nordic design ski jumper, from his strangely combed hair that appeared to have been taped down flat against his head and glued into place, to his overly shiny Oxford shoes with plastic soles. His glasses were less sexy professor and more son-of-John Major, and framed a face that certainly couldn't be described as ugly, but wasn't even on *nodding* acquaintance terms with 'handsome'.

'You must be Joy,' he said, beaming at her nervously.

'I am!' She beamed back, stoically preventing her disappointment from making an appearance on her face. 'And you're George.'

'Correct!' He forced his hands into the pockets of belted jeans and increased his smile. 'Well, isn't this surreal?'

She laughed, appreciating his frank and immediate summarization of their situation. 'Bizarre,' she agreed.

'Shall we?' He indicated the door of the restaurant.

'Of course.'

He leaped ahead of her and held the door ajar. 'Thank you,' she said, trying to recall the last time a date had held a door open for her.

They were led downstairs to a basement room by a waitress in a skin-tight red silk dress and shown to a table in a corner. Joy glanced around the restaurant, which contained two other couples and a small group of friends. She wondered if it was obvious – could they tell that she and George had only just met, that they'd placed and replied to lonely hearts ads? Was it obvious that they didn't *match*? Were they wondering what this young girl in chic black Lycra leggings and an oversized ribbed sweater from Warehouse was doing having lunch with a man who looked like an off-duty vicar? They shuffled around for a moment, unfolding napkins, opening up menus. Joy peeked at George quickly while he wasn't looking. His mouth was a touch too full for Joy's liking and his eyes rather bizarrely widely spaced, but he wasn't ugly. He had lovely skin, smooth and poreless, like pale-pink suede, and his eyes were a striking shade of pastel green. But really, truly, whichever way she looked at it and however hard she tried, he just wasn't her type.

'D'you like it spicy?' he said, his glasses looming over the top of his menu.

'Er . . . yes,' she replied. 'Fairly.'

'Good,' he grinned, disappearing again.

A couple of hours, thought Joy, staring blankly at her menu, that was all this was. A couple of hours out of her life. A mere blink of an eye, flap of a wing, beat of a heart. Two hours, then she could bring out her pre-designed excuse (a suddenly remembered promise to feed her friend's cat) and scarper. And no one need ever know . . .

'So,' said George, smiling benignly, 'you work in the arts?'

Joy laughed. 'Er, no. Not exactly. I work for a repro company. I'm a screen printer.'

'Well,' he said, 'that's art, isn't it? Of a kind.'

'Of a kind,' she allowed, smiling.

'And do you like your job?'

'No,' she said, bluntly, 'I hate it.'

'Well, snap!' said George. 'I hate mine, too!'

They laughed and felt the ice begin to thaw.

'What do you hate about it?'

'Oh, the whole stinking thing. It's just bloody awful. Awful people, awful place. Just the smell of it,' he shuddered. 'You know, that dreadful office smell of Formica and coffee machines and lives being wasted in the pursuit of somebody else's profits. Every morning, from the moment I arrive and see those parking spaces in the car park – *Reserved for Managing Director, Reserved for Senior Partner* – and realize that they represent, for some, the pinnacle of their lives' achievements, my heart sinks. And it doesn't rise again until I get into my car at the end of the day, put on the radio and head homewards.'

'So you don't want to be an accountant, then, I take it?'

'No,' he smiled, 'I don't want to be an accountant. I want to be a writer.'

'Really?'

'Yes. Does that sound ludicrous?'

'No,' she said, 'it doesn't sound at all ludicrous. What sort of writer?'

'Well, I've played around with poetry for a while now. And I've done a creative writing course. And one day . . .' He paused and took a sip from his lager. 'One day I'd like to write the Great British Novel.' He laughed out loud. 'Now that really does sound ludicrous! What about you? Do you have an escape route planned? Any ridiculously overblown ambitions?'

'No. I used to want to be an actress when I was little. Then I wanted to be an artist. Now I'd be happy doing just about anything apart from what I'm doing now.'

'Well, you're only young. You're at the stage of your life when you can try out all sorts of different things – dip in and out of things. But I'm nearly thirty. It's now or never for me. The doors to the Last Chance Saloon are about to slam in my face! Here,' he said, picking up his lager, 'let's make a toast. A toast to shitty jobs and getting out of them.'

Joy picked hers up and clinked it against his, smiling.

And then he smiled at her, a sweet, unaffected smile, and she noticed that he had a tiny dimple on his left cheek. And as she noticed this, she also noticed that she was actually enjoying herself here in this restaurant with this man with the strange hair and the John Major glasses, and that she no longer felt the desire to go to the bathroom, climb on to the cistern and escape through the toilet window.

After lunch they emerged into a dazzling autumn afternoon and George suggested that they go for a walk somewhere in search of ice cream. Joy gave less than a second's thought to her imaginary friend's imaginary cat and agreed immediately. As they walked, heading informally towards Green Park, Joy discovered that George was an Aquarian, that his mother was dead and his father was a distant and unpleasant memory, that he'd bought his Stockwell flat with his mother's inheritance, that he'd just split up with a long-term girlfriend whom he described as a 'complete psycho' and that he had an older sister called Mirabel who'd died of a heroin overdose when she was nineteen years old.

He and his sister had been brought up by their mother in a beautiful fifteenth-century half-timbered house with turning staircases, wall-hanging tapestries and a minstrel's gallery, just outside Rye in Sussex. He'd gone to boarding school in Kent from the age of seven, which he'd hated, particularly after his mother met an overly tanned but genial estate agent called Lionel and moved to the Algarve with him when George was twelve years old, meaning that holidays and weekend exeats were suddenly spent flying across the Channel to stay in a stark, marble-floored apartment in Faro, instead of the beautiful, snug, carpeted house in Rye. His sister took an irrational dislike to Lionel and refused to go to Portugal during her school holidays. Instead she stayed with a friend called Genevieve who lived a totally unsupervised adolescence with her delinquent artist parents in a rambling, unhygienic house in Chelsea, and it was here that Mirabel first began her long and unhappy relationship with drugs by putting her head over a plastic bag full of Superglue and inhaling.

By the time George and Joy arrived at the top of the steps to Green Park, the dull and unassuming man she'd first met three hours earlier was starting to accumulate layers of colour and depth, and Joy was less and less concerned with the incongruity of their pairing and more and more concerned with finding out everything she could about George Edward Pole.

They found an out-of-season ice-cream van parked outside the park. George had a Mr Whippy with a Flake in it, proclaiming, possibly disingenuously, but certainly charmingly, that he'd never had one before in his life and expressing great excitement at the prospect. Joy had a small tub of Loseley's vanilla, and they continued wandering in the aimless, meandering manner of newly acquainted people with a whole lifetime of memories, anecdotes and opinions to share with each other in a single afternoon.

Joy had been out on a dozen dates with a dozen men keen and eager to share their histories and opinions with her, men who'd felt no compunction whatsoever about hogging the conversation and failing to ask her one solitary question about herself, men with the ability to talk and talk until she lost the will to live. But with George it was different. He talked about himself in a soft, melodious voice, with a charming turn of phrase and just the right amount of detail. He didn't force his history on her like extra homework, or offer it to her uncertainly as if it was a slightly soiled pair of underpants, but instead revealed himself to her page by page, like a beautifully written, unputdownable book.

She began subconsciously to redesign him while he talked: contact lenses to replace the unfashionable glasses, a good short-back-and-sides, a new wardrobe, maybe a leather jacket or a cashmere overcoat. She imagined placing her fingertips against his scalp and giving his over-tamed hair a damn good mussing. She imagined gently plucking his spectacles from his ears, putting them to the floor and grinding them up under her shoe.

They sat together on a bench by the lake at Buckingham Palace Gardens, and Joy found that there was very little physical space between the two of them. George's arm brushed against hers and their rumps were firmly bedded together on the wooden bench. But she didn't find this unnerving or awkward in any way. She glanced down at his hands where they rested on his lap and decided they were his best feature, large and solid with square tips and a smattering of hair. You could forgive a man a dozen physical shortcomings if he had a decent pair of hands, she decided.

He asked her questions about herself and she told him about her birth in Singapore, her subsequently unexceptional upbringing, her unlovable parents, her three years at Bristol University, her crappy job, her most recent love life and her new flatmate. And he watched her while she talked as if she was quite the most fascinating woman he'd ever encountered.

When it started to get dark they decided to prolong the day and find somewhere warm to have a drink. The first place they stumbled upon was the ICA, a place that Joy had visited twice previously in her life, once as a fourteen-year-old, with Kieran, to see Orange Juice playing live, then as a nineteen-year-old fresher, on a weekend trip to London with a dozen overexcited and partly drunk art students. Joy liked revisiting places after a long interval – it gave a sense of time and perspective to her existence. She tried to remember that fourteen-year-old girl as she crossed the threshold with George Pole, tried to remember what she was wearing, how they'd got there, what she'd had to drink, but all she could remember was staring up at Edwyn Collins, wishing that he were her boyfriend instead of the unfortunate Kieran.

They sat on high stools around a high table and sipped designer beer from bottles, surrounded on all sides by the chatter and enthusiasm of people who'd spent their Sunday morning in the pursuit of culture and knowledge, and their Sunday afternoon in a bar. They toyed with the idea of heading across town to see a film, but never quite got round to doing anything about it, happy just to sit and chat the evening away.

He told her more about his 'psycho' ex, a manic-depressive PE teacher called Tara who once knocked him out cold with a rounders bat and accused him of having affairs with every woman in their social circle. And in return, Joy told him about Ally and his decision to leave the country without her, about the man who'd left her standing outside the Swiss Centre on a Wednesday night and about how every man she'd met since she was fourteen years old had been, in one respect or another, a huge and soul-destroying disappointment.

At nine o'clock they decided they'd both drunk enough for a Sunday night and meandered towards the nearest Tube station, and it wasn't until they came to say goodbye to each other that Joy began to feel awkward again, aware of her situation, on a blind date with a man she didn't find attractive. Would he try to kiss her? And if he did, how would she respond?

'Well,' he said, smiling down at her with evident pleasure, 'that really was a most unexpectedly enjoyable day. I've had a truly great time.'

'Me, too,' she said, deciding that, no, she didn't want to kiss him, and subconsciously rearranging her body to make herself look unavailable for any kind of unannounced physical approach.

'And might I just say,' he continued, looking at her

intently, 'and I do hope you won't take this the wrong way, but you really did undersell yourself on the phone last week. You aren't pointy in the slightest. In fact, I'd go so far as to say that you're the least pointy girl I've ever met. And I have met an awful lot of pointy girls in my time, I can tell you. No – I'd describe you more as . . .' – his eyes roamed her face for a second – 'more as . . . delicately, *spectacularly* pretty – like a beautiful Meissen teacup. If that makes any sense.' He didn't blush as he said this, or laugh, or display any signs of embarrassment, just stared straight into her eyes with a sort of wide-eyed wonder, like an art collector unexpectedly coming upon the finest example he'd ever seen of a favoured artist's work.

'Well,' said Joy, laughing, 'thank you. That's lovely.'

'And if it's all right with you, I'd like to phone you some time this week. But only if you want me to.'

'Oh!' she said, so used to dates that ended in a confused, ambiguous mess of mixed messages and unclear intentions. 'Of course you can call me. I'd like it very much.'

His soft face melted into a broad smile, and he grabbed her hands and squeezed them. 'Good,' he said forcefully, imbuing the word with every ounce of its meaning, 'that makes me feel very happy.' He beamed at her, and she beamed back, his joy strangely infectious. 'Right, then. I'll be off. And I'll call you. Probably mid week – say, Wednesday? Would that be OK?'

'Wednesday's fine,' she smiled.

'Excellent.' He gave her hands one last squeeze, turned and walked away.

Joy watched his receding figure for a second or two, a

layer of objectivity returning to her as the physical space between them increased. He really was a funny-looking fellow, she decided, gauche, unfashionable, middle-aged in his manner and appearance, yet so switched on to the modern world. He was a walking dichotomy. And Joy had absolutely no idea what to make of him.

Julia was sitting cross-legged on the sofa, wearing some kind of African tunic top and smoking a pink cigarette when Joy got back to the flat on Wilberforce Road later that night.

'Thank *God* you're back,' she said, pressing a hand to her huge chest. 'I'd been about to call the police.'

'Sorry,' Joy grinned, 'went a bit better than I thought it would.'

'Well . . .' Julia's look of maternal concern immediately turned to unbridled glee, '*ob*-viously!' She scooched across the sofa and patted the cushion next to her. 'Now tell me absolutely everything.'

'Oh, God.' Joy flopped down next to her.

'Was he delicious?'

'No. Not quite.'

'Oh.' Julia's face dropped in disappointment.

'He's not very good-looking at all. Kind of awful-looking, actually.'

'Oh, dear. What a shame.'

'But really sweet,' Joy interjected defensively. 'A real old-fashioned gent. But with an edge, if you get my drift. Kind of quirky. Very intelligent. Very interesting. Very on the ball.'

'So not a psycho, then?'

'No – not a psycho. Not at all. Though he did tell me that I reminded him of a beautiful porcelain teacup.'

'Aw,' said Julia, squeezing her mug of tea, 'sweet! So he's nice and sane, and he says lovely things to you. Are you sure he's not gorgeous?'

''Fraid not.'

'But you liked him?'

'Yes,' nodded Joy, 'I did. Very much.'

'Well, then, that's all that matters.'

And Joy nodded and smiled, and wondered to herself if maybe it was.

Seventeen

While Joy's date with George hadn't exactly been a precursor to burning passion, true love and happily ever after, it had at least provided her with a timely and much-needed ego boost. So three days after their date, buoyed up by George's flattery and talk of teacups, she decided to call Stuart Bigmore.

Stuart Bigmore was a friend of hers from Bristol and the object of the greatest crush of her life. He was tall and gangly with jet-black hair and an almost girlishly pretty face. She'd fallen in love with him during their first week at Bristol, at precisely the same moment that he'd fallen in love with a beautiful and insecure girl called Vivica, leaving Joy stranded on the sidelines in the somewhat vague and unsatisfactory role of 'best female friend'. They got on like old friends and people often said that they looked like brother and sister, but their friendship was always compromised by the existence of the beautiful, insecure girlfriend.

They swapped numbers at graduation and promised to stay in touch, but then real life kicked in and they hadn't seen each other since. She'd often wondered what would have happened if the beautiful, insecure girlfriend hadn't staked her claim on him so early and so cloyingly, but felt too shy to contact him, worried that he might think she was stalking him in some way. But it had been three years since uni. Maybe the time was right. Maybe he was single. Maybe he was lonely. Maybe he would look at her afresh and be put in mind of delicate porcelain teacups.

She called him on Wednesday afternoon.

'Well, well, well,' he said, 'Joy Downer. What a blast from the past.' He shouted at her over the din of music playing loudly in the background. He was working in the art department of a record label in Soho Square. It sounded like a nightclub.

'Christ,' she said, 'how do you get any work done?'

'Headphones,' he shouted. 'Private noise instead of public noise. How are you doing?'

'Great,' she said, 'really great. You?'

'Excellent. Life is sweet.'

'Oh,' she gushed, 'great. Where are you living now?'

'Clapham,' he said, 'or should I say, *Claarm* . . .' He laughed and she gulped, wondering how she was going to bring up the subject of beautiful, insecure Vivica without sounding predatory.

'Are you . . .' she began. 'Have you got your own place, or are you sharing?'

'Sharing,' he said.

She breathed a sigh of relief, fondly imagining him in a flat full of unhygienic single men, watching *Baywatch* and peeing in the shower. 'Me, too,' she said. 'It's a nightmare, isn't it?'

'Yeah, but not for much longer. We're moving out next week.'

'We?'

'Yeah. Me and Viv.'

'Oh.' She felt her heart plummet with disappointment. 'So you're still together, then?' She drew her hand into a tight fist.

'Uh-huh. Got married last summer.'

'Wow,' she said. 'Married? That's really . . .'

'Grown-up?'

'Yeah. Really.'

'I know. But we just thought, fuck it, we're soul mates. We're going to be together for a very long time, maybe even for ever. Why not just go that extra step, make that commitment. You know.'

'Yes,' she said, even though she didn't. 'God. I can't believe it. Married. At twenty-four. You're very brave.'

'Is that a polite euphemism for "very stupid"?' he teased.

She laughed. 'Maybe a bit.'

'I know. I never thought I'd want to settle down so young. But you know, sometimes you just have to go with the flow, not question things too much. Follow your heart . . .'

'Indeed.'

'And what about you? Anyone special in your life?'

She hesitated, thought about telling him about George. There was a time in her life when Stuart would have been the first person to know that she'd replied to a personal ad, there was a time in her life when he'd have helped her word her reply, but now, among all this talk of marriage and big grown-up jobs, her little adventure on Sunday afternoon suddenly struck her as sad and pitiful. 'No.' She shrugged. 'Not really. There was someone. But we split up a few months ago.'

'Ah, well,' said Stuart, 'don't suppose you'll be single for long. Here, look, what are you up to tomorrow night?'

'Nothing,' she said, trying to make it sound like a happy coincidence, rather than a woeful pronouncement on the state of her social life.

'Cool. We're having a leaving party. Me and Viv.'

'Leaving?'

'Yes. We're emigrating. To Spain.'

'What? Seriously?'

'Uh-huh. We've bought a wreck in Andalusia. No water. No roof. We must be fucking mad.' He laughed, although Joy couldn't really see what was funny about it.

'But – what are you going to do in Andalusia?'

'I'm going freelance and Viv's going to set up her own pottery. We want to start trying for a baby soon, and neither of us wants to bring up children in this miserable fucking country, so we just decided to get out while we were still young. Make a real life for ourselves.'

'God, I can't believe it. You're so brave.'

'Is that another euphemism?' he teased.

'No. Seriously. I really think that's incredible.'

'Yeah. I know. Terrifying. But brilliant. So we're all packed up, all sorted. I finish work here on Friday, then next Thursday we're off. Jesus. I cack myself every time I think about it! So, you'll come? Tomorrow night?'

'Yes. Definitely. Who'll be there?'

'Oh, everyone.'

'Everyone?' she asked uncertainly.

'Yeah. Karen, Dymphna, Toby, Jim, the twins, Helena, Conor. The whole crew.'

'Wow. You mean you're still in touch with all those guys?'

'Yeah. Of course. We see each other all the time. Me and Viv have been living with Helena and the twins for the past two years.'

'Wow,' she said again, 'I can't believe you've all stayed in touch with each other. I tried, but everyone seemed to be doing different things.'

'Yeah. We lost touch with people, too. But then we bumped into Conor in Sydney and he was sharing a place with Toby and Jim, and Jim was going out with Helena who was sharing a place with the twins, and blah-de-blah, and somehow it all fell back into place . . .'

Joy gulped and felt her pulse quicken with a sort of indescribable and unwarranted rage. These were *her* people. This was *her* circle of friends. When she'd moved down to London three years ago, she'd tried to stay in touch with them, but it had been too difficult. Some took a year off to go travelling; some moved back home; some went on to do MAs in various parts of the country. Eventually they'd all given up trying to get together, and Joy hadn't minded because she thought that that was what happened to friends from university – that they bonded, then scattered like beads from a snapped neck- lace. But now she was being told that actually the circle was still intact; that they'd carried on functioning per- fectly happily without her for years.

Why didn't you call me? she wanted to yell at Stuart. Didn't you miss me? Didn't you care about me? Didn't one of you ever think that it would be really nice to call up dear old Joy and get her back in the circle? And then she thought with a plummeting, nauseating surge of dis- appointment that maybe they'd never really wanted her in the circle in the first place, that maybe she was the expendable person hovering in the periphery, pleasant enough but not really part of the gang. Everything about her three years at Bristol suddenly went out of focus. She'd arrived so full of confidence after her experience with Vince in Hunstanton. She was a sexually experienced woman. She'd been with a man. She'd given and received love. She was never again going to accept second-best; she was never again going to pretend to be something she wasn't.

She'd been accepted into the in crowd immediately without once questioning whether she was cool enough or clever enough and, when she left university, she'd taken that confidence with her into the outside world and used it to build herself a life in London. And now, just as it was starting to run low, she was being made to feel like an outsider again.

'Well,' she said, childish tears stabbing at the back of her throat, 'it'll be really great to see everyone again.'

'Yeah,' said Stuart, 'it'll be cool. I can't wait to see you. I've really missed you.'

But it was too late for pleasantries and platitudes.

Stuart and Vivica were married. Stuart and Vivica were successful artists. Stuart and Vivica were leaving the country to start a family in Spain. Stuart and Vivica had a social life. Stuart and Vivica saw all her oldest friends on a regular basis. Stuart and Vivica were a stark and painful reminder that Joy's life was a pile of shit.

She gritted her teeth and wrapped up the conversation in as few words as possible, then hung up the phone and cried until her tears ran out.

Eighteen

The cat was there again when Joy got home from work on Friday night. It had first turned up on Monday night, mewing plaintively from the kitchen door, a tragic-looking individual with a sad, squashy face and mad apricot fur.

'Oh, look,' Julia had exclaimed as she opened the door, 'it's Bagpuss!'

The cat – they hadn't managed to determine whether it was a girl or a boy because there was too much fur in the way to be able to check – had immediately sauntered in and started inspecting the kitchen, like a snooty guest at a five-star hotel, ensuring that the facilities were up to scratch.

'It looks very posh,' Joy had said. 'Do you think it might be a pedigree?'

'Hmmm.' Julia peered at the cat over her reading glasses. 'Possibly a Persian. Not very Finsbury Park, I must say. Well,' she addressed the cat, 'you're very beautiful and you can hang out here for a while, but you're not getting anything to eat. Not in this house anyway.'

The cat had then proceeded to follow Joy around for the rest of the evening, lovingly entwining itself around her legs, purring loudly and attempting to climb on to her lap every time she sat down. Julia had finally kicked it out just before she went to bed at midnight, but it had returned early the following day, a delicate puff of golden fluff, sitting outside the kitchen door, looking almost as if it had forgotten its keys. Again it spent the entire evening following Joy around before slipping out through the back door at around midnight and disappearing into the darkness.

But Joy didn't have time to fuss over the mysterious cat again this evening. This evening she was in a hurry. She had less than forty minutes to get herself ready, back on the Tube and into town. Because tonight Joy was meeting up with George for their first official date.

He'd called, just as he said he would, on Wednesday evening, precisely three hours after Joy hung up on Stuart Bigmore.

Even though Joy had given over a very generous amount of time since Sunday to pondering the issue of whether or not she actually *wanted* to go on an official date with George, she still hadn't decided by the time the phone rang on Wednesday evening, so she'd ended up applying the same approach to decision-making she used in restaurants when she couldn't decide what to order: she waited until the waiter – or, in this case, George – was hovering over her with pen poised, and made her choice under pressure. And in the heat of the moment, with her conversation with Stuart Bigmore still fresh in her thoughts, she'd decided that actually, that sounded rather nice and said, 'Yes, I'd love to.' To which George had responded, with unbridled delight, 'Ah, now I shall smile for the rest of the day!'

Two days later and she still wasn't entirely sure she wanted to be sauntering down this particular avenue, but it was too late to do anything about it now. In approximately half an hour George would be hovering outside the Hippodrome in Leicester Square, pink-cheeked and Barbour-ed up and, having been stood up so recently herself, she wasn't about to inflict the same insult upon another poor soul. So she ran around the flat, throwing off clothes, pulling on boots, spraying herself with Obsession and raking a quick coat of mascara through her eyelashes while the fluffy cat watched her quizzically from its position on top of her unmade bed.

'What do you reckon, Mr Cat?' she said, brushing her hair back into a ponytail and scouring the room for an elastic band to secure it with. 'Do you think I'm mad going out with this funny man who I don't fancy?'

The cat flicked its bushy tail, which Joy took as a sign of disapproval.

'Hmmm,' she said, 'you're probably right. But, hey, it's only one night. And he *is* a very nice man.' The cat flicked its tail twice, but it was already quarter to seven and Joy didn't have the time to argue.

Joy was only about three minutes late when she emerged into the Friday night throngs outside Leicester Square Tube twenty minutes later. Even when she was running really late she still managed to be on time.

The atmosphere was frenetic with expectation as dozens of people loitered under the tremulous mirrored lights of the Hippodrome on the corner of Leicester Square. It had stopped raining, but the pavement was dark and damp underfoot, throwing out muted reflections of amber street-lights and the on-off flash of multicoloured neon. The thump of 'Relight My Fire' by Take That bled from the doors of the Hippodrome, and Joy had a sudden sense of being out of place, out of time, as if she should be meeting up with a group of fun-loving friends for a night of drinking cheap wine and dancing, but she pushed this feeling of dislocation to the back of her thoughts and turned her attention instead to trying to find George in the crowd.

She didn't need to look too hard. He was there at the front, partly obscured by a bouquet of flowers the size of a small Christmas tree, looking very smart indeed in a navy double-breasted suit and tie, and beaming at her over a fat chrysanthemum like the most blessed man in central London.

'Joy,' he said, stepping towards her, 'you came!'

'Of course I came!' she exclaimed, noticing that he looked much chunkier in a suit and that his hair didn't look quite so glued-down tonight. 'Did you think I wouldn't?'

'Absolutely,' he smiled. 'I fully presumed I'd be standing here in the rain watching my flowers wilt, then trundling despondently home to a leftover takeaway and an early night. I'd already decided what I was going to do with these flowers.'

'Which was . . . ?'

'I was going to find the saddest, ugliest-looking girl in Leicester Square, hand them to her and silently walk away.'

Joy laughed and thought that every time she'd decided what kind of a person George was he did or said something to completely change her mind.

'But now I don't have to,' he said, passing her the enormous bouquet. 'I hope you like gigantic, ostentatious flowers. I'm afraid I went rather over the top.'

Joy stared into the vast open faces of stargazer lilies, pom-pom dahlias and fat tangerine roses. 'I love gigantic, ostentatious flowers,' she smiled. 'Thank you very much. I've never been given flowers before – well, not proper flowers anyway.'

'I find that very hard to believe,' said George, as they started to walk. 'Now,' he said, 'I thought we might head over to Kettners – I hope that's all right with you?'

'Kettners?'

'A-ha!' he said, clapping his hands together. 'I was hoping you wouldn't know it. That way I can hoodwink you into thinking I've taken you somewhere grand for at least a little while.'

Joy threw him a quizzical look.

'You'll see,' he said, taking her elbow to steer her round a puddle. 'It's London's greatest illusion!'

'Here we are.' George stopped outside a building that looked like a smart hotel, with a New York-style glass canopy over the front entrance. Inside was all oak pan-elling, hushed chatter and the sound of a pianist gently tinkling away on a grand piano.

'I thought we might start with a bottle of champagne. You do like champagne?'

He asked this in a tone that suggested he'd just offered to share a bottle of prune juice with her.

'I *love* champagne,' she said.

'Good,' he smiled, and led her through to a small bar furnished with little brown leather armchairs around low tables and absolutely heaving with people.

'So,' she said, 'what's this great illusion?'

'You'll see when we sit down to eat,' he smiled. 'Here, let me take your coat.'

'Oh,' said Joy, 'thank you.' She twirled round to let him access her sleeves and felt suddenly flustered in the face of all this opulence and chivalry – it was all so alien to her. 'Thank you,' she said again as he smoothly disengaged her from her coat and folded it neatly over his arm. 'And let's get those flowers out of the way, too, shall we?' He scooped them up with his other hand and ferried all her hindersome belongings out of the bar, returning a few moments later empty-handed. She didn't ask him what he'd done with them, having surmised by now that George was simply one of those rare young men versed in the secret art of adulthood.

George picked up a wine list. 'Now,' he said, 'do you have a preference?'

'No,' she said, 'just as long as it's got bubbles in it's fine with me.' Joy had come into contact with champagne on only a very few occasions in her life, and even then there'd never been a choice involved. She'd heard talk of 'Bollinger', 'Taittinger' and 'Perrier Jouët', but in her experience the matter of choice had never extended beyond 'House'.

George returned a few minutes later with a dewy wine bucket and two full glasses. He sat down and raised his slim glass by its stem. 'I have to say, it really is a pleasure to see you again. You're even more lovely than I remembered.'

Joy flushed and smiled, and felt his flattery seeping through the gaps in her soul like Polyfilla. She raised her glass to his, clutching it by its stem in a subconscious attempt to mimic his sophistication. 'It's lovely to be here,' she said.

'So, how's your week been?' George straightened the legs of his trousers, sank back into his leather armchair and laced his fingers together, readying himself to absorb every last detail of the past six days of her uneventful life. There was something about the way he looked at her that made her feel as if maybe she really was as interesting as he seemed to find her, and she relaxed a little as the champagne bubbles hit the bottom of her empty stomach, and told him all about her week.

She told him all about living with Julia, about the overflowing ashtrays, the crumpled piles of pallid underwear on the bathroom floor, the stained bath towels, unflushed toilets and used tea bags that sat on kitchen counters until the Formica was stained dark ginger.

And then she told him about her night out with her old university friends. She didn't mention the fact that she'd felt insecure and paranoid because they'd all been hanging out together quite happily without her for two years. She didn't mention the fact that they all felt like strangers to her. And she didn't mention the fact they all had better jobs than her and better flats than her and better relationships. Instead she told him how much fun it had been and how they'd all felt really old with their sensible jobs and their enormous overdrafts, and how distant the good old days of student life seemed. George laughed and said, 'You don't know the meaning of the word "old". Just wait until you're nearly thirty.'

Joy felt that she was being dull with a capital D, but the way George looked at her as if he was an alien hearing about life on Planet Earth for the very first time gave her the confidence to keep rambling on.

At some point they finished the bottle of champagne and moved seamlessly through to the restaurant. The drink had bypassed Joy's stomach and gone directly to her head, and the evening was starting to take on a kind of dreamy, unreal quality. A waiter showed them to a table on the far side of the restaurant and Joy slid on to a velvet banquette.

'That's a lovely top you're wearing,' said George, pulling his napkin on to his lap.

'Thank you,' said Joy, fingering the duck-egg lambs-wool. 'It's ancient, though. Look, it's all pilled under the arms.' She raised her arm to show him her pilled armpits. 'I really should throw it away, but I'm emotionally attached to it for some reason.'

George stared at her, smiling with intense warmth. 'I love that about you,' he said, his eyes never leaving hers.

'What?' said Joy, dropping her arm.

'That . . . that . . . not self-deprecation as such, more your ability to throw insults at yourself at the same time as exuding vast amounts of self-confidence. It's a nifty trick, you know.'

'It is?'

'Absolutely. Not many women could make the pilled armpits of their sweater appear so delightful.'

Joy laughed. She didn't normally take to flattery – it made her feel exposed and uncomfortable – but there was something about the sincere way George looked at her through his big glasses that made her feel like someone she really wanted to be.

The menus arrived and the 'illusion' became apparent.

'Pizza Express?!'

'Indeed,' smiled George. 'It's the world's swankiest pizzeria. I just love this place. I mean, don't you think it's utterly fantastic to be able to eat proley food in such grand surroundings? Imagine if all fast-food restaurants were like this – wouldn't the world be a better place for it? Don't you think a Big Mac would taste so much better sitting on velvet?'

Joy nodded and laughed, and agreed that it would, and for a moment she forgot that George was a strange man she'd met in a newspaper and found herself feeling almost excited to be out on a date after so long. But then her gaze wandered for a while to other couples smiling at each other over their doughballs and capricciosos, couples who looked as if they'd met under normal circumstances, couples who *matched*, and she suddenly wondered to herself yet again what the hell she was doing here and where the hell she was headed.

By the time George and Joy left Kettners that night they'd had a bottle of champagne, a bottle of Pinot Grigio and a tot of Chivas Regal each after pudding.

'I've got a confession to make,' said George, as he helped Joy back on with her coat in the foyer. 'I rather forwardly, but also, I hope you'll believe me, entirely *appropriately*, put a bottle of champagne in my fridge before I left for work this morning. I just thought that if we'd reached this stage of the evening and we were still having fun together it might be nice to carry on in more comfortable surroundings. Would you like to share it with me?

No pressure. Absolutely none. You are under no compunction to say yes just to be polite. And I would of course see you safely into a cab at the end of the evening . . .'

'Oh,' said Joy, sobering up briefly to consider this proposal. 'Well, I, er . . . I don't know.' Ever since she'd first set eyes on George a week ago, she'd felt strangely like a ship that had come loose from its moorings and was moving slowly adrift from port. Up until this point the twinkling lights of the harbour had still been in view. If she accepted his invitation to go back to his flat and get even more drunk than she was now, she had a feeling that she'd be swept away by the tide and never find her way back.

But if she said no, then she'd be implying that the evening hadn't been as enjoyable as it indubitably had, that George wasn't as charming as he had every right to claim to be and that being a perfect date simply wasn't enough.

'Er, yes,' she found herself replying, 'why not.'

'Really?' he looked at her with surprise.

'Absolutely,' she said, wondering what strange, unworldly force was compelling her to keep going in this bizarre direction, 'I've never been to Stockwell.'

'How wonderful!' he exclaimed, beaming at her in amazement for a moment, before springing back into action. 'Well, then,' he said, holding the door open for her, 'let's see if I can get us a cab.'

They stepped out on to the pavement of Romilly Street and a cab appeared, and as Joy slid onto the back seat she turned to look out of the rear window and say farewell to the harbour for ever.

Nineteen

In much the same way as George's face hadn't quite lived up to his description of 'handsome', his description of his 'comfortable but somewhat unruly' flat in Stockwell had also turned out to be a bit wide of the mark.

It was the sort of flat that called for some kind of apology, a disclaimer. A 'Sorry for the mess', an 'I've been meaning to decorate' or an 'It's just temporary', but none was forthcoming. The first thing that hit her was how cold it was. She hoped he might pass some comment about the Arctic temperature and run to put on the central heating, but he didn't.

The hallway was carpeted in something greenish and swirly, painted a shiny avocado, and led to a living room which boasted two sofas clad in anaemic grey velour, a very small television balanced on a huge cardboard box, two walls of bookshelves constructed from unpainted chipboard and some blue stripy wallpaper with a sheen to it. The 'comfortable' element was served by a scattering of tartan cushions, some strange red velvet curtains and a green woollen blanket thrown over a coffee table in the middle of the room. She scanned the room for some source of warmth – a gas fire, a blow heater, a radiator – but found nothing. She shivered slightly and went in search of the bathroom.

The toilet was housed in a tiny room to the left of a

draughty-looking bathroom. It was white, with a black seat, a high cistern and a plastic handle on a long rusty chain. There was an out-of-date calendar on the wall opposite, and the seat was so icy cold that it left Joy breathless when she sat down. When she returned to the living room, George was busy with a bottle of champagne, wearing a pair of belted jeans and a thin green T-shirt. Joy missed his smart blue suit already.

'Oh,' he said looking at her with concern, 'here, let me take your coat.'

'Oh, no, no,' she smiled, hugging it to her protectively, 'I'm a bit chilly. I think I'll keep it on.'

This failed to prompt an offer to dispense some kind of heat, so she tucked her frozen hands into her pockets and lowered herself on to one of the sofas, loath to take them out even when he handed her a long glass of chilled champagne.

'Here's to inauspicious beginnings,' he said, raising his glass to hers.

'Indeed,' she smiled, her teeth chattering slightly.

'Oh, dear,' he said, 'you really are cold, aren't you?'

'Yes,' she nodded. 'I'm absolutely freezing.'

'I'm so sorry,' he said. 'One of the reasons this place was such a steal was that it needed a central heating system put in, but it was summer when I moved in and by the time winter came round I'd kind of got used to living without it. It's boarding school,' he smiled apologetically. 'Toughens you up. Here, let me see if I can dig out my old blow heater. I won't be a tick.'

George came back a few minutes later clutching a big metal box that looked as if it would burst into flames the moment it was plugged in. The acrid smell of burning dust accompanied the first few creaking wafts of warm air, but after a few minutes the small room started to thaw, and fifteen minutes later Joy finally felt warm enough to remove her coat. George put on an Arrested Development CD and poured them some more champagne. He lifted the green blanket on the coffee table and pulled out a small wooden box.

'I don't know how you feel about this,' he said. 'I'm afraid it's a rather big part of my life.' And then he did something incredibly unexpected. He pulled out a packet of Rizlas and proceeded to knock together a gigantic spliff.

'You know something,' said Joy, watching his hands in action, 'you really are a very unexpected person.'

'I am?'

'Yes. You just keep confounding all my expectations. I mean, the first time I saw you, I thought you looked like a vicar, then tonight, well, you looked like the archetypal accountant in your suit and tie, and now you're sitting here in your jeans, listening to Arrested Development, making a spliff. I just don't know what to make of you.'

George smiled, as if he'd been told this before. 'And would it surprise you even more if I told you that I was once a punk?' he said. 'Have a look at these.'

He pulled another box from under the coffee table and handed it to Joy. Inside the box was a big wadge of photographs, mainly the small square ones on matt paper from the 1970s. She leafed through the pictures, groups of gawping 1970s and 1980s public school youth, a plethora of batwing tops and narrow jeans, army surplus jackets and cap-sleeved T-shirts, cigarettes, stuck-out tongues, stilettos and plastic earrings, too much hair, electric guitars, mopeds, drum kits and spotty chins.

'Which one's you?'

'Can't you tell?'

'No.'

'There,' he said, pointing to a thin boy with back-combed hair, a horizontally striped T-shirt and a German shepherd dog wearing a bandana.

'No!' she exclaimed, looking closer at the blurred image.

'And that one.' He pointed at another picture of an even thinner boy with bleached blond tufty hair and a sulky-looking teenage girl with pink hair sitting on his lap.

'God,' she said, 'you look so different. And who's the girl?'

'That's Phoebe – my teenage sweetheart.'

Joy studied the girl closely, subconsciously trying to validate her own unexpected presence in George's life with the existence of other women who'd taken the same path.

'She's very pretty.'

'Yes,' he said, peering over her shoulder at the picture, 'she was. I'm afraid I'm terribly shallow. I only date very pretty women.' He smiled at her and lit the spliff, and Joy suddenly realized that this whole physical attraction thing was totally relative. Compared to other men she'd dated, George wasn't especially good-looking. But in his *own* estimation he was 'handsome' and therefore attractive enough to be able to stipulate that he would date only pretty women. And hence, in his mind, there was nothing incongruous about Joy agreeing to a second date and sitting here now drinking champagne in his flat. And if he thought that they made a good match and Phoebe thought that he was a good catch, then maybe *she* was the one with the problem.

And just then, as if to compound this train of thought, the phone rang and George tutted. 'Oh, God,' he said, 'that'll be Tara.'

'Tara?'

'Yes. The psycho ex, remember? I'll get rid of her.'

Joy sat and listened in wonder as George fended off what sounded from her point of view like a barrage of hysteria and tears from the other end of the line before finally hanging up with a terse, 'Please don't call here again.'

'Woah,' said Joy, all agog with the drama of it, 'what was that all about?'

'Oh, God,' he said, flopping down on the sofa and running his fingers through his hair, 'she's heard through the grapevine that I'm seeing someone and she's freaking out about it. I knew this would happen.'

'Oh,' she said, 'so she's not over it yet?'

'Sadly not. She's convinced herself that we're going to get back together, and I suppose the fact that I've been single for so long just added fuel to her conviction. And now she's finally having to accept that it's over. And if I sounded a little cruel just then, it was very much to be kind, I can assure you. She's been deluding herself for too long now and it's not healthy. She needs to move on . . .' He shook his head sadly as he considered the mental state of his poor, lovesick ex-girlfriend, and Joy felt her suspicion growing that maybe there was nothing wrong with George at all and that her resistance towards him was entirely a matter of a bad first impression and her own narrow-mindedness.

So when George finally made a move and kissed Joy on the lips, she'd already decided that she was going to go with the flow and see what happened. And when it came fifteen minutes later to the practicality of getting Joy back to Finsbury Park at nearly one in the morning, it was inevitable that the option of Joy staying the night was going to arise.

'You take the bed,' he said. 'I can curl up here on the sofa.'

But Joy had already decided that even though she didn't have any overwhelming desire to have scx with him right now, that if she could accept the possibility of scx with George at some point in the near future, then she wasn't putting herself in a particularly hazardous position by agreeing to share a bed with him. And so she found herself ten minutes later, wearing one of George's T-shirts and huddled under a rather damp duvet in George's ice-cold bedroom watching him getting undressed and realizing with a start that he actually had a very nice body – well-formed pecs, a smattering of chest hair, lovely skin with a lingering hint of summer tan.

'I thought you said you had an "unimpressive" physique,' she teased. 'You've got a lovely body.'

'Thank you,' he said, beaming with delight, 'I've been going to the gym quite regularly since I've been single. You're the first person to see the results, so I suppose

I didn't want to comment without objectivity. Now, would it make you feel more comfortable if I were to wear a T-shirt to bed, too?'

Joy shrugged. 'What would you normally wear?'

'Well, that would be nothing.'

Joy eyed him in his boxer shorts and decided she wasn't quite ready for that. 'Shorts are fine,' she said.

He hopped under the duvet with her and turned his head to face her.

'Do you know something?' he said, smiling at her like a small boy. 'I've had this fantasy ever since I was a teenager . . .'

'Oh, yes . . .'

'No – not that sort of fantasy. A chaste fantasy. A fantasy about the girl I'd end up with. And I know this probably sounds terribly asinine, but I knew that she would have black hair and a one-syllable name. And ever since I got your letter I've just had this feeling, quite overwhelming, that you're her . . .'

And for some reason the idea of living up to the exacting adolescent fantasies of a teenage George struck her as an enormous compliment, so when he looked at her with his soft green eyes and asked her for a hug – 'Purely platonic, I promise.' – she acquiesced. And the hug, inevitably, turned into a kiss, and the kiss tuned into a passionate embrace and, before she knew it, she was staring at the back of George's neck while he rifled frantically through his bedside cabinet for a condom.

Joy didn't regret sleeping with George when they awoke the following morning. Joy never regretted sleeping with anyone. The only sort of sex you should regret, she believed, was the sort you'd given to someone who didn't deserve it.

He brought the death-trap blow heater into the bedroom and made her a cup of tea in an attempt to warm her up, but even under a thick duvet she was still too cold to even contemplate getting out of bed.

'Look,' she said, making an oval of her mouth and breathing out, 'you can see my breath.'

'Oh, God,' George said, dropping his head into his hands, 'this is dreadful. Here I am with the most radiantly beautiful woman in the whole world lying naked in my bed and I can't even give her the basic luxury of bodily warmth. Here!' he exclaimed, brightening. 'How about a nice hot bath? The boiler here churns out gallons of hot water. You could just lie there and keep topping it up until your bones get warm.'

'But what about getting there?'

'I'll get you a blanket.'

He returned and wrapped her chivalrously in a rather scratchy blanket, then ushered her into a steamy bathroom.

'No bubbles?'

'Oh, God.' He slapped his head. 'I'm such a disaster. I can't believe I didn't think of bubbles.'

'It doesn't matter,' she smiled, hopping into the steaming hot bath and feeling her bones melt with relief.

'Now, I've put a towel in the tumble dryer to warm up,' he said. 'Just let me know when you want to get out and I'll fetch it for you.' He stopped and folded his arms, a smile spreading across his face as he stared at her. 'You really are quite exquisite,' he said. 'The most perfect, perfect thing I've ever seen.' He smiled at her for a bit longer, before snapping out of his reverie. 'Now. Can I get you another cup of tea?'

Joy lay in the bath for nearly an hour while George brought her cups of tea, slices of toast and a steady stream of compliments. They then spent the rest of the day in bed where they talked and had sex and talked and had sex until the streetlights outside the window flickered on at four o'clock and threw amber shadows over the bedclothes.

The world had shrunk over the course of the past twenty-four hours. Where once there had been a thriving city heaving with millions of bodies, there were now just two people huddled together under a duvet in a small, dark room in the corner of a flat, floating alone in the blackness of the cosmos.

Everything had lost its context, and Joy no longer knew where she was going. And it wasn't until their stomachs started growling at eight o'clock and Joy found her way back into the clothes she'd discarded the previous night in order to leave the confines of the flat and find something to eat that any semblance of objectivity returned to her, and she suddenly remembered that, even though she'd now been on two dates with George, spent twelve hours in bed with him and had sex with him four times, she still didn't find him in the least bit attractive.

Twenty

Julia's strange friend Bella was round again on Saturday night when Joy got back from George's. There were many strange things about Bella, but by far the strangest was the fact that he was a man.

Joy had first encountered Bella (apparently his given name was Barry) the day after she moved in. He'd been sitting on the sofa watching *Songs of Praise* when she walked through the living room on her way to the kitchen to get her morning cup of tea, an emaciated little creature in black leggings and a huge black jumper that nearly swallowed him whole. He had thin brown hair worn in a blunt shoulder-length bob, eyebrows plucked to the point of almost nonexistence and the scrub-faced, exposed look of a man who was often to be found in full make-up.

He'd made a big show of jumping when Joy walked into the room, clutching his heart and exclaiming about what a fright she'd given him. Then he'd uncoiled himself from the sofa like a little grass snake and introduced himself. 'I'm Bella – Julia's little sister.' Joy had been at a loss to know what to say. 'I know,' he'd said, 'we don't look anything alike.'

It turned out of course that he was neither Julia's sister nor her brother, but was, in fact, her 'very best friend in all the world'.

Julia absolutely adored him, but as far as Joy could make out he was vain, neurotic and totally fucked up. In his head he was a captivating, glamorous but ever-so-slightly tragic queen living the urban homosexual dream. In reality he spent all his time hanging out with Julia eating Hobnobs on her sofa and bitching about everyone on the telly. Apparently he had a drag act – Bella Bella – but he'd fallen out with the management at the club where he had his spot and nobody else had seen fit to book him since. He'd never had a boyfriend because, according to Julia, he hated gay men, and he struck Joy as one of the most inherently unhappy people she'd ever met in her life.

'Well, well, well,' he purred over a can of Strongbow when Joy walked in that night, 'look what the cat dragged in.' That was another thing about Bella – he was incapable of saying anything even vaguely original.

'Darling!' Julia leaped from the sofa. 'Thank God! I was starting to think you'd been abducted. You should have phoned!'

'I'm sorry,' she said, pulling off her coat and flopping down on to the sofa. 'I didn't think.'

'I *bet* you didn't . . .' Bella pursed his lips in mock disgust.

'Darling,' Julia said as she perched herself on the edge of the sofa and lit a powder-blue cigarette, 'I want you to tell me everything. I want to hear every last gruesome detail . . .'

'Oh, please,' Bella tutted and looked away, letting it be known that the mere concept of heterosexual sex was too much for him to stomach.

Joy started at the beginning, with the huge flowers and the posh pizza, and as she retold the story she began to see it through the eyes of her audience and it suddenly didn't seem so strange and off-centre any more. A lovely man whom she'd met in unconventional circumstances had taken her for dinner and treated her like a queen. They'd enjoyed each other's company so much that they'd gone back to the lovely man's flat, drunk champagne and had sex. It looked great on paper, sounded wonderful in relation, but the reality? Well, she still wasn't entirely sure about that.

'Looks aren't everything,' said Bella, slapping Julia's hand away from a spot on her chin she was fiddling with. 'It's what's inside that counts.'

'Yeah, I know,' said Joy, thinking that not only was he trite, but also he was wrong. Looks weren't *everything*, but they were definitely, significantly, *something*. 'But it's not just his looks, it's just . . . it all just feels, I don't know . . .'

'Oh, invite him over,' said Julia. 'Let's have him over for dinner and have a look at him. We'll tell you whether he's good-looking or not.'

'Oh, I don't know,' muttered Joy. 'I mean, I haven't even decided if I want to see him again or not.'

'Er, sorry?' Bella clasped his hand to his chest and let his jaw drop. 'You've just spent twenty-four hours shagging this poor bloke to within an inch of his life and you're not sure you want to see him again? There's a name for girls like you, you know . . .'

Joy was too tired and too disoriented to want to find out exactly what name he was thinking of and decided to play it a bit more positive. 'Maybe,' she said, 'it's all to do with expectations. You know, maybe if he'd said in his letter that he looked like a dog's arse, then I would have been pleasantly surprised when I saw him and my whole perception of him would have been different. Maybe it's the fact that I was expecting "handsome" and I had a very particular image in my mind of what "handsome" looked like and, when he wasn't it, it just cast a negative vibe over the whole thing.'

'Yes,' soothed Julia, whose whole being was openly consumed with the desire for Joy's romantic liaison to work out. 'That'll be it. You just need to look at him afresh. I mean, he can't be that bad if you had sex with him four times, can he?'

Joy nodded, but then thought back to the two years she spent being fondled in Kieran's bedroom and wearing his engagement ring as a teenager and the two months she spent kissing Miranda and fiddling with her nipples in the sixth form. And then she thought of that bloke, the one who'd stood her up outside the Swiss Centre on a Wednesday night – she hadn't fancied him at all, but she'd accepted a date with him because he'd asked her so nicely. She thought of pretty much every man she'd ever slept with or been out with and realized that, with the exception of Vince and Ally, she had a long and painful history of being intimate with people she wasn't sexually attracted to. The fact that she'd slept with George – more than once – was no indicator of sexual attraction. It was an indicator of the fact that she was a complete moron with an apparently pathological inability to say no.

'Look at it this way,' said Julia, 'when I first came to see this flat my gut reaction was that it wasn't the place for me. I'd always said that when I found the right flat

I'd know immediately – that I'd just walk in and fall in love with it. But then I got an offer on my place in Cambridge and I needed to move quickly so I thought, fuck it, just buy the fucking flat and worry about it later. And it took me a few months, just putting my mark on it bit by bit, and now I adore it – couldn't imagine living anywhere else. And that's what you need to do with poor old George. Put your mark on him. *Personalize* him. Men are very impressionable when it comes to clothes and stuff, you know – they're just gagging for some woman to come along and tell them how to dress and how to do their hair.'

'It's true,' nodded Bella. 'Straight men are missing a gene. The *style* gene. Poor lambs. It's tragic.'

Joy looked at Bella, who was wearing red denim bell-bottom jeans, a skintight grey jersey polo neck that showed every rib in his chest and a red bandana with a skull and crossbones on it. She opened her mouth to say something, then shut it again.

'And I guarantee you, darling, once you've got him exactly how you want him you'll fall instantly in love with him and marry him. I mean, he sounds *divine.*'

And he was. He was gentle and polite and old-fashioned. He was funny and eccentric and clever. He was chivalrous and interesting and made her feel like not only the girl of *his* dreams, but of the dreams of every living man.

And after months of feeling herself fading away like an old Polaroid left in a shoebox in the loft, George's fulsome, fervent and soft-focused attentions were exactly what she needed.

Twenty-One

Over the course of the next two weeks, George took Joy to a stupidly posh restaurant in a Chelsea back street where they were the youngest couple by about twenty years, to the Renoir to see a Czechoslovakian film with subtitles, to the RNT to see *Arcadia* and to the Café Royal for afternoon tea.

He bought her two pairs of vintage diamanté earrings, an art deco marcasite bracelet and a silver Edwardian pendant in the shape of an angel, and he sent her flowers at work on three separate occasions.

After their second official date they went back to George's flat and Joy discovered that he'd bought her a brand-new blow heater which he insisted she have switched on wherever and whenever she wanted it. 'I don't care about the cost – I just can't bear the idea of you being cold,' he said when she commented on the effect that this might have on his electricity bill.

On their third date he'd brought along a huge pile of Dulux colour cards and told her she could redesign the flat to her own specifications, even if that meant pink polka dots and leopard skin. 'It is quite clear that you have a surfeit of good taste, whilst I, unfortunately, have none. I trust you implicitly.'

And on their fourth date the subject of clothes shopping had arisen and he'd handed himself over to her on a plate. 'I've bought no new clothes in four years. I haven't had any awareness of fashion since I was a punk. You, on the other hand, are hugely stylish, so if at any point you were to feel like steering me in the direction of a particular shirt or pair of trousers, I would not take the slightest offence.'

George claimed that he'd started looking at life completely differently since he'd met Joy. 'My aesthetic sense has been completely transformed,' he'd said. 'I just have to look at you and I suddenly want to buy new curtains!'

In the three weeks that they'd been seeing each other George had swiftly and effectively eliminated the source of every single one of Joy's misgivings about him. The only misgiving that now remained was the not insignificant fact that Joy wasn't physically attracted to him, but they were having so much fun together that Joy had kind of forgotten about that little impediment and was going with the flow.

Everyone at work knew about George now.

Joy had told one of her regular customers, a chatty girl called Mimi who worked across the road at Sony, and within two days everyone at ColourPro knew that Joy had met a man through a personal ad who was now completely sweeping her off her feet. Not that she minded everyone knowing her business – she wasn't a particularly secretive or mysterious person – but it was just that the more people knew about it, the more real it became.

Men on the whole seemed a bit perplexed that a perfectly normal, presentable girl such as Joy had been reduced to scouring the classifieds for a bloke, but women were overwhelmed by the notion of finding love in the lonely hearts. Girls who'd never shown that much interest in Joy before were cornering her in the staff room to ask all about it.

What was it that had attracted her to the ad, what did she think the first time she saw him, which restaurants had he taken her to, what plays had they been to see?

She was being accosted now, by Jacquie and Roz, incredulous eyes bulging over chicken mayonnaise sandwiches.

'So, has he told you that he loves you yet?' said Roz.

'No, not in so many words.'

'Bet he will though – bet he'll tell you soon. God, it's so romantic. I can't believe it. I've never met anyone who actually *met someone* through an ad before.' She shook her head in wonderment.

'What does he do?'

'He's an accountant.'

'Oh, my God, an accountant!' squeaked Jacquie. 'Bet he's really rich, isn't he?'

'Well, sort of.'

'What car does he drive?'

'Oh, it's just a company car. A Ford something.'

'Is it big?'

'Ish.'

'Christ.'

Both girls stopped and stared at her for a moment, letting the existence of a big-ish company car sink in.

'What does he look like?' said Jacquie.

'Oh, just kind of ordinary really. You know . . .'

'Have you got a picture of him?' said Roz.

'No.'

'Oh, you should get one.'

'Yeah,' agreed Jacquie, 'you should get one. Let us have a look at him.'

'I'll see what I can do.'

'Has he got a nice flat?'

'Well, you know, it's OK. Needs a bit of work doing to it.'

'Yeah, but it's *his*. He *owns* it. That's the important thing. No flatmates. God, Roz, can you imagine going out with a bloke who had his own place?'

'No way,' Roz shook her head slowly. 'Or a bloke who takes you out to fancy restaurants. Or a bloke who buys you antique jewellery. Or a bloke who sends you flowers at work for *no reason*. Christ.'

'Christ,' said Jacquie, 'you're so lucky.'

They both stared at her in awe.

'Do you love him?' said Roz.

'No!' she exclaimed. 'Of course not. We've only been on five dates.'

'That doesn't mean nothing. My cousin met her husband on the Tuesday and was on honeymoon in Lanzarote by the following weekend.' She shot Joy a look that suggested that there was virtue in such foolhardiness. 'They've got four kids now *and* they still love each other.'

'Well, that's lovely, but really, I don't think that I'm headed down that particular road.'

'God, makes you want to answer an ad yourself, doesn't it, Roz?'

'Yeah,' Roz nodded, 'too fucking right.'

And then a strange thing happened – Big Lee spoke to her.

'Erm, hello,' he said, 'erm, Joy.' He disgorged her name as if he'd only just learned how to pronounce it. 'There's a, er . . . phone call for you. Urgent. Er . . .' Then he disappeared again.

She locked herself into the tiny office off the supplies room and lifted the receiver to her ear. 'Hello.'

'Joy, love. It's mum.'

'Mum. What's the matter?' Her mother never called her at work.

'Oh, love . . .'

'Oh, God,' Joy felt her bloodstream fill up with adrenalin. 'What?'

'It's your dad . . .'

'What about him?'

'He's gone.'

'Gone where?'

'He's left. With Toni Moran.'

'What!'

'He's left me, Joy.'

'But, when? Where? I don't understand.'

'Just now. I was microwaving some soup for him. It had just pinged and he walked into the kitchen with a suitcase. Told me he was going.' She sounded flat, like someone had their foot on her larynx. 'It never stopped,' she said, 'all these years – it never stopped. They've been . . . *doing it*, all along.'

Joy could almost hear her shaking her head in disbelief as she talked.

'Stay there, Mum,' she said. 'I'm coming straight home.'

Twenty-Two

Joy and Barbara sat in the early gloom of the afternoon, sipping sherry from musty crystal glasses, letting the reality of the day's events sink slowly in.

Alan was gone.

He wanted a 'quickie' divorce.

He loved someone else.

He'd been lying for years.

Barbara was a single woman again at the age of sixty-five.

'Mum,' said Joy, a sudden need for confidences and answers overwhelming her, 'why did you choose Dad?'

'What do you mean?'

'I mean, what was it about him? Why did you fancy him? Fall in love with him?'

'Fancy him?!' she laughed.

'Yes.'

'Well, your father was the most handsome man I'd ever set eyes on. You'd be better asking *him* why he chose *me*.'

'Mum! That's awful. How can you say that?'

'Well, it's true. I was thirty-five years old. Practically middle-aged in those days. Naive. Inexperienced. And not exactly the prettiest thing you'd ever seen. And your father – well, he swept me off my feet.'

'He did?' Joy's mind boggled at the very thought.

'Yes. Flowers. Gifts. Compliments. I'd never known anything like it.'

'Wow.'

'Yes. He was a true romantic back then. He wasn't always such a . . . well, you know,' she sighed, and turned to face Joy. 'And then we got married and we got posted out in Singapore and . . . well, he changed. We both changed, I suppose.' She got a faraway look in her eye.

'Why?'

She shrugged, picking absent-mindedly at the slubs in her tweed skirt. 'Very competitive place Singapore back in those days, the 1960s. Very stressful. He worked twelve hours, fourteen hours a day sometimes. So much money. And then there was drink, drugs – all the beautiful people. Everyone wanting to be in on the action all the time. Anything you wanted in Singapore was there for the taking, on a plate. I think it turned his head, to be honest.'

'And was he having affairs there? In Singapore?'

Barbara suddenly looked wistful, got a pinched look about her cheeks. 'Oh,' she said lightly, 'I don't know. Probably. I'm sure he was. All those beautiful women. The stress at work. All the problems we were having, you know, conceiving. I'm sure he was.'

'Didn't you ever think about leaving him? Didn't you ever think you deserved better?'

Barbara turned on her seat and stared at Joy for a while, a terrible haunted look suddenly overcoming her. 'Yes,' she said slowly, 'plenty of times. But I couldn't.'

'Why not?'

She turned back to the window, stared into the darkness. 'Well,' she said, 'I didn't want to hurt him.'

Joy looked at her in surprise. '*Hurt him?* After all the affairs. After what happened in Hunstanton. After he treated you like shit all your life.'

'It wasn't that simple.'

'Wasn't it?'

'No. Your father . . . he had his reasons. I wasn't perfect.'

'Yes you were. You *are*.'

'No, love. I wasn't. Nobody is. There are two sides to everything.'

Joy flinched slightly. She could feel something beyond this conversation, something she wasn't sure she wanted to hear.

'What are you trying to say, Mum? Is there something you're not telling me?'

'No,' her mother smiled, rubbing the back of Joy's hand. 'No. Of course there isn't. I just don't want you blaming your father for everything, that's all.' Barbara stood up. 'More sherry?'

Joy nodded and looked at the back of her mother's head, at the curler-rolled sausages of Wella Warm Mahogany hair that had deflated slightly over the course of a long, hard day, and felt a surge of love overcome her.

'You know I love you, don't you, Mum?'

Barbara turned to her and smiled wanly. 'Of course I do, love. I just hope you always do. Whatever happens . . .'

The following morning, while her mother sat in the kitchen peeling the last of the summer windfall for apple sauce, Joy pulled on her jacket and headed over the road to Number 18. Toni Moran answered the door. She was wearing a plum-coloured polo neck and beige trousers, and her hair was cut short and sleek. Black kohl ringed her turquoise eyes and gold chains circled her elegant wrists. She smelled of Poison. She was tall and lean. She was fifty-one. She was everything Joy's mum wasn't.

'Joy!' she said, as her ruby-hued lips stretched themselves into a smile of genuine pleasure. 'How lovely to see you. And looking so beautiful. Come in. Come in.'

She ushered Joy into a hallway that smelled of cigarettes, damp dog and clean laundry. A leggy red setter ambled towards her, wagging its tail lazily. Joy put out a hand to pet it, then snatched it back. She couldn't go back to her mother's house smelling of Toni Moran's dog.

'Is he here?' she said, woodenly.

'Yes. Of course.' Toni threw her a look of sympathy, as if this whole rotten scenario had absolutely nothing to do with her. 'Al,' she called up the stairs, 'Joy's here.'

She showed Joy through to the living room. Her house was exactly the same shape as Joy's parents', but felt completely different. Instead of damp wisps of nylon net hanging across her windows, she had folds and flounces of thick oatmeal jacquard. Instead of fields of ancient, patterned carpeting covering her floor she had shiny beech-effect parquet. And instead of a solitary hanging light bulb housed under a dusty paper shade she had rows of twinkling halogen lamps embedded in her ceiling.

Joy sat down on a plump sofa in green and white stripes and listened to her father's footsteps, heavy on the stairs behind her. She could hear him whispering with

Toni in the hallway, and took a deep breath. She knew what she'd come here to say. Now she just wanted to say it and leave.

'Joy.' Her father stood in the doorway. He was wearing a blue T-shirt with some kind of logo on it. She'd never seen him in a T-shirt before.

'Dad.' She got to her feet.

'I hope you haven't come here to cause any trouble.' His face looked tight and defensive.

'No,' she snapped, 'I haven't come to cause *trouble*. I've come here to say something – then I'm going.'

'Fine.' He folded his arms across his chest and stared at the floor.

'Mum is in there,' she pointed across the road, 'with a broken heart. She's done nothing but love you and care for you and look after you, and you've done nothing but treat her like shit.'

Alan opened his mouth to say something, but Joy was on a roll.

'I ended up on a psychiatric ward because of you and that woman. You swore to Mum that you'd never see her again, and now it turns out that you were lying the whole time. And then there was Hunstanton. You humiliated me and made me lose the only person who'd ever made me happy and I've tried my hardest to forgive you for that, but I can't. Mum deserves a better husband than you and I deserve a better father. I never want to see you again. I don't want you to phone me, write to me or visit me. As far as I am concerned you no longer exist. As far as I'm concerned I no longer have a father.'

Joy stopped and caught her breath. Adrenalin fizzed

through her veins and she could feel her left eyelid twitching. She stared at Alan and waited for his response.

He nodded slowly and lifted his gaze from the floor. 'Fine,' he said again, 'I understand. Now go.'

'What?'

'I said – go.'

'Is that it? Is that all you've got to say?'

'You heard me.'

Joy glanced uncertainly at the door, sure that at any moment her father would say something else, display some emotion, beg her forgiveness. But he didn't. Instead he held the door open for her.

'You say you don't want me,' he said stiffly as she walked past him into the hall. 'Well, that's fine because I don't want you, either. I never wanted you in the first place. Have a good life.'

Joy turned at these words and stared at her father looking for a sign that they had caused him any kind of pain, but his eyes were dead. She opened her mouth to say something, but nothing came close to expressing what she was feeling, so she closed it again.

And then she turned to leave Toni Moran's house and walk out of her father's life for ever.

Twenty-Three

Joy stood on a stepladder wearing an old tracksuit of George's that was twice the size of her, with a paint roller in one hand and a tray in the other.

George was squeezing tea bags in the kitchen and about to do something quite extraordinary. He knew he was going to do it. He'd known he was going to from the moment he first set eyes on her. He'd meant to do it the previous night, but had lost his bottle at the last minute. He'd thought maybe he shouldn't do it at all, but just now when he'd asked her if she wanted a cup of tea and she'd beamed at him from the top of her stepladder and said, 'Ooh. Yes, please,' and she had mint-green paint splattered across her cheek and she was painting *his* flat in *his* tracksuit on a Saturday afternoon, he knew more than ever that he was going to do it.

Joy knew he was going to do it, too. She could feel burning particles of his intent floating round the flat, like tiny fireflies. Everything had been building towards it, all weekend.

He'd met her from work on Friday night in his car and stared at her for a full minute before starting the engine.

'You don't mind, do you?' he'd said. 'I just want to look at you for a while.'

'No,' she said, 'feel free.'

He'd looked as if he was going to say something then, but eventually he'd started the car and driven away.

They went for dinner at a tiny French restaurant behind the opera house in Covent Garden, where they ate fat snails curled up in pools of garlicky butter, teaspoons of salty cod roe and soft, flaky duck legs with golden slivers of almond. They talked about the unsatisfactory mess of their past relationships.

'You know,' Joy had said, 'if this doesn't work out, then I truly think I'll become a nun.'

'Do you mean that?' he said.

'Yes. This is the best relationship I've ever been in.'

And it was. George wasn't the love of her life, but then she wasn't entirely sure what that meant anyway. She did know that she enjoyed every moment in his company, that he phoned when he said he'd phone, that he treated her with a respect bordering on reverence and that she knew exactly where she stood with him. She'd also discovered that a lack of aesthetic appeal was no obstacle to an enjoyable sex life, proved indisputably by the fact that George had treated her to her first purely penetrative orgasm the previous night.

'I can't believe it's taken me seven years to do that,' she'd said breathlessly afterwards. 'They make it look so easy in the films.'

'To be honest,' George had said sheepishly, 'I was rather under the impression that you'd been having them all along.'

'Oh, no,' she'd said, 'that was definitely the first. Couldn't you tell the difference?'

'Not really, no,' he'd admitted. 'You're always rather, er . . . noisy.'

'Am I?'

'Well, yes, but not in a bad way. In a very good way.'

'Oh, no – do I sound like a porn star?'

'No,' George laughed, 'not at all. Just very enthusiastic. Which is good. Which is lovely. And yet another thing that I love about you.'

It was one of a few oblique mentions of the 'L' word that weekend, mentions which made her feel happy because, although Joy definitely wasn't *in love* with George, she most certainly wasn't *not* in love with him. She loved being with him. She loved the way he looked at her. She loved the way he felt about her. She loved the way he treated her. And, more pertinently, she felt that one day, if everything about him were to shift a degree or two in another direction, she could learn to love *him*.

George was teaching her how to be grown-up at a time in her life when she really needed to be an adult. It was as if he hadn't noticed that Joy was still a child, had seen some inherent maturity in her and had welcomed her into his adult world without any doubt that she'd be able to conduct herself properly. They had a grown-up life together; they drove around in a big grown-up car doing big grown-up things. They talked about politics, philosophy, feelings, life. They cooked for each other from recipe books – two-course meals with prawns and crab claws and complicated sauces that they ate by candle-light with music playing in the background. They spent twenty minutes in Oddbins, choosing wines based on the weather patterns that had brought the grapes to fruition rather than on how much change they'd get from a tenner. They drove into the countryside on Sunday afternoons and took photos of the landscape with George's massive Nikon.

George had grown-up friends, friends with children and mortgages, friends who got married in the Home Counties and had huge receptions in marquees in their parents' gardens.

He even managed to make his spliff-smoking habit seem grown-up. A skinny forty-year-old woman called Marian came to his flat every couple of weeks with a little lump of resin for him. She wore her hair in a bun and talked about her kids and her holidays while she made a spliff to share. After half an hour she folded George's £20 note carefully into a purse she wore around her waist, got into a shiny Toyota Corolla and drove back to her terraced house in Catford.

Joy didn't feel like an overgrown teenager any more. She was ready to leave that phase of her life behind her. She wanted to read big, intense books written by dead Russians, make her own pâté, learn to play chess, stay in National Trust properties, read broadsheets and use long words in passing conversation.

She didn't want to get back on the merry-go-round of bars and clubs and having to be charming to stupid boys who smelled of cigarettes and wanted sex more than they let on. She didn't want to go to another party and find herself stuck in the kitchen with the boring bloke that everyone else was avoiding, too polite to make her excuses because he'd know that she didn't *really* need to go to the toilet and was just saying it so that she could get away.

She didn't want to be stood up again, ever, as long as she lived, and she didn't want to sit in a pub with her friends wondering if the man of her dreams was just around the corner.

She wanted stability. She wanted commitment.

And George was just about to offer it to her in its purest, most concentrated form.

'You look so lovely up there,' he said, placing her tea on the top step of the ladder.

'Mmm,' said Joy, wiping her hair out of her eyes with the back of her hand, 'I'm sure. Paint-splattered tracksuits have always been my best look.'

'It's a sort of Felicity Kendal thing, I suppose. The tousled hair; the tomboy demeanour. No British male can resist.' He smiled and offered his hand to help her down the steps. 'Well, at least I can't. Look,' he said, turning her round to face him, 'I'm going to say this quickly in case I run out of steam, but did you mean what you said yesterday, about becoming a nun if this doesn't work out?'

'Yes,' she said, suddenly feeling slightly breathless.

'Good, because I feel the same way. Without the nun part – obviously, I'd become a monk. Well, an agnostic monk, anyway. And there I go, rambling again, when what I mean to say, *want* to say, is this –' He stopped, took a deep breath in. 'Would you like to get married? To me?'

And even though Joy had always maintained that she would never get married before her thirtieth birthday, even though she'd only known George for eight weeks and even though she wasn't entirely sure she wanted to spend the rest of her life with him, she looked into his green eyes, absorbed every particle of his unconditional and undisguised love for her, realized that he would never reject her, that he would always want her, that to him she would always be the girl of his dreams . . . and said yes.

Twenty-Four

'Look,' said Cass, removing herself from a decrepit-looking Afghan coat and dropping a carrier bag on to the coffee table in front of him, 'I've bought you a present. Budge up.' She shifted Vince along the sofa with her bum and reached for the bag.

Vince stared at the object for a second or two, his brain firing blanks as he tried to identify it. 'It's lovely,' he said, reaching out to touch it, 'is it a, er . . . does it . . . what is it exactly?'

'It's a crystal ball, doofus. A very expensive crystal ball.' She rested the globe on a carved wooden stand and caressed it lovingly. 'I've always wanted one, so I thought I may as well get the top of the range.'

'But I thought you said it was for me?'

'Well, it is, kind of. It's for me to help you. It's for finding Joy.'

'Oh, for God's sake.' He threw her one of his special 'Cass, you are a total fruit' looks, and flopped back into the sofa.

'Seriously,' she said, stroking the ball, 'this little beauty will tell us where to look. I promise.'

He raised his eyebrows and opened a magazine.

'Vince – work with me. Think positive. This will work.'

'Cass, do what you want. Just don't ask me to get involved.'

'You don't need to – just get me that letter she wrote you. That's all I need.'

Vince tutted, but got to his feet and retrieved the letter. When he got back Cass was constructing a roll-up while reading a paperback called *Ball Gazing for Beginners: Tapping into the Supersensory Powers of Your Subconscious.*

'Don't you need to have years of experience to do this kind of thing?' he asked sceptically, handing her the note.

'No,' she said defensively. 'If the power's within you, if you've got *the gift*, then things like this –' she indicated the ball – 'are just vessels.'

Vince stifled a derisory snort and picked up his magazine. 'Cassandra McAfee, you are full of shit.'

Cass sniffed and threw him an injured look. 'So, if I find her, what do you want me to do? Keep it to myself?'

'Cass, my lovely, witchy fruitcake,' he said, putting an arm round her shoulder, 'if you find her in that lump of glass, then I will give you a hundred pounds *and* make you godmother to our first-born child.'

'Really?' she smiled.

'Yes, really.'

'Cool,' she said, then she turned off all the lights, lit a candle and started being spooky.

Half an hour later and all Cass had divined from thirty minutes of frantic rubbing and intense concentration was that Joy was living near a stream or possibly a river, that she was wearing something green and that she had something to do with horses – or possibly cows. She also saw red shoes, a small chair and a packet of Silk Cut.

'So,' said Vince, 'sounds like Joy's a chain-smoking milk-maid, then?'

'Oh, stop taking the piss.'

'No, I'm serious. If I'm going to find her, then I really need an accurate picture of her. Was she actually *milking* a cow when you saw her?' He indicated the ball.

'No, Vincent, she wasn't *milking* a cow. I didn't actually *see* her. This isn't a fucking *video*,' she said, pointing at the crystal ball.

'So what did you see, then?'

'Just *stuff*. Ephemera. Like feelings, floating around.'

Vince could tell that Cass was floundering – she'd left behind the comfort zone of her tarot cards and was completely out of her depth. There was a slight edge of panic about her.

'And even if it's true – even if she is a milkmaid living near a stream – how does that help me track her down? She could be anywhere – maybe not even in this country. She might be milking cows in Yugoslavia or Argentina for all we know.'

Cass shook her head defiantly. 'It was definitely England,' she said.

'And you know that, how?'

'Just do,' she said sullenly.

'Right.' Vince nodded, and sighed.

'Look. OK. Maybe the ball wasn't that helpful,' Cass conceded, 'but I still think you should keep looking anyway. The sooner you start looking for her, the more time you'll have together. You say you want to find this girl – but what have you actually done about it, eh? Absolutely fuck-all. I mean, you're still going out with

Magda, for fuck's sake. What the hell's that all about?'

'Oh, Jesus, Cass — will you please get off my case. You're doing my brain in.'

'No, I'm serious. What the fuck are you doing going out with Magda when you don't love her and you love somebody else?'

'I don't know,' he replied, lamely. 'I don't know. It just wasn't the right time to finish it. But when the time's right, I will finish it, *then* I'll start looking for Joy. One thing at a time . . .'

'Yes, but –'

'No, yes but. Just not. OK? When I'm ready, I'll start looking for Joy.'

Cass was about to answer back, when the familiar sound of Madeleine's claws clacking against the wooden floors distracted her.

'Oh,' she said, turning to glance at the cat, 'it's you.'

The relationship between Cass and Madeleine had soured somewhat over the course of the past few weeks, as the latter's absences had grown longer and more frequent. There was no doubt in Cass's mind that Madeleine was now living a double life. She had entered into an unauthorized shared-ownership arrangement with some overperfumed woman in the local vicinity and was patently quite happy with this situation.

Cass, on the other hand, was deeply hurt and very confused.

'It's just bad etiquette,' she sniffed. 'Anyone who knows anything about cats knows that you just *don't* feed someone else's cat. It's rude.'

'How do you know they're feeding her?'

'Oh, of course they are. Why else would she be spending all that time there? At the end of the day, cats are mercenary creatures – they're only where the food's at.'

'Maybe you should try feeding her something else, then.'

'Oh, for God's sake,' Cass said, throwing her hands up in exasperation. 'She already gets tuna chunks and roast bloody chicken – what the fuck more could she want?'

'Have you tried Whiskas?'

'I am not feeding my cat that manufactured gunk – it's nothing but cereal and additives mixed up with a bit of meat juice.'

Madeleine had come to a halt in the middle of the room and was in the latter stages of grooming her haunches. She sat for a while, licking her lips and appraising the lap options on the sofa, looking from Vince to Cass and back again, before trotting towards Vince and landing on his knees with a loud and contented purr.

This latest betrayal seemed to tip Cass over the edge.

'That's it,' she said. 'That is it! I am taking tomorrow off work and I am going to follow that fucking cat everywhere she fucking well goes. I am going to find this Obsession woman and I am going to have *very, very* strong words with her. I'm prepared to have a fist fight, if necessary.'

Vince stared at her and sniggered. 'Don't you mean a cat fight?'

'Ha, ha. Very funny.' She kicked his leg with the heel of a socked foot. 'I'm serious, Vince. I want my cat back. And I'm going to get her back. By any means necessary.'

And with that she got to her feet and stalked theatrically out of the room.

Vince and Madeleine exchanged a bemused glance and carried on watching the telly.

Twenty-Five

Cass followed the tip of Madeleine's orange tail as it skipped over garden walls, disappeared under hedges and scooted round corners.

The cat came to rest for a while on top of a wheelie bin, surveying the lay of the land before continuing on her way.

As she reached 44 Wilberforce Road, she slowed her pace slightly, stopping again on the front lawn to arrange herself for a moment, before striding up the front steps and scratching furiously at the front door.

Cass tensed, waiting for someone to come to the door, but after a minute or two Madeleine leapt on to a wall, where she stretched out and adopted a 'happy-to-wait' pose.

Cass felt sick. Who was this woman who was so special that Madeleine was happy to sit outside in the damp cold of a November afternoon waiting for her to return?

The minutes ticked by slowly enough for Cass to watch the entire contents of the flat next door being packed into a removal van and driven away, but finally, at half past one, a couple stopped outside the house and turned to go in. Cass caught her breath, feeling like a suspicious wife about to witness her husband's infidelity.

The woman was one of those women with skinny ankles who got progressively wider the higher up you got, like an upside-down triangle. She was wearing an old 1950s print summer dress, with thick black tights, a vintage astrakhan coat and red plimsolls. She also had a kind of Margo Leadbetter turban thing on her head and was smoking a blue cigarette through blood-red lips.

Her boyfriend was about four inches shorter than her, a foot or two narrower and dressed in ripped jeans, a fringed suede cowboy jacket and a grubby baseball cap. His hair was long and lank and parted in the middle, and he appeared to have no eyebrows to speak of.

They were the sort of people who looked like they didn't change their bed sheets unless they spilled something on them. Cass shuddered. 'Please, don't let it be them. Please, don't let it be them,' she muttered under her breath as they mounted the front steps.

'Mou-Shou! Darling!' The large woman swooped upon Madeleine and enveloped her in a cloud of cigarette smoke, upon which Madeleine raised herself on to her tiptoes, stretched and allowed the repellent woman to pick her up and carry her inside.

The door slammed behind the trio and Cass jumped slightly.

Mou-Shou?

They called her cat Mou-Shou?

She shook her head in disbelief and numbly lifted herself off the garden wall. She was so furious she could barely remember how to breathe. She was so furious in fact that she could do nothing other than turn around and walk home very, very slowly, thinking about all the things she wished she'd said to the pair of freaks who'd stolen her cat.

Twenty-Six

Julia peered disconsolately at Joy from beneath the plastic cap covering her hair, which was in the process of being virulently hennaed. 'But you can't possibly move out. You're the best lodger I've ever had. Bella, tell her. Tell her she can't move out.'

Bella lifted the edge of the plastic cap and pulled out a lock of copper hair, turning it to the light to examine it before tucking it back under the plastic. 'Julia says you can't move out,' he said. 'So therefore you can't move out.'

'I'm really sorry,' said Joy, 'but it just seems a bit strange to be engaged to someone and not living with them. And obviously I had no idea when I moved in here that I'd be getting married three months later.'

'Well, no,' flashed Bella, '*obviously*. I mean, who would?' He curled himself up into the corner of the sofa and fiddled with his plastic gloves.

They'd decided, last night, she and George. There was no point in hanging around, waiting for a long-distant summer's day that may or may not be blue-skied and balmy. If they were going to do something as spontaneous as getting engaged after eight weeks, then why not go the whole hog and marry in haste? Christmas Eve meant nothing to George since his mother had died, and it would be a sensitive date this year for Joy and her mother. Why not make it something to be truly celebrated, create a new anniversary?

Joy had been surprised by the proposition, but not averse to it. It was only when George had suggested, quite rightly, that if they were to be married by the end of the year, then they really should think about moving in together, that Joy had felt a tremor of uncertainty. Wilberforce Road was her link to her independence. It was the place she came home to, drunk after a night out with her colleagues; the place where she lounged around on the sofa, picking her toenails and watching rubbish television (George only used his TV for watching videos and *Newsnight*). It was the place where she swore, freely and liberally (George had decreed fairly on in their relationship that swearing was the 'lowest form of communication' and Joy had immediately dropped five words from her vocabulary). It was where she drank lager and had stupid conversations about soap stars and hairstyles. Up until now, her grown-up life with George had been one strand of her existence; when she moved in with him, it would become the *only* strand of her existence.

But she could hardly have said, 'I'm prepared to marry you – but live with you? No, thanks.' So she'd nodded and said, 'I'll give Julia my notice tomorrow.'

And the boat drifted ever further from the harbour lights.

Julia pointed at the cat with a pink Sobranie. 'Mou-Shou will be devastated. Won't you, Moushy?'

Joy ruffled the cat's head and smiled. The name Mou-Shou had nothing to do with her. It was a stupid bloody name and Joy could only assume that Bella had had something to do with it, but in her present state of mind she really wasn't prepared to enter into a debate on the subject. Mou-Shou. Dim Sum. Crispy bloody Duck. Whatever . . .

'He'll get over it,' she said. 'He manages without me five days out of seven as it is.'

'Yes, but he's not the same. Not really. He comes every day, you know. Goes into your room, looking for you. Sits there on the sofa, waiting for you. Totally ignores me, though, the bastard,' Julia sighed, and examined her hair in the mirror. She had a violent orange splodge on her left cheek, which she rubbed at with a spitty finger. 'I've been thinking about getting a cat flap put in. Poor thing was drenched when I let him in yesterday – God only knows how long he'd been waiting out there.'

'You know he's not our cat, don't you?' said Joy.

'Yes, I know. He belongs to the patchouli person with the curry smells. But he definitely prefers it here.'

Joy sniggered. 'How do you know?'

'Well, of course he does – he wouldn't spend so much time here otherwise. And we don't even feed him. But anyway, that's not the point. The point is that you're leaving us. Lovely, beautiful, precious Joy is leaving us,' she sniffed dramatically. 'It's too sad.'

Bella raised a plucked eyebrow, clearly feeling no sadness at all at the prospect of no longer having to share his beloved Julia with someone thinner and prettier than himself. 'I think you're mad,' he said, 'getting married to someone you've only just met.'

'Bell!' Julia threw him an appalled look. 'Don't say that!

217

Don't listen to him,' she said to Joy, 'he's just jealous. It's wonderful that you're getting married. The most romantic, wonderful thing. And on Christmas Eve, too. Will you wear red velvet? White fur? A cape?'

'Oh, and why not a big white beard while you're at it, too?' Bella uncurled himself and stalked over to Julia to examine her hair.

'No, not fur and capes,' Joy ignored him. 'I'm going to get something made up for me. I've got pictures. Do you want to see?'

'Ooh, yes.'

Joy pulled out a stash of pages torn from the wedding magazines a girl at work had brought in for her, and handed them to Julia. 'I want something short,' she said. 'It's only a registry office do, so I didn't want to go over the top.'

'Oh, I like this one.' Julia pointed at a little 1960s-style shift dress with enormous buttons. 'Very Jackie O.'

At the mention of one of his all-time icons, Bella flopped on to the sofa next to Julia, chanting, 'Let me see, let me see,' and for the next half an hour they lost themselves in a frenzy of dresses, rings and flowers.

The past week had been an ongoing frenzy of dresses, rings and flowers. Every time she told someone the news they immediately started asking a million questions about the minutiae of her upcoming nuptials, and in spite of the fact that Joy had never really been a particularly wedding-y girl, hadn't spent her teenage years fantasizing about tulle and tiaras, and even now was hoping for something low-key and simple, she couldn't help but get carried away by the force of other people's enthusiasm.

Having blended into the background at ColourPro for more than a year, Joy had suddenly achieved celebrity status. Jacquie and Roz had made it their business to tell everyone her news: clients, the girls at the sandwich shop, couriers, the managing director – even the managing director's wife was in the know. Joy would never have guessed how strongly people felt about weddings, how much pleasure such a simple piece of news could bring to people who barely knew her and how much interest virtual strangers would suddenly take in what seemed to her mere frippery.

People had started foisting things on her, too – bridal magazines, lists of venues, offers to organize hen nights, anecdotes, advice and congratulations. People smiled at her more and the atmosphere was enhanced wherever she went. Her mother had smiled for the first time in four weeks when she went home to tell her the news. Everyone at work seemed to have an extra spring in their step. Even the acidic Bella was sweetening slightly at the prospect of having some input into the design of her dress.

'Oh, let me make it. Please, let me make it.'

Joy had never seen Bella so excited before – he was almost smiling.

'I'm really good, aren't I?' he turned to Julia. 'Tell her how good I am. Show her that bustier I made you for that slags party. Go on.'

Julia heaved herself and her bosom from the sofa and trundled off to her bedroom in fluffy socks.

'Honestly. I'm really good. I mean I've not been to fashion college or anything, but my mum taught me to sew and she was a proper seamstress and look –' He grabbed the bustier from Julia's hands. 'Look at the detail in that.'

She examined the voluminous piece of red satin in awe. It really was quite beautifully made, covered in tiny red sequins and squiggles of black lace.

'That's real whalebone, that is,' he said, turning the bustier inside out and showing her the seams, 'like they used to make them, in the old days. Properly. You know.'

'Bella,' said Joy, fingering the tiny hook-and-eye fastenings, 'I don't understand. Why are you working as an usher when you've got this talent? This is just amazing.'

Bella shrugged and rolled his plastic gloves back on. 'Don't know, really. Just like hanging around in theatres, I s'pose. The smell of the crowd. The roar of the greasepaint. You know.'

'Well, you could have been a costume designer, then. God, just think. You could be running up tutus for the Royal Ballet. Imagine that.'

He shrugged again, and pulled the transparent cap off Julia's head. 'Nah,' he said, 'I don't think so.'

'Why not?'

'I dunno. Just not really very me. Anyway,' he changed the subject, 'can I or can't I? Make your dress?'

'Yes,' she said, 'why not? I can't afford much, though.'

'Well, then, I won't charge you much. How does £200 sound? Plus materials and stuff.'

'Sounds amazing. Are you sure?'

'Positive,' he said. 'Now, Miss Julia, it's time to get you to the bathroom, before your hair turns Day-Glo.' With that he ferried Julia out of the living room, leaving Joy alone to contemplate the commissioning of her wedding dress and the taking of her first faltering steps on the wide, open road to her wedding day.

In bed that night, Joy thought about what Bella said, about her being mad getting married to someone she barely knew. Maybe he was right, she mused. Maybe she was insane. She had no idea. Joy had lost the ability to differentiate between fantasy and reality, and the whole 'engagement' scenario was now so plump with positive energy that Joy found it impossible to give any thought to the negative aspects. Like the notion of leaving her lovely warm bedroom in Wilberforce Road and taking up permanent residence in George's ugly, chilly flat. Like the fact that she hadn't met any of his friends and he hadn't met any of hers. Like the shadowy sense of dislocation that she still hadn't managed to shake off. All she knew was that, at a time in her life when everything had felt grey, empty and bleak, George had come along and made it colourful again.

And now she found herself in a position where the light emanating from her state of betrothal was so bright that it had somehow blinded her to everything – including her own incipient, dazzling folly.

Twenty-Seven

'Sorry, Mummy, I missed my potty!'
Tiffany Rose is a big girl now and when nature
calls she knows it's time for her potty. But even
the biggest girls can make mistakes. One look into
Tiffany Rose's big blue eyes and you can't help
but forgive her for her little puddle. Tiffany Rose
is a joyous delight from the tips of her silky
blonde hair to the toes of her real leather bootees.

One day, thought Vince, there'd be an awards ceremony for this sort of thing and, if there were any justice in the world, he would get the top prize. The Heinous Tat Marketeer of the Year Award or something.

No one could quite believe their eyes when they'd come into Melanie's office on Monday morning and seen Tiffany Rose sitting on the boardroom table, her cotton poplin skirt hitched up to her thighs, a sag of jersey knicker around one ankle, perched over a tiny plastic potty with a shiny 'puddle' to the side – thankfully not in lifelike yellow, but discreetly transparent. On pulling up her skirt they ascertained that the designers had indeed given her a proper bare, dimply bottom and even the faint suggestion of a fanny at the front.

'Urgh, Jesus, that's disgusting,' had been the general consensus.

'Surely that's illegal,' had been another observation.

Vince, meanwhile, sat her on his desk, his tiny porcelain muse, and waited for the words to come.

'Vince,' came a voice from the other side of the office, 'phone for you. It's Cass.'

Vince picked up the phone, thankful for the diversion. 'Cass.'

'I've found her.'

'Who?'

'The woman. The Obsession woman.'

'Oh. Right. And?'

'And, she lives on Wilberforce Road and she's very fat and she's got an ugly little boyfriend who looks like a girl.'

'And what did you say to them?'

'Nothing. I lost my nerve. Just watched them from the other side of the road. They call her Mou-Shou.'

'Sorry?'

'Madeleine – I heard them talking to her and they were calling her Mou-Shou.'

'As in pork?'

'Yes,' she hissed, 'as in pork. I mean, they've named her after *meat*, for fuck's sake. Why didn't they just go the whole hog and call her Sirloin? Or . . . or, you know – *Rump*. I'm so furious I could . . . I could . . . Jesus. I'm furious.'

'So, what are you going to do?'

'I'm going to go back tonight. Have it out with them. But I want you to come with me.'

'*Me?* But why?'

'Because they're weird-looking and I don't want to go on my own.'

'And what exactly do you think might happen to you?'

'Christ, I don't know. I mean I read this book once about this girl who was given a lift by this really normal-looking couple who ended up keeping her in a box under their bed for ten years. The world is full of scary fuckers. Why take a chance?'

'OK,' he said, 'but I'm not very good with confrontation. Promise me you won't go ballistic.'

'Of course I'm going to go ballistic. They've kidnapped my fucking cat.'

'Cass, aren't you supposed to be a hippy?'

'Yes. And?'

'Well, what happened to good karma and being mellow and all that.'

'Fuck that,' she said. 'This is war.'

Cass and Vince didn't make it to 44 Wilberforce Road that night. A howling gale arrived in Finsbury Park at around seven o'clock, accompanied by horizontal rain and a wind-chill factor of minus two degrees.

'We'll go tomorrow night,' said Cass, wearing a scarf and hat, and stirring a steaming pan of something green and pungent on the hob.

'Can't tomorrow night. I'm busy. And Friday night.'

'Well, then, we'll go at the weekend. Saturday afternoon?'

'Why don't you just write her a note instead? That way you don't have to come into contact with her?'

'No,' said Cass. 'That's too easy. I want to see the whites of her eyes. I want her to feel the full force of my fury.'

'Fine,' said Vince defeatedly. 'Fine. Saturday afternoon. We'll go on Saturday afternoon.'

Twenty-Eight

Joy glanced down at her left hand and fiddled with a small silver ring on the third finger. It was embedded with a dozen small diamonds clustered around a larger diamond, and had originally belonged to the wife of the man who wrote *Charley's Aunt*, according to the man with the handlebar moustache from whose antique jewellery shop on the New King's Road they'd bought it.

'Don't even think about the cost,' George had said. 'Just choose the one you love the most.'

As it happened, the one she'd loved the most had cost exactly a quarter of the amount of £50 notes George had folded up into his wallet, and he'd proclaimed her a cheap date.

The ring had been the centre of attention all week long.

'Let's see it, then.' She would dutifully hold out her left hand, in a faintly regal manner, while some over-excited girl or other oohed and aahed and turned the ring this way and that to catch the light.

'It's a bit puny,' had been Bella's response. 'Thought you said he was rich.'

So the ring had been chosen and paid for in cash, the dress was a work in progress, the banns had been posted at Chelsea Town Hall, a classified had been placed in the announcements section of the *Daily Telegraph* (her mother's idea), the last few remaining boxes of her possessions were squashed into the boot of her mother's car and she was an hour away from leaving her single life behind for ever.

Joy felt curiously numb as she emptied her lovely room, took pictures off the walls, pulled photos from the mirror frame, hoovered away the detritus of ten weeks of her life. If she thought too much about what she was doing she'd have to stop to think about everything else, and if she did that, then . . . well, it was too late to do anything about anything now, so there was no point.

She watched her mother trundling down the path towards the Volvo estate carrying a box of shoes – she looked about ten years younger than she did the day those same shoes had arrived at Wilberforce Road more than two months earlier. Barbara had barely had the puff to perform a three-point turn then, but now here she was marching briskly back and forth between the car and the flat with all manner of boxes and bags, barely breaking out into a sweat.

She'd lost a few pounds since Dad left. She'd taken to walking the half a kilometre to the local shops and back every day, to pick up a paper or a lottery ticket – just to get her out of the house, just for something to do. And she couldn't be bothered to cook properly, not for herself, so she tended to graze her way through the day on Rich Teas, Cuppa Soups and Golden Delicious.

She'd changed her hair, too – decided to try a new salon, just for a change. It was still old-lady hair, but softer, warmer, less sausagey old-lady hair. It hadn't taken her long to recover from the shock of Alan's departure and, now that Alan and Toni had moved into a new house three miles away and she no longer had to watch their silhouetted forms disrobing at night through their bedroom window or watch Alan gallantly helping Toni into the passenger seat of his Jag or see him happily pushing a shopping trolley around Asda in a way he'd always resolutely refused to do for her, she finally felt as if she could get on with her life.

'Well,' said Joy, letting herself fall into Julia's marshmallow embrace, 'it's been fantastic. Short but very sweet.'

Julia pulled back and regarded her fondly. 'You're a very special girl,' she said, 'and George is a very lucky boy.'

'See you next week, for your second fitting,' Bella swooped towards her and hammered a birdlike peck on to each cheek before swooping briskly away again. 'And don't forget to invite us to your hen night.'

'I won't,' she said.

She got into the passenger seat of her mother's car, belted herself in and waved goodbye to Julia and Bella, feeling strangely as if she'd forgotten something.

She racked her brain for the full forty minutes of the journey from Finsbury Park to Stockwell, but couldn't think what it was.

And it wasn't until they pulled into the access road behind George's mansion block, and saw him beaming at them from the kitchen window on the third floor, that she realized – it was herself she'd left behind.

Twenty-Nine

'This is it.' Cass forced her hands into the pockets of her Afghan coat and came to a halt outside one of the fat red-brick houses on Wilberforce Road.

'Very nice,' said Vince appreciatively.

Cass threw him a withering look and walked forcefully towards the front steps. 'Come on,' she said as she turned to him impatiently, 'let's get this over with.'

Vince whistled nervously under his breath while they waited for the door to be answered. A few seconds later a large woman in a not-quite-long-enough T-shirt and pink angora socks appeared at the door. She had bright orange hair tied up in a ponytail and was smoking a green cigarette.

'Hello,' she said, smiling at them widely.

'Hello,' said Cass, whose hands were bunched up into fists at her sides. 'I'm Cass and this is Vince. We live over there –' she said, indicating behind the woman. 'On Blackstock Road. We've come to talk to you about my cat.'

'Oh, yes?'

'Yes. Madeleine. The big Persian tabby. *My* cat.'

'Oh, well, how utterly hysterical – he's a girl! Bella! Bella!' the woman shouted into the hallway behind her. 'Guess what! Mou-Shou's a girl!' She turned back to them. 'We thought he was a boy,' she said, somewhat unnecessarily. 'Would you like to come in?'

The woman's flat was high-ceilinged and cluttered. Wine

glasses and unemptied ashtrays littered every surface. A large duvet was folded on top of a red sofa, and a very thin man was curled into the corner of a very large leather armchair on the other side of the room, wrapped in a blanket and halfway through a chocolate Hobnob.

'Told you it was a girl,' he said to Julia, unfurling a thin leg and eyeing up Vince and Cass with undisguised disdain.

'This is Vince and Cass. They live on Blackstock Road. Mou-Shou – sorry, *Madeleine* – is their cat.' She turned to smile at them, and Vince smiled back at her extra hard to make up for Cass's deadpan belligerence. 'This is my friend Bella.'

Vince and Cass both turned as one to reassess the thin man in the armchair. He had long hair and thin eyebrows, but was indubitably a man.

'Can I get you a coffee?' asked Julia, jamming her green cigarette into a tray of multicoloured stubs.

'Actually,' said Cass, 'this isn't a social visit.'

'Oh,' Julia looked disappointed.

'No. I've come here to tell you to stop feeding my cat. I mean, it's just not on. I've had her for five years. I've paid all her vet's bills, taken time off work to take her there, fed her, loved her, been there for her when she needed me. I mean, me and Madeleine – we've got this *connection*.' She tapped her temple with her finger. 'Do you see? She's not just some cat – she's, like, my best friend. And ever since you started feeding her whatever the fuck it is that you're feeding her, I hardly ever see her and, even when she does come home to me, there's this . . . *distance*. It's not the same as it was. And anyone who knows about cats knows that you *just don't feed other people's cats. It's rude and it's cruel and I want you to stop!'*

Cass was a livid shade of red by the time she drew breath at the end of her tirade. Her hands were shaking and she'd started crying.

Vince held his breath and listened to the ringing silence. The thin man called Bella had retreated even deeper into his blanket, with a Hobnob suspended halfway between the packet and his mouth.

'Oh, you poor, poor darling.' Julia steamed towards Cass with her arms outstretched. 'I had no idea.' And then she buried Cass between her bosoms and squeezed her tightly. 'If I'd thought for a moment . . . oh, God, I feel dreadful, so utterly dreadful.'

Cass started sobbing properly then, and buried her face deeper into Julia's T-shirt. 'Bella,' said Julia, 'coffee, please, darling – and make it strong.'

She ferried Cass towards the sofa and sat her down. 'Now,' she said, 'you must tell me what we can do to sort this out.'

'I told you,' gulped Cass, 'stop feeding her.'

'But, sweetness, we don't feed him – *her*. I would never do such a thing. From the moment she appeared at the door, I said to her, "You're very pretty, but we're not bloody well feeding you." But she kept coming back. She's in love, you see, in love with my lodger.'

Cass turned to look at Bella in bewilderment.

'No, not with him. With Joy.'

'Joy?'

'Yes. Lovely Joy. My ex-lodger,' she sighed.

Cass and Vince exchanged a glance.

'She just moved out this morning, actually. We're feeling very sad.'

'Weird,' said Cass. 'We've been looking for a girl called Joy.'

'Have you, really?'

'Yes. I don't suppose . . .' She looked at Vince. 'It couldn't be the same one?'

'Of course it's not the same one,' muttered Vince.

'What did she look like, your Joy?'

'Slim,' said Julia, 'dark. Very pretty, very pale.'

Cass threw Vince a questioning look. He shrugged and nodded.

'How old?'

'Mid twenties. Thereabouts.'

'Surname?'

'Downer.'

'Oh. My. God.' Cass slammed her hand over her mouth and began hyperventilating.

'Is it her?' said Julia. 'Is it the same girl?'

'Yes,' breathed Cass.

'Spooky,' said the man called Bella, coming back into the room with a fistful of mugs.

'Fucking hell,' said Vince.

'Sugar?' said Bella, plonking mugs of coffee on to a table.

'I mean,' Cass got to her feet and began pacing the room manically, 'we've done nothing but talk about this Joy girl for ages. She came up in a tarot reading I did for Vince and he admitted that he was still in love with her . . .'

'I am not *in love* with her,' he interjected.

'. . . and that was why he was so crap at relationships, then he decided to find her and I even bought a crystal ball, you know, looking for this girl, this mysterious Joy, and all the time she was here. *Here.* Just around the corner. This is just, like, the *freakiest thing ever.*'

'Sugar?' demanded Bella again, wagging the teaspoon up and down impatiently.

'Vince, can you believe this?' Cass flopped back on to the sofa, quivering with excitement.

'No,' he said, 'it's unbelievable.'

He couldn't decide what to feel. He subconsciously sniffed the air, searching for physical evidence of Joy's recent presence in this strange flat with these bizarre people.

'How is she – *was* she?' he muttered. 'Is she well?'

'She's getting married,' said Bella, abruptly.

'Oh,' said Vince.

'Next month. To a bloke she met in the classifieds.'

'Oh,' said Vince again.

'You're joking,' said Cass.

'No. It's true,' said Julia, whipping the teaspoon out of Bella's hand and ladling three spoons of sugar into her coffee. 'She moved in two months ago, then she met this fellow called George through a personal ad and he's completely swept her off her feet, got engaged last week and now they're getting married. Frankly, it's the most romantic thing I've ever heard . . .'

Vince gulped. 'But isn't she, a bit *young* to be getting married? I mean, she's only twenty-five. I would have thought . . .' He trailed off. What would he have thought? That someone as special as Joy wouldn't be snapped up while she was still fresh? That every man she met wouldn't fall insanely in love with her and want to marry her on the spot? Of course she was getting married.

'Yes, she's young. But she's very mature.'

'And what's he like, this George?'

'Never met him,' said Bella, 'I reckon he's got three eyes and a wart on the end of his nose.'

'Bell!' Julia reprimanded. 'Stop being awful. I'm sure George is lovely.'

'Bet he's not. Bet he looks like a hyena.'

'Oh, God – just ignore him,' said Julia. 'He's just a horrible person. No, I'm sure George is completely divine. And I know that Joy is totally head over heels in love, and that is all that matters.'

'When's she getting married?' Vince ventured.

'Christmas Eve,' hissed Bella. 'Chelsea Town Hall. Will you turn up and stop the wedding?'

'Er, no,' said Vince, feeling genuinely taken aback by the suggestion.

'Oh, you should. You should hurtle in when the vicar says that bit about any persons here present and say, "She can't marry him – he looks like a warthog and he's got no central heating!"'

'Eh?'

'Well, that's what she said. Said his flat's like a blooming meat packer's. *And* it's in south London.' Bella shuddered theatrically. 'Imagine living in *south London* without heating. Urgh. It doesn't bear thinking about. And then you should pick her up and run down the King's Road with her, as fast as your little legs can carry you.'

'Bella!' said Julia. 'Will you stop being so awful.'

'Seriously, though – what are you going to do?' said Cass.

Vince shrugged. 'Nothing,' he said. 'She's happy. That's all that matters.' And that was all that mattered. He'd simply left it too late, he thought. Joy had been living round the corner, ripe for the plucking and ready to fall in love, and he'd got here nine weeks too late. Someone in the Big Boardroom in the Sky had obviously had a good hard look at his record and decided, on this occasion, not to offer him a promotion.

They stayed for another half an hour, discussing the Incredible Coincidence and drinking Julia's shockingly strong coffee. By the time they got up to leave at four o'clock, Cass and Julia appeared to be in love with each other, and Bella had finished the entire packet of Hobnobs without offering one to anyone.

At the front door they swapped numbers and made promises to keep in touch. Bella threw them a half-hearted farewell from his crumb-strewn blanket. 'See you on Christmas Eve,' he said to Vince, tapping his nose. 'Chelsea Town Hall. Don't forget.'

Vince smiled wryly. 'I don't think so.'

'Oh, go on,' he said, 'stir it up. Life's too short.'

'No,' said Vince, 'I'll leave it. It wasn't meant to be.'

Bella pursed his mouth. 'Your loss,' he said.

And as he and Cass wandered round the corner back to the flat on Blackstock Road, Bella's last words to him echoed in his head, and Vince wondered if maybe he was right.

Thirty

Joy felt a shiver of excitement as she boarded the north-bound Victoria Line at Oxford Circus on Thursday evening. She was on her way to Bella's bedsit on Seven Sisters Road for her second dress fitting. It was the first time in over a week she'd headed north after work, and for some reason the very notion filled her with a sort of nostalgic longing. Not that she wasn't happy living in Stockwell – Stockwell was very nice, and she and George were very happy – but it was nice to get a bit of space, a bit of distance from which to view her new existence. And, poignantly, her new journey home seemed to reflect the general direction her life had taken over the course of the past three months as she turned left instead of right, went south instead of north.

She grabbed a seat and looked at her fellow passengers, feeling a comforting sense of kinship, of being among her own people again – north London people. She glanced at her reflection in the black of the window opposite as the train hammered its way from Kings Cross to Highbury and Islington, and wondered if it showed, her new state of foreignness.

And then she glanced down at her ring, the only outward manifestation of the new world she inhabited and she twisted it back and forth and round and round her finger until the train pulled into Finsbury Park.

*

Bella's bedsit was a full and complete explanation for the fact that he spent most of his life sitting round at Julia's.

In a room that could not have been much bigger than ten feet by ten feet, there were no fewer than three separate clothes rails, a wardrobe and a chest of drawers. Clothes were piled on the floor and hanging from picture hooks on every wall. Yet more clothes hung from the curtain rail, from the back of the door and over the radiator. There was even a plastic clothes drier underneath the sink festooned with an eclectic variety of pants, socks and underwired bras.

'I collect them,' he explained. 'They speak to me. "Bella," they say, "Bella, take us home. We want to come and live with you."' He fingered a lime-green chiffon cocktail dress while he talked. 'I just can't resist them.'

He made her some tea by microwaving a mug of water, chucking a tea bag in it, then pouring in some milk, which he kept on his windowsill. It was overly creamy, slightly tangy, but Joy sipped the tea politely and perched herself on the edge of Bella's single bed, careful not to crush an ostrich feather hat.

'Have *I* have got *the* most amazing thing to tell *you*.' Bella removed the ostrich feather hat and squeezed up next to Joy on the bed. He was squirming with excitement.

'Ooh,' said Joy, 'what?'

'If I said the name "Vince" to you, what would you say?'

Joy choked on her tea.

'So you know who I'm talking about, then?'

'I don't know,' said Joy, wiping tea off her chin. 'Who *are* you talking about?'

'Tall, fair, handsome. Still in love with you.'

'What?'

'You know exactly who I mean. I can tell by the look on your face.'

'Well, there was a Vince . . .'

'Yes. Tall, fair, handsome, still in love with you and living on Blackstock Road.'

'Bella, can you start again? I'm all confused.'

'Right.' Bella brought his legs up on to the bed and crossed them. 'Door goes Saturday afternoon, just after you moved out. There's some hysterical witch in a patchwork hat standing there with the most *gorgeous* man. They come in and she starts screaming at Jules about that sodding cat . . .'

'Cat?'

'Yes. Mou-Shou. Turns out the cat's hers and also that he's a she, but anyway, she's going, "Ooh my cat, it's the centre of my tiny petty little world and you're so horrible for letting him come in here and blah-de-blah-de-blah," and Jules explains that the reason the cat's always round at hers is because it's in love with *you*. Joy. And then witchy woman says, "Ooh, Joy, we've been looking for a girl called Joy." And it turns out that this bloke Vince used to go out with you and thinks he's still in love with you and the witch woman's been doing tarot readings and gazing into crystal balls and God knows what else trying to trace you so that he can proclaim his undying for you. And he's there, in your flat, literally like an hour after you've moved out. I mean, is that the freakiest thing ever, or what?!'

'Oh, my God,' said Joy, clamping a hand over her

mouth. 'That is unbelievable. Vince Mellon. I don't believe it.'

'So – what are you going to do? Are you going to see him?'

'God. I don't know. I mean . . . *Christ!* Did he really say he was still in love with me?'

'Yes! No. Well, the girl said he was in love with you, and he only disagreed a little bit. But I think he was just embarrassed.'

'So this girl wasn't his girlfriend, then?'

'No. She was just a friend.'

'Vince Mellon.' She sighed and rested her chin on her hand as she brought his face into her mind's eye. 'God, he was gorgeous.' She recalled his gentle hazel eyes, the way his hair fell on to his forehead, his big, solid skull and wide-set shoulders. She hadn't thought about him properly for so long she'd almost forgotten that he existed in flesh and bone. Whenever she thought about him she tended to shudder with embarrassment and stop the train of thought in its tracks before the notion of her father manhandling Vince's mum made its way into her head.

She still didn't know exactly what had happened that night. All she knew was that her mother was clammy with shame, using words like 'disgusting', 'ashamed' and 'humiliated', while her father was bolshie and defensive, using words like 'a bit of fun', 'overreacted', 'too much to drink', 'prick tease' and 'working-class scum'.

It had been her mother's idea to leave that night.

'I can never face that poor woman again,' her mother had said, throwing clothes into a suitcase, while Joy's father examined his bandaged nose in the mirror, a picture of exquisite self-pity.

Joy had almost knocked on Vince's bedroom window before they left, to say goodbye, to give him her note, but she'd changed her mind at the last minute and left it pinioned under a pebble on the outside step.

It took nearly six months for Joy finally to resign herself to the fact that Vince wasn't going to get in touch. She liked to think his lack of communication was due to loyalty to his mother rather than any lack of affection for her. She didn't blame him – what man would want to get involved with a family like hers?

Because their relationship hadn't ended, but had instead evaporated slowly in a hazy blur of passing days, she hadn't been left with a broken heart, but rather a strange sense of longing for something she couldn't quite describe. In her heart, Vincent Mellon existed as a vague, sun-dappled montage of fairground smells and cawing seagulls, of sweaty hands and Monopoly pieces and of feeling madly, deliriously in love for the first time in her life. He was the person she referred to when she told people she'd lost her virginity at eighteen to a man she met in Hunstanton. He was a part of her history that lived in its own dimension, separate and distinct from everything else, like a film or a book.

But now he was living just around the corner. He still existed. In three dimensions. She gulped.

'How was he?' she said.

'Fine, I guess. But then I don't know what he's normally like.'

'What was he wearing?' She didn't know why she'd

asked that – she just wanted to picture him, she supposed.

'Jeans. Grey jumper. Grey overcoat. Very minimal. Very smart. Very fucking sexy.'

'Did you tell him I was getting married?'

'Uh-huh. Should have seen his face. Poor boy was *devastated*.'

'No!'

'Yes. Couldn't believe his bad luck. I told him to come to the wedding and whisk you away.'

'You didn't!'

'Of course I did.'

'Bella, that's awful.'

'He won't come. Don't worry. But I thought he at least deserved the option. And talking of options –' He brought out a leather bag from beneath his bed and unzipped it. 'Here. You deserve the option, too.'

'What is it?'

'It's his phone number. Just in case you change your mind about Georgie Porgie.'

Joy looked down at the crumpled piece of paper. 'Is that his handwriting?'

'No. It's mine. I copied it down for you.'

She studied the numbers on the paper as if they were magic hieroglyphics, the key to the gates of a secret civilization. 'What makes you think I'm going to change my mind?'

Bella shrugged. 'I don't. But, you know, it's all a bit sudden, isn't it?' He picked at the corner of his duvet cover, then looked up at her. 'I wonder,' he began, 'do you think maybe you're rushing into it because of your dad?'

'My *dad*?'

'Yeah. You know, maybe this wedding thing, maybe it's your way of dealing with your parents splitting up?'

Joy frowned.

'It's just, when my dad died I know I went off the rails a bit. Got obsessed with this man. He was married. Completely unobtainable. But I was just craving a bit of stability, a bit of attention, you know. And I wondered if maybe you were doing the same. Trying to replace your dad, kind of thing.'

Joy shook her head. 'I know this sounds awful,' she said, 'but I don't really care. I don't miss him. Not at all.'

'Yeah, well I wasn't that close to my dad, either, but your parents, you know, they're part of you, make you who you are, whether you like it or not. And when part of that goes, however it happens, it leaves a big hole. And it's only natural to try to fill it.'

Joy nodded, and ran a finger along Vince's phone number. 'I don't know,' she said. 'I feel like I should be sad, but I'm just not. My mum seems to be coping really well with it and I don't miss him and it's almost better in a way. Better without him. And George . . .' she paused, 'George is just the nicest, kindest, sweetest, most intelligent man I've ever met. He loves me and cares for me, he respects me . . . oh, and *he makes me come* . . .' She grinned.

'Oh, per-lease,' Bella grimaced.

'Well, seriously. What more could a girl ask for?'

'And you?'

'What about me?'

'Well, do you love him?'

Joy gulped and cast her eyes downwards. 'Of course I do.'

'As much as he loves you?'

'Yes,' she said.

'Really?'

'Of course I do. Wouldn't be marrying him otherwise, would I.'

'And do you love him as much as you loved that Vince?' He pointed at the piece of paper.

Joy's eyes strayed to the note, to the angles and curves of the letters that made up his name. She remembered the way her heart had pumped when she first saw him, the intensity of her desire to undress him, to be naked with him, the way she'd felt like she could say whatever she wanted and be fully understood and do whatever she wanted and be totally accepted. She remembered how easy it had all been, how open and bright, like being in an empty whitewashed room with all the windows wide open. She remembered the feel of his hand around her bare shoulder, the way they'd fit together so snugly as they walked along the seafront and how she'd truly believed she'd found her soul mate on a Hunstanton caravan site.

'Well,' she said, 'that's different. That was a holiday romance. I was a teenager. You feel things more intensely when you're a teenager.'

Bella pursed his lips. 'Well, anyway, maybe once the dust's settled and you've had a chance to think about things, you might decide to wait. And maybe one day you'll think about old Vince and wonder what he's up to and what might have been. And at least you'll have that –' He pointed at the paper. 'The option.'

They fell silent for a second. A door slammed across the landing. Joy stared at the paper.

'Well,' she said, as she folded it in half and slipped it into her coat pocket, 'thank you. I'll put it somewhere safe.'

And then they both put the notion of handsome, local, lovelorn Vince somewhere safe while they concentrated on the altogether less thorny issue of what exact shade of cream her wedding dress was to be.

All the lights were off in the flat when Joy got home at 9.45 that night. She tiptoed towards the bedroom, expecting to see the outline of George tucked up under the duvet, but the bed was flat.

She pushed open the door to the living room and found George sitting on the sofa, reading a book by the light of a solitary candle. He failed to glance up as she entered the room.

'Has there been a power cut?' she said, removing her coat.

'No,' he said, slowly turning a page.

'Then why are all the lights off?'

George shrugged and stared at his book. 'I like it like this.'

'Are you all right?' She sat down next to him and grasped his knee.

'Yes. I'm fine.'

'Are you sure?'

'Yes,' he hissed, 'I'm fine.'

'Are you pissed ... *annoyed* with me?'

'No. I'm not *annoyed* with you. I'm just reading, that's all.'

'Do you want me to leave you alone?'

He shrugged again. 'I don't really care.'

'Fine,' said Joy, now certain that George was angry with her for some unknown reason and torn between wanting to give him the cold shoulder and demanding to know what the hell his problem was.

She spent a few minutes clattering around the flat, pretending to be fine before she could no longer control herself.

'George,' she said, marching into the living room, 'you are obviously not happy about something and, if it's something I've done, I want you to tell me.'

George sighed and closed his book, as if Joy were the most tiresome person it had ever been his displeasure to encounter. 'I just think,' he began, 'that it's really very rude to tell someone you're going to be home at one time, then just waltz in an hour late with no explanation.'

Joy glanced at the clock over the mantelpiece and frowned with confusion. 'I didn't say I'd be home at any particular time,' she said.

George just sighed again and picked up his book.

'George, I did not say I'd be home early. I said I was going to Bella's —'

'*Bella* — huh!'

'What?'

'Well, it's ridiculous — a man called Bella.'

Joy huffed and ignored him. 'I said I was going to Bella's for my dress fitting and that I'd be home after that.'

'Which would lead one to assume you'd be home at a reasonable hour.'

Joy looked at the clock again in amazement. 'It's not even ten o'clock!'

'Did it occur to you I might have had plans for tonight?'

'Er . . . no. Why would you make plans if you knew I was going to be out?'

'Oh, I really have no wish to pursue this risible line of conversation for another moment. I'm going to bed.' He slammed his paperback down.

'No,' said Joy, grabbing his arm, 'this is ridiculous. We need to talk about this.'

'No,' he peeled her hand from his arm, 'we do not.' He stalked from the room and slammed the door behind him.

Joy stood statue still for a while, unable to comprehend what had just happened. And then she let herself flop on to the sofa and stare in dismay at George's horrible sitting room as the first of the nameless fears she'd felt hovering at the edges of her consciousness for the past two months finally came home to roost.

At ten-thirty the following morning a vast arrangement of delicate flowers in autumnal shades of burgundy, gold and henna was delivered to ColourPro Reprographics, addressed to Miss Joy Downer.

The card, attached to the cellophane wrapper by a pin, read:

I am so blessed to have found you. I never want to lose you. I love you. I adore you. I worship you.

And despite the glaring absence of the word 'sorry', Joy decided to take this as a full and heartfelt apology, and to carry on as if the previous night had never happened.

Thirty-One

The words just wouldn't flow today. It didn't matter how hard Vince stared at little Katy-Clare, with her soulful blue eyes and shiny auburn hair, he couldn't think of a single original thing to say about her. Every description he brought to mind had been used before. And even though he knew that Coalford Swann collectors and readers of the *Sunday Mirror* colour supplement had no recollection of the exact turn of phrase he'd used two years ago to describe Millicent Amanda's mischievous smile or Tabitha Jane's adorable dimpled cheeks, that wasn't the point. It was a matter of personal pride.

Something was blocking the flow of his creative juices this morning, something in the atmosphere, something strange. Melanie's secretary, Polly, had been in a weird mood all day, trotting around officiously, refusing to join in with the usual Friday japery. Melanie herself had been locked in her office for most of the day with the Personnel Director, wearing a sharp black suit and looking very grim. The effect of all this on the marketing team was a sort of low-level hysteria, like an electric undercurrent of unspoken panic, and nobody seemed to be doing any work at all.

Vince decided to remove himself momentarily from the unsettling vibrations of his office and phone Magda.

'Mags, it's me.'

'Hello, me. How's it going?'

'Weird. Everyone's in a strange mood.'

'Business as usual, then,' Magda joked.

'No. It's even weirder than usual.'

'Not possible, surely.' Magda had never been to Vince's office, but found the whole notion of a bunch of twenty-something graduates sitting around discussing ways of selling spooky china dolls utterly bizarre.

'What do you fancy doing tomorrow?' she said. 'Shall we go Christmas shopping?'

Vince groaned inwardly. Vince didn't mind shopping per se. He quite enjoyed a gentle wander around Covent Garden or Kensington High Street, casually trying on shoes and coats, flipping through CDs and exploring bookshops. But Christmas shopping was something completely different. Christmas shopping was the pentathlon of shopping events, involving, as it did, five different disciplines: memory, stamina, strength, patience and prioritizing. Carrying all those different people around in your head, their tastes, their preferences. Finding just the right gift for someone, but realizing it was too heavy or cumbersome to carry around for the rest of the day. Deciding at one end of Oxford Street that the gift you wanted to get for your mum was at the other end of Oxford Street. No, no, no. It was hell. And the thought of carrying out such a gruesome task with Magda, the Shopping Queen, made his skull ache.

'You know something,' he said, 'I kind of promised Mum I'd see Kyle tomorrow.'

'Oh, well, then that's perfect! He can come with us!'

'What!'

'Yes – we can take him to see the Christmas lights and take him to Hamleys to see Father Christmas. Oh, it'll be brilliant.'

And actually, when he thought about it, Vince found the idea strangely thrilling, too. He'd never taken Kyle out anywhere without Chris or his mum being there, too. And he'd probably be too nervous to take a small child into the West End on his own, but if Magda was there . . . and Kyle did like Magda, and frankly, any excuse to visit Hamleys was good enough for him.

'That's an excellent idea,' he said. 'I'll phone Mum first thing and see if it's all right.' For a moment, Vince felt full of optimism and enthusiasm. Until Magda went and spoiled it.

'Won't it be funny,' she said, 'being out with you and Kyle. Like a proper family.' Which was fine in itself, but it was the accompanying tone of maternal longing and wistfulness that made Vince's stomach churn. It wasn't the tone of a woman enjoying a no-strings, casual-fun relationship. It wasn't the tone of a woman who just wanted sex and laughs. It was the tone of a woman who wanted diamond rings and a future.

And it was just another reminder that he was still trundling along dejectedly down the wrong path and that at some point he was going to have to turn round and walk all the way back.

The reason for the strange atmosphere in Vince's office made itself known after lunch.

Melanie announced a departmental meeting at three o'clock, which was unheard of on a Friday afternoon.

The team filed into her office exchanging questioning looks and shrugged shoulders. Gill Pearson, the scary Personnel Director, was stationed at the head of the table, smiling benignly in a navy polka-dot blouse.

'Hello, everyone,' she said. 'Thank you all for coming at such short notice.' Her smile was so forced it looked as if it had been stapled on to her face.

Vince fiddled with the pointy bit at the bottom of his tie and glanced around the table. Everyone was engaged in some kind of displacement activity – nibbling at finger-nails, twiddling hair, drumming Biros, shuffling papers. Everyone knew something bad was about to happen. That's what personnel directors were for.

'As you might be aware, Coalford Swann Collectibles has experienced something of a downturn in profits over the course of the past eighteen months. This is in no way attributable to the quality of the product or the ded-ication and hard work of our staff, all of which are beyond reproach. The economy simply isn't healthy enough to support our customers' luxury spending, and collectibles are always hardest hit in tough times like these. So, inevitably, we have had to look to the bottom line.'

Vince felt his gut clench.

'Coalford Swann is renowned throughout the world for the quality of its marketing and publicity. And rightly so. Melanie has worked incredibly hard over the course of the past three years putting together the finest team of marketeers in the industry. Which is why the decision we've reached has been so painful.'

Oh, for God's sake, thought Vince, just get on with it.

'As of Monday morning, the marketing and publicity departments will cease to function. Therefore, I am sincerely sorry to announce, your jobs are effectively redundant as of today. I'll be speaking to you all individually over the course of the afternoon, so if you'd like to return to your desks and stick around until I've had a chance to have a chat, that would be very much appreciated. In the meantime, please keep this to yourselves. An official announcement will be made on Monday morning. And can I just take this opportunity to say how much I and the rest of the directors appreciate all your hard work and commitment over the years.' And with that she smiled tightly, gathered her files and left the room.

The whole team collapsed like a snapped elastic as the door closed behind her and exhaled as one.

'Fucking hell,' said Demetrius.

'Shit,' said Sian.

'Fantastic!' said Billy.

Vince didn't know what to think. He'd fantasized about something like this happening so many times, dreamed of the rush of adrenalin that sudden freedom would unleash, the things he could do, the places he could go, but now it had actually happened he just felt vaguely hurt. They didn't want him. They hadn't made an exception for him. They were happy just to let him disappear into the sunset and for some nameless, faceless person at an agency somewhere to write their advertisements for them instead. He'd been dumped. By someone he wasn't even in love with. And he felt crushed.

*

His meeting with scary Gill later that afternoon helped to heal the wound a little. They were giving him three months' tax-free salary and a glowing reference. He wouldn't have to work out his notice and would get all his untaken holiday leave backdated and paid in full. He would, in other words, be getting a tidy sum and an unplanned holiday. And looking at it like that, Vince couldn't help but feel slightly celebratory.

Magda, he thought, you'd better hold on to your hat, girl, for tonight we shall be drinking champagne.

Thirty-Two

Joy and George were having dinner at a Chinese restaurant in Norbiton. Norbiton wasn't a place that Joy had ever thought she'd find herself doing anything other than driving through en route to somewhere else, but life, as she was rapidly coming to understand, was strange and unpredictable.

She was eating gigantic prawns, with chopsticks. She'd never managed to master the art of chopsticks before and had decided it was a skill she could easily get through life without, but George had been so appalled the first time they'd gone to a Chinese restaurant together and she'd asked for cutlery that she'd felt shamed into learning.

He'd taught her how to hold the top one like a pen and rest the bottom one in the crook of her thumb and forefinger; how to keep the bottom one still and use the top one as the pincer. George had taught her lots of other things, too, over the weeks.

He'd taught her how to open champagne (Twist the bottle, not the cork. Let the cork pop into your fist, not towards the ceiling.) and how to drink champagne (Hold the glass by the stem, not the bowl. Otherwise the champagne gets warm.).

He'd taught her how to order in posh restaurants (Just ask for the main ingredient of the dish – i.e. 'I'll have the lamb' not 'I'll have the lamb fillet with couscous and spiced aubergine.') and how to taste the wine (If it's not corked just say 'fine' and put your glass down – no need to comment any further.).

He'd taught her to say 'sitting room' not 'lounge', to say 'napkin' not 'serviette' and to ask for the 'loo' not the 'toilet'. He'd taught her none of these things explicitly of course – that would have been far too rude – rather she'd picked them up by osmosis, by reading between the lines. George, she was coming to realize, though he saw himself as liberal and free-spirited, was a stickler for etiquette and tradition. He winced when someone swore loudly in his vicinity; he expected impeccable service wherever he went and complained heartily if he didn't get it; he found the whole notion of *EastEnders* repellent, hated regional accents and got very angry about misprints in newspapers.

He wasn't a snob, exactly, but there was certainly a big, fat stratum of society that existed outside of his consciousness. People who read tabloids and went on package holidays. People who washed their own cars and sat down to eat at service stations. And in a strange way, Joy felt that he found a kind of invigorating novelty in the fact that she had come to him from this mysterious stratum. He'd seemed fascinated by her parents' house when Barbara had insisted on throwing them an engagement party, intrigued by life in an Essex cul-de-sac, by the steady stream of people with names like Rita and Derek who processed through the house in Marks & Spencer's casualwear, by the sausage rolls and processed ham sandwiches that had passed for canapés and the shaggy towelling hat that sat atop the toilet seat.

He'd laughed, affectionately, but somewhat patronizingly, when Joy's mother had suggested placing an announcement in the forthcoming marriages section of the *Telegraph*. He used words like 'plebeian', 'arriviste' and 'gauche', and swirled his wine around his glass before he drank it.

Joy was learning many things about George as time went by – some of them good, some of them not so good – and she was just about to learn something new.

'So,' he said, beaming at her across the table, 'my beautiful wife-to-be, have you contacted your bank yet about changing your details?'

'What do you mean?'

'Well, your new surname. You'll have to change your passport, too, remember.'

Joy gulped. Along with her teenage vow to herself not to marry before her thirtieth birthday, she'd also decided that, when she did eventually marry, there was no way she would ever consider changing her surname to that of her husband. It was archaic and outmoded. It went against all her principles. Her name was her identity; it was who she was. It was the name that had been called out every morning at school, the name she filled out on forms. It wasn't a great name and it didn't fill her with ancestral pride, but it was *her* name and she wanted to keep it.

'Erm, George. You do realize I have no intention of changing my name, don't you?' Joy wasn't sure what she was expecting to happen next or how she'd imagined George might react. But laughter wasn't it.

'Oh, very funny,' he guffawed.

'No, George. I'm serious. Ever since I was a little girl I vowed that I would never change my name.'

The smile dropped from George's face and was replaced by a sort of blank horror. 'But we're getting married. You *have* to change your name.'

'No, I don't. Not in this day and age.'

'No. You do. It's hugely important.'

'But why? Why is it important? I don't understand.'

'Good God – we're getting married. You're going to be my wife. You can't have a different surname to me. I'd be a laughing stock.'

Joy snorted. 'With who exactly?'

'*Whom*,' he snapped. 'With my friends. My colleagues. My family.'

'Oh, George, they're not going to care whether I've got your name or not.'

'Of course they will. They'll think you don't respect me.'

'*Respect* you? George – it's 1993. That sort of thinking went out with pocket handkerchiefs.'

'Maybe in *your* world,' he sniffed, and Joy chose to ignore the oblique reference to their differing social stations, 'but in my world marriage is defined as an official, legally binding *union* between two people. We become *as one*. We become *family*. With a shared surname.'

'OK, then, why don't we take *my* surname. Let's both be Downers.'

'Oh, don't be ridiculous.'

'Why is that ridiculous? You just said that once we're married we should share a surname – so let's share *my* surname.'

He sneered and pinioned a straggle of spring onions

between his chopsticks. 'Now you're being juvenile.'

'Why? What's wrong with my surname?'

'There's nothing wrong with your surname. But it's *your* surname. That's not how it works. And besides, it would be disrespectful to my dead mother.'

'Your dead mother! What about my living parents?'

'Oh, come on now – that's a bit low.'

'Well, you started it.'

'Oh, now, this is just turning into a rather vulgar slanging match . . .'

'Let's go double-barrelled.' Joy attempted a compromise.

'Good God, no.'

'Why not?'

'Do you really have to ask? Quite apart from the fact that it is quite gut-churningly nouveau – Downer-Pole? I've never heard anything so ghastly.'

'Yes, well, what about Joy Pole? I mean, that just sounds *rude.*'

'Ah,' said George, 'I see. Now we're getting to the crux of the matter. This has nothing to do with your high-flying feminist ideals. You just don't like my surname.'

'I *do* like your surname. And if I really wanted to take your surname, I'd take it even if it was . . . was . . . *Willy*, or something. But I don't want to take it. Because I don't believe anyone, regardless of their sex, should have to change their name for any reason whatsoever. I just wouldn't be *me* any more.'

George raised his eyebrows sardonically, and dabbed at the corners of his mouth with a napkin. 'Me, me, me,' he muttered under his breath.

'Sorry?'

'Nothing,' he said, 'absolutely nothing.'

And a heavy, impenetrable silence fell upon them.

There were so many points of concern to be pondered as a result of the preceding conversation that Joy could barely think straight. Concerns about differing value systems, about pedantry and snobbishness, concerns about their compatibility and concerns about whether or not they actually liked each other very much.

Joy had never liked confrontation and had an almost pathological fear of silences. A combination of the two was too much for her to bear. She was also terrified by the prospect of the final destination that pursuing these concerns would inevitably take her to – because once she started to air her misgivings there was only one possible conclusion to be reached: that they were both in the grip of some strange madness and about to make a terrible mistake. That they shouldn't get married. And whether or not that was true, she wasn't ready to face it. So instead of addressing these issues head on in a grown-up fashion, Joy decided to sidestep them entirely and change the subject.

'We should sort out wedding rings next week,' she gushed, breaking into the silence like a drunk at a funeral. 'It's one of those things you usually need to do six weeks in advance, apparently.'

'Oh,' said George, a hint of sulkiness still clinging to the corners of his mouth, 'fine. Where do we need to go for that?'

'Oh, just a high-street jeweller will do for wedding rings. Nothing fancy.'

'Good,' said George, 'fine. We'll go on Saturday.'

'Actually,' said Joy, 'I was planning on going into town on Saturday. Christmas shopping.'

'Fine. Then we won't order rings on Saturday.'

'I can go in the morning,' she offered, sensing yet another conflict about to hatch. 'Early. Be back by lunchtime. We can go in the afternoon.'

'Good. Fine. Saturday afternoon.'

'Good,' said Joy, her napkin screwed into a tight knot on her lap. 'Fine.'

As another silence threatened to engulf them, she chimed, 'These prawns are absolutely fantastic, aren't they?' heroically navigating her runaway boat through treacherous seas.

The following afternoon a courier arrived at ColourPro with a small parcel wrapped in gold paper and addressed to Miss Joy Downer.

Roz and Jacquie watched in awe as she peeled off the paper to reveal a black leather box. Inside the black leather box was a beautiful art deco marcasite bracelet, which sparkled under the halogen spotlights like a night sky full of stars.

The note inside said:

To my darling Joy, I am so honoured to be marrying you and so impatient to call you my wife. You make my world beautiful. I love you, frantically, foolishly, infinitely . . . for ever.

'Oh, my God,' said Roz, one hand clasping the note, the other pressed against her heart. '*You are the luckiest fucking bitch in the whole wide world.*'

Thirty-Three

It was two weeks before Christmas, and Selfridges was heaving with festive bodies. Couples, young families and gangs of friends marauded through the aisles exuding body heat through outdoor clothes and an overwhelming, slightly alarming sense of purpose. Apart from her weekly visits to Bella's bedsit in Finsbury Park, this was the first time she'd been out on her own since she'd moved in with George three weeks earlier and, instead of feeling unfettered and free, she felt small and lost, like she'd cancelled her membership to the world and was about to be asked to leave.

George had been slightly gloomy this morning as she'd pulled on her coat and wished him farewell. He hadn't said anything explicit, just been meaner with his pleasantries, used less syllables, shorter sentences.

'Are you OK?' she asked.

'Yes. I'm fine. Why do you keep asking me if I'm OK?'

'I don't know,' she'd said. 'You just seem as if you're annoyed with me.'

'Well, I'm not.'

He could have proved this by wishing her a fun day out, by hugging her at the door or by cracking a joke. But he did none of these things. Instead he sat on the edge of the bed in his bath towel, staring at his toenails, like an abandoned puppy.

Joy took her handbag from her shoulder and sat down next to him. 'George. What is it? You always seem so cross when I go out without you.'

'I can assure you I am not "cross".'

'Then what? Why are you being all sulky?'

'Sulky?'

'Yes. Sulky.'

'Good God,' he snapped, pulling himself off the bed, 'I've been awake for less than an hour, I haven't even had a coffee yet and you're already throwing accusations at me. I can't take this.' He strode angrily towards the kitchen, where she could hear him filling the kettle.

'So,' she said, standing in the doorway, 'you're not cross with me; you're just tired?'

'Yes,' he hissed, without turning to address her.

'Good,' she said, 'fine. So give me a hug.' She circled him with her arms and felt him stiffen slightly at her touch. His arms hung limp at his sides.

What! she wanted to scream, *What is it?! Talk to me!*

But it wasn't in Joy's nature to question other people's behaviour; it wasn't in her nature to demand explanations – it was in her nature to soothe, to remove the root of others' displeasure. It was in her nature to make everything better. So she fussed over George and she stroked him and promised she wouldn't be late, diminishing her enjoyment of the day ahead of her before she'd even set foot out of the door.

And now here she was darting around Selfridges, feeling time falling through her fingers like grains of rice. She'd bought her mother a dressing gown, in plain cotton lawn, and a sachet of potpourri. She'd bought Maxine,

260

her best friend from school who lived in San Diego, a tin in the shape of a London bus and filled with treacle toffee, and her cousin Tracy who lived in Poole a book about iguanas because she collected them.

It was already twelve o'clock and that was as far as she'd got. She hadn't bought anything at all for George yet, and he'd been her primary target for the day. She let the price tag of an overpriced silk tie fall sadly from between her fingertips and made a decision.

A wok.

She would get George a wok. A proper steel, round-bottomed wok from Chinatown. And some of those bamboo steamers. And nice chopsticks and some rice bowls. He'd love them.

She didn't have time to walk to Chinatown, so she hopped on a bus outside Selfridges with the intention of getting off at Piccadilly Circus.

The lower deck was jammed full, half with humans, half with carrier bags, so she hoisted her own bags to one side and made her way up the narrow staircase to the top deck. She grabbed a window seat to the left of the bus, tucked her bags under the seat in front of her and turned to stare out of the window. The pavements of Oxford Street were awash with humanity. They streamed across junctions, so heavy in numbers that they overrode the traffic lights – cars came a poor second in these circumstances.

The sky above the rooftops of Oxford Street was a chalky white. The Christmas lights strung across the road on steel gibbets creaked gently back and forth as the bus passed under them. On the corner of Oxford Street and

Regent Street a man in a donkey jacket baked chestnuts over a glowing brazier, scooping them into paper bags for tourists. Joy felt a sudden surge of excitement at her state of relative freedom and hugged it to herself. She loved travelling by bus. All there was to look at on the Tube were rows of ugly people and the floor. The bus, on the other hand, was a moving theatre, and after her claustrophobia in Selfridges just now it was nice to get some distance from other human beings.

The bus turned right into Regent Street, and Joy stared down on to the tops of strangers' heads, trying to imagine lives for them, wondering what it felt like to be them. As the bus passed Hamleys her gazed passed briefly over another stranger standing by the front doors, before being dramatically snapped back towards him.

A man. A hugely handsome man. A handsome man in a charcoal grey overcoat and Levi 501s.

Vincent Mellon.

Her heart bounced up towards her throat, and she sat bolt upright.

He had one hand in his pocket and the other was clutching a mass of carrier bags. He turned slowly to watch the window display, a family of robotic dinosaurs arranged on a snow-covered hill behind a window emblazoned with the *Jurassic Park* logo, before turning back again.

The bus came to a halt behind a long line of traffic that extended well beyond the next set of traffic lights. It occurred to Joy that she could pick up her bags, climb off the bus and go to say hello. That maybe this was some kind of sign. That maybe she wasn't supposed to be staring at him, but talking to him instead, turning the page in the book, finding out what happened next. This all occurred to her in the space of two seconds. It took another four or five seconds for her to think of all the reasons why she shouldn't get off the bus and say hello – she'd be embarrassed, not know what to say. He'd be embarrassed, not know what to say. She didn't have time. She'd be late home.

By the time she'd persuaded herself that this was much more than a coincidence, that she had at this very moment a piece of paper with his telephone number on it in her coat pocket and that maybe there was a *reason* for Vince being there, another five seconds had elapsed. She glanced ahead to reassure herself that the traffic wasn't about to start moving again and was about to lift herself from her seat when the doors to Hamleys opened and a beautiful girl emerged, carrying a small boy in her arms. She was tall and slim, dressed in a shiny black leather jacket and jeans. Her hair was an oil slick of black that hung halfway down her back and was held from her face with black sunglasses. She beamed at Vince, and he beamed at her. She passed the little boy to him and reached to kiss him on his cheek. The little boy threw his arms around his neck, the beautiful girl slipped her hand through the crook of his arm and the three of them turned and strode away towards Oxford Circus looking like an impossibly glossy template for modern family life.

Joy let her grip loosen on the shopping bags and caught her breath.

Of course, she thought. Of course.

Vince was married, had a beautiful little boy. Of course.

His wife looked like a model.

It made sense.

She'd thought he was out of her league that first time she'd seen him in Hunstanton. He must have been feeling a bit desperate, nearly nineteen years old and still a virgin. And it wasn't as if he'd had a lot of girls to choose from at the Seavue Holiday Home Park. He must have decided that she'd do for a holiday fling, taken advantage of her willingness to sleep with him, found her note the morning after and been thoroughly relieved that he wouldn't have to take things any further.

But then, she thought, what about that story Bella had told her? What about the friend with the crystal ball and the tarot cards? What about him being 'in love' with her?

It was a joke, wasn't it? They'd been mucking about. Maybe he'd told his friend all about the girl he'd lost his virginity to and they'd been laughing about her, about her perverted father and her awful family and her pathetic little note with its declaration of undying love. It all made sense.

And now he'd moved on and upgraded to pneumatic, chiselled model girls, while she'd moved on and down-graded to moody accountants who placed personal ads. She thought about Stuart Bigmore and Vivica and their wreck in Andalusia and their plans to start a family. She imagined their children, beautiful, ethereal, dark-eyed angels. And then she thought about Ally. He'd probably met someone, too, she mused, probably met some beautiful woman in New Zealand whom she wanted to spend the rest of his life with and have children with. Someone extraordinary. Someone special. Someone completely different to her.

For weeks, she'd been living under the delusion that she was somehow *better* than George – that she was out of his league. But now, as she watched Vince and his beautiful family disappear into the Underground, the dislocation suddenly shifted and her life fell into place. She and George were the same; she and George were made for each other. And when she thought of George now, she felt soothed by the knowledge that to him she was every bit as beautiful as the girl with black hair who'd given Vince a son, that to him she was every bit as special as moody, artistic Vivica who'd lured Stuart down the aisle and out of the country at such a young age and that to him she was extraordinary enough for him to want to marry her and be with her for ever to the exclusion of all other women.

She slipped her hand into her coat pocket and felt around for a piece of paper. She pulled it out and stared at Vince's phone number for a moment, before folding it in half, screwing it into a small ball and letting it fall to the floor of the bus.

And then she took Vince Mellon and put him in a little box in her mind, labelled it 'the past' and focused afresh on her future.

Thirty-Four

Vince finally finished with Magda the following week.

It happened when she arrived at his flat bearing holiday brochures and talking enthusiastically of Tenerife. Talking about June. Scaring the living daylights out of him.

It had been one of those awful, clichéd, 'We need to talk', 'It's not you; it's me' type of conversations. Magda had cried the whole way through, huge glassy tears that seemed to emanate from every part of her eyeballs and streaked her face brown with muddy mascara. That was the worst thing about girls crying, Vince felt. It didn't just make you feel like a prize bastard, but it made them look ugly as well, and when a girl looked ugly it made you feel sorry for them, and once you felt sorry for a girl then the whole dynamic of the thing changed completely. The girl ceased to be a proper human being and became instead an asexual object of pity, like a little old man with a dowager's hump or a tiny puppy with a broken paw.

The whole awful scenario had lasted about four hours. Four wholly unnecessary hours as far as Vince was concerned. Everything that needed to be said got said within the first ten minutes; after that it was all pointless hypothesizing, recriminating, regurgitating and questioning. But because the dumping had taken place at *his* flat he'd had no choice but to keep going until *she* called a halt to it – asking her to leave, he felt, would have been beyond the pale.

There'd been a foul thirty-minute wait for the minicab he'd called to collect her, mainly because they'd said it would only be ten minutes and he and Magda didn't have an extra twenty minutes' worth of conversation left between them. And then she'd gone. He'd stood at the window to watch her leave, as he'd done a hundred times before, checking out the minicab driver, making sure he didn't look like a sadistic rapist, memorizing his number plate. And then he'd let the curtain fall back, collected his empty mug and some wine glasses, and gone to bed. Single and alone.

Single and unemployed.

It was the first time he'd been either since he was nineteen years old.

And suddenly finding himself both at the same time was a very peculiar feeling indeed.

He woke up the following morning in the full knowledge that nobody cared where he was. There would be no chirpy phone call from Magda asking what he was up to, no call to the office to explain his absence. It was like he'd suddenly ceased to exist. The sensation was as scary as it was liberating.

He spent that week doing all the things that he'd always imagined he'd do if he didn't have to go to work. He read an entire book in a day. He ironed five shirts, six pairs of trousers and a bed sheet. He went to the supermarket and spent forty-five minutes deciding what to cook for his dinner. He drank beer at lunchtime. He met up with friends in their lunch hour, friends who smelled of offices and the Underground, feeling smug as they watched hands racing round clocks and hurtled back to their desks at one o'clock. He discovered shops in Finsbury Park he'd never known existed before and came home clutching exotic-smelling jars of Moroccan chilli paste, strange vegetables he didn't know what to do with and cans full of things called 'foul mesdames'.

After a few days of this, the novelty began to wear off and he remembered that there were other things he'd always dreamed of doing in the absence of having the stupidest job in the world.

Like writing a book.

Like learning something new.

Like travelling.

Like having a job that made him really happy.

He bought a copy of *Floodlight* and perused it for self-improving evening classes, but never got further than circling a few options before losing it under a cushion on the sofa.

He bought a book called *How To Write a Bestseller* and read the introduction.

He went to Trailfinders and picked up some round-the-world brochures, realized that he couldn't afford to go and gave them to Cass to read in the toilet.

He bought the *Guardian* and searched the recruitment pages for the perfect job, only to discover that it didn't exist, and that, even if it did, he wouldn't get it because he was too young and too inexperienced.

And every single day, without fail, he fabricated some

excuse or other to walk past 44 Wilberforce Road and glance nonchalantly at the front door.

He wasn't sure what he was looking for. He knew she'd moved out, that she was living in south London somewhere. But you never know, he reasoned with himself, she might have left something behind, come back to visit, *changed her mind*.

He saw the big woman, Julia, occasionally. He ducked out of view if he happened upon her, not really wanting to have to explain his presence outside her house to her, not wanting to have any kind of discourse with her at all, really. But he liked to see her. It gave him a kind of warm glow to catch a glimpse of someone who'd been on such recent intimate terms with Joy, made him feel connected in a way, as if, if he really wanted to see Joy, he could. Not that he did want to see Joy. That was off the agenda for now, obviously. He'd totally missed the boat there.

Cass, of course, hadn't stopped going on about the Incredible Coincidence since, and was now completely convinced that Madeleine not only had been a famous monk in a former life, but had also had dozens of former lives and been someone hugely wise, important and mystical in each and every one of them. She was furious with Vince for not following Madeleine's lead and making contact with Joy.

'She's in love with someone, for fuck's sake. She's getting married.'

'Christ,' she muttered, 'so what if she's getting married? What's that got to do with anything? This is destiny we're talking about. Fate wants you to be together. You can't ignore the signs. The minute you put that note into my hand — no, in fact, the minute you even mentioned her name — I knew it. I just knew that you and she were meant to be. It was overwhelming. Overpowering. And Madeleine knew it, too. She found her for you, found your one true love. And you're just going to throw that away?'

'What do you expect me to do?'

'Talk her out of it, of course.'

'No. I can't. I can't mess with her head like that.'

'Her head *needs* to be messed with. It's crying *out* to be messed with. She's making a heinous mistake and you need to stop her.'

'And what if I do, eh? What if I see her and tell her not to marry this George character and she listens to me and then we realize a week later that we don't have anything in common.'

'You won't.'

'How do you know?'

'Because it's fucking obvious, you fucking fuckhead. Do you think cats just *always* end up hanging out with people's ex-girlfriends whom their owners just happen to be in the process of looking for? Don't you believe in fate? In signs? In *magic*?'

'Magic?'

'Yes — magic. Not everything makes sense, you know. Not everything is just a *coincidence*. Some things are powered by *outside forces* — beyond our control.'

And Vince was sure that there were men out there, men who would stop at nothing to be with the woman they loved, men who would crash weddings and wreak havoc in other people's lives, but he just wasn't one of them. It wasn't his style. He was too cautious. And maybe he simply didn't feel things strongly enough.

But something was about to happen to him that would change the way he felt about things for ever.

On Saturday morning Vince packed a few things into a bag and caught the train to Enfield. Chris was away on a stag weekend in Blackpool, and Vince had promised his mum he'd come and stay to help her out with Kyle.

They'd just put Kyle to bed on Saturday and were about to order a pizza when Kirsty had come back from the toilet looking ashen.

'I'm bleeding,' she said, 'quite a lot.'

Twenty minutes later, Kyle was in his pyjamas in the back of Kirsty's Renault 5 and they were halfway to Chase Farm Hospital.

'How many weeks are you?' said an obstetrician with half his arm inside Kirsty.

'Thirty-six.'

'And are you in any pain?'

'Well, not really. I've had a bit of indigestion. But nothing serious.'

'Hmmm.' He removed his hand from inside Kirsty and snapped off his latex glove. 'It looks like a placental abruption.'

'A what?' said Vince.

'A placental abruption means that the placenta has started to pull away from the wall of the uterus . . .'

'What's a placenta?' Vince had heard the word before, but would have been hard-pushed to define it.

'The placenta is the connection between the mother and the baby – it's where the baby's nourishment comes from – so the fact that it's coming away from the mother – the source of the nourishment – could potentially be a very serious problem indeed.'

Vince looked at Kirsty, hoping for reassurance that she knew exactly what this meant and that it really wasn't such a big deal. But her face was as blank and uncomprehending as his own.

'Is the baby all right?' she whispered.

'We'll run some checks.'

Her massive belly was wired up to various pieces of machinery, and Vince stared in wonder at the huge dome of skin. He'd never been so close to a naked pregnant belly before and wasn't sure whether he found it beautiful or really quite disgusting.

'I can't have the baby now, you know,' Kirsty pleaded with the midwife who was doing the wiring. 'My husband's in Blackpool. I can't have it now.'

'It might not come to that,' soothed the midwife. 'We'll know more in a minute.'

Kirsty reached for Vince's hand and squeezed it so hard it made his eyes water. Suddenly the room was filled with a sound that brought a lump to his throat.

A vital, insistent thump.

A heartbeat.

'Baby's heart rate is good,' said the midwife. 'No signs of foetal distress.'

'Oh, my God,' he breathed, 'that's the baby?'

'Yes,' said the midwife, 'and it's doing fine.'

'Wow,' he said, 'I can't believe it. It sounds so . . .'

'Real?' suggested the midwife.

'Yes,' he said. 'It's amazing.'

'Well' – the midwife pulled the ultrasound gun from Kirsty's stomach and immediately the miraculous sound of new life disappeared – 'the baby's fine. But you are losing a lot of blood. I think it's very likely that we'll have to induce labour.'

'What – now?' pleaded Kirsty.

'Well, we'll see what Mr Patel says, but if he agrees with me, then, yes, we'll have to move quite quickly. You can't afford to lose any more blood.'

'But I told you. My husband's in Blackpool. I can't have the baby without him. I can't . . .'

'I'm sorry, Mrs Jebb, but, unless your husband can get back here within the next few hours, I don't think we have any choice.'

The obstetrician seconded the midwife's opinion, and within minutes Kirsty was being induced.

Kirsty's father arrived an hour later and took Kyle home, and Vince called the guesthouse in Blackpool where Chris was staying and left an urgent message for him. But apart from that there was nothing left for him to do but to sit and wait while his mother went through the early stages of having a baby.

It took another four hours for anything of any significance to happen. Various people kept coming in to stick their hands up Kirsty and pronounce measurements as if they'd gone in there with a tape measure. An anaesthetist arrived and stuck a needle in Kirsty's back, which made Vince's knees go all quivery and funny, but seemed to make his mum feel a hundred times better. At around midnight the midwife told Kirsty she was nearly nine centimetres dilated and that it was time to start pushing.

Vince had already made the decision that at this point in the proceedings he would probably make his excuses and disappear. But just as he was about to take his leave, his mum grabbed his hand and whispered urgently in his ear, 'You will stay with me, won't you, love?' She looked so scared and so alone that he sighed, and said, 'Of course I will. I'm not going anywhere.'

Three people had stationed themselves at Kirsty's helm, almost as if the baby was due to be shot out like a cannonball and they were primed to catch it. His mum had her knees pulled up to her collarbone and was making noises like the ones an injured horse makes just before someone shoots it. Mr Patel swooped in, peered briefly between Kirsty's thighs and proclaimed her good to go. And Vince stood there awkwardly, feeling torn between wanting to see the baby coming out and not wanting to see his mum's apertures.

'The head's coming,' smiled a red-haired nurse. 'Do you want to see?'

'Er . . .' he hesitated.

'Oh, go on,' she urged. 'It's the same place you came from. Nothing to be scared of.'

He glanced at his mum to make sure she didn't have a problem with him gazing at her nether regions, but she was concentrating so hard on pushing that she seemed to have forgotten he was in the room.

'Go on, Kirsty. You're doing great.' The midwife had hold of each of Kirsty's kneecaps and was staring intently at the activity immediately below. 'Nearly there now, Kirsty. Just a couple more big pushes. Oh,' she smiled, 'look, lots of lovely dark hair.'

And at the mention of lots of lovely dark hair, curiosity got the better of Vince and he craned his neck to have a look. And just as he craned his neck to have a look, his mum made another dying horse noise and the baby's head popped out.

'Oh, my God,' he said, looking from the damp, bloody skull to his mother's puce, sweaty face and back again. 'Oh, my God – it's incredible.'

'Right, Kirsty, the head's out. Now just one more big push and your baby's arrived.'

'Oh, my God,' said Vince again. 'Mum, it's amazing. It's got hair. Push, Mum, push.' And Vince gripped her bare thigh and completely forgot that he was staring at his mother's genitalia, as he felt overcome with a sudden impatience to meet his new sibling. And then, ten seconds later, his mother's body kind of shook and went floppy, and a little person slithered from her and into the hands of the midwife. Vince stared in awe as the little person was sucked free of fluid with a teat pipette and rubbed down with a white towel.

'What is it? What is it?' said Kirsty.

'It's a little girl,' said the midwife, 'a beautiful little girl.'

'Oh, my God,' Kirsty said, clamping her hands over mouth and stifling a cry. 'A little girl. I've got a little girl.'

'Would you like your son to cut the cord, Kirsty?'

Kirsty smiled and nodded.

'God – are you sure?' said Vince, feeling slightly nerve-wracked at the prospect of such a huge responsibility.

'Of course,' laughed his mum. 'Who else would I want to do it?'

'OK, then. What do I have to do?'

The midwife handed Vince an enormous pair of L-shaped scissors. 'Just cut there, between the two bands.' He snipped gently through the pearlescent tube, feeling the enormity of what he was doing even as his thoughts raced through his head in a blur. And then the tiny person was placed on Kirsty's T-shirted chest, and Kirsty smiled at her and said, 'Hello, my little queen – I've waited a long time for you.'

The midwife took the little queen to a set of scales lined with green paper and placed her gently in it. 'Five pounds thirteen ounces,' she said, proudly. 'A whopper considering she's four weeks early.'

Vince watched as they planted the baby's feet in an inkpad and took a set of footprints, then swaddled her tightly in a white blanket and handed her to his mother. 'You're beautiful,' she whispered to her new baby, 'just absolutely beautiful. Your daddy is going to love you so much when he sees you.'

Vince peered at the little Eskimo face peeping out of a gap in the blanket and felt waves of something he couldn't explain washing over him.

'Do you want a cuddle?' Kirsty offered.

Vince nodded, and held his hands out for the little white bundle. 'Hello, baby sis,' he said, staring into a pair of ink-black eyes, 'I'm your big brother. Your very big brother.' The ink-black eyes blinked at him and a tiny rosebud mouth formed a circle of surprise. And as he stared at her, Vince felt the strongest connection he'd ever felt with any human being in his life, stronger than the first time he'd seen Kyle, stronger even than the bond he shared with his mother. He suddenly felt the meaning of the word 'relation' in its purest, strongest form. He'd seen this person's first entry into the world; he'd seen her body leaving his mother's body; he'd disconnected her from her first source of life. She was truly, completely, eternally a part of him, and the overwhelming love he felt for her brought his whole life instantaneously into focus.

Nothing mattered but this, he thought. This was the true essence of life, of existence. This was what love was for.

'What are you going to call her?' asked the midwife.

'Ashleigh,' said Kirsty, 'Ashleigh Rose.'

'Ah,' she smiled, 'that's beautiful.'

And Vince smiled at Ashleigh Rose, watching his face imprinting itself on to her brand-new consciousness, and decided that it was time to start shaping his own destiny.

Thirty-Five

Joy's hen night wasn't turning out quite as she'd imagined.

After weeks spent discussing concepts such as party buses, nightclubs, stretch limos, weekends in Amsterdam and male strippers, they'd ended up at George's flat eating pizza. With George. And his best friend Wilkie. And his drug dealer Marian.

It was like an anti-hen night.

Joy wasn't quite sure what had happened. It had all started going wrong when George sneered disdainfully at the suggestion of a stag night.

'I have absolutely *no* intention of having a *stag* night. The whole concept is utterly repellent.'

'But don't you want to see your friends? Have a laugh?'

'I can do that any night. I don't need to dress it up with a ludicrous name and make a fiasco out of it.'

'It doesn't have to be a fiasco. You could just go out for dinner.'

'No. It's something I've always found distasteful, whatever form it takes.'

'Oh.' Joy felt a small gulf opening up between them.

'But don't let that stop you having fun. I had an idea, actually. I thought, maybe' – he smiled excitedly and grabbed her hand – 'you might like to have your party here.'

'Here?' Joy glanced around the living room and felt her soul sag in the middle.

But he'd said it in such a way that it was plainly an offer, not a suggestion. He was *giving* her his flat. It was a gift. And though there were probably at least a hundred different ways in which she could have sweetly turned the gift down, she couldn't think of a single one of them at that precise moment.

'Oh,' she said, 'I hadn't thought of that. But what about you? What would you do?'

'Oh,' he said airily, 'I'll find something to do. Don't worry.'

Her girlfriends had been a little bit surprised when she'd mooted the plan for the night, but gamely bounced back with enthusiasm, talking about the clothes they'd wear, the cocktails they'd make, the games they'd play. Someone suggested an Ann Summers rep. Someone else talked about a strip-o-gram. And somewhere along the line Joy started to think that, actually, it could be quite fun.

But then two days before the big day, George had come home and announced that his friend Wilkie was in town for the weekend and that they wanted to get stoned together and that, really, the only place they could do that was at the flat. And somewhere in the process of trying to fill yet another gulf before it turned into an 'issue' she found herself somehow negotiating a kind of hybrid hen/stag night. She tried to retrace the conversation in her head, to find the exact point at which she'd agreed to such a bizarre compromise, but she still had no idea how it had happened.

*

Wilkie had been first to arrive, a small, wiry person with slightly too much hair and wire-framed spectacles. He wore an aged bobbly jumper with a white polo neck underneath and talked in a soft Edinburgh accent, so quietly that Joy could only catch one in every three words he said. He was a friend of George's from public school and worked as a science reporter for the *Scotsman*, and Joy thought he was very nice, if slightly damp-smelling. He obviously saw George as the leader of the pack, some kind of throwback to school days, and laughed heartily at anything he said that was even halfway funny.

Ten minutes after Wilkie arrived, Marian the drug dealer turned up. She was wearing a strange hand-knitted jumper that appeared to have been fashioned from straw and a long denim skirt with cat hair all over it. Her incredibly long hair was rolled up into a sort of mushroom, and her eyeliner was smudged halfway down her face.

Joy, who had the ability to get on with pretty much anyone from pretty much any walk of life, could have carved a pleasant enough evening for herself out of this selection of slightly vague but fundamentally decent people, but it was the prospect of the terrible human chemical collision that was about to occur that made her feel edgy.

Joy had given a lot of thought over the weeks to how she imagined it might be the first time George met her friends. She'd imagined him meeting her nice, normal friends, the ones from university. She'd imagined jolly meals in friendly brasseries, lovely drinks in warm, smoky pubs. What she hadn't envisaged was a basque-clad Julia arriving at the front door with her bosoms presented in front of her like two enormous blancmanges sitting on a windowsill, followed by Bella in a red sequinned dress, waist-length nylon hair and heels that rendered him six feet tall. Both of them were festooned with shocking pink feather boas and dildos on chains, and had obviously had more than a couple of pre-party drinks as they came crashing through the front door screaming and whooping at the tops of their voices.

Joy had never seen Bella in drag before and the transformation was terrifying. Bella's sexuality was fairly ambiguous in his day-to-day guise, his manner low-key and his appearance androgynous. But the act of putting on a dress had somehow turned him into the campest, gayest person Joy had ever met. He spoke at twice his normal volume and did lots of unnerving sashaying, twirling and pursing of his (vermilion) lips.

'I've got my thermals on,' he stage whispered, nudging Joy sharply in the ribs. 'I'm prepared.'

'Shhhh,' she whispered urgently, 'George is here.'

'What – *the* George? He's here?'

'Yes. He's got some friends with him. They're, er . . . joining us.'

'What do you mean, they're joining us?'

'I mean George and his friends are staying. Here. With us.'

Julia's face crumpled with horror. 'But darling, they can't – this is your *hen night*.'

'I know, I know,' she hissed, 'but what could I do? It's his flat. I couldn't very well tell him to piss off.'

'Well, it's not actually,' said Julia. 'It's both your flat. You both live here.'

Joy shrugged feebly, and Julia and Bella exchanged a glance, which told Joy everything she needed to know about their opinion of her man-management skills.

'Oh, well,' breathed Julia, 'at least we finally get to meet him, the enigmatic *George*.'

And with that they both charged down the corridor and burst into the living room where George, Wilkie and Marian were sitting in the far corner, sharing a bottle of claret and talking very quietly.

'Now which one of you two lucky, lucky men is *George*?' said Bella, standing in the doorway with his hand on his hip.

Wilkie gulped so hard that his Adam's apple looked as if it might roll out of his mouth, and Marian just sat and blinked.

'Er, hello,' said George, looking more like an accountant than he'd ever looked in his life. 'I'm George.'

'Georgie Porgie, pudding and pie!' squealed Bella, and launched himself at George with his arms spread open. 'We've heard so much about you.' He kissed George firmly on both cheeks, leaving lipstick kisses, which George immediately rubbed off with the backs of his hands.

'Hi,' said Julia, steaming towards George with gently undulating breasts, 'I'm Julia, Joy's old landlady. Oh, God, that makes me sound terrible, an old landlady, like Annie Walker or something, but you know what I mean. It's *gorgeous* to meet you.'

The colour visibly drained from George's face as Julia wrapped her arms around him, squashing her bosom flat against his chest.

'It's er, very nice to meet you, too,' he managed before gently extricating himself from her embrace.

Julia stared around the room, trying and failing to find something nice to say about it while Bella adjusted his feather boa.

'Toke?' said Marian, passing Bella the bum end of a spliff.

Bella turned to her and sneered. 'Oh, no,' he said, 'disgusting stuff. Never touch it.'

'Oh,' said Marian, sadly, 'never mind.'

For a second the room resonated with the silence of people wondering what to say next, until it was finally broken by the timely chime of the doorbell. Joy breathed a sigh of relief, praying that she was about to open the door to Dymphna and Karen, her lovely sane friends from Bristol, but in the doorway stood Roz and Jacquie, swaying drunkenly and carrying a bunch of blown-up condoms and two bottles of tequila

'Aargh! Happy Fucking Hen Night!' They both crashed through the door, forcing a cheap nylon veil over Joy's head and attaching L plates to her back as they went. 'Fucking nightmare, finding this place,' said Roz, looking around the damp hallway uncertainly. 'Cab driver said he'd only come south if we showed him our tits. So we got out and got on the fucking Tube. God, it's fucking freezing in here. Have you got a window open?'

Joy disgorged them from their coats, revealing extremely short skirts and Lycra tops with cutout panels. 'No,' she whispered, 'it's just cold. It's warmer through there.' – she indicated the living room – 'We've got a blow heater.'

'Thank fuck for that,' said Jacquie, passing Joy a bottle of tequila and wrapping her skinny arms around herself.

In the living room, Roz and Jacquie clung vaguely to the wall as introductions were made, clearly horrified that they'd got all dressed up and trekked halfway across London to sit in an ugly room full of freaks.

'All right,' they said in unison, gazing numbly around the room, before backing out and dashing into the safety of the kitchen. This left Joy torn between feeling she should stay in the living room, where Bella was completely freaking George out by flipping vigorously through his CDs as if he was browsing in Our Price, and heading into the kitchen to make sure Roz and Jacquie were OK and to get everyone a drink. She decided that they'd probably all survive a few minutes on their own and went to get some drinks.

'He's not staying is he, your George?' said Roz, grabbing her arm urgently.

'Yes. He is.'

'You're fucking kidding me,' said Jacquie. 'It's your fucking hen night.'

'I know. But he kind of landed it on me unexpectedly, and I didn't handle it very well.'

Jacquie snorted and lit a cigarette. 'Christ, you're not joking.'

'I'm really sorry. It'll be fine. Honestly. I promise.' Joy could feel herself shrinking in their estimation as she spoke. And when she thought for a moment about the ludicrous situation she had somehow allowed George to orchestrate on what was supposed to be *her* last night of freedom, she couldn't really blame them.

*

By the time Dymphna and Karen arrived ten minutes later, it was too late – their normality was lost in a fug of overwhelming weirdness. The night was a disaster. It was hanging on to itself by a thread. Joy's skin itched with the discomfort of it all.

Julia, Bella, Karen and Dymphna were all trying their hardest to pretend that this was a perfectly acceptable excuse for a hen night, talking slightly too loudly and verging on the hysterical. Roz and Jacquie sat smoking furiously in one corner, making no attempt to hide their disappointment, while George sat cocooned by Marian and Wilkie, making absolutely no effort to engage with her friends.

The loud ones grew louder as the night drew out and the quieter ones grew quieter, and when Bella put on a 1970s disco compilation and started dancing on the coffee table Joy had to physically remove herself from the room for a while.

She went to the kitchen and washed some glasses, staring numbly at her reflection in the kitchen window as she did so. She was torn halfway between two existences – pre-George and post-George – and the realization that there was to be no meeting point between the two worlds left her feeling cold with dread.

'Hi, honey.' Julia squeezed in behind her and stroked her hair. 'You all right?'

'Yes,' she beamed, 'excellent.'

'Having fun?'

'Fantastic!'

'Good. George is lovely.'

'Do you think so?'

'Yes. And he's not ugly at all, you know.'

'Really?'

'No. He's nice. I don't know what you were worrying about.'

'I'm really sorry,' she began, 'sorry he's here. Sorry I didn't organize things better.'

'Ah, well. It's not the end of the world. And everyone's having a lovely time.'

'No, but really. I feel awful. You've all made such an effort and I haven't made any. I mean, I didn't even buy any mixers,' she gestured at the fridge.

And it was true. She'd had all day to organize things, to make the flat look nice, but instead she'd spent the entire day in bed with George. It was what they *did* on Saturdays. George bought breakfasty things the day before – croissants, expensive bread, exotic honey from some far-flung corner of the globe – then they lay in bed, sleeping off the ill effects of the two or three bottles of wine they'd drunk the previous night, listening to the radio, having sex and talking. All day. Until it was time to go out for dinner. And even though today was different, even though they were having a party, for some reason it hadn't really occurred to either of them to break the pattern and do something about it. George had bought a case of ponderous-looking wine from Oddbins the night before and seemed to think that that constituted a party, but some skewed internal logic had made Joy feel that suggesting a trip to the supermarket to stock up on crisps and mixers would in effect have been suggesting that pushing a trolley around Tesco was a more appealing prospect than spending the day in bed with him and that her friends were therefore more important to her than him, and she'd pushed the notion to the back of her mind and gone with the flow.

'Are you sure you're OK?' said Julia, turning to face her.

'Yes. Honestly. It's just not what I expected, that's all.'

'You know you can change your mind, don't you?'

'What?'

'About getting married. You know no one would be cross.'

'Oh, Julia,' she said with a brittle laugh.

'Seriously, hon. If you're having any doubts, any doubts at all, don't do it. It's too important not to be 100 per cent sure.'

At these kindly words, Joy felt the tear ducts at the bridge of her nose pinch together tightly, followed by a painful scratching at the back of her throat. She turned away to rearrange the glasses on the draining board.

'I'm not saying you *should* have any doubts,' Julia continued, obviously feeling she'd inadvertently offended her. 'Just that if you did, you should, you know, *act* on them.'

And Joy knew then that Julia was implicitly telling her that in her opinion she *was* making a mistake and that she was offering her a winch back to dry land, but the prospect of discussing her impending folly, here, tonight, now, was too much to handle. 'Well,' she said softly, controlling an urge to gulp, 'I hear what you're saying.'

'It's just something I always say,' said Julia, looking suddenly flustered. 'To all my friends, before they get married. You know.'

Joy smiled, relieved that Julia was backtracking. 'Bless

you.' She draped an arm around Julia's soft, bare shoulder and pulled her towards her for a hug. 'You're the nicest person in the whole world.'

'No,' said Julia, 'you are. And you know what they say about nice girls, don't you?'

'No. What's that?'

'They finish last. Oh, and they get cancer. So don't be too nice – eh?'

And then Julia hooked her arm through Joy's and they headed back into the living room, just in time to see Bella fall on to George's lap, loop his arms around his neck and slur at the top of his voice, 'Joy said you were really ugly, but you know what? I don't think you're ugly at all. I think you look just like a lovely big fluffy teddy bear.'

Joy listened to the echoing shards of Julia and Bella's laughter as they left the flat at midnight and got into a rumbling taxi outside the building. She clicked the door closed slowly and headed towards the living room.

George was sitting with his knees brought up to his chest, surrounded by empty wine bottles and smoking a spliff. He didn't turn around when she entered the room, just stared into the distance, exhaling doughy cushions of smoke. Joy perched herself uncertainly on the edge of the sofa and looked at him. She hadn't the first idea what to say, what to apologize for first. Every arrangement of words that came to her mind seemed destined to aggravate the situation further, so it seemed safer to say nothing at all. She placed a hand on George's knee, which he ignored. A moment's silence passed, then

George pressed his spliff into a jumble of butts and uncurled himself.

'Well,' he said, reaching to switch off a table lamp, 'I can honestly say that that was the most appalling night of my entire life. Good night.'

He stalked from the room, leaving Joy sitting in the dark watching an orange circle burn its way through a Rizla in the ashtray and turn to colourless ash.

Thirty-Six

Bella took a pin from his mouth and pressed it firmly into the cream fabric.

'You've lost weight,' he said, tugging at the dress. 'You can't keep losing weight. I'm not going to have any fabric left to stitch together.'

'I can't help it,' said Joy, balanced precariously on top of a stool in the middle of Bella's bedsit. 'I'm just not hungry.'

'Yes. And why's that? Because you're miserable, that's why.'

'I am not miserable.'

'You are. I can tell.'

'I am not. I'm getting married in four days. It's stressful. There's so much to organize. And anyway, why would I be miserable?'

'Because you live in a pigging disgusting flat in south London, because your first love is married to a super-model, because your fiancé hasn't spoken to you since your sorry excuse for a hen night . . .'

'Bell . . .' Joy glanced down at him pleadingly, 'you do promise you won't tell Julia about that, won't you?'

Bella raised his eyebrows and snorted. 'Of course I won't tell her. We wouldn't want to burst her lovely, big, pink, romantic bubble now would we?'

'And anyway – it's not that he's not talking to me; it's more that he's not using very many words when he does.

And I can't really blame him. I mean, who wouldn't be upset if they found out that their future wife had been going around telling all and sundry that she thought he was ugly.'

Bella shrugged and blanched. 'Yeah, well. I'm really sorry about that. I shouldn't drink. I'm no good at it. And anyway, I still don't understand why you didn't just tell him that I was lying. I wouldn't have minded.'

'Because it would so obviously have been a lie. Why would you say something like that if it wasn't true? George isn't stupid. It would just have made it worse if I'd tried to deny it.'

'So, how much longer do you think this silent treatment's going to go on for?'

'Oh, God,' tutted Joy, 'I don't know.'

'Because he'll have to start talking to you again at some point or he won't be able to say his vows, then all this . . .' he said, gesturing at her dress, 'would look pretty fucking silly, wouldn't it?'

'Look. He'll come round in the end. This is just his way of dealing with things. He's hurt. And there's absolutely nothing I can say to him to make it any better. Even if I tell him that I've changed my mind, that I think he's the most handsome man in the whole world, nothing can take away the fact that I used to think he was ugly. I keep expecting him to call off the wedding, but he's still going through the motions.'

'And what about you?'

'What about me?'

'Are you still going through the motions? Do you still want to go through with it?'

'Of course I do.'

'And you still love him?'

'Totally. I mean he's not perfect or anything, he can be moody and stuff, but it's still the best relationship I've ever had.'

'Yeah, but . . .' Bella took the final pin from his mouth and embedded it into the hem of her dress. 'You say it's the best relationship you've ever had, but that doesn't mean to say it's the best one you'll *ever* have. I mean, you might meet someone tomorrow who just blows you away, you know, someone who doesn't only make you feel *amazing*, but someone who makes you feel *complete*. Someone with a warm flat, someone with straight hair. Someone a bit more . . . *you*. I just don't understand why you're settling for second best, I really don't . . .'

Joy stared at Bella in surprise. 'Second best?'

'Yes. Because, Joy, my sweet girl, I know this is neither the time nor the place to be saying this, but I really think you could do so much better than Georgie Porgie.'

Joy felt herself stiffen defensively. 'Well,' she said tersely, 'you say that, but actually, could I? Could I really do better than George? I used to think maybe I could. When I met him, it was like he was someone from another planet, I thought he was totally beneath me, but actually he's about a hundred times cleverer than me, he's got a really nice body, he's really good in bed, he's romantic and sensitive and kind. All his family are dead or missing, he's had to look after himself since he was eighteen and it's not surprising that he gets a bit moody from time to time. And I'm not exactly perfect myself. And if I do decide to hang around waiting for some "perfect man", where will that get me, anyway?

Men like that always leave you in the end, they always find someone *better* to be with, someone more beautiful.'

'Men like *what*, exactly?'

'Men like Vincent Mellon. Men like Stuart Bigmore. Men like my fucking father . . .'

'Ah, yes,' said Bella, folding his arms across his chest, 'your father . . .'

'Oh God, please don't start that again. This has got nothing to do with my fucking father.'

'Oh, of course it has. It's got everything to do with your father. How else would you explain that a week after he left your poor downtrodden mother for a glamorous younger woman, a week after you cut him out of your life, you bizarrely accepted a proposal of marriage from a man you barely knew and didn't fancy? It's because you think that if you marry someone who puts you on a pedestal, then you'll never end up like your mother. But the problem with pedestals, Mrs Pole, is that you can fall off them.' He grabbed the legs of the stool she was balanced on and shook it from side to side.

'I am not on a pedestal,' she tutted, and gripped Bella's bony shoulder for support. 'And I am not afraid of ending up like my mother.' She climbed gingerly off the stool. 'All I want is to make George happy and have a lovely life. And I really think that once we're married, all this insecurity and sulking, it'll stop, because then he'll know that I'm not going to run off with someone else, that I'm not going to leave him.'

'That's what you think, is it?'

'Uh-huh. He just needs a show of commitment. That's all . . .'

'Well,' said Bella, 'you know what they say. Make a show of commitment in haste, repent at fucking leisure. It's your funeral.'

Joy threw him a withering look and started to climb out of her dress.

'Don't you want to see it?' said Bella. 'Don't you want to see what you like look in it?'

'No,' said Joy, 'not yet. I'll wait until it's finished, till all the pins are out.'

'Fair enough,' said Bella, appraising her slowly, and adjusting the neckline slightly, 'but for what it's worth you are officially the most beautiful thing I have ever seen. In fact, if you had a cock, I'd marry you myself.'

George didn't start talking to Joy properly again until two days later when she came home with her wedding dress in a huge white bag.

Spitting in the face of matrimonial tradition, Joy disappeared into the bedroom and slipped into the dress to give George a preview. She stood on the bed in an attempt to catch a full-length glimpse of herself in the small mirror on the opposite wall, but all she could see were her knees and shoulders.

'Are you sure you want to see?' she shouted from behind the living-room door.

'Absolutely!'

'Da-da!' she said, making her entrance. 'What do you think?'

'Oh, wow,' said George, getting up from the sofa. 'Wow, wow, wow, *wow*.'

'Is it nice? I couldn't really see in the mirror.'

'Nice?' he said, circling her appreciatively, 'it's absolutely stunning. You look like . . . God, I'm lost for words. You look spectacular. Utterly. Come here,' he said, opening his arms to her. 'I am the luckiest man in the whole world. Totally and utterly blessed.' He kissed the top of her head and Joy hooped her arms around him and felt all the tension of the past week instantly leave her body. He'd forgiven her. He still loved her. He still wanted her. He still thought she was perfect and beautiful. She was still the girl of his dreams.

And she clung on to him for dear life in her beautiful new dress, a bare-footed princess in cream linen, not wondering for a second why it was so important to her that she remain the girl of George Pole's dreams, not thinking one inch beyond the realms of his momentary approval.

Thirty-Seven

Vince paid more attention than usual to the weather forecast on the day before Christmas Eve.

Dry, cold and sunny.

Perfect, he thought, a perfect day for a wedding.

The forecast was proved 100 per cent accurate when he awoke the next morning to a brilliant blue sky blemished only by a solitary jet-engine trail. He attempted a lie-in, but something made him restless. He could hear Cass snoring in the room next door as he made his way to the bathroom, where Madeleine was asleep on the bathmat, a new favourite place. He watched her out of the corner of his eye as he peed, her belly rising and falling with each breath. She extended her claws and scratched lazily at the turquoise loops of the towelling mat. And then she turned to gaze at him, suddenly and unnervingly.

'What?' he said, turning away to check his aim.

She opened her mouth and issued a plaintive 'ow'.

And of course the cat wasn't talking to him, of course the cat didn't know what was going through his mind, but it was all the encouragement Vince needed to throw on some clothes, sort out his hair and get on the first Tube to Sloane Square.

The King's Road on the day before Christmas was thick

with teenagers. They cruised in groups of three or four, arms linked, back from boarding school for the holidays, reclaiming their territory. They weren't here buying gifts for friends and family; they were choosing outfits for raucous teenage parties in rambling Chelsea town houses and voluminous Fulham mansion flats.

Vince didn't peer through shop windows as he walked. He wasn't tempted by the sharp suits and designer clothes hanging from rows of angular plastic men. He had only one destination in mind as he strode purposefully westwards, and that was Chelsea Town Hall.

Someone else was getting married as he stopped on the other side of the road, outside Habitat, shielding his eyes from the sun. A man shaped like a currant bun had just married a woman shaped like a pencil. She wore a hat made of brown feathers and a narrow dress in purple velvet. He wore tails, but no top hat. They looked joyously happy as elderly people in expensive-looking coats threw paper confetti at them.

Vince glanced at his watch. It was ten-thirty. He darted across the road, ducking to avoid appearing in the newlyweds' photographs and followed the signs to the registrar.

'Excuse me,' he said, 'how can I find out what time someone's getting married today?'

He was pointed towards a board under glass. The banns. Inside, cards were pinned to green felt listing every wedding registered in the borough. He skimmed the display with his finger, primed for the word 'Joy'. And then he saw it:

Joy Mary Downer
George Edward Forbes Pole
24 December at 12.15

He found a coffee shop, where he consumed three cups of tea and a chocolate muffin, then at midday he paid his bill and returned to his post outside Habitat.

The steps outside the town hall were empty and speckled with confetti. After a few moments a dark Mercedes dressed in white ribbon pulled up outside and a youngish-looking man got out. He was wearing a black suit with a brightly embroidered waistcoat and a satin tie. His hair was brown and on the frizzy side of curly, and he looked as if he took life very seriously. He smiled at the person left in the car, turned and straightened his tie. He looked softer when he smiled, like a vet or a children's doctor. Vince could see him clearing his throat. He looked nervous but happy. He looked like a groom.

A smaller, youngish-looking man got out after him wearing a job interview suit and inappropriate rubber-soled shoes.

The two men climbed the stairs together, sharing a joke. The taller man, the groom, turned at the door to scan the street, before heading inside. If this was George, as Vince suspected it was, then Joy had done well for herself. He looked like he'd be good to her. He looked decent and intelligent and kind. He looked like he'd make a good husband. Vince felt a grudging approval.

Over the course of the next few minutes more guests arrived. Vince recognized the big woman and the poof

298

from Wilberforce Road. She was bursting out of lime-green tweed and oversized pearls, and he looked sallow and uncomfortable in a sombre grey suit, with his hair scraped back into a ponytail.

And then, five minutes later, at exactly 12.15, another Mercedes arrived. This one was white and slightly bigger than the first. The driver leapt nimbly from the front to open the back door.

Vince caught his breath.

She looked like something from a dream. Her dark hair was cut into a sharp, geometric bob and held back on one side by a small cream rose. Her lips were painted a sherberty mauve and she wore a simple cream dress with three outsized fabric-covered buttons running down the front, which ended just above her knee. She clutched a small posy of mauve and cream roses tied with mauve paper ribbon between her breasts, and smiled at the driver. She was the bride that every man dreamed of. Young, pure, simple, untainted. If all brides looked like this, thought Vince, men wouldn't be nearly as fearful of wed-dings.

She was followed from the car by Barbara, slightly slimmer than he remembered, but still perspiring lightly, in a pale blue skirt and jacket with a pillbox hat perched inelegantly on top of her head. She tugged at the hem of Joy's skirt and straightened a pendant that hung from her neck. Vince watched the car, waiting for the abom-inable Alan to emerge, but the driver clicked the door closed, returned to his seat and drove the car away.

He stared across the road as Joy mounted the steps to the town hall. A passing car hooted its congratulations at her, and she turned and waved at the driver, embarrassed, slightly goofy. And that was the image that imprinted itself on to Vince's memory for the next six years: a beautiful young woman in a plain linen dress, flushed with excitement, turning to smile at a stranger on her wedding day.

The doors to the town hall closed behind Joy and her mother, and Vince turned and headed into Habitat, thinking that, while he was here, he might as well pick up a set of shot glasses for Chris's Christmas present.

Al & Emma's Kitchen, 1.27 a.m.

'So you didn't say anything?!' Natalie squealed in horror.

'No. I bought the glasses and went home.'

'You didn't even wait to see them come out? To make sure they actually got married?'

'No. I'd seen everything I needed to see. He looked like a nice bloke and she looked deliriously happy. I didn't go there to *stalk* her. I just wanted to have a look, that was all.'

'But did you still think she was "the one"? Did you still love her?'

Vince shrugged. 'I don't know. It was nice to see her. It was nice to know she was happy. I don't think it really hit me how much she meant to me until the next time I saw her.'

'You saw her again?'

'Yes. Three years ago. The day Jess told me she was pregnant.'

'No way!'

'Yes way.'

May 1999
The Wrong Bus

Thirty-Eight

Vince hadn't had sex for eleven months when he met Jess.

He hadn't had a girlfriend for fifteen.

His last serious relationship had ended when he proposed to her.

'Fuck,' had been her panic-stricken response to his heartfelt request. 'Jesus. Shit.' She'd said she'd think about it, but when after three weeks she still hadn't made up her mind they took it as a sign that they weren't destined to grow old together and went their separate ways. Vince's heart had been properly broken. Smashed to smithereens. He mended it temporarily with four back-to-back one-night stands, then decided to pull out of the whole relationship thing entirely.

He lived in Enfield now. He'd spent nearly six months looking for a job in London after he was made redundant by Coalford Swann, but, strangely, nobody wanted to employ someone whose only experience involved finding words to describe porcelain dolls. Eventually his redundancy money had run out and he'd been forced to hand his notice in on the flat in Finsbury Park and move back to Enfield. And then one day, he'd been leafing through the local paper and chanced upon a recruitment advert for BSM.

A free car. No admin. Decent money, if he was

prepared to put in the hours. And even though teaching people to drive wasn't exactly the worthy career path that Vince had fantasized about pursuing all his life, it was still better than stringing together words to make people buy things they didn't need.

So here he was, almost thirty-two years old, sharing a poky flat in Enfield Town with a fifty-year-old mature student called Clive, teaching people to drive for a living, and he'd already started losing his hair. Not so that anyone else would notice, but it was definitely going. It seemed to be departing his skull in ever decreasing circles, from the outside in, leaving him to conclude that at some stage he would be left with just a tuft in the centre of his head, like a troll.

He felt as if he was on the cusp of middle age and about to lose his looks for ever. No one had fancied him for ages; girls no longer held his gaze for that split second longer than necessary. He was just the 'driving instructor' and he felt like a driving instructor. He'd even started to dress like a driving instructor. He'd had 'it' and now he was in the process of losing 'it'. And without 'it', Vince didn't really know how he was supposed to find a girl-friend.

So when Jess had folded herself into the passenger seat of his Vauxhall Corsa one sunny Tuesday afternoon and fluttered, *literally* fluttered, her eyelashes at him, he'd experienced a jolt of sexual energy he hadn't thought his body was still capable of producing.

'Hi,' she'd said. 'Vincent Mellon?' She appraised him briefly, like she was measuring him up for curtains. 'Great name,' she said eventually, letting his hand drop.

'Oh,' he said, 'thanks. It's, er . . . my dad's.'

'Yes,' she said, tucking a golden tendril behind her ear, 'surnames usually are.' And then she laughed, a thick, rich, wholesome soup of a laugh, and Vince thought it was the most incredible noise he'd ever heard.

Jess didn't have the slightly quavery edge that first-time drivers usually had. She handled the gear stick like a pro and chatted away as they drove with all the confidence of a black-cab driver.

She was tall, about five foot ten. She had brown shoulder-length hair streaked with gold that she wore clipped back with a plastic claw. Her skin had a natural olive glow, which, Vince would later learn, she accentuated using a brush and some multicoloured metallic beads in a pot.

She wasn't his usual type. Physically she wasn't as quirky or girlie as any of his exes. She wasn't into fashion and mostly dressed in drawstring jersey trousers that sat below her hipbones, or faded jeans, which she wore with tight T-shirts and flip-flops. She didn't appear to own any shoes with heels, and the only jewellery she wore was a small silver heart around her neck. She went to a tanning salon once a week and wore white G-strings, which emerged like bleached wishbones from the backs of her trousers.

She was harder than the girls he'd fallen for in the past. She'd had two abortions in her early twenties and there was some kind of history of drugs and Ibiza and clubs and unsavoury sexual liaisons, but she'd been through a sea change when she turned thirty and now lived a life of yoga, Pilates, steamed fish and celibacy. She referred to herself as a 'reformed hedonist'.

Her explanation for the fact that she'd only just decided to learn to drive at the age of thirty-one was typically Jess. 'There was no point in me driving before. I was always fucked.'

She was a producer for the hospital radio station at Chase Farm, and was paid next to nothing. She lived over a pet shop in Enfield, in a one-bedroom flat which was infused with a slight tang of urine-soaked straw. She had a black cat called Pasha and two stripy fish called Es and Whizz, and all her houseplants lived in a permanent state of semi-dehydration.

Vince learned all of this within ten days of her first driving lesson, first through the steady stream of chatter she fired his way while they inched around the back streets of Enfield and secondly when he awoke in her flat on a Sunday morning after a night of truly life-altering sex.

Their shared celibacy had been both a meeting point and an incitement to break the deadlock. They talked about sex like two dieters circling a pile of profiteroles, mutually respectful of each other's self-control while silently awaiting permission to cave in.

'Christ,' said Jess, flinging herself backwards against her pillow afterwards, 'remind me again why I haven't done that for two years?'

Vince couldn't think of one good reason. He had no recollection of sex ever having been this good before and was sure that, if it had been, there was no way he'd have abstained for nearly a year.

Jess was the sort of girl who knew tricks, who had props, who used swearwords during sex. It was the first time in his life that Vince hadn't felt even partly in control of the process, and he'd loved it.

He'd been half-expecting her to kick him out the next morning, for her to be standing over him with his shoes dangling from her fingertips and his coat draped over her arm, but instead she'd made him breakfast – perfectly poached eggs on wholemeal toast with sour cream and a splash of sweet chilli sauce.

'Kind of huevos rancheros, Jessie-style,' she said, sliding back into bed with him. 'Can I watch you break the yolk?'

Her bedroom was painted white and was only just big enough for the superking-sized bed wedged behind the door. There was a blown-up canvas print of an arum lily over her bed and a view of a William Hill betting shop through the window opposite. The kitchen was tiny and white, and full of towering bottles of oil and vinegar and the sort of very expensive pasta that comes in boxes. The bathroom was equally tiny and white, and came to life with a thunderous hum when the string for the light switch was pulled on. There was a small ash dining table in the living room, bearing chrome candlesticks with a kink in the middle, and two small, cushion-strewn yellow sofas huddled around a TV housed in an ethnic-looking cabinet.

She was renting the flat from a friend who was living in Sydney, and it was impossible to tell where her friend's tastes ended and Jess's began, but Jess's style of living definitely veered towards the chaotic. Clothes were hanging to dry from radiators and the backs of chairs. Last week's Sunday papers sat in a rifled splat on the coffee table, and a dinner plate smeared with something greasy and orange sat on top of the TV.

'Where did you get those scars?' she said, running her finger along his jawline.

'I didn't think they still showed,' he said.

'Yeah,' she said, 'they're faint, but they're there.'

'Plastic surgery,' he said. 'I had an underbite, like this –' He pushed his jaw out, as he'd done so many times before. 'They took some bone out there.'

Jess winced. 'Ow,' she said.

'I wouldn't have thought you'd have been squeamish, judging by those,' said Vince, pointing at tattoos on her upper arm and hip.

'Those are just pricks,' she said, 'not cuts. There's a big difference between pricking and cutting. So what did you look like before? Were you really ugly?'

'Yeah. It wasn't a good look. Didn't exactly get the girls chasing after me.'

'Oh, bless,' she said as she chucked him under the chin. 'Well, at least it gave you a chance to develop a personality. If you'd been this good-looking all your life you'd have been shallow and boring.'

And Vince almost wanted to say, 'But I *am* shallow and boring. I've got no interests, no hobbies, no ambitions. I don't know anything about politics or sports or world affairs. I just watch TV and teach people to drive,' but decided that it would be better to preserve the flawless perfection of her compliment by saying nothing at all.

'I always thought I'd lose my virginity to a woman like you,' he said.

310

Jess looked suddenly aghast. 'What? You mean . . . ?'

'No! No. I mean, *before* I lost my virginity. I imagined I'd lose it to someone like you, someone experienced and . . . and . . . *into* it. You know.'

'Ooh,' her eyes lit up, 'I wish you had. It's a little fantasy of mine. Deflowering an inexperienced young man. Who was the lucky girl?'

'Joy,' he said, abruptly.

'*Joy?* What was she – seventy-five?'

'No. She just had an old-fashioned name. She was the same age as me.'

'Which was?'

'Eighteen. Ish. She was a virgin, too.'

'Oh, my God – that must have been a disaster!'

'No, it was great, actually. Really, really great.'

'I don't believe you! How could it possibly be great? Neither of you knowing what you were doing?'

'I don't know,' he said. 'It just was.'

They spent the rest of the morning in bed and had sex five times. Only ten hours into their relationship and Vince already knew that this was going to be the greatest sexual pairing of his life. Whatever happened after this, Vince knew he would always use the sex he had with Jess as a yardstick by which he would judge all subsequent couplings. And as the minutes ticked by, second by second, shag by shag, it occurred to him that this might not just be a one-off thing, an aspic-set experience to be stored in a corner of his memory and brought out on lonely winter nights. It occurred to him that Jess and he had more in common than just a base need to call a halt to their states of celibacy, that they were sort of *bonding*.

There was a kindness between them, a gentleness. They discussed family and history and childhood memories. Jess had no secrets, no side; she told him everything, almost issuing a challenge to like her in spite of all her faults.

They shared a bath, and Jess washed Vince's hair, massaging his skull tenderly with smooth fingertips. They had lunch at a café across the road and played with each other's feet beneath the table. And when, after they'd eaten, Vince suggested that maybe he should be getting back, Jess looked at him and asked, simply, 'Why?'

So he didn't go back and they spent the rest of the day together, and the rest of the night, and by the time Vince finally made it back to his gloomy flat to collect some clean underwear three days later, he was fully, totally completely and rampantly in love.

Thirty-Nine

Vince knew for sure that Jess was going to be the mother of his children the first time she met his little brother and sister.

Previous girlfriends had been sweet to Kyle and Ashleigh. They'd patted them, held them, run around the garden with them, bought them presents, talked nonsense to them on the phone. There'd even been favourite girlfriends. The last one, the Rejected Proposal, had been a big hit with Ashleigh in particular, as she knew how to do complicated things with Ashleigh's hair and make her look like the girls in Steps. And the one two back from Rejected Proposal had been Kyle's favourite because she could make up great stories about dragons from off the top of her head.

But the minute Jess set eyes on Ashleigh and Kyle some chemical reaction occurred that transcended everything. She turned into a magic person. Her eyes lit up and she lost her outer crust of hardness, and Ashleigh and Kyle were sort of pulled magnetically towards her. She didn't actually have to *do* anything to win their affection; it was instantaneous.

'Are you going to marry my brother?' said Ashleigh, climbing on to Jess's lap and playing with a strand of her hair.

Jess smiled sagely. 'Well,' she said, 'that depends. I've only known him for a few days. Do you think I should?'

'Yes,' said Kyle, 'you should. Because otherwise he'll be old and lonely.'

Jess stifled another smile. 'Do you think he'd be a good husband, then?'

Kyle and Ashleigh both nodded vigorously. 'Yes,' said Ashleigh, 'definitely. He's really clever and he's really kind and he likes animals and small children.'

'And do you think maybe I'd make a good wife?'

'Yeah,' Kyle shrugged, 'you'd be perfect.' And as he said it a red flush crept up his cheeks and swallowed him whole. He turned away abruptly, and Jess and Vince smiled at each other across Ashleigh's shoulder.

'Vincent nearly got married before,' said Ashleigh. 'He asked her and she said no.'

'Yes. He told me about that. What a cow, eh?'

'Yeah,' said Ashleigh, eyes opened wide with surprise at someone finally telling it as it was. 'I used to really like her, too, but now I hate her.'

'Too right,' said Jess. 'You should always be loyal to your family. Particularly your big brother.'

'Yeah. She was horrible. I never really liked her anyway – I just *pretended* to like her because she was good at hair. But that doesn't matter any more because now he's got you and, if he asks you to marry him, you'll say yes.'

'Well,' said Jess, 'people really need time to get to know each other properly before they do something as serious as getting married. But maybe one day when your brother and I have spent some more time together we might get married.' She looked up at Vince and winked at him, and he winked back at her and, even though it should have been terrifying listening to this conversation only eleven days into their relationship, it wasn't. It was amazing and incredible because it was exactly what he wanted.

'She's great,' said Kirsty, loading the dishwasher after a raucous lunch.

Jess had been dragged up to Ashleigh's room to play with her Barbie mansion, and Kyle was in the front room watching Nickelodeon.

'Fucking knockout,' said Chris, rubbing his belly lightly. Chris had expanded slowly but substantially over the years. He still had his long, slim legs and broad shoulders, but his six-pack was a long-distant memory, cowering somewhere beneath a comfortably settled layer of fat.

Kirsty was still as trim as ever though, looking remarkably youthful at forty-nine in neat size 10 jeans and a pale blue knitted top with three-quarter-length sleeves. She said it was the kids that kept her young, but it was an obvious case of good genes.

'How come she's learning to drive so late?'

'She's a reformed hedonist,' quoted Vince, scraping congealed gravy off a plate and into a bin. 'She spent her twenties off her face.'

Chris laughed. 'Figures,' he said, 'she's got that sort of edge to her.'

'What do you mean?'

'I don't know. She's just got that twinkle in her eye, you know, a bit wild, like she might be trouble.'

'Do you think?'

'Yeah. But in a good way. Not a bad way. And she's great with the kids.'

315

'She is, isn't she?' Vince smiled.

'Oh, look at you,' teased Kirsty. 'You've gone all dreamy.'

'Oh, yes,' Chris joined in, 'look at that. Vincent's *broody*!'

'Oh, fuck off!' Vince threw a screwed-up paper napkin at him and smiled.

Jess walked back in, Ashleigh clutching her hand.

'Jess has been teaching me yoga. Look.' She slid one foot slowly up the opposite calf and balanced on one leg while pressing the palms of her hands together. 'It's called the Tree.'

'Oh, the Tree, is it?' said Chris. 'You'll be wanting macro-bloody-biotic sandwiches for your lunch next.' He grinned at Ashleigh, who stuck her tongue out at him and dragged Jess out into the garden to learn some more positions.

Vince stood at the window and watched them for a while. Kyle emerged a minute later and asked what they were doing. Within seconds he was joining in, too, contorting his body into strange shapes, mimicking Jess's languid movements.

The sun was just starting its descent overhead, throwing vibrant shadows through the tendrils of a small weeping willow in the middle of the garden. Next door's cat sat on the interconnecting wall, playing with a tiny green butterfly. It was the second warm weekend of the year, warm enough for short sleeves, but not quite warm enough for bare feet, the soil beneath the grass still holding its wintry chill.

Vince watched Ashleigh arranging her limbs into the Lotus position. She was at that foal-like stage of her development, all lanky limbs and knobbly knees, the woman she was going to become hovering shyly in the wings, not quite ready to take centre stage. Vince felt a moment of sadness as it occurred to him that in a few short years Kyle and Ashleigh would be adolescents, their childhoods a distant memory, and when that happened there'd be no children in his life at all. None of his friends had reached that stage yet. They were all still enjoying their middle youth, spending their money on fancy holidays, meals out and cabs home. Children were just a topic of conversation, a vague concept, something inevitable but safely distant. 'We're going to start trying next year, once we've bought a bigger place/been promoted/got married/given up smoking.'

But watching Jess now, gently rearranging Kyle's legs, tall and strong, healthy and vital, Vince could already tell she wasn't like his friends. She wasn't clinging on to anything, scared of losing anything. He could envisage her eight months' pregnant, stroking her bump, glowing with health and hormones. She wouldn't bemoan her imminent loss of freedom, her inability to get drunk on cocktails, the physical changes in her body. She would thrive as a mother. She would *bloom*. And suddenly, the thought of planting a baby in that long, strong body, of making her a mother, struck Vince as the sexiest, most exciting thing imaginable.

A seed of broodiness had been sown in Vince's belly the moment he first set eyes on Kyle. That seed had started sprouting roots when he watched Ashleigh arrive in the world three years later. But here, in his mother's kitchen, on a sunny Sunday afternoon, for the very first time in his life he felt genuinely ready to be a father.

*

317

'They're gorgeous,' said Jess, as they drove home an hour later. 'Absolute angels.'

'I know,' Vince smiled, proudly. 'Mum and Chris have done a great job. They're great kids.'

'Such a responsibility, isn't it? Bringing kids into the world. So many different ways you can fuck up.'

'Yes. It's the greatest challenge of them all.'

She turned and looked at him. 'Do you ever wonder if you'd be up to it? You know, if you've got what it takes?'

Vince shrugged. 'Yeah. I think about it. But I reckon I'd be good at it. I've had a bit of practice.'

Jess nodded, her lips pursed. 'You're lucky,' she said. 'I've never really had anything to do with kids. None of my friends have got any and when I got pregnant, you know, *before*, I was nowhere near ready for it. The thought of giving up my independence, of having some screaming, shitting kid attached to my ankles all day, just freaked me out. But lately . . .'

Vince threw her a look.

She smiled. 'Oh, I don't know. It's nice, isn't it? Having kids. Being a family. It's real . . .'

'I think it's what we're all here for,' he teased.

'Yes,' she said thoughtfully. 'It is, isn't it?'

She turned to stare out of the window, and they continued the journey in a contemplative silence.

Forty

They started trying for a baby two months later. It was still early in their relationship, but once they'd discovered their mutual desire to become parents they decided that there was no point in hanging around. They didn't tell anyone they were doing it. Vince's friends were still at that teasing stage about proposals and weddings – it hadn't occurred to any of them that Vince and Jess might bypass that formality entirely and go straight to the main event. And they didn't look at ovulation charts or take temperatures. They just followed Jess's mother's advice to have 'as much sex as possible'.

It had felt strangely liberating the first time they'd had unprotected sex, an overwhelming sense of doing precisely what nature intended, of being in tune with the universe. Both of them had been utterly incredulous when Jess's period arrived the following month.

'God,' Jess had sighed, ripping open a box of SuperPlus tampons, 'you spend your whole sexual life trying so hard not to get pregnant – it just seems unthinkable that you can have sex *fifty times* without a condom and not make a baby.'

But they hadn't felt sad that first time. It would have been too soon. It still felt experimental.

When Jess's period arrived the following month, they were less bewildered.

'It's hardly surprising,' said Jess. 'You know, two abortions, all those drugs – I'm probably not as fertile as I could be.'

By the third month, they philosophically settled themselves in for a long wait. 'Even if it takes another year, I'll only be thirty-three by the time the baby comes. That's still relatively young.' So they carried on having as much sex as possible and stopped imagining that every single symptom Jess displayed in the run-up to her period was a sign that she might be pregnant.

They weren't even officially living together yet. Vince spent most of his time at Jess's flat, because it was ten times nicer than his and Clive didn't live there, but he was still paying rent on his flat share and spent the occasional night there, when Jess wasn't around. He didn't have keys to her place and he didn't stay there when she was away. He didn't even keep a toothbrush there; he used Jess's.

It was as if they were both subconsciously waiting for the thin pink line on the plastic stick before they made any kind of formal commitment to each other. The suggestion implicit in this arrangement was that if they failed to make a baby then they would drift apart as easily as they had drifted together. And even though this should have given Vince pause for thought, should have caused a shaft of disquiet to pass across his consciousness, it didn't – because he was so in love that it hurt.

Jess had a smattering of male friends in her life. Most of them were exes of one form or another. Kevin was her teenage sweetheart (and the father of one of her aborted babies). He was married now and lived in Brighton with his wife and two children. They talked on the phone from time to time and got together for a drink whenever Kevin found himself in London without his family. Vince had met him once. He was tall and ginger with a slightly flabby paunch and represented no threat to him whatsoever.

Carl was one of her Ibiza exes. He lived on the island permanently and phoned occasionally when he was off his face to tell her that he loved her. Jess always smiled when she put the phone down to Carl and shook her head despairingly. 'Mad,' she'd say fondly, 'completely mad. I pity his girlfriend, I really do.' Vince had seen a picture of a youthful Carl, all long, shaggy hair and over-sized shorts. He was good-looking but vacant. He was also 500 miles away and living with a model. Vince didn't lose any sleep worrying about Carl.

Nor did he concern himself much over Bobby. Bobby was the man who turned Jess celibate. He was forty-five and had just married the woman he'd refused to leave for Jess. He'd messed with Jess's head so badly that she'd spent three months in therapy after they finished. Part of that therapy involved going for dinner with him every now and then and talking about 'neutral' things. 'Don't know what I ever saw in him,' Jess said when she came back from one of these occasional meetings. 'He looks more and more like a toad with every day that passes.'

The only one of Jess's exes who worried Vince in the slightest was Jon Gavin. Jon Gavin had been the love of her life – and the father of her second aborted baby. She always referred to him by his full name – Jon Gavin –

because there'd been three other Johns in the big gang of friends they'd hung around with in their twenties. Jon Gavin had been Jess's partner in crime during her Ibiza days, the one she stayed up all night partying with, the person she associated most with the 'good old days' of her youth.

There were pictures of him in various locations around the flat. He was tall and lean and handsome in that Paul Newman way that other men could appreciate. He was a music producer and lived in a beach house-cum-studio just outside LA. But more worrying than the good looks and the sexy job was the fact that Jess never said a word against him. If only she'd just once said something disparaging, even if it was something petty like that he had horrible feet or that he snored, Vince might have felt more relaxed about him. But she didn't – far from it.

'I *adore* him,' she said, 'absolutely adore him. He's the most amazing person. I wish you could meet him – I know you'd love him, too.'

The one thing that Jon Gavin had in his favour as far as Vince was concerned was his physical distance from the two of them. He was deeply indebted to Jon Gavin for choosing to live on the other side of the Atlantic and would have happily paid him maintenance to stay there for ever.

So when Vince met Jess in the pub across the road from her flat one night, and she beamed and said, 'I've had some really exciting news – Jon Gavin's coming back to London,' Vince had had to take three very deep breaths to compose himself before he could find a proper reaction.

'How come?' he managed eventually.

'I don't know,' she said, still glowing with excitement, 'something to do with work. I don't believe it – you're finally going to meet Jon Gavin!'

'Yes,' said Vince, 'it's great. When's he back?'

'Next Monday! I'm going to collect him from the airport. Surprise him.'

'Cool,' he said, 'great idea.'

'I'd ask you to come along, too, but, you know . . .'

Vince didn't really know but could only presume and nodded mutely. 'No, no,' he said, 'that's fine. I understand.'

'But you'll meet him on Tuesday.'

'Oh, yes?'

'When you come over.'

'Oh, right.'

'I've asked him to stay with me. Just until he gets himself settled in, finds somewhere to live.'

'What? Seriously?'

'Yes. Is that a problem?'

Vince wanted to say, yes, that is a fucking problem, actually. But he was still, ludicrously, at the stage in his relationship with Jess where he wanted her to think that he was cool, that he was secure with a capital S.

'God. No. It's not a *problem*. It's just . . . isn't it going to get a bit cramped? With the three of us?'

'No,' she scoffed, good-naturedly, 'Jon doesn't take up much room.'

She said this, as she said everything about Jon, as if it was yet another unique virtue that he possessed.

'But where will he sleep?'

'On the sofa bed,' she said.

'Oh. Right.' Vince sniffed. He imagined the three of them lined up on the sofa watching a DVD. He imagined Jon yawning at nine o'clock and Jess leaping to her feet to unfold the sofa bed with him. He imagined waiting outside the bathroom to brush his teeth as Jon emerged wrapped in a towel with his six-pack rippling at him and his gigantic pecs twitching. And then a fantastic idea occurred to him. 'I just had a thought!' he said, brightening. 'Why doesn't Jon stay at my flat! He'll have his own bedroom, and it's only a five-minute walk away.'

Vince expected to see Jess's face light up with pleasure at this suggestion, but instead she frowned. 'Oh,' she said, 'no. I don't think so. That flat's so miserable. And I can't quite imagine what Jon would make of dear old *Clive*.' She said Clive's name is if it were slang for a sexually transmitted disease and, for the first time in his life, Vince felt defensive of his dreary flatmate.

'What's wrong with Clive?'

She threw him a questioning glance. 'Oh, come on,' she said, 'you know exactly what's wrong with Clive. He's old and he's weird ...'

'He's not weird.'

'OK. Not weird, exactly – but he wears strange clothes and he talks so ... slowly ... it ... makes ... you ... want ... give ... up ... living. And besides, I haven't seen Jon for four years. I *want* him to stay with me. He's good for my soul. He makes me happy.'

Vince gulped. He knew Jess wasn't deliberately trying to upset him. Jess had no guile, no notion of game playing. People had total responsibility for handling their own emotions, as far as she was concerned. It wasn't her job to censor her actions, to edit her feelings. It was the other person's job to grow up and take it. She had no interest in dealing with other people's insecurities and that was why Vince was sitting here, taking deep breaths and behaving in a reasonable fashion, when what he really wanted to do was have a full-blown tantrum and storm off like a girl.

'Fair enough,' he said, finally. 'It was just a thought.'

Jess beamed at him and clasped his hand. 'My two best boys, under the same roof,' she said. 'So exciting!'

And as she said it, a mental stopwatch clicked on in Vince's head, painfully ticking down the seconds until Monday night . . . until Jon Gavin.

Forty-One

George stood beside his car, outside the station.

He was wearing the shirt he'd worn on their wedding day six years earlier. The top two buttons were undone and the white of the piqué cotton against his olive skin looked cool and fresh. He'd done something different to his hair, too. It was cut shorter, closer to his skull. It looked good. His hands clasped a large bunch of white flowers, unidentifiable from this distance, but probably arum lilies.

Joy pulled her coat tightly around her and smiled uncertainly. In her left hand was a Selfridges carrier bag containing some toiletries, her pyjamas, her diary and a packet of Lil-lets. She'd packed them on Friday while George was in the garden, thrown things into the bag randomly, urgently, fuelled by adrenalin. She'd forgotten her moisturizer and had to use her mother's cold cream that smelled of damp porches. And she'd brought only one change of clothing, a black Lycra shirt that was now in her mother's linen basket. She'd intended to come back for everything else, fill the boot of her mother's car, drive across London yet again.

Instead she was coming back to stay – to make another go of it. Her heart filled up with disappointment, drip by drip. Disappointment in herself. All the planning, the subterfuge, the courage she'd had to muster to leave the house on Friday lunchtime, all the nerves and the tension and the sheer terror of getting on that train three days ago, all for nothing. One phone call from George and she was back. One ten-minute conversation filled with promises of change and improvement, declarations of love and adoration. That was all it had taken.

George had bought flowers.

She was back at square one.

She flashed her Travelcard at the young man with the pied hair, the young man she saw every day on her way to and from work, the young man she thought she'd never have to see again after Friday, and took a deep breath. She felt shy as she approached George, awkward. She couldn't remember which muscles to use to make her face smile.

He beamed at her, his face wrinkling into soft folds of happiness. 'You look beautiful,' he said, handing her the flowers and taking her carrier bag from her in one smooth movement, 'absolutely beautiful.'

She smiled tightly, no longer sure how to accept a compliment from George after so many years. 'You're wearing your wedding shirt,' she said, fingering one of the buttons.

'Yes,' he said, glancing down at it, 'I've been waiting for an opportunity to wear it again – now seemed as good a moment as any. I found a piece of confetti, caught under the collar. It was a horseshoe. It struck me as rather portentous.' He grinned and held the passenger door open for her. 'It's lovely to see you,' he said, 'really lovely. I've missed you.'

Joy slid into the passenger seat and smiled up at George. 'I missed you too,' she said. And in a strange way, she had. She hadn't missed his long, painful silences or their ritual Saturday-night sex. She hadn't missed the smallness of their life together or the near-squalor that they had somehow managed to end up living in. But she'd missed *him*. In the days before she left, as she contemplated the enormity of what she was about to do, she'd opened the wardrobe and sniffed one of George's suits, and as his scent hit the back of her nose she'd hugged the suit to her and cried into the lapels.

Another time, she'd caught a glimpse of the back of George's head, the softness of his neck, the little trickle of a burgundy birthmark just peeping from his hairline, a tuft of unruly hair sticking up at an angle, and had suddenly and overpoweringly seen him as a little boy, a small, lonely child with no parents, no friends, no one at all apart from her. She'd wanted to get up and hug him, bury his face in her shoulder, but he would have looked at her as if she'd taken leave of her senses and shrugged her off. They didn't do affection any more.

She should have seen these as signs that she wasn't ready to go, that even though every bone in her body ached with the desire to escape from the tiny, messy, cold and suffocating world that she had somehow found herself in, her head wasn't ready to make the leap back to shore. She'd been adrift at sea for so long, she'd lost her land legs. She couldn't remember how to be without George. She was lost with him and lost without.

'So,' said George, buckling up his seat belt, 'I've booked us dinner at the new Japanese place. Is that OK?'

'Lovely,' she said, 'I'm in a fishy mood.'

'Good,' he said. 'Excellent. But first, let's get you home.'

Forty-Two

Jon Gavin arrived on the same day as Jess's fourth period.

He was sitting on Jess's sofa when Vince got to her flat at seven o'clock that evening. He got to his feet the moment Vince walked in and shook him vigorously by the hand.

'Vince. It's an honour to finally meet you.'

'Yeah,' said Vince, staring into a pair of the most dazzlingly blue eyes he'd ever seen in his life, 'you, too.'

'Jessie's really been talking you up – Vince this, Vince that . . .' He smiled and let Vince's hand drop.

Jessie? How come he was allowed to call her Jessie? Vince had called her Jessie once and she'd snapped that only her father was allowed to call her that. 'Well, that's nice to hear,' he said, smiling back.

Jon was shorter than he looked in photos, but that was the only thing about his physical appearance that Vince could take any comfort from. He was dressed casually in combat type trousers and a crewneck in soft grey lambswool. His hair was shorn into an all-over number two, but not because he was losing it – it was thick and covered his scalp densely like plush velvet – it was shorn because it suited him shorn, because he had incredible bone structure and a well-shaped skull. It was shorn because it set off his ridiculously blue eyes and thick, dark eyelashes so well.

He even had nice feet.

The one part of the anatomy that was more often than not to be found lacking in aesthetic appeal, the one bit that was allowed, *expected*, to be horrible, and Jon's were, like the rest of him, tanned, shapely and toned.

Vince wished he'd made more of an effort getting dressed this morning. Spending all day sitting in a car, his primary concern regarding clothing was comfort. He wished he'd had his hair cut, too. It always tended to look thicker when he'd just had it cut. He felt pasty, British, bald and old. He felt totally and utterly inadequate.

Jess emerged from the kitchen in jersey trousers and a tight vest top with no bra. Vince stared helplessly at the profile of her nipples. Yesterday they'd been *his* nipples; today he was sharing them with another man.

'Good evening, my lovely man.' She planted a warm kiss on his cheek and cupped his right buttock. 'I see you've made your acquaintances?'

They both nodded and smiled.

'Bloody period just started,' she tutted, arranging cutlery on the dining table. 'Just now – about half an hour before you got here.'

'Oh,' said Vince, glancing at Jon to see how he would react to this unexpected and somewhat personal announcement.

But Jon looked completely unfazed. 'Oh, shit, Jess,' he said, 'I'm sorry.'

'Erm, does Jon . . . have you told him . . . ?'

'Yes,' she said lightly.

'But I thought we said we weren't going to tell anyone.'

'No – *you* said you weren't going to tell anyone. I just *chose* not to. Until now.'

'Oh,' said Vince, 'right.'

'Hey, look,' said Jon, 'don't worry about it. If you guys are trying to keep it low-key, you can trust me. I won't blab.'

'No, no, that's fine. It's just, you know, if people know then they start wondering why it's taking so long and it's just added pressure, and we just want the whole thing to be, you know, *fun*.'

'Fair enough,' said Jon, 'I totally understand, I really do. I just think it's fantastic. I'm so excited for you guys. Little Jessie, going to be a mummy.' He beamed at Jess and she beamed at him. 'No one deserves it more than you.' And then they suddenly swooped on each other and hugged for a full twenty seconds.

'Oh, Jon,' said Jess, her arms circled loosely round his waist, 'it's so good to have you here.'

'It's so good to be here.' He kissed her on the forehead, then hugged her again. They both made squeezy bear-hug noises while Vince stood and watched, feeling completely excess to requirements.

'Promise me you'll never go away again.'

'Ah, now. You know I can't promise that. But I do promise not to leave it so long between visits next time.'

'That'll do for now,' she smiled, and pulled away from him, but not before tapping him lightly on the bum with the palm of her hand.

Vince cleared his throat, not to draw attention to himself, but out of sheer embarrassment. He felt like he was watching young lovers. He felt like he should excuse himself from the room. Instead, he fell to the sofa and picked up a copy of Jon's in-flight magazine.

'How was your, er ... flight?' he managed, flicking mindlessly through the thick, glossy pages.

'Good,' said Jon, joining him on the sofa, 'yeah. Not bad. Bit of turbulence coming in, but otherwise it was cool.'

'Virgin any good?' he asked, pointing at the magazine. He didn't know why he'd asked this, had no idea whatsoever. He had no intention of flying anywhere any time soon, but the image of Jess's hand on Jon's arse was stuck in his mind like a paused video and he couldn't think of anything else to say.

'Yeah,' he said, 'great. Upper Class – not first class as such, more like business, but pretty good value for money, I thought.'

Vince gulped. Jon was the kind of guy who flew first class as a matter of course. He'd feared as much. He'd suspected that that casual, understated lambswool sweater had a glimmer of something expensive about it, that those worn-out combats weren't from Gap. And that tiny silver hoop in his left lobe was starting to look more and more platinum by the minute.

He was working-class boy made good.

He was handsome and rich and successful.

He was warm and friendly and confident.

He was everything that Vince wasn't. And everything that he wanted to be.

'Right. I hope you two are hungry. I've made enough for at least eight hungry men.'

'What are we having?' Vince rubbed his hands, trying to work some enthusiasm into himself.

'Spaghetti and meatballs.'

'Oh, you beauty!' said Jon. 'My favourite! I can't believe you remembered.'

'How could I forget!' Jess winked at him and disappeared into the kitchen.

'Wow,' said Vince, his voice cracking slightly with the strain of not sounding peeved, 'you *are* honoured. All I ever get is steamed fish and vegetables.'

Jon shrugged. 'Ah, well,' he said, 'maybe you should try leaving the country for four years.' He smiled at Vince, as if to underline the fact that he wasn't being serious, but it didn't matter anyway.

Vince was way too far down Insecurity Avenue to be guided back now.

Forty-Three

Jon was perfect. Absolutely perfect, in every way.

He didn't walk around in skimpy towels and he didn't get in Vince and Jess's way. He didn't talk through *The Sopranos* and he didn't watch *Ri:se* in the mornings. He didn't hog the phone and he didn't flirt with Jess. He didn't show off about his sexy job and he didn't flash his cash.

His sofa bed was folded away every morning before Vince and Jess had even stirred, the cushions replaced in the exact configuration in which he'd found them. He watered all of Jess's desiccated plants and somehow brought them back to life. He made the best cup of tea this side of Vince's grandmother and was always in a good mood, the kind of good mood that rubbed off on Vince and put an extra spring in his step when he left Jess's flat in the morning. Vince had used the bathroom one morning after Jon had been in there for long enough to suggest a bowel movement and the room had smelled, literally, of roses.

He even complimented Vince on his skills as a driving instructor.

'Jesus,' he said, 'I never thought I'd live to see Jess behind the wheel of a car, let alone *survive* with Jess behind the wheel of a car! But she's really good. You must be a great teacher.'

Vince didn't want to tell him that Jess was actually a natural driver, that his teaching had nothing to do with it, and smiled nonchalantly instead, gratefully absorbing his approval.

Vince was walking a tightrope between love and hate. Some days he wanted to slap Jon on the back and tell him how great he was. Other days he wanted to throw acid in his face.

At a time in his life when Vince had finally started to feel like a man, when everything was falling into place, Jon had come along and made him start questioning everything. He'd accepted that someone as sexy and cool and charismatic as Jess wanted to be with him because he had only one context in which to view her. Without Jon, Jess was just a low-paid hospital radio producer who lived in a small rented flat in Enfield, went to yoga three times a week at the local church hall, shopped at Budgen's, drove a Micra, cut her own hair and liked having a lot of sex.

In the context of Jon, however, she suddenly became an exotic creature who could have married a successful music producer and spent her life flitting between LA, Sydney and Cape Town. She could have had platinum credit cards, diamond earrings and beautiful children with thick hair. She could have had her own yoga instructor, a macrobiotic chef and a four-wheel drive Jeep. In the context of Jon, everything about Jess looked different. In the context of Jon, she and Vince made absolutely zero sense as a couple, and the whole notion of them making a baby together seemed somehow comical.

In the context of Jon, Jess, basically, was completely out of Vince's league.

'Why did you and Jon split up?' he asked her one night. He held his breath, hoping for an explanation that would put his mind at rest – that they'd split up because Jon was impotent, because she stopped fancying him, because he was a brutal serial killer – anything. He should have known that he wouldn't get what he wanted.

'I don't know, really,' she said, running her fingertip around the curves of his ear. 'Jon was really ambitious when he was younger. I just wanted to party. I think we kind of went on different journeys, drifted apart.'

'Ha,' he said, attempting to sound blasé, 'ironic, really, isn't it?'

'What is?'

'That you split up because you were too much of a party girl and now you're so abstemious – maybe if you'd stuck together for a bit longer you would have drifted back together again.' Say no, he thought, his teeth clenched tightly together, say no. Laugh sardonically. Shrug it off. Pooh-pooh the very notion. Please.

'Hmm,' she said, 'I never really thought about that before. It's possible, I guess. But, you know, life has its own agenda. Jon and I split up for a reason. You and I met for a reason. It's all predestined, isn't it? No point wondering what if . . . ?'

Vince nodded, but inside he was shouting, 'Bull*shit!*' He hated all that destiny bollocks. His old flatmate Cass had tried to shove it down his throat. All that business with Joy and that stupid bloody cat. She'd tried to per-

336

suade him that it was a *sign*, that it meant something, when all it had meant was that Joy had chosen to live in the same part of London as him for a while and that Cass's cat had good taste in people.

If destiny could bring two people together, then it could just as easily tear them apart, and, if it could tear two people apart, then it could just as easily bring them back together again. There was no beginning, middle and end to destiny. It wasn't neat and manageable. It was random and scary. It did what it wanted. And if it wanted to bring Jon back into Jess's life so that she could suddenly wonder what the hell she was doing trying to make babies with a loser like Vince, then it would.

'So, if Jon had come back six months ago, before I met you, what do you think might have happened?'

Jess made a noise that suggested that she was much more interested in sleeping than discussing what-ifs.

'You see,' Vince persisted, 'there's no bad history between you, is there. You're best friends; he's a really good-looking bloke; you used to be in love. What would have stopped you?'

'Oh, Christ.' Jess turned over on to her side. 'I don't know. I just don't see him like that any more. He's a mate. He's just . . . Jon.'

Exactly, thought Vince, *exactly*. That was the whole point. Jon was just Jon, and Jon was total and utter perfection.

Forty-Four

Joy slid her Switch card back into her purse and pulled the carrier bag off the end of the counter.

It had started to rain, suddenly and heavily. A crescent of people stood in the entrance to the supermarket, peering at the sky through the glass doors, while their shopping sat in flaccid bags at their feet.

Joy, having expected rain, pulled her umbrella out of her handbag and unfurled it. Car tyres fizzed over the wet tarmac and people walked with an added urgency. A man ran past Joy, bumping her with his elbow.

There's no point in running, she wanted to shout after him, they've done tests and you only stay 5 per cent drier if you run through a rain shower than if you walk.

Joy's bag was full of food for dinner. It was her turn to cook. That was how it worked. George cooked on Monday, Wednesday and Friday, Joy cooked on Tuesday, Thursday and Saturday, and on Sundays they went out for dinner. Tonight she was making something from *The Naked Chef* – a big bowl of soup with chicken and noodles. George was recovering from a cold and it had sounded nice and medicinal.

It was amazing to Joy how quickly they'd slipped back into their old routines.

For the first couple of days George had been on best behaviour. He'd agreed with her that things needed to change; he'd promised he'd do something about his mood swings; he'd gone so far as to suggest having her mother over for Sunday lunch. They cleaned the house and talked about holidays and made plans for the future. They even had sex on a Tuesday. The relationship felt fresh and clean – it felt like it had felt back in the early days when George had adored her, before he'd decided that she was the cause of all his woes.

But then, as the days drifted by, everything settled down. The house returned to its state of squalor. The plans came to nothing. George retreated back into himself. And life continued as if Joy had never packed a bag and left him alone in this suburban prison.

They lived in Esher now. They'd moved here three years ago when George decided to give up working to write his Great British Novel. It was a tiny two-up-two-down cottage off the high street and had cost half as much as he'd sold his three-bedroom flat in Stockwell for. The rest of the money was sitting in a high-interest account paying for George's extended sabbatical. It was supposed to have been for only a year. George had moved here full of hope, bristling with excitement as he plugged in his laptop and flexed his fingers. He'd been convinced that by the time the New Year arrived he'd be sitting on a big fat manuscript and a publishing deal. But by the following January he was eleven pages into his fourth attempt, three previous books aborted halfway through and sitting in cold storage.

His money had started to run out a few months earlier, and he'd been forced to take on some accounting work to keep himself out of debt – his clients ranged from a local florist to a piano teacher and a mobile hairdresser. He hated every minute of it, resenting the intrusion of these random elements of the outside world into his writing time and his domestic cocoon.

George and Joy never had guests to their house. Joy's mother pretended to understand, but was patently baffled by the fact that the man she'd so happily watched her daughter marrying six years earlier had never so much as rustled up a bowl of pasta for her and only ever came to see her in her own home for fleeting, impatient visits, usually en route to somewhere else. When Barbara did manage to pin them down for the occasional Sunday lunch, George would start glancing at clocks and watches the moment he'd swallowed his last mouthful of apple crumble, making no attempt to hide his uneasiness at being so far outside of his comfort zone.

For one allegedly so well brought up, George could be incredibly ill mannered.

Julia and Bella had turned up one Friday night a few weeks earlier. It was transparently a rescue mission masquerading as an impromptu 'we were just passing' visit. Joy and George had just finished dinner and were about to watch a video. The doorbell rang and George twitched the front curtains, his body bristling with irritation and dread.

'Oh, my God,' he said, letting the curtain fall, 'it's your dreadful friends. That vile little man and the loud woman with the chest.'

'Julia and Bella? You're kidding.'

'Unfortunately not.'

Joy gulped. She hadn't seen Julia and Bella for nearly two years. They spoke on the phone from time to time, but both of them had grown bored with trying to get her to come out with them. Joy had given up her social life a long time ago. It wasn't worth the long silences and the sulking and the grief. It was easier just to make her excuses and stay at home with George. It had been better when she was still working in town, at ColourPro. She'd been able to see people in her lunch hour. Now she was based in Surrey, even that tiny little social avenue had been blocked off and she saw no one but George.

In any other circumstances, in a relationship with a normal man, she would have felt surprised but pleased by the unexpected arrival of two of her oldest friends on her doorstep. As it was, the news of their uninvited presence sent a shockwave of dread through every bone in her body.

'Did you invite them?'

'No,' she exclaimed, 'of course I didn't.'

The suggestion was ridiculous. Her home was hermetically sealed against the world. The only people who crossed its threshold were plumbers and gasfitters. Their Friday nights had a rhythm, a shape borne out of ritual. Joy suspected that most couples sharing a home had similar shapes and routines, but with a sort of in-built flexibility, like tall buildings designed to withstand high winds. Their routines, however, were so rigid and unyielding that the slightest hint of change could send the whole thing toppling over into a mass of shards and splinters.

The doorbell rang again. Joy opened her mouth to say

something. 'Shhh.' George put his finger to his lips. 'Quiet,' he whispered. Joy closed her mouth.

Everything she said and did now was designed to keep George happy. Even her style of dressing was informed by his opinions. When miniskirts had come back into fashion a couple of years earlier George had expressed discomfort at the amount of leg that Joy had started displaying, so she'd immediately gone back to trousers. She could have stood her ground and taken an 'I'll wear what the damn hell I like' kind of attitude, but she knew exactly where that would have led, and she didn't have the energy or the conviction to go there.

She was compliant in every aspect of her life with George. She no longer saw her friends, used swearwords, watched trashy TV, wore short skirts, referred to toilets as toilets, dropped her aitches, dyed her hair, referred to her past, discussed her family, held her knife like a pen or gave him oral sex. She had systematically and surgically removed every source of potential displeasure and irritation from his life, and under these extreme circumstances they had somehow salvaged a good marriage from what remained. Left to their own devices, following their own routine and without any incursion from the outside world, they lived a pleasant and amiable life. They watched videos every night, ate good food, read good books and talked for hours over excellent wine about politics and philosophy and things that really mattered. They never argued and life ticked along pleasantly, so much so that Joy had come to resent attempts by friends to lure her away from this domestic stranglehold.

Most of them had stopped trying years ago, but Julia

still plugged away at it. 'We're going to see Take That at Wembley – you must come, darling. I'll buy you a ticket.' 'Bella and I are off to Stratford for the weekend – staying at a lovely B & B. Please, say you'll come.' 'Come and meet us in town – we're going to a new bar on Rupert Street.' And every time Joy was forced to find some way of saying no that didn't involve admitting that George wouldn't let her.

In the past Julia had occasionally been able to bully Joy into saying yes. Her acceptance would be immediately followed by a couple of anxious days, gearing herself up to break the news to George that she was going out. Once she'd decided that the time was right to make her dreadful announcement, there would be at least five minutes of deep breaths and mental arrangements of the exact words she intended to use before finally spitting them out in what she hoped was a nonchalant fashion, usually accompanied by promises not be late. A dark mood would then ensue which would last for hours or sometimes days, reaching a crescendo on the actual day of her engagement and lifting the moment they awoke the following morning and life returned to normal. This pattern had become so painful to Joy that she no longer saw social invitations as a pleasant part of adult life, but as a poisonous and insidious disruption of her hard-earned domestic harmony.

As far as Bella and Julia were concerned, when they turned up unannounced that night, they were coming to see a friend whose husband didn't let her come out to play. There was no way they could be expected to understand the implications and ramifications of their actions and, even if Joy tried to explain, they still wouldn't have the first notion of what she was going through. She could explain about George's long, drawn-out silences, but they could just bat that away with a flippant, 'Oh, just ignore him. He's a grown man. He'll survive.' She could try to explain the way these silences made her feel – excluded, abandoned, imprisoned, oppressed – and the atmosphere that his moods lent to her environment – bleak, gothic, ponderous, endless – but they would never really understand why she let him make such a huge impact on her psyche.

And the truth was that Joy didn't understand either, not really. She'd worked out a long time ago that George was an inherently unhappy man and that all that stood between him and this ever-looming state of unhappiness was her. She was the key to everything and, without her compliance, George, through no fault of his own, started sailing close to a place where there was nothing to live for and no reason to exist, a place that Joy knew better than most, a place where suicide lurked. She made excuses for him because she recognized the way in which he viewed the world, and she stayed with him because if she left there'd be no one to stop him falling.

Joy stared at the blurred outlines of Julia and Bella through the opaque glass of the front door and felt blood pumping through her body. 'Christ,' she muttered, 'I don't understand what they're doing here.'

'I'm not letting them in,' he whispered, sitting on the arm of the sofa and folding his arms.

'What?'

'I'm sorry, but it's gone nine o'clock and I just think it's really very rude to turn up uninvited.'

'But they've come all this way . . .'

'That's not my problem.' He glanced at the front door. 'They should have given us some warning.'

The doorbell rang again and the flap of the letterbox lifted. Four fingertips appeared inside the door.

'We know you're in there,' trilled Bella's voice. 'We can see you.'

George glanced at the door in horror, and Joy shrugged at him before arranging her face into an expression of surprised delight and opening the front door. 'Oh, my God!' she gasped. 'What are you two doing here?'

'We were at Waterloo station seeing Julia's sister off, and we saw this platform display and it said Esher, and it was leaving in ten minutes so we thought, fuck it, let's go and see our lovely little Joy. Ooh – I love your little house,' he said as he looked around. 'It's really cute.'

'Oh, yes,' said Julia, coming up behind him, bringing with her an aroma of cold air and warm pubs. 'Very nice. Very homely.'

George sat where he was, staring mutely at the TV screen, which displayed a paused image of the video they'd been about to watch.

'Oh!' said Julia. 'You're watching *Dumb and Dumber*. I love *Dumb and Dumber*.'

'No,' said George slowly, 'that's a trailer.'

'Oh.' Julia spun round to address George, having only just noticed him in the corner. 'George! Hello there! How are you?'

'Fine,' he muttered.

There was a microsecond of silence as Julia waited, in

vain, for him to say something further. 'We're not inter-rupting anything, are we?'

George said nothing.

'Er, no,' said Joy. 'Not really. Just a video.'

Julia and Bella both nodded and looked around. 'Here,' said Joy, finally snapping out of her shocked reverie and realizing that they had guests. 'Sit down.' She moved last week's papers off the sofa and took the dinner plates off the coffee table.

They both sat down, squashed together on the tiny sofa, and Joy could see their high spirits deflating like punctured space hoppers as they absorbed the palpable tension in the air. George moved and sat down cross-legged on the floor, where he picked up a stray maga-zine and started flicking through it.

'Can I get you a drink?'

Julia and Bella both nodded. 'What have you got?'

'Wine. Beer. Water.'

'I'd love a glass of wine.'

'We haven't got any wine,' said George.

'Yes, we have.'

'No,' he said. 'We haven't.'

'Oh. Right.' Joy tried not to look flustered. 'No. I forgot.'

'Don't worry,' soothed Julia. 'A beer will be fine.'

She brought them each a bottle of Hoegaarden and sat on the floor.

'So,' said Julia, 'you look well.'

'Thank you,' said Joy, 'so do you.'

'And you, George. I haven't seen you since your wed-ding day. I must say, married life seems to agree with you. You look very well.'

George glanced up from his magazine and smiled tightly at her before letting his head drop again.

The expression of friendly interest froze on Julia's face and a small silence descended. It dawned upon Joy that George was going to deal with this invasion of his Friday-night routine by pretending that it wasn't happening. He'd obviously decided that if he extended no hospitality to these people that not only would they leave sooner, but also that they were less likely to ever visit again.

The conversation was stilted and uncomfortable. It was impossible to chat normally while George sat seething in the corner of the room, ostentatiously turning the pages of his magazine, and the visit had so obviously been engineered to check up on Joy, to see what sort of life she was living, that once their guests ascertained that, yes, George was as controlling and antisocial as they'd suspected and that, yes, Joy was as brow-beaten and submissive as they'd feared, there hardly seemed to be any point in them being there. But the charade of the 'impromptu visit' needed to be played out until the bitter end, and so the three of them hung on stoically until the last dregs of beer had been drunk from the bottles and the last train was about to became a viable excuse to leave.

Joy saw them to the door.

'Sorry,' she said.

'What for?'

'For . . . *that*. For everything. You know. It's just. . . .'

'Don't you worry about a thing,' said Julia, hugging her tight. 'Just remember, we're here. We're always here. Whenever you're ready for us. Yes?'

'Yes,' Joy nodded gratefully. 'Thank you.'

'Sorry to turn up unannounced,' said Bella, leaning in for his customary cheek pecks. 'We just really wanted to see you.'

'I know,' said Joy, 'it's fine.'

'It's my thirtieth next week,' he said. 'I've booked a table at Mezzo. Wednesday night. D'you want to come?'

Joy smiled tightly, feeling tears prickling at her nose. 'I don't know,' she said, 'I'll see. I'll let you know.'

He smiled at her with a hint of disappointed resignation. 'Cool,' he said.

And then they went, Bella with his arm looped through Julia's, headed towards the train station and back to reality. Back to a world full of thirtieth birthday parties and friends and spontaneity. Back to a world that Joy had left a long time ago. And for a split second Joy wanted to run after them, shouting, 'Take me with you! I want to come, too!' Instead she turned and went back inside, steeling herself for another long and painful silence.

George didn't talk to her that night. He didn't talk to her until around five o'clock the following day, but by the time he finally came out of his sulk and started being civil again it was too late – Joy had already decided to leave. On Wednesday night she'd sat in front of the TV and envisaged a table full of happy people in Mezzo, people who'd written 'Bella's birthday' on their calendars and caught the tube to Tottenham Court Road and Leicester Square in their best clothes ready for a night of drinking, eating and laughing. She imagined someone making a toast to Bella and Julia making a speech and someone else popping a bottle of champagne. She'd conjured up this vignette from thin air and it probably bore no relation to reality, but it was enough to convince her that she didn't want to turn down another invitation as long as she lived.

But more than that, the dreadful evening with Julia and Bella had made her acknowledge that she could no longer live with a man who was so terrified of the outside world that he would refuse to offer wine to guests. There seemed to Joy something so fundamental about the sharing of wine with friends, so innate and primal, so natural and joyful, and the thought of never being able to do it again was more than she could bear.

So she'd packed a bag and she'd left.

Then she'd come back.

And now here she was, two weeks later, on Esher High Street, in the rain and back where she'd started. Nothing had changed. She was no closer to accepting invitations to parties than she'd been before she left. She was trapped, by George's insecurities and her own weakness. And for the very first time since she'd first set eyes on George all those years ago, she stopped imagining herself as lost at sea on a runaway boat and accepted instead that this was her destiny. Being with George, living in the suburbs, working in a photo lab. No one was going to rescue her. There was no alternative, parallel existence. This was her life. This was her journey. And as she absorbed this frightening realization, she glanced around her at the people of Esher and saw two women walking towards her. They were her age, early thirties, averagely attractive, blandly dressed in Next and Debenhams, and each pushing a pram. The prams were hung with carrier bags, the babies inside obscured by rain-splattered plastic covers. She stared at the women and another realization hit her, more powerful than the first. The only way she could survive this journey, she suddenly knew, was to become one of those women. To become a *mother*. Because a baby was the only thing that made any sense of this scenario, of her life, of her and George.

She had to have a baby.

George would respect her again. She would respect herself. She would know who she was. She wouldn't be lost any more.

And with that thought, she turned left off the high street and headed home towards George and her destiny.

Forty-Five

Jon and Vince went to the pub together the following week. It was Jon's idea. Jess was at yoga and it was the first Monday after the clocks went forward. Enfield Town felt vaguely exhilarated by the thrill of an extra hour of daylight. People sat outside pubs in their overcoats savouring the first tentative moments of summer. Jon and Vince went to the King's Head by the market place and ordered pints of Heineken Export.

Jon didn't look out of place here at all, with his shaved head, his earring and his designer street wear. He could just as easily have been one of these boisterous market traders, a silver-tongued purveyor of outsize nylon underwear, knock-off CDs or strawberries. He was, like Vince, an Enfield boy through and through, and, like Vince, he'd got out of Enfield at the first opportunity to sample life elsewhere. Unlike Vince, he'd made a career and a reputation, was respected throughout his chosen industry and probably had awards on his toilet wall to prove it. He'd lived in different countries, worked with different people, gathering momentum as he went. Vince, on the other hand, had moved to London with some vague idea of working in the media, moved back to Enfield when that didn't work out and taken the only job he could find that made him feel even vaguely grown up. Jon was a year younger than

Vince, but at least ten years older in terms of life experience and status.

'So,' Vince opened, 'what's your plan?'

'You mean in London?'

Vince nodded.

'None really. Just having a break.'

'Funny,' Vince smirked, 'leaving a beachside house in California for a break in Enfield Town.'

'Yeah,' Jon nodded and smiled, 'it's all the wrong way round, isn't it? But living somewhere like that, somewhere spectacular, doesn't stop you loving the place you come from. Makes you appreciate it even more if anything.'

'Which bit of Enfield are you from?'

'Turkey Street.'

'Turkey Street. Blimey,' said Vince, an eyebrow raised in acknowledgement of one of the roughest parts of Enfield. 'You've really come a long way.'

'Yeah,' Jon laughed. 'Can't say I've ever run into anyone from my estate on my travels.'

'And your folks. Are they still there?'

'Yeah. Well, my mum is. I would have gone and stayed with her, but she's up to her neck in teenagers. Four of them, between fourteen and eighteen. In a three-bedroom flat. Can you imagine it?' He grimaced.

'Brothers and sisters?'

'Yeah. Well, half-brother and half-sisters. Mum's second time round. There was just me for the first fourteen years, then she met Richie and popped out another four pretty much one after the other. From two of us to seven of us in the space of five years. If that wasn't an incentive to get my arse out of the flat, out of Enfield and into the big wide world, then I don't know what was.'

'Weird,' said Vince. 'Same thing happened to me, sort of. Lived with my mum for fourteen years, then she met Chris and now they've got two kids. They waited till after I'd left home to have theirs, though, thank God. I was twenty-three when Kyle came along.'

'Now that's a bit more civilized – you can appreciate them that way when they're not keeping you awake all night and scratching your records and throwing up on your best shirt. Jesus,' he said, 'it was a nightmare – nearly put me off kids for life.'

'So you've never contemplated having a family of your own?'

'Oh, God, yeah – of course I have. I'd love a family. That's my next big plan.'

'Oh. Right.'

'Just haven't met the right girl. Yet.'

'So you and Jess never thought about it, after the – you know – the abortion?'

'She told you about that?'

'Yeah.'

He smiled wryly and nodded. 'No,' he said, 'that was pretty much the end for us, the abortion. Jess was wild back then. She wasn't ready to be a mother. It would have been a disaster. Half the reason she had that abortion was because she didn't realize she was pregnant until she was ten weeks gone and the amount of drugs and booze she must have put inside herself during that time – Christ knows what harm that would have done to the baby. No. Jess was never the mothering kind. Well, until

353

now that is.' He raised his glass to Vince's in a congratulatory manner. 'I've got to say,' he continued, 'I'm pretty impressed with the way you've managed to tame her.'

Vince grimaced. 'Nothing to do with me,' he said. 'She was like this when I met her. It was just timing.'

'Yeah. I know what you mean. Jessie sets the pace. Always has done. Jessie's one of those people, right, she's like a *bus driver*.'

'What?'

'OK. Let's say that life is a trip across town. Some people are cab drivers – their destination is dictated by their passengers. But other people are bus drivers. They set the course. People can get on and off the bus, but ultimately the bus is only going in one direction and there's nothing a passenger can do to change that. And that's Jess.'

Vince nodded, feeling that, although Jon's analogy was faintly ridiculous, it also rang very true.

'But having said that, it still says a lot about you, that she's chosen you. Having a baby – that's a huge thing. She must think you're pretty fucking special to want to share this leg of her journey with you.'

An alarm bell rang violently in Vince's head. 'Leg?' he said.

Jon paused again. 'Yeah,' he said, '"cause that's the thing about Jess – and I really hope you don't think I'm saying this because I'm jealous or anything, 'cause really, mate, trust me, I'm not – but the thing about Jess is that if you don't want the same things as her at the same time as her for the rest of your lives, then at some point you'll get kicked off the bus. And if someone gets on who *does* want the same things – well, you know . . .'

Vince nodded tautly.

'You've got to be prepared to play second fiddle from hereon in if you want to make it work. Jess is the boss. Accept that, accept her, accept everything she does, and you're laughing. Otherwise, well . . . I suppose what I'm trying to say is just, be careful. Jess is a dangerous person to fall in love with. And I should know . . .'

Vince blanched slightly. He was torn between wanting to smash a glass over Jon's head and asking him to explain further. As it was, all he could manage to do was to pick up his empty glass and ask Jon, wanly, if he wanted another drink.

'Sorry, Vince, I went too far, didn't I? I talk too much. Always have done. It's none of my business. You and Jess are great together, and you'll have great babies and that's all that matters. End of story.'

Vince nodded and took their empty glasses to the bar, his head full of buses and babies.

He thought back to the first time Jess had slipped into his car and introduced herself. What had she seen when she looked at Vince? Had she seen a vibrant sexy man or a sperm donor? The man she wanted to spend the rest of her life with or someone who'd give her what she wanted right now?

He thought about their life together. Was it a love affair? He loved her, he knew that without a doubt. And she *acted* as if she loved him. She looked after him and cared for him. She was affectionate and warm. But was she committed? Were they doing the right thing, making a baby together when they barely knew each other? Jess would be a great mother, there was no doubt in Vince's mind about that, but would they work as a *family*?

He glanced at himself in the carved mirror above the bar. He looked tired. He looked old. He *was* old. There was no time for prevaricating. If he wanted a family, he needed to start now.

He pushed Jon's comments and his own lingering doubts to the back of his mind and handed the barman a £5 note.

Forty-Six

Vince sat in his car outside 10 Ladysmith Road.

It was nine-thirty on a Saturday morning, and he was waiting for Charlene Okumbo to emerge for her driving lesson. Charlene was seventeen years old and this was her third lesson. Vince liked Charlene because she talked nonstop about herself and her friends and her life, and made him feel vaguely tuned in to the youth of today. Her mum was a teaching assistant from Perthshire and her dad was a bus driver from Ghana. She went to Enfield College where she was taking A levels in English and Business Studies, and eventually she wanted to run her own retail empire.

She was also always at least ten minutes late for her lesson, so Vince turned off his engine, pulled out his phone and called Jess.

'Oh, hi, Jon, it's Vince.'

'All right, mate? How you doing?'

'Good, thanks. Is Jess there?'

'Yeah. I think so. Let me just see . . .' Vince heard him calling down the hallway. 'Hang on a sec, mate. Jess? Jess?' It went quiet for a moment. 'Er, Vince. It doesn't look like she's here.'

'What?'

'Yeah. Doesn't look like she came home last night. Her bed's not slept in.'

'You're kidding me.'

'No. Seriously. She's not here.'

Vince gulped. Jess had said she was going out last night with people from work. She'd said they were going to have a few drinks at their local pub, then she fancied an early night.

'I don't understand it,' Jon continued. 'When I left her she said she was just having one more drink, then she'd be leaving.'

'Left her? What – you mean you were there?'

'Yes.'

'At her work do?'

'Yeah. I didn't have anything on so she asked me to come along.'

'Oh,' said Vince, 'right.' He felt his gut clench with jealousy. He hadn't had anything to do last night either, but Jess had made it very plain early on in their relationship that her work life was totally separate from her private life. He'd never met any of her colleagues from the radio station and he'd never pushed it because he thought it was fair enough – he approved of them having separate social lives, thought it was healthy and mature. Jess did lots of things without him and it didn't bother him. But the thought of her inviting Jon along to one of her Friday nights out, while he sat in with Chris and his mum watching *Friends* and eating Domino's pizzas made him want to throw something very hard against a wall.

'Do you want me to call her?'

'No,' snapped Vince, 'no. I'll call her. Do you think I should be worried?'

'No,' said Jon, 'I'm sure she's fine. Probably just had a bit too much to drink and crashed at someone's house.'

'She was *drinking*?'

'Yeah. She had a couple.'

'But she's teetotal.'

Jon laughed. 'Last night she was drinking. Tomorrow she'll be teetotal again. That's the thing with Jess. She does what she wants.'

Vince bridled at yet another insight borne out of an intimacy he increasingly felt he didn't share with his girl-friend, sighed and switched off his phone.

'Morning, morning!' Charlene's beaming face appeared at his window.

Vince sighed again and conjured up a smile.

'You all right?'

'Yeah,' he said, slipping out of the driving seat to let Charlene take over. 'I've just got to make a quick call. I'm really sorry. I won't be long.'

'Cool with me,' she said as she slipped into the driving seat and examined her eyeliner in the rear-view mirror.

Vince pressed his mobile tightly to his ear and listened to the ringing tone.

'Vince! My angel boy!'

'Hi,' he said, feeling thrown by her exuberance. 'Where are you?'

'I'm at Frank's place.'

'Frank? Who's Frank?'

'Frank. Franco. He's a chef. You know.'

'No,' he muttered, 'I don't know. What the hell are you doing there?'

'Oh, please don't get all arsey with me, Vincent –'

359

'I'm not getting arsey,' he hissed, 'I'm just worried about you. What happened last night? Jon said you were supposed to be coming home . . .'

'Yeah, well. I was, but then some of the girls were going up to Eros . . .'

'You went to *Eros*?' Vince's mind boggled at the thought of clean-living, miso-soup-slurping Jess getting down and dirty at Eros on a Friday night.

'Yeah. It was great. Haven't been there for years. And we bumped into Franco – he's a cook up at the hospital.'

'Oh. Right.' An image of a swarthy, muscle-bound Italian wearing nothing but a chef's hat and apron flitted briefly through Vince's mind.

'Got chatting, had a line or two. Suddenly it was four in the morning. Couldn't get a cab so I came back here with Frank. Bless him.'

Vince didn't know which element of this shocking story to question first. The inviting of Jon to one of her precious work dos. The drinking of alcohol. The taking of drugs. Or the going back to a strange Italian's flat in the early hours of the morning. His mind raced with a million grievances and concerns. 'Christ, Jess . . .' he managed.

'What?' she said. 'You're not angry with me, are you?'

'Jess,' he said, taking a deep breath in an attempt to sound measured and reasonable, 'I can't talk now. I'm in the middle of a lesson. I'll see you tonight. OK?'

'You sound pissed off. Are you pissed off?'

'Yes. I'm pissed off.'

'Oh, Vince. Please don't give me any grief. My head's fucking pounding. I really don't need it.'

Vince sighed again. 'Look. I'll see you later.' And he hung up.

Charlene threw him a look. 'Whoah,' she said, her mouth an agog O, 'that was a bit heavy.'

'Hmmm.'

'Wanna talk about it?'

Vince glanced at his phone, then at Charlene. Yes, he thought, he did want to talk about it. 'If you were seeing someone,' he began, 'and that person went out on a Friday night without you, but with their best friend of the opposite sex, then ended up in a nightclub taking drugs – while you were supposed to be trying for a baby – met up with another person of the opposite sex from work and ended up going home with that person at four o'clock in the morning, what would you do?'

Charlene popped a fruit pastille in her mouth and looked him squarely between the eyes. 'Dump him,' she said, simply.

Vince stared at her for a second, waiting for her to soften the bluntness of her pronouncement. She didn't.

He nodded slowly, and turned to find his seatbelt, feeling a strange numbness suffusing his body.

'OK,' he said, 'Mirror, signal . . . and manoeuvre.'

Forty-Seven

Freedom came in strange forms and from unexpected directions.

The last time Joy had had a day and night to herself was two years ago when George had spent the night in hospital with an ingrown toenail – the particular little window of freedom that Joy was about to enjoy had been afforded by the fact that George had decided that he needed to kick-start his writing career with a creative writing course. He found one in Winchester that fitted the bill – mainly because it promised plenty of one-on-one meetings with top literary agents. George was convinced that all he needed to do was find someone who appreciated what he was trying to do, someone to champion his embryonic work, and success would be guaranteed. 'Publishing – it's all a matter of who you know,' he explained to Joy. 'It's all about making contact with these people.'

Joy had nodded sagely, unsure whether his theory was right or wrong, but not wanting to do or say anything that might make him change his mind about leaving her alone for an entire weekend.

Joy could barely believe it when the door closed behind George on Friday afternoon and she watched his car pulling out on to Esher High Street. She half expected him to come back, to bowl through the door saying, 'What was I thinking? I can't possibly go through with it – I might have to talk to people I don't know and you might end up having fun somewhere.' She hadn't moved from her position on the sofa for a full ten minutes after he left, just in case he came back and found her looking like she was up to something.

Which she wasn't.

Not really.

She'd met Dymphna and Karen on the South Bank last night. They had a drink at the Royal Festival Hall, then headed down the river to a pizza restaurant on Gabriel's Wharf. It was a pleasant evening, nothing special, nothing that thousands of other people in the capital weren't doing, too, but for Joy, sitting in a restaurant with her friends on a Friday night, sharing a bottle of Pinot Grigio and not having to check her watch once all evening had felt as close to ecstasy as she'd ever been.

This morning she'd woken up in an empty bed, the day had opened up in front of her free of strictures and routine and she decided that what she wanted to do more than anything was spend the day mooching around London on her own.

London had once been the epicentre of her existence. Wherever she lived, whoever she went out with, wherever she worked, London had been her constant companion. It was solid and dependable and never let her down. Different parts of it fitted different moods. It could make her feel small and anonymous, or brave and conspicuous. It could make her feel young and carefree or old and past it. London had been there, solid in the background, through every chapter of her life for the past ten years. London was her friend.

Before she moved to Esher, she'd been able to maintain her friendship with London, albeit in a somewhat abridged fashion, but since they'd moved to the suburbs London was somewhere she saw only fleetingly through the windows of trains and cars, with barely a chance to wave hello.

She pulled on a pair of her most comfortable shoes, bought a one-day Travelcard and caught the first train to Waterloo.

She walked across Hungerford Bridge, glancing at people as they passed her. They were grim-faced, unimpressed to find themselves walking across the River Thames on a perfect April morning.

You're all so lucky, she wanted to shout, so, so lucky. You can do this whenever you want. This is just normal to you. You don't appreciate it and you should. Being able to walk through the heart of your city on a Saturday morning, to see it spread out in front of you and behind in all its magnificent glory, to have somewhere to go and nobody to stop you going there. Embrace every moment. Savour your freedom.

On the other side of the river she walked through back streets, marvelling at rows of Georgian town houses, at the notion of people actually living here in this secret little triangle nestled between Trafalgar Square, the Strand and the river. She caught a random bus to Knightsbridge, glanced at her watch and relished the feeling of time being on her side for once. It was still morning. She wasn't due to meet Julia and Bella until seven o'clock. She had time to burn.

As she stared out of the window, vignettes presented themselves to her, moments from her own history.

The corner of Jermyn Street and Haymarket where she and Ally had had a stupid, drunken row on her twenty-third birthday.

The Odeon on the Haymarket where she'd been to see *The Rachel Papers* with some bloke whose name she couldn't remember one Valentine's Day.

The first-floor Chinese restaurant next to the flashing lights on Piccadilly where she'd eaten lunch alone when she couldn't get back to work because of a bomb scare.

The church courtyard at St James where she'd sat one incredibly hot summer's day and been chatted up by a homeless guy with no teeth who quoted Wordsworth to her.

The underpass at Hyde Park where she'd been mugged trying to find her way to a game of company softball.

The exact patch of grass near Park Lane where she'd been sitting when Ally had chosen to dump her.

The corner of Knightsbridge and Sloane Street where she'd finally caught a cab at two in the morning after walking all the way from a Christmas party in Islington in a party dress and heels.

Every corner of London meant something to her. Every corner held a memory, however inconsequential or mundane. It was an affront to her that she wasn't free to visit her city whenever she felt the need. It was an injustice greater in some ways than being unable to see her friends and family.

She got off the bus at Sloane Square and wandered down the King's Road until she found herself outside

Chelsea Town Hall. Confetti dotted the steps. Tiny brides-maids in lilac fluttered around behind glass doors. Somewhere beyond them Joy could see a bride.

She stopped outside Habitat and stared for a while. It was unthinkable to her that that had been her, that she'd once been a bride, waiting in the lobby of Chelsea Town Hall in a beautiful white dress about to get married. And no matter how she herself had felt on her own wedding day, no matter how jumbled her emotions, how ambiva-lent her feelings, she felt nothing but joy and excitement for the girl behind those doors. Because she knew without a doubt that the chances of there being two girls in the world stupid enough to get married to someone they weren't in love with at Chelsea Register Office were so remote as to be nonexistent.

She waited for the wedding party to emerge before resuming her travels. The bride was older than her, prob-ably in her mid thirties. The groom was about the same. They'd probably lived together for years, Joy mused, prob-ably had a joint mortgage, a shared car, a long history. They'd waited until they knew all of each other's flaws and foibles, weaknesses and strengths, until they knew without a doubt that there was no one better for them out there. They'd waited until they were grown-ups. They'd done it properly.

Joy watched them smile for their photographer and disappear in a vintage Jaguar, then she wandered slowly down to the World's End, considering her own existence as she walked. It felt bleaker than ever in the light of this beautiful, weightless, freewheeling day. Those mothers with their plastic-cocooned babies on Esher High Street seemed a million miles away from the beautiful girls and boys strolling around Chelsea with nothing to do and Joy felt completely removed from the life she'd found herself living. She didn't feel like a tourist or an out-of-towner; she felt like she was home. And she had no idea how she was supposed to reconcile this feeling with the future that destiny seemed to have in store for her, with George and babies and living at the furthest outposts of life.

She hadn't mentioned her baby revelation to George, and now, as she felt some of the colour returning to her cheeks, she wasn't entirely sure she ever would.

She caught a Number 328 bus on the New Kings Road, with a vague notion of getting off at Ladbroke Grove and having a wander around Portobello Market. The bus filled and emptied as it passed through the back streets of Earl's Court and High Street Kensington. More snapshots from her past flashed through her mind. The day she'd come to Kensington Market with her father's money burning a hole in her handbag and the perverse euphoria she'd felt as she surfaced from the crepuscular rabbit warren of stalls laden down with carrier bags. And a flat she'd been to see in a mansion block off Earl's Court Road where ten Australians were living in three bedrooms, with a bed in the kitchen.

She changed her mind about Portobello Market when the bus got to Notting Hill. The sunshine had brought the tourists flocking here in their thousands, and she wasn't in the mood for crowds. Instead she jumped on the tube and decided to head towards Covent Garden.

She wasn't sure why she decided on Covent Garden. She didn't have enough money to go shopping and it didn't hold any particularly fond memories for her, but the day was dictating its own path so she went with the flow.

Half an hour later she was sitting outside a café in Neal's Yard, reading the paper and just about to bite into a prosciutto and sun-dried tomato ciabatta roll, when she looked up and saw a man walking towards her, smiling uncertainly.

'Joy?' said the man.

'Oh, my God,' said Joy, letting her sandwich fall on to her plate, 'Vince. I don't believe it.'

Forty-Eight

He'd been taking a shortcut between Shorts Gardens and Earlham Street, heading down towards Seven Dials. He hadn't even really been paying any attention to people around him as he walked, engaged as he was in an argument with Jess on his mobile phone. He'd stopped in the middle of Neal's Yard briefly to make a particularly important point, then he'd seen her.

Joy.

His Joy.

Sitting outside a café, turning the pages of a newspaper and about to bite into a sandwich.

He'd known it was her immediately, even before he saw her face. The delicate way her hands handled the unruly broadsheet, the kick of brown hair across her high cheekbones, the narrow feet beneath the table, crossed elegantly at the ankle. He told Jess he'd call her back and folded his phone back into his coat pocket.

As he approached her table his pace quickened. She looked up when he called her name, and it was like that moment all over again – that moment in Hunstanton when he'd first seen her through his bedroom window, sitting on a deck chair, reading a magazine.

She hadn't really changed. Her hair was slightly darker and worn longer. She was wearing jeans, trainers, a fitted corduroy jacket in olive green and a fat woolly scarf in baby pink. She still looked chic, slightly exotic. She still looked out of his league.

'Shit,' he said, 'I never thought I'd see you again.'

'Me neither,' she beamed back at him. 'What are you up to?'

'Oh, just a bit of clothes shopping.' He showed her his carrier bags. 'What about you?'

She shrugged, folded up her newspaper, 'Just mooching around, really.'

'Are you with your . . . husband?'

'No. Not today. He's in Winchester. Doing a creative writing course.'

'Oh,' said Vince, 'right.'

'And your wife?'

'She's not my wife yet,' he laughed.

'Oh. Sorry. I just presumed because you had a kid and everything . . .'

'Kid?'

'Yes,' she blushed slightly, 'I saw you once. A few years ago. Outside Hamleys. You had a little boy . . .'

Vince racked his brain for a second, trying to remember a day when he'd been outside Hamleys with a little boy. 'Oh,' he said, suddenly remembering. 'You mean *Kyle*. He's not my son . . .'

'Oh,' said Joy.

'No, Kyle's my little brother.'

'You've got a little brother?!'

'Yes. And a little sister. Not so little now, though. Nine and six.'

'Oh, my God. So your mum and Chris . . . ?'

'Yeah. They're still together.'

'Wow,' Joy smiled, 'that's so great. I always thought they were one of the best couples *ever*.'

She smiled at him and he smiled back at her. There was a moment's silence.

'Are you in a hurry?' Joy asked eventually. 'I mean, are you on your way somewhere?'

'No,' smiled Vince, 'just more clothes shops.'

'D'you fancy a cup of tea?'

'Yeah,' he said, pulling a chair out and pushing his shopping under the table. 'Yeah, that would be great.'

They called over a waiter, and Vince ordered himself a latte and a piece of chocolate truffle cake.

'So,' he said, 'you're still married, then?'

'Yes,' she grimaced slightly. 'It'll be seven years in December.'

'I saw you,' he said, not sure why he was telling her, but unable to stop himself. 'I saw you getting married.'

'What!'

'Yeah. That bloke, that weird bloke you were living with, with the weird name . . .'

'Bella.'

'That's it. He told me you were getting married at Chelsea Town Hall, so I came along and watched. From over the road.'

'You didn't!'

'Uh-huh. What kind of a sad stalker does that make me?'

'But why?'

He shrugged. 'I don't know. It was something to do with that cat . . .'

'Oh, God – that cat! How spooky was that? Your cat being in my flat . . .'

'Yeah. My flatmate Cass thought it was a sign . . .'

'What sort of sign?'

'Oh, I don't know – a sign that we should be together or something.' He laughed to show how ludicrous he thought this was. 'But that morning, the morning of your wedding, it just looked at me and made this weird noise, and the next thing I knew I was on a tube to Sloane Square.' He wriggled his shoulders, trying to exorcize the memory of his behaviour being influenced by a cat. 'You looked amazing,' he said. 'Really, really amazing.'

Joy blushed a little. 'Thank you.' She ran a finger around the edge of her plate and opened her mouth to say something. 'Can I just ask you a question?'

'Of course.'

'All those years ago, before I married George, when all that business with the cat was going on. My friend Bella told me that you'd been looking for me. And then I saw you outside Hamleys that day and I thought he must have been lying. But he said he was telling the truth. Was he? Were you looking for me?'

'Yes,' he said, exhaling the word and wincing. 'I was. We were. Me and Cass.' He picked up Joy's paper and hid behind it.

Joy batted it out of the way and smiled. 'Really?' She looked embarrassed, but pleased.

'Uh-huh. She was trying to work out why I was such a loser in love and decided that it was because I'd never had closure with you.'

Joy blinked at him.

'Yeah. Now there's a whole 'nother conversation. Hunstanton. Our parents. Your note.'

372

Joy folded her arms and waggled her head. 'You don't need to explain.'

'No,' he said, 'I do. I've been wanting to explain for years. Your note. It rained in the night. I couldn't read it. All I could make out was "I feel so ashamed." I thought you'd dumped me. And then I was talking to Chris about it a few years later and he told me what happened between my mum and your dad, and I'd had no idea. No one told me at the time. I thought you'd really regretted what happened that night, you know, what we did. I thought you'd left because you couldn't face me.'

'Oh, my God,' said Joy, 'no. That night. What happened that night, what we did, it was incredible. The whole thing, the time we spent together. It was ... I was devastated when we had to go. I nearly woke you up to give you the note, to tell you what was happening, but I thought you'd be angry with me.'

'Angry?' said Vince. 'Why would I be angry with *you*?'

'I don't know. I just thought it would be better in a note. I wanted to give you the option of whether or not you wanted to see me again. And when you didn't call, I just thought, fair enough. I just thought, I wouldn't want to be involved with my family either.'

There was a silence then as they both took on board the series of mixed messages and bad fortune that had led them to where they were today.

'So, when your cat found me, when you came to Wilberforce Road, how come you didn't say anything?'

'You were getting married in three weeks' time. I couldn't help but feel that my timing was a little off.'

'But then you came to the town hall. Came all the way to Chelsea. Why didn't you say hello?'

'I don't know,' he said. 'It was your wedding day. Your special day. I didn't want to freak you out.'

She laughed. 'I don't think anything could have freaked me out any more than I already was.'

He threw her a questioning look.

'My wedding day was . . .' – she picked at a frill of prosciutto hanging from her ciabatta – '*strange*. To say the least.'

'Strange in a good way or strange in a bad way?' He moved away to let the waiter put his coffee and cake down.

'Bad, I guess,' she smiled. 'Bad wedding. Bad marriage.'

'No. Really?'

'Uh-huh,' she nodded and smiled again. 'I married in haste. Now I'm repenting at leisure.'

'Oh, shit. Joy, I'm sorry. He looked really nice, your husband – you both looked so happy. I thought . . . I thought you'd got it sorted, you know, found your Mr Right, settled down.'

'And I thought you had, too, when I saw you with your brother. Thought you'd already got a family together. And that woman. That beautiful woman you were with – are you still together?'

'What – *Magda*? Oh God, no. That finished about two weeks later. And it should have finished a lot earlier than that.'

'So, who are you with now, then? Who's the woman you're not married to *yet*?'

'Jess.' He felt awkward, wishing for some reason that

374

he could say he wasn't with anyone, that he was available. 'I'm with Jess.'

'Jess,' Joy nodded.

'That's who I was talking to. On the phone just now. Or *arguing* with, more accurately.' He wasn't sure that Joy needed to know this, but he wanted her to know that things weren't perfect, that things weren't right.

'What were you arguing about?'

'Oh, God – just . . . *stuff*. Jess is – she's *difficult*.'

'Is she nice?'

Vince was about to nod, but then he stopped. 'She can be,' he said. 'She can be really nice.'

'Would I like her?'

'Probably not. Girls don't tend to like her very much. She's not a girls' girl. She doesn't do clothes or gossip or confidences. She can be blunt, you know – thoughtless. And she's quite . . . *self-centred*.'

Joy sent him a look that he translated to mean, so tell me why you love her if she's so awful.

'But she's cool,' he shrugged. 'She's loyal to her friends. Loving. And really great with kids . . .'

'So you're going to marry her, then?'

Vince laughed. 'I don't know.' He scratched the back of his neck. 'Maybe. We're trying for a baby right now, so, probably, you know, eventually . . .'

'Wow,' said Joy, nodding, 'so it's really serious?'

'Yeah. I guess so.'

'*So* – what were you arguing about?' she asked him with a twinkle in her eye.

He laughed. 'Christ. I don't know. We're going through a bit of a tough time right now. Her friend came back

375

from the States a few months ago and, ever since he's been here, she's changed. She was teetotal before, didn't take drugs, did yoga, ate healthy food, early nights, all that. And all of a sudden she's turned into this party animal. And it's not this friend's fault. He's a really good bloke. But it just seems to have been a catalyst for her to go back to her old ways. And she was supposed to be meeting me in town this afternoon, but now she's going to see her new friend *Franco*. I don't know, she says he's gay, but I'm not so sure. The thing with Jess is that she does whatever *she* wants to do. If it happens to fit in with your plans, then that's fine. If not, then . . .' He shrugged his shoulders.

'And how will all this partying fit in with being a mother?'

'Exactly,' he said smoothing back his hair, 'exactly. I don't know. It worries me. The whole thing worries me. I just think . . .' He was about to say that maybe they were making a mistake, that maybe they should take time to get know one another better before they headed towards parenthood, but he stopped himself. He wasn't ready to take that turning off the path. Not yet. 'Oh, I don't know.' He smiled and dug his fork into his cake. 'It'll all work out in the end, won't it. I'm sure once she's pregnant . . . What about you? What's the deal with your "bad marriage"?'

She smiled wryly. 'Christ,' she said, 'you got all day?'

'Not all day,' he said, 'but I've got at least . . .' He looked at his watch. 'Oooh – three hours.'

And so she told him a heart-breaking story, a story of a young woman looking for stability and security after the breakdown of her parents' marriage and finding it with a man who gave it to her with one hand before snatching it back with the other. A man who mistook marriage for possession. A man who had no idea how to give or receive love. A man who wanted Joy to wither away and crumble into powder so that no one else would want her, not even him.

She smiled stoically throughout the telling of her tale, but there was a weakness around her bottom lip that told of a deep-seated misery and a sense of bitter resignation.

'I even went to Relate once,' she said. 'About a year after we got married. It was all just so awful, we were arguing all the time – this was before I'd submitted entirely to his will and I was still maintaining this pretence of the fabulous fairy-tale wedding to all and sundry. I just really needed to talk to someone, I think, tell someone what was happening to me. And I went and sat in this room in Portland Place, just behind the BBC, and this lovely woman with chopsticks in her hair asked me all these questions about my childhood and George's childhood. And as I was talking to her I started feeling really sorry for George, thinking of this poor damaged little boy who had no one in his life but me, no one to care about him, no one to look after him, and I suddenly couldn't say anything bad about him. It was so weird.

'She said, "you're very defensive of him, aren't you?" And I said, "Yes. I am." She told me to try to talk to him, get him to come along to the next session. But there was no way I could ever have done that. If George had known that I'd been talking about his childhood, *our marriage*, to a complete stranger he'd have been devastated. So that was it. I never went back. I was on my own.'

'And you've never told anyone how unhappy you are?'

She shook her head.

'Not even your mum?'

She shook her head again. 'I wrote a letter once,' she said, 'to my best friend in the States, Maxine. She hadn't been at the wedding and she'd never even met George. She was so distant from it all, it felt safe telling her. It was ten pages long that letter. Maxine said she burst into tears while she was reading it, then she gave it to her friend to read and she burst into tears, too! And she'd never even met me!'

'But surely your friends, your family – they must know you're not happy.'

'Yes,' she said, 'they know. It's just not spoken about, that's all. It's as if I don't want to let everyone down. My mother who stood by my side so proudly on my wedding day, who made George so welcome into our family. My friends who wanted so much to believe in it, the whole love story thing . . .'

'And do you? Love him?'

She looked up at him and smiled, an embarrassed smile. 'No,' she said softly, 'not really. I never did.'

'Not even when you married him?'

'No – not even when I married him.'

'So *why*? Why did you marry him?'

'That,' she said, 'is the hardest question I will ever have to answer. Because I really and truly don't know.'

He stared at her for a moment in shock. The idea of walking into a register office and making those vows, saying those words in front of your family, in front of your friends, with someone you didn't love was completely horrific to him. He was appalled. 'You have to leave. You know that, don't you?'

She nodded.

'More than six years, Joy — more than six years of your life. Your twenties. Gone,' he clicked his fingers. 'Just like that. Shit.'

'I know. I know. It's a big old mess. But I made it and I've got to clean it up.'

'Look. Whatever happens, we'll have to keep in touch. I need to know what happens to you. I need to know you're all right.'

'Definitely,' she said. 'But you can't call me.'

'Why not?'

'Because we haven't got a phone.'

'What!'

'Yes. I know.' She pursed her lips. 'George thinks that they're an infringement of his privacy. He hates them. Therefore we don't have one. And I'm not allowed personal calls at work.'

'Jesus.' Vince shook his head in numb disbelief. 'Well, then, you'll have to call me. Look,' he said, scribbling his mobile number on to a napkin, 'promise me you'll stay in touch.'

'Yes,' she said, taking the napkin and staring at it, 'but what about your girlfriend. Won't she mind?'

'Oh, God, no — not Jess. She's thinks I'm a freak because I haven't stayed in touch with any of my exes. She thinks it's a character flaw.'

'So,' she said, folding the napkin into her handbag. 'Do you think I'm pathetic?'

379

'Well, I can't pretend to understand. I certainly don't think you're pathetic. But if you phone me in a month's time and tell me that you're still married to someone who keeps you imprisoned in your own home, who you don't even *love*, then, yes, I might start thinking you're a bit on the flaky side.'

She laughed and covered her face with her hands. 'This is such great timing,' she said, 'bumping into you today. I've just been walking around London with all these thoughts in my head. I haven't been able to make sense of anything. But really, it's simple, isn't it? I just leave.'

'Yes,' Vince nodded enthusiastically.

'Because he's just a man. And he's not going to die and he's not going to explode.'

'He might even be glad.'

'Yes. He might even be glad. And there's nothing to be scared of.'

'Nothing at all.'

'And I can come back to London.'

'Indeed.'

'And see my friends.'

'Absolutely.'

'And do whatever I want whenever I want.'

'You can.'

'Fuck.'

'Exactly.'

And then they both laughed, a long, loud release of nervous energy that faded gently into a companionable silence.

They chatted for another hour. They chatted about his

brother and sister, and laughed about his job as a driving instructor. They chatted about Joy's mother and father, and laughed about her job in a photo lab. They talked about food and films and family and feelings. They talked, basically, about everything they might have spent the past ten or so years talking about if it hadn't rained that night in Hunstanton, if Joy hadn't written her note in ink, if Alan hadn't put his hands up Kirsty's top and down her shorts, and changed the paths of their lives so dramatically and irrevocably.

At five o'clock Vince's phone vibrated in his coat pocket and he pulled it out just as it burst into a tinny rendition of the Bond theme. He smiled apologetically at Joy and flinched slightly when he saw Jess's name flash up on the display. He was tempted not to answer it. Big, bold Jess with her shiny white teeth and visible G-strings, her mysterious male friends and shady past, suddenly seemed a million miles away from where he'd been this afternoon with Joy. Jess was sitting in a flat somewhere with a man called Franco who may or may not be gay, but who Vince was certainly destined never to meet. She was probably taking drugs with him or possibly having sex with him – nothing about Jess could really surprise him these days – but whatever she was doing it had nothing whatsoever to do with him.

The phone rang on, getting louder and louder. People turned to see who was failing to answer the phone with the incredibly annoying ring tone.

Vince pressed accept.

'Hello, Angel boy. What you doing?'

'Having a coffee in Neal's Yard.' He was tempted to

add, 'with a stunningly beautiful ex-girlfriend whom I used to be madly in love with', but decided that he was too old for game playing at such an infantile level.

'Cool,' she said. 'How soon can you get home?'

He shrugged and glanced at his watch. 'In an hour?'

'I'll see you at mine, then,' she said, 'I've got something to tell you.'

'What?' he said, a feeling of dread trailing down his spine.

'I'll tell you when you get here. And don't be late.' And then she hung up on him.

He snapped his phone shut and glanced at Joy. 'I'm going to have to go,' he said.

Joy shrugged. 'That's OK.'

'I'm sorry. I was really enjoying our chat.'

'Don't worry about it.'

'Jess says she's got something to tell me.'

'Ooh,' she said. 'Sounds mysterious.'

'Hmmm.' Vince pulled his wallet out of his pocket and peeled out a £10 note. 'It does, doesn't it.'

This was it, he mused, she was going to dump him. She was going to say that she and Franco were having an affair, or that she'd realized she was still in love with Jon, or that she'd simply decided that going out with a balding driving instructor had lost its appeal. His relationship was about to end. And there was a small part of him, buried deep down inside, that felt almost relieved, as if he was being let off the hook. He'd fallen in love with one Jess, but was currently conducting a relationship with a completely different Jess – and even though he was still stupidly in love with her, he wasn't sure he particularly liked her any more.

'Well,' he said, regarding Joy fondly, 'you've got my number now. Don't let it get caught in the rain.'

Joy laughed. 'I won't,' she said.

'And promise me you'll call, the minute you've decided what to do.'

'I promise. I need to call anyway – find out what Jess's big announcement is. Maybe she's pregnant.' She shoved her hands into the pockets of her jeans and grinned at him.

'No,' he said, 'unlikely. We missed her fertile period last month – she had the flu.'

'Ah, well,' she said, 'maybe she's going to ask you to marry her.' She laughed, a little bit too loud. 'I'm so glad this happened,' she said. 'The timing, it couldn't have been better. It feels almost . . .'

'Predestined?'

'Yes,' she said, 'as if there are forces at work. Maybe that cat was trying to tell us something, after all.'

Vince grinned back at her. 'Maybe,' he said.

And then they leaned towards each to say goodbye, and it suddenly felt inadequate to close such an intimate episode with a perfunctory peck on the cheek, so he opened up his arms for a hug, and the minute she stepped into his embrace a hundred memories stampeded through his head. He remembered the feel of her and the smell of her and the taste of her. He remembered Cameo and candy floss and silky calves and sand dunes. He remembered picture postcards and sweaty car seats and warm Coca-Cola. He remembered feeling whole and complete for the first time in his life. He remembered feeling as if he belonged somewhere, as if he fitted. He remembered that he'd once had a soul mate.

He stared at the crown of Joy's head as he hugged her and, even though decorum was telling him to let go of her, his heart wouldn't let him. And besides – she was holding him tight, too.

They finally separated after a few moments and laughed nervously.

'Well,' he said, feeling suddenly awkward. 'Lovely to see you. Just amazing.'

'You, too,' said Joy. 'I'll call you. Definitely.'

'Good,' he smiled, and picked up his carrier bags. 'I look forward to it. A lot.'

And then he went, turning once at the entrance to Neal's Yard, just to take one last look at her, just to see if she was looking at him, too.

She was.

Forty-Nine

'Look!' said Jess, the second Vince walked through the door that afternoon. 'Two lines! I'm pregnant!'

Vince had imagined this moment so many times in the months leading up to it, imagined how complete and overjoyed he would feel when Jess uttered those magic words. The reality, unfortunately, hadn't quite lived up to his expectations.

For a start, Jon was in the room when she made her announcement.

'Oh, my God.' Vince stood rooted to the spot, holding the white stick, staring in awe at the first visible, outward manifestation of the child Jess was carrying.

'Oh, Jesus! Jess! That's amazing!' Jon leaped to his feet and bundled himself at Jess, lassoing her in an effusive embrace. 'Vince! Mate!' He held his arms out to Vince, who stepped numbly into them and found himself suddenly crushed between Jess and Jon like an overgrown child. 'You guys! You did it! That's the best! The best thing ever!' And then he started crying. Crying properly, like a woman.

Vince stared at him in disbelief. This big, hard-nut Turkey Street boy, this cosmopolitan sophisticate, this *man*, was sobbing his heart out. And it wasn't even his baby. And that was when Vince started to think about the logistics of the scenario.

'Wow,' he said, 'so that's positive, is it?' He handed the plastic wand back to Jess.

'Oh, yes,' she said, disentangling herself from Jon's second embrace. 'These tests are pretty much 100 per cent reliable these days. It's official. I'm up the duff!' Her face shone with excitement and pride, but Vince felt strangely numb.

'How did you know?' he said. 'I mean, what made you decide to take a test?'

'It was Frank's idea,' she said happily. 'I said I was feeling a bit sick when I woke up this morning, and he said I looked different – persuaded me to go to the chemist. Get a test kit. I peed on the stick and he was right!'

'What – you did the test with *Frank*?'

'Uh-huh.'

'So Frank was the first person to know?'

'Yes. He was *so* excited. You should have seen his face. Me finding out I was pregnant right there in his flat. I said he'll have to be the godfather. Along with you, too, of course,' she said as she grabbed Jon's hand and beamed at him.

'Christ. Jess. I can't believe you did the test with *Frank*. With a stranger. I mean – didn't you think you should have waited? Done it with me?'

Jess bit her bottom lip. 'God. Yes. I suppose so. I didn't think. But isn't it great? Aren't you pleased?'

'Of course I'm pleased. I'm just a little bit surprised. I thought we'd missed our chance this month – you know – when you had the flu.'

'Oh, yes, but that fertile window – it's only a guideline. I mean, Christ, you can get pregnant when you've got your period. And besides, there's something beautiful about it. The fact that we weren't trying and it happened anyway – like this baby really wanted to be. Like it made my body fertile just so that it could exist.' She beamed and cupped her belly with her hand.

'Oh, God,' said Vince, as another discomfiting thought occurred to him. 'What about the drugs?'

'What drugs?'

'You know. All the coke you've been doing lately.'

'*All* the coke? You mean the two lines I had last weekend and the dab I had last night?'

'Yes.'

'Oh, come on, Vince. That's hardly enough for us to be worrying about. It's only a little blob of cells . . .'

'Yes, but don't you think you should make sure? Ask the doctor?'

'Oh, my God – I've known my doctor since I was five years old. I am *so* not telling him I've been taking drugs.'

'Well, then, maybe you could phone a clinic – see someone impartial.'

'Jesus, Vince – this is the happiest moment of my life. This is what we've both wanted since the minute we set eyes on each other and all you've done since you walked through the door is whinge. Aren't you happy? Have you changed your mind?'

'*No.* No. Of course I haven't changed my mind. This just isn't how I thought it would be. I thought we'd do the test together, *alone.* I thought it would be intimate and romantic. I thought it would be this . . . this *great* moment. And instead you've done your test with some

387

bloke you've known for less than a month, whom I've never even met and who may or may not be gay –'

'I can assure you that Frank is gay –'

'Whatever. And then you tell me that I'm about to be a father in front of Jon. No offence, Jon, but I'm sure you understand.'

'Of course. Of course.' Jon slapped his hand to his forehead. 'Christ. What an insensitive twat. I'm really sorry.' He grabbed his jacket and made for the door.

'No,' said Jess, folding her arms across her chest. 'Jon. Don't go. Vince is being ridiculous.'

'No. Really,' he said, 'I'm going. Vince is right. I shouldn't be here.' He smiled apologetically at Vince and left the flat.

'Good grief,' snapped Jess, turning to face Vince as the door closed behind Jon. 'I had no idea you could be so *childish*.'

'Childish! Me! Are you kidding. I'm not the one who's been out clubbing every weekend and taking drugs and drinking while we've been trying for a baby.'

'Oh, for God's sake. I've been out four times in the past month. I only got drunk once. And as for drugs, I really don't think a couple of lines and a few dabs constitutes a problem.'

'Well, it does to me.'

'Well, then, we've obviously got very different outlooks on life. I'm two weeks' pregnant, Vince. All that's in there is a few cells that are not going to be harmed by a couple of drinks and a sniff of coke. If that really were the case then 50 per cent of the kids in the world would have something wrong with them. Obviously now I know I'm pregnant, I'll stop drinking immediately. But it was taking so long to get pregnant and I just really needed to let my hair down. I've got it out of my system now, and from hereon in my body is a temple. But I am not going to let you make me feel guilty about a couple of nights out.'

'But it's not just that, is it?' said Vince collapsing on to the sofa. 'It's not just that.'

'Then what is it?'

'It's everything. It's you. It's us. It's . . .'

'Christ, Vince. What are you saying?'

'I don't know what I'm saying.'

'Are you getting cold feet?'

'No. Of course not. It's just . . . I don't know. You and I. We're so different. So completely different. How are we going to raise a child together?'

'You are! I don't believe it! You're getting cold feet!'

'I am not. I'm just thinking about things from a different perspective. Ever since Jon arrived I've seen another side of you and, to be honest, it's scared me.'

'*Scared* you?'

'Yes. I don't feel as if I know you any more. In fact, I don't feel as if I've *ever* known you.'

'Of course you know me.'

'No. I don't. I knew a girl who liked a quiet life, who liked early nights and lie-ins. A girl who respected her body, possibly a little too much, but that was the girl I knew.'

'But I told you – I told you the sort of person I used to be, the sort of person I *am*. I was honest from the outset.'

'Yes, I know you were. But I thought that part of your life was over . . .'

'Yes. And so did I. But seeing Jon. It just reminded me of the good times, you know. Being young and reckless. I suppose I just wanted a bit of a last fling, a bit of fun, before settling down.'

Vince nodded tersely. She was starting to make sense, but there was still a part of him that couldn't quite accept that everything was going to be all right, just because Jess was 'over' her party phase. There was still so much to consider. The stale old boyfriends hanging around in her life like unwanted party guests. Her ability to compartmentalize her life with an almost pathological exactitude. Her inability to empathize, to put herself in other people's shoes. Their informal living arrangement. And the fact that after nearly a year together, she'd never even told him that she loved him ...

And now there was this. Two pink lines. A baby.

It was what he'd always wanted, but it couldn't have come at a worse time.

He looked at Jess. She was sitting perched on the edge of the sofa, her hands clasped together between her knees, staring at him imploringly. She was scared. Fearless, cocky Jess was scared. She'd expected Vince to come home this afternoon and whoop with delight when she told him her news. She'd expected champagne and celebrations. She hadn't expected doubt and confusion. She lived so firmly in the World According to Jess that she was unable to deal with the imposition of other people's reality. She was thrown. She was terrified.

'It's going to be all right, isn't it?' she said softly. 'We're going to do this together, aren't we?'

Vince took a deep breath and took Jess's hands in his

own. 'Yes,' he said, pulling her in towards him, 'it's going to be fine.'

Jess brightened as she felt Vince softening. 'So can you get excited now, please.'

Vince turned and smiled at her. 'Oh,' he said, cupping her belly with the flat of his hand, 'all right, then.'

Fifty

Joy studied the papers, then picked up a black Biro and started writing.

1) On the second day of our honeymoon the respondent stopped talking to me. He didn't talk to me again until the fourth day of our honeymoon at which point he explained that he'd been angry with me because some local men had been looking at me outside a temple. He claimed it was my fault because I'd been wearing shorts, although our tour guide had assured me that the shorts would be perfectly acceptable attire for visiting a Thai temple. The respondent then suggested that my behaviour was so unacceptable that we should probably consider getting a divorce.

She sighed and continued.

2) Three years after our marriage the respondent and I moved house. The respondent oversaw the move. He asked me what I would like to be done with some personal effects in a cupboard in the spare bedroom – diaries, old photographs, schoolbooks etc. I said that some of it could be thrown away, but that I wanted to keep the photo albums, diaries etc. I was very clear about exactly what I wanted to be kept. When I arrived home that night, he told me that he'd disposed of everything in the cupboard except one

photo album. He maintained that he had followed my instructions and refused to apologize, even though he could see how devastated I was by the loss of so many elements of my personal history.

This was harder than she'd expected. She had to give five examples of George's unreasonable behaviour, but there were just so many countless examples that she didn't know where to start. George had said she could claim infidelity as a basis for her divorce action, but she didn't want to lie. She wanted to state for the record, in black and white, for evermore, the truth about their marriage. She took a deep breath and continued.

3) In January of this year, two friends of mine arrived unexpectedly at our house at around nine o'clock. The respondent initially refused to open the door to them, but relented once he realized that they knew we were in. He then refused to talk to them, and when I attempted to offer my guests wine told them that we didn't have any even though there was a bottle open in the kitchen. My guests left an hour later after which the respondent didn't talk to me for over twenty-four hours.

4) In 1995 I was invited by my mother to join her for a weekend at a health farm. She was in need of some pampering and some quality time with her daughter. When I broached the subject with the respondent he claimed to have made plans for the same weekend that I planned to spend with my mother, but when I asked him what his plans were he refused to elaborate. On the morning of my trip the

respondent claimed he felt unwell and suggested that I should cancel my trip. There was no outward manifestation of his illness, so I went ahead with my plan for a weekend with my mother. The respondent claimed that my neglect was grounds for divorce, then refused to talk to me for nearly a week.

5) In 1996, during a casual conversation about sex, the respondent claimed that I was 'not particularly good in bed'. I asked him to explain what he meant by this and he went on, quite enthusiastically, to describe me as unspontaneous, unpassionate and not very sexy. He failed to understand how hurtful I found this and claimed I was overreacting when I began to cry.

She read back through what she'd written and felt a wave of dissatisfaction engulf her. These titbits, these tiny crumbs of anecdotes, did nothing to describe the full tragedy of the past six and a half years of her life. They didn't explain how two people had come together and imploded into a mulch of insecurity and resentment. They didn't depict the devastation on George's face after Bella told him that Joy thought he was ugly or the overwhelming sense of grief she experienced when she learned that ten years' worth of her diaries were sitting on top of a rubbish tip somewhere in Blackheath.

The court wanted examples of George's unreasonable behaviour. They weren't interested in how that unreasonable behaviour had made her feel. As she read back through the form she had a sudden fear that maybe the faceless, nameless people whose job it was to read these paper representations of such intimate moments between people they'd never met might decide that George's behaviour hadn't been unreasonable at all. Maybe they would read her form and think that she was a silly girl who was overreacting to a bit of harmless sulking and childishness.

She passed the form to her mother who was sitting on the sofa opposite her, watching *Coronation Street*.

'What do you think?' she said, as her mother pulled on her reading glasses.

Barbara turned to her with tears in her eyes as she read. 'Did he really say that to you?' she said. 'About not being sexy?'

Joy nodded.

'Oh, Joy,' she shook her head sadly, 'how any man could look at you, my beautiful girl, and tell you that you're not sexy. I just can't bear to think about it . . .'

'But do you think it's OK? Good enough for the courts. Good enough for a divorce? I mean, does it sound unreasonable enough to you?'

'Oh, yes,' said Barbara, nodding enthusiastically, 'it's unreasonable. You'll get your divorce. Don't you worry.'

'Can you believe it?' she said. 'Can you believe that your daughter's getting divorced?'

Barbara chuckled. 'No,' she said, 'I've only just got used to the fact that *I'm* divorced. What a disastrous pair we are, eh?'

Joy smiled and took the forms back from her mother. This was it, she mused, she was on her way back to shore. George was in Esher and she was in Colchester. All her possessions were here. She'd changed her name back to

Downer. She'd given in her notice at the photo lab. She was filling in her divorce papers. She was nearly there. All she needed to do now was move back to London, get a job, get her life back and she'd be home and dry.

Fifty-One

Two weeks after Jess's big announcement, Vince saw a documentary on Channel 4.

It was about the fact that one in eight babies was conceived by a man other than the man who thought he was the father. Apparently, women were hormonally programmed to play away from home while they were ovulating. It was nature's way of making sure that their children were born out of as large a genetic pond as possible. The documentary makers interviewed a man somewhere in the Midwest of America who had five sons. After one of them was struck down with a mysterious genetic condition it became necessary to test the DNA of all five of the boys, upon which it was discovered that of the five boys, only one of them had been sired by their 'father' and that the remaining four had been sired by four different men – including the 'father's' brother.

The men in this documentary haunted Vince for days after he watched it, as did the thought of rampant, ovulating women, scouring the streets for potential ingredients to throw into their genetic soups. Studies had shown that not only did ovulating women feel more predisposed towards sex with men other than their partner, but also that they favoured men with a typically 'masculine' appearance – square jaws, triangular torsos and strong, white teeth. Men, Vince had concluded bitterly, not unlike Jon Gavin.

There was nothing about Jess's general aura or mood to suggest guilt or doubt about the paternity of the child she was carrying, but then, as Vince now knew only too well, she was very gifted in the art of turning a blind eye to anything that didn't quite suit her. Equally, Jon seemed to be very buoyant and light-hearted around the subject of Jess's pregnancy. Maybe it wasn't his. Maybe Jess had found some other chisel-jawed hunk on the streets of Enfield to impregnate her while simultaneously battling the flu and rejecting Vince's advances.

And maybe, of course, Vince was being a paranoid idiot and the baby Jess was carrying was his. But until it arrived, until he finally set eyes on the child, he would just have to live with the painful little seed of doubt growing fat and swollen in his heart.

Fifty-Two

Joy finally called Vince three weeks and six days after their meeting in Neal's Yard.

It wasn't that he'd been counting the days or anything, just that once Jess told him that she was pregnant, time suddenly came and went in strongly defined parcels of weeks. Jess was two weeks' pregnant when Vince met Joy and almost six weeks' pregnant by the time Joy called on Friday afternoon. Therefore it had been three weeks and six days since he'd given her his number.

He'd barcly thought about her in that time.

The shock of discovering that he was nine months (or forty weeks) away from becoming a father had sort of obliterated his previous existence. Anything he'd said, done or thought in the weeks leading up to Jess's big announcement disintegrated into white noise the minute Jess showed him the two pink lines on a white plastic stick.

He'd just dropped a student at the testing centre when she called, and was about to tuck into a cheese-and-ham toastie at a caff around the corner.

'Vince. It's Joy.'

His heart literally skipped a beat, and he let his toastie fall to the plate. 'Wow. Joy. You called.'

'Well, I said I would, didn't I? Sorry it's taken so long, though. I've had a lot on.'

'No. No. Don't worry. I have, too. God. How are you?'

'I'm good. I'm great. Really great.'

'And did you . . . are you still with your husband?'

'Nope.'

'Seriously?!'

'Yup. I left him the day after we met.'

'No!'

'Yes. I waited till he got back from his creative writing course the next day and told him I was going.'

'Oh, my God. What did he say?'

'He was cool, actually. I'd really psyched myself up for it. It was incredible, as if I was possessed by some kind of demon spirit. As if after all those years of being so submissive, so scared of him and his moods, I was suddenly somebody else, someone strong and fearless. There was nothing and no one that could have stopped me leaving him. I was so impatient for him to get home, I was literally pacing back and forth. I just wanted to do it. To say it.'

'So what did you say? How did you tell him?'

'I said, "George, I'm leaving you." Just like that. And it was weird because he didn't look at all surprised. He tried persuading me to stay for a few minutes, but it was a bit half-hearted. And he asked me if there was anyone else. But after that we just talked. We talked for five hours and it was great. It was as if he'd been expecting it, as if he was relieved. I think he felt the same as me. I think he thought when I came back last month, that things could change, that he could be different, that I could be different, that we could still live up to this big romantic ideal he had in his head. But then he realized that it was impossible, that we'd gone too far to ever get back to where we were – or, at least, where he *thought* we were. It was all really, really civilized.'

'Wow. Joy. That's great. I'm so pleased for you. You must feel extraordinary.'

'I do. I feel amazing. To be out of that situation. To know that I never have to go back. To know that he's happy, that I haven't ruined his life. I just sent off my divorce papers. And I've told him to keep the house and the furniture and everything. I really don't want anything material. I just want a clean break. I just want my freedom.'

'Well, you deserve it. Totally. I'm really pleased for you.'

'And I just wanted to thank you. That day, when we met. I think I was at my lowest ebb ever. I'd even thought about getting pregnant, having a baby, just to give it all some sense of purpose. It felt as if ... I don't know ... ever since I met George I've had this weird feeling, as if I was veering off course, taking the wrong path. In my head I felt like a ship that was out of control, in the middle of the ocean, no land in sight, but always with the hope that I'd find my way back to dry land eventually. But just recently, before that day we met, it was like the ship had capsized ... and I was drowning. And then you turned up in Neal's Yard and all of sudden I was rushing up through the water, I could see the light above, I could breathe again. Does that sound stupid?'

'No. Not at all.'

'You rescued me. Do you see? You pulled me out of the water and plonked me on a life raft.'

'Like that bloke at the end of *Titanic*?' he laughed.

She laughed, too. 'Yes. Exactly. Like that bloke at the end of *Titanic*.'

'Well, I'm glad to have been of assistance.'

'You really were in the right place at the right time. Although, if you'd marched into Chelsea Town Hall on the 24th of December 1993, bundled me into a cab and taken me home then, you would have been a real hero!'

'Oh, God,' he said, 'I feel awful.'

'Oh, don't feel bad. I was only joking. I had plenty of opportunities to bail out. I just chose not to take them. I wanted somebody else to make the leap for me. You know, sometimes I used to sit in George's car, outside the off-licence, or outside the video shop, and wish that someone would kidnap me, wish that some big brute of a man would leap into the driver's seat and take me away somewhere. Anywhere. Isn't that tragic?' She laughed.

'That's one of the saddest things I've ever heard,' said Vince.

'I know. It's pathetic, isn't it.'

Vince smiled. 'So, where are you staying?'

'Back at my mum's. Which isn't so great.'

'Yeah – I moved home for a while when I came back to Enfield. It's weird, isn't it? It feels like such a step backwards . . .'

'Yeah. Exactly. And my mum's doing her best to make it feel all right, but it doesn't make any difference. I just want to get myself a place as soon as possible. Get my life back.'

There was a brief silence, during which Vince contemplated suggesting to Joy that she come to stay in his flat, the one he shared with Clive. He was only there a couple of nights a week and it wasn't anything special, but it was better than living in Colchester with her mum.

But then he thought of his own circumstances, of Jess, the baby, of everything that was about to happen to him in the coming months, and he decided against it. Joy took the continuing silence as a sign that Vince was tiring of the conversational theme and broke it.

'Anyway,' she said. 'That's *more* than enough about me. How about you? What was Jess's big announcement?'

'Aah, yes,' he said, dropping a sugar cube into his tea. 'The announcement. You were right.'

'What – she's pregnant?'

'Uh-huh.'

'Oh, Vince! That's fantastic! That really is brilliant news!'

'Yes.' He stirred the cube idly around his cup, watching it shrink away to nothing. 'It's amazing, isn't it?'

'You must be so excited. And so terrified, too.'

He smiled wryly. 'A fair amount of the former and shitloads of the latter.'

She laughed. 'So have you sorted out your problems, you know, with Jess's partying and staying out and everything?'

'Yeah, kind of. I mean obviously now she's pregnant she's not exactly going to be clubbing and drinking anyway. She's feeling pretty ropey, so it's not really an issue at the moment. God knows how it's going to work out for us in the long term, but right now it's good. It's exciting. It's an adventure . . .'

Joy made a strange noise, halfway between a snort and laugh.

'What?'

'Sorry. Nothing. It's just, George's best man, Wilkie.

Bless him – he was so flummoxed and so bewildered by the whole thing, really didn't have a clue what was going on. And that was what he said in his speech. He said, "If nothing else, it'll be an adventure."' And boy, was he right.'

'Well, yeah, it's all a learning curve, I guess . . .'

'But you love her, don't you? You do love Jess?'

He nodded. 'Yeah,' he said. 'I do.'

'And she loves you?'

'Yeah. Well, I think so. I mean, she's not actually said it, but she shows it. She's loving, you know.'

'Well, then – that's all that matters. If you love each other, whatever happens you can deal with it, you can work it out. Because if there's one thing I've learned, it's that it's really not much fun having an adventure with someone you're not in love with.'

'Yeah,' Vince smiled. 'I can see that.' He looked up at someone hovering in his peripheral vision. It was Terry, another BSM instructor. He was looking at Vince expectantly, a mug of tea in one hand, his paperwork in the other. Vince patted the seat next to him and Terry sat down.

'And whatever happens between you and Jess,' Joy continued, 'whether you stay together or split up, if you love each other there'll always be that strong foundation there for your child.'

'Yeah,' said Vince, 'you're right.' He was feeling self-conscious now, with Terry sitting next to him bristling with his desire to strike up conversation.

'And it's funny,' Joy went on, 'how people always say that marriage is the greatest commitment you can make to another person, the biggest decision you'll ever make in your life. And maybe once upon a time it was. And obviously, I stayed with George a lot longer than I would have if I hadn't married him, but, once I'd decided it was over, all I had to do was pop into WH Smiths, pick up a DIY divorce kit, fill it in and I never, ever have to see George again as long as I live. But babies – they're the real commitment, aren't they? The real glue that keeps people together. Without babies it's all just paperwork . . .'

'Yes,' said Vince, 'indeed. Look. Joy. I'm really sorry, but I'm going to have to go.'

'Oh, right.'

'Someone needs to talk to me.'

'No, that's fine. I've chewed your ear off for longer than I intended to anyway. It's just that I promised I'd call and I never break promises – oh, except ones I make in register offices, that is.'

Vince laughed. 'I'm glad you called. Really glad. A lot's happened to both of us since that day in Neal's Yard.'

'A lot's happened to us since *Hunstanton.*'

'It certainly has, it certainly has. Look, let's stay in touch this time, eh?'

'Definitely. I've got your number. And now you've got mine – it'll be on your phone.'

'Yeah. Of course. I'll save it. And I'll be in touch. Maybe we could get together one night, for a drink?'

'I'd love that,' said Joy. 'I really would.'

'Excellent. Well then, I'll call you or you call me, and we'll arrange something. Definitely.'

'Cool. I look forward to it.'

'Me, too. And, look – well done for leaving. You're very brave.'

'And congratulations to you. And Jess. You're very brave, too!'

They said goodbye and Vince slipped his phone back into his shirt pocket and turned to Terry. 'Old friend,' he said, by way of explanation.

Terry nodded, clearly entirely uninterested.

Vince picked up his somewhat limp toastie and ate it unenthusiastically. The cheese inside had turned cold and rubbery, and he didn't feel particularly hungry any more.

He listened to Terry banging on about his new conservatory and thought about Joy, free, unencumbered and ready to grasp her new life firmly with both hands. It was as if she'd been reborn, as if she was getting a second stab at life. And as he thought about her he felt a sudden sense of loss that he wasn't able to join her on her journey. He wanted to help her find a flat, help her find a job, celebrate every moment of her new-found freedom with her.

Because, even though he adored Jess, even though he was as proud as hell of his impending state of fatherhood and even though this was everything he'd always wanted, there was still a small but powerful part of him that felt overwhelmingly like he was a passenger on the wrong bus, heading towards the wrong part of town.

And if he was to follow Jon's bus analogy to its logical conclusion, then he couldn't help feeling that the day he'd bumped into Joy, the day Jess had told him she was pregnant, he'd actually been standing on the platform of the bus, ready to get off. And maybe if Jess hadn't told him she was pregnant he'd have somehow ended up on the same bus as Joy. Because every instinct in his body was telling him that that was exactly where he was supposed to be.

He stared at his phone as Terry talked. Joy's number was on there. He could call her tonight. Make plans to see her. Place himself firmly back in her life. But he knew that he wouldn't. Because Joy wasn't just an 'old friend' – she was his first love, his soul mate and someone he still had frighteningly strong feelings for.

He'd leave it up to her. If she called, then he'd see her. If she didn't, then he'd take it as a sign. Not that he believed in signs, but sometimes leaving things to fate was the simply the easiest option.

Vince didn't save Joy's number on his phone, and Joy didn't call him.

Al & Emma's Kitchen, 1.50 a.m.

'You're kidding!' exclaimed Natalie. 'After all that. Bloody psychic cats and predestined meetings and lost ships and wrong buses and God knows what else, you just lost touch?'

'Yup.'

'But that's terrible,' said Emma. 'I mean, you two were so obviously destined to be together.'

'Do you think?'

'Er – *duh* – what do you think? I know you don't believe in destiny and, actually, I don't either particularly. But sometimes you've just got to think that God's trying to tell you something.'

Vince smiled and topped up his wine glass. All the men had left the table one by one as Vince's story had unfolded. He could hear them now in the living room, chatting loudly about Balamory and colic. Having children had made women out of all of them.

The girls remained, however, enraptured by this story of missed chances, crossed wires and lost loves.

'But you're single now, Vince. What if she was, too? What would you do?'

'God, I don't know. Go out for a drink, I suppose. Get to know each other again. See what happened. But that's not going to happen, is it, because I didn't keep her number. I've got no way of contacting her.'

'God, you *anus*,' said Natalie, slapping her hands against the tabletop with frustration. 'God keeps throwing this woman in your path and you don't even keep her fucking phone number. You really are a dickwad.'

Vince smiled. 'Well,' he said, 'if God wants me to get it together with Joy so badly, maybe he'll throw her into my path again.'

'Ah, so, you don't believe in destiny, but you do believe in serendipity?'

'Is there a difference?'

'God knows,' slurred Emma, 'but I tell you what. Next time she comes into your life, you'd better do the right thing or frankly you deserve to end up alone and unloved.'

There was a brief, uncomfortable silence as it dawned on the group that this was a little insensitive in the light of Vince's current circumstances.

'Oh, shit,' said Emma, 'I'm sorry, Vince. I didn't mean to . . .'

'Don't worry about it,' he said. 'Really, it's fine.'

'So,' Natalie glanced briefly at Emma, and began cautiously, 'what happened? With you and Jess? Why did you split up?'

Vince smiled. It was blatantly obvious that the girls had spent hours speculating about the abrupt end of his marriage to Jess and had only found the courage to ask him about it at the bottom of a bottle of Cabernet Sauvignon.

'I mean, you don't have to talk about it if you don't want to . . .' she added, taking his silence as a sign of discomfort.

'No,' he said, 'really, it's fine. I don't mind talking about it. It all started going wrong when Lara was six months old . . .'

August 2001
Teen Spirit

Fifty-Three

Lara May Mellon-James was delivered in Jess's mother's living room in the very small hours of a windy February night, to the sounds of Nirvana's 'Smells Like Teen Spirit'. Vince had loaded 100 of his and Jess's favourite songs of all time on to his MP3 player, and left them playing on a loop throughout the labour. The idea was that whatever song was playing when the baby was delivered would be his or her theme tune for the rest of his or her life.

Lara had failed to arrive during 'We Have All the Time in the World' or 'Perfect Day' or 'Golden Brown' or 'Dancing Queen' or 'Nobody Does It Better', and had emerged instead just as Kurt Cobain started screaming, 'Here we are now, entertain us.'

Neither Jess nor her mother, nor even the midwife, had been aware of which song was playing in the excitement of the moment. It was only a few days later that Jess asked Vince if he'd noticed. 'I'm not sure,' he said, 'I think it was "Wonderful World".' He'd tell her one day, maybe when Lara was a teenage rebel with body piercings, but in the midst of the existential perfection of having a newborn baby in their lives he didn't feel she needed to know.

Lara's birth marked the end of a nine-month period of ongoing tension between Vince and Jess. Jon was still living at Jess's when she was nearly eight months'

413

pregnant, and Jess refused to enter into any serious discussions on the subject of their long-term living arrangements. Jon moved out suddenly and messily one afternoon, after a row that Jess refused to elaborate on, adding even more fuel to Vince's loitering suspicion that he might have had something to do with Jess's pregnancy. In the days leading up to Lara's birth Vince had seriously entertained the prospect of finishing things with Jess and becoming a part-time father.

But the days and weeks following the birth of Lara May Mellon-James turned out to be the happiest of Vince's life. He and Jess floated around in a big pink bubble of delight and amazement, completely oblivious to the world around them. And any lingering doubts he might have had about the paternity of his child were extinguished the minute he first saw her face. It was like looking at a miniature version of himself.

'It's a genetic trick,' said Jess. 'Nature makes a newborn baby look just like its father so that he knows it's his and doesn't mind going out and spearing a few wild boar for the mother. Clever, isn't it?'

Lara May had thick yellow hair and legs like a chicken's, and was covered all over in a soft layer of white down. 'She looks just like a baby duck,' said Kirsty when she saw her for the first time.

Lara and Jess took to breastfeeding like a pair of pros, and Vince would watch in amazement as his tiny daughter attached herself so confidently to the lifeline of her mother's body. Kirsty hadn't breastfed any of her children and this was the first time that Vince had watched the process at such close quarters. He'd seen women feeding their babies from a distance, in restaurants and parks, but always averted his gaze, as he would if he saw two people kissing passionately or a man urinating against a wall. But watching Lara and Jess nestled silently together against a cloud of cushions, Vince decided that it was one of the most beautiful things he'd ever seen in his life.

If Vince had been a bit on the soft side before Lara was born, he transmogrified into a human marshmallow the moment she arrived. Everything Lara did filled him with amazement and awe. He bathed her every night in lavender-scented bubbles and gently patted her dry with a soft towel, which he snatched from the radiator at the very last minute to prevent it from losing even a degree of heat. He paraded proudly around Enfield Town with Lara strapped to his chest in a sling and showed pictures of her to all his students, whether they expressed an interest or not.

Fatherhood had lived up to all his expectations, and more. He felt complete for the first time in his life. Jess was the most incredible mother, and the two of them had never been happier together. Seeing her with Lara, so gentle and loving, so strong and nurturing, reminded him of exactly why he'd fallen in love with her in the first place. The subject of their living arrangements hadn't ever been formalized, but 80 per cent of his possessions now lived at Jess's, so it was as near as dammit.

For the first six months of Lara's life, everything was perfect. It wasn't until one sunny Sunday the following summer that everything started to go wrong.

*

It was the end of Jess's maternity leave and rather than get involved in the time-consuming business of expressing milk for Lara to have during the day, Jess decided it would be easier to stop breastfeeding completely. She phased out Lara's feeds, one by one, until she was entirely bottle-feeding her.

Once she was free of the restrictions of being her child's only source of milk, she asked Vince to look after Lara for the day. She was starting back at work the following week and needed a day to herself. Vince didn't hesitate in saying yes. He loved spending time with Lara, especially now he could feed her himself.

'I'm going into town,' she said, applying mascara for the first time in six months. 'I need some new clothes for work. None of my pre-pregnancy ones fit me any more.' She cupped her still rounded belly. 'And I want to have a pedicure. Look –' She showed him her feet. They looked fine to Vince, but were, apparently, 'minging'. 'And then I'm meeting Jon in Regent's Park, for a picnic . . .'

'Jon?'

'Yes.'

'*Jon* Jon?'

'Yes,' she hissed, '*Jon* Jon.'

'But, I thought you two had fallen out.'

'No,' she looked at him as if he was slightly retarded. 'Where on earth did you get that from?'

'From the fact that you haven't seen him since he moved out . . .'

'Of course I've seen him.'

'What?'

'I see him at least once a week. He comes over here or we go to see him in his new place.'

'But when?'

'God, I don't know,' she muttered, stuffing keys into her handbag. 'During the day, while you're at work.'

'But I don't understand. The last I heard, you two had had a row, he stormed off and you've not mentioned him since.'

'Good grief, Vince. Did you honestly think that Jon and I would let a stupid little argument kill off our friendship?'

'Christ, I don't know. I just *assumed* . . .'

'What – and not let him see Lara?'

'So when did you two make it up?'

'When he got back from the States.'

'He went to the States?'

'Yes, just after he moved out of here. And he phoned the minute he got back and came straight round to see Lara.'

'But why didn't you mention it?'

'I don't know,' she shrugged, and leaned down to pick Lara up from where she'd been sitting on the sofa watching her parents argue. 'It just didn't seem important. You don't tell me everything you do every day . . .'

'That's because I don't do anything worth telling you about. I teach people to drive, then I come home.'

'Yes. But you don't talk about your students or what you talk about or where you have your lunch.'

'But what about *me*?' he said. 'I really like Jon. I'd like to see him, too. Show him my daughter. Show off a bit, you know. Why do you have to see him on your own?'

She smoothed down Lara's tufty hair and stroked her cheek. 'Look,' she said, 'it's no big deal. I'll invite him over next weekend. We'll have lunch. Just chill out, my angel boy. Why do you always have to get so worked up about things?' She put her hand to his face and cupped his cheek tenderly.

The feel of her hand against his skin softened him immediately. 'I'm not getting worked up.' He kissed the palm of her hand. 'It's just, I really like Jon . . .'

'I know you do, my angel.'

'And I want us to do things as a *family*, you know.'

'I know you do.'

'And I'm so proud of you both, of *us*.'

'Aww . . .' She pulled him towards her and they engaged in a family hug. 'Look,' she said, 'I promise. I'll talk to Jon today. Arrange something for next weekend.' She handed Lara over to him, looped her handbag over her shoulder and left the flat with a cheery 'See you later.'

Vince and Lara had a lovely day together. After her morning nap, he put her in the car and drove round to see Chris and his mum. Vince's grandmother was there and it was a beautiful sunny day, so they all sat out in the garden watching Chris light the barbecue.

'So where's Jess off to today?' said Kirsty, rubbing sun cream into her knees.

'Into town,' said Vince, bouncing Lara on his lap. 'Said she needed some new clothes for when she goes back to work tomorrow.'

'Aw,' said Gran, 'is this the first time she's left the little one?'

'For a whole day, yeah,' said Vince. 'She's left her with me for the occasional hour or so before, but she's been breastfeeding so she hasn't been able to go out for too long.'

'Bet she's missing her,' said Kirsty. 'Has she been phoning you every five minutes?'

'No,' said Vince. 'Well, not yet, anyway.'

'Oh, I'm sure she will,' smiled Gran. 'No mother can resist checking up.'

Jess didn't phone once the whole time Vince was at his mum's.

'Oh, that's a good sign,' said Kirsty. 'Means she's really relaxing.'

At four o'clock, just before Lara woke up from her afternoon nap, he sent her a text message.

Everything OK here. Lara sleeping. Had 250 ml at lunch and a strawberry yoghurt. What time you home?

He watched the phone for a while, but nothing happened. She still hadn't replied to his text message by the time he got home that afternoon, and he tried his hardest not to be bothered about it. His mum was right. It was good that Jess was really taking some time out. She'd been a completely devoted mother for the past six months, put her life on hold entirely to give Lara the best possible start in life. She deserved to let her hair down. He resisted the temptation to phone her and got on with getting Lara ready for bed, but when Jess still wasn't home at seven-thirty that evening, and still hadn't called,

Vince decided he couldn't be cool for another minute and phoned Jess on her mobile.

As he waited for her to answer, he heard her ring tone coming from the bedroom and followed it to the pocket of her jeans hanging on the back of a chair. He pulled out her phone and sighed heavily.

Jess had gone out without her mobile. The first time she'd left Lara for a full day and she hadn't even thought to ensure that she had some form of emergency contact with him. It was flattering in one way that she had such confidence in Vince's abilities as a substitute mother – but frightening in another that she was able to sever the umbilical cord so fully and completely. Vince made sure he had his phone fully charged and about his person everywhere he went these days. He hated the idea of being out of contact with his family for even a minute.

He went to bed at eleven o'clock, fully expecting to hear her key in the lock as he drifted off to sleep, but when Lara woke up briefly an hour later and he realized that she still wasn't home he finally lost his cool.

He stormed into the living room and snatched Jess's phone off the coffee table, scrolled through her phone-book until he got to Jon's number and dialled.

His jaw was set tight with the effort of containing the words he wanted to spit out to whoever answered the phone. Jon's phone rang four times and went through to voice mail. Vince snapped the phone closed and threw it across the room. His insides were bubbling up into a molten, volcanic rage. He didn't object to Jess taking off for the day and sharing a romantic picnic with her ex-boyfriend on a beautiful sunny bank holiday, and he didn't object to being left to look after their daughter for a whole day and night. What he objected to, more than anything, was the fact that she hadn't felt the need or the desire to speak to either of them once all day to find out how they were doing.

He sighed and rubbed the palms of his hands down his face. It was 12.15 a.m. Lara could well be awake and ready for a bottle in six hours. He should get back to bed, get some sleep.

He collected Jess's phone from the other side of the room and rested it on the coffee table. He stared at it for a while, wondering what secrets were contained there, inside that little phone, what clandestine messages and covert phone calls.

During his long days at work, Vince had enjoyed imagining Jess and Lara at home together, going to the shops, visiting her mother, going to baby massage classes. But now it turned out that they were involved in secret meetings with Jon. What else had they been up to, his girlfriend and his daughter? Where else had they been while he was teaching seventeen-year-olds to reverse around corners all over Enfield?

He picked up the phone, flipped it open, then stopped in his tracks. Lara May smiled out at him from the LCD screen, a picture Jess had taken of her on the first sunny day of the year, sitting in his mum's garden, wearing a white cotton sun hat. He remembered the moment vividly – Jess pulling the hat out of the enormous bag they never went anywhere without these days and tying it gently underneath Lara's chin. He remembered the look of complete adoration on her face as she looked at her daughter sitting on a blanket in her first sun hat, and he suddenly realized that he didn't want to know what was on Jess's phone. She was a great mother. He was a great father. Lara was lucky to have such loving, competent parents, and she deserved to have them for ever. Together. If he started poking around, he might find something that he couldn't live with, something that might tear them apart, and he didn't want that – for any of them.

He snapped the phone shut and tiptoed back to bed. On the way he stopped to glance down at Lara.

She was lying in her Moses basket, flat on her back, with her head turned to the side and her hands bunched into loose fists next to her ears. Her breathing was slow and regular, and every now and then she smacked her lips together and made a tiny sucking sound. She was magnificent, he thought, magnificent in every way. And so was her mother.

He would allow Jess this infraction. She was with someone he liked and respected. She deserved a proper break. This was part and parcel of the person she was and, if he wanted them to be together for ever, then he would have to learn to accept that.

He kissed the air above Lara's cheek, then fell into bed, where he drifted into a deep and immediate slumber.

Jess was out cold on the sofa when Vince awoke at seven o'clock the following morning. She was naked from the waist down, but was still wearing her T-shirt and one red sock.

She opened her left eye slowly as he hovered over her. 'Morning, angel boy,' she croaked.

'Morning,' he replied in a mock-stern tone.

'Are you angry with me?'

He perched himself on the edge of the sofa and took her hand. 'No,' he said, stroking her fingertips, 'not really. I wish you'd taken your phone, though.'

'Oh, God,' she groaned, 'I know. I couldn't believe it when I realized I'd left it behind. So annoyed.' She glanced behind him at the bedroom door. 'Is Lara awake?'

'Nope. Not yet.'

'I came in and looked at her when I got home. I couldn't resist it. Did I wake you?'

He shook his head.

'God, she's lovely, isn't she?'

He smiled and nodded. 'She's fantastic.'

She beamed at him. 'How come you're not angry with me?'

Vince shrugged. 'I'm not *not* angry. I'm just . . . accepting. You've been incredible these past few months. You needed to get away, properly. I understand that. Kind of wish you'd at least phoned . . .'

'I know. I'm sorry. I'm totally crap. Did you have a nice day?'

'Lovely,' he said. 'Really, really nice. And you?'

'Brilliant,' she said. 'I spent nearly £300 on clothes, then had the most brilliant time with Jon. Went to a club in Hoxton. Had a celebratory pill or two . . .'

Vince bit his tongue against the admonishment that was straining at the leash to break free, and smiled stiffly.

'. . . ended up back at this bloke's flat in Shoreditch – incredible place, converted cannery or something. Didn't get home till five . . .' She glanced at the clock on the video player. 'Jesus – *two hours ago!* Oh, my God. I've only had two hours' sleep!' She groaned and flopped back on to the sofa.

Vince smiled at her and stood up. 'Look. Why don't I get Lara up and you go back to bed for a while?'

'What – are you serious?'

'Uh-huh.' Vince felt inflated with good grace. It was a nice sensation.

'Vincent Mellon,' she said, 'you really are an angel.'

'I know,' he said, 'I'm a total fucking saint.'

'No, really. You are, and I'm so fucking lucky to have you. You're just this amazing father and this beautiful, kind, gentle person. I really love you, d'you know that?'

Vince stopped in his tracks. His stomach flipped over. She'd said it. Finally, after more than two years, Jess had told him that she loved him. He gulped and tried to look nonchalant. 'Yes,' he said, 'I know that.'

'D'you think . . . ?' she began, then stopped.

'What?'

'I was thinking. Maybe when Lara's a bit older. Maybe when she's old enough to leave with my mum for a few days, you and I could go to Las Vegas. You and I could . . . get married?'

'What?!'

'Yes,' she laughed, 'why not? I've never really fancied a big wedding and I've always wanted to go to Las Vegas. That way Lara gets proper parents, like we didn't have – you know – *married* parents. And we get to spend some time by ourselves. And I get the coolest surname ever.'

'Jessica James,' he said, smiling, 'are you proposing to me?'

'Um, yes,' she smirked, 'I guess I am.'

424

'Fucking hell.'

'I know. I've shocked myself.'

'Jesus.' He rubbed his chin and grinned at her.

'Well,' she demanded, 'are you going to reply or not?'

'Christ,' he said, 'yes. Of course. Definitely. Definitely. Let's get married.'

She smiled and slid off the sofa. 'Good,' she said. 'Now I'm going to kiss my beautiful daughter very hard on both her fat little cheeks and go back to bed until lunchtime.'

Vince watched the mother of his child and future wife as she sauntered towards the bedroom. She loved him. She wanted to marry him. Jessica James who could have had anyone she wanted, who could have had Jon Gavin and a life of five-star international luxury, had chosen him. And for now, in spite of all his misgivings and deep-rooted concerns about their future as a couple, that was all that mattered.

Fifty-Four

Joy had spent very little time in her parents' loft. It was accessible only by a stepladder that had to be hauled out of a shed in the garden, and it was full of spiders and mouse droppings.

But she was moving out next week and she wanted to have a nose around at all the stuff they'd brought back with them from Singapore, see if there was anything up there she might want for her new flat, a tiny one-bedroom conversion in Southgate. It was nothing special, but it was her first step on the property ladder. Her mother had handed over almost her entire divorce settlement for Joy to put down as a deposit on it, and Joy had had to negotiate a substantial pay rise from the photo shop she managed to be able to afford the mortgage, but as of Tuesday, 4 September 2001, Joy would be an official homeowner.

Before she dared venture into the shadowy cavities of the loft she emptied a whole can of insect killer through the hatch and left it to do its work for two hours. Then she put on a polo neck and gloves, and tucked her trousers into her socks, careful not leave a gap anywhere on her person into which any form of insect or rodent might find its way, flicked on her torch and mounted the steps.

It was the day of her father's wedding.

He was marrying Toni Moran in a chapel on the edge of a cliff in Cornwall. Apparently, because he'd married

426

her mother in a register office and not in the eyes of God, he was still entitled to a religious ceremony, even though he'd fornicated and adulterated his way through every year of his first marriage. The invitation had turned up three months ago. It was incredibly twee, with paper roses in sugar pink and curly writing.

Alan Trevor Downer and Antonia Patricia Moran
joyfully request the pleasure of your company
at their wedding on Saturday, 25 August 2001.

It made Joy want to throw up. Ridiculous, she thought, getting married at his age. He'd be dead before their fifth anniversary.

Barbara claimed not to be upset by it. 'I'm happy for them, I really am.'

'How can you say that?' she'd demanded. 'How can you feel like that?'

Barbara shrugged and sighed. 'Because,' she said, 'not everything is your father's fault. Because I want him to be happy.'

But Joy couldn't stand it. She'd sent a reply the same day.

Dear Alan and Antonia,

Many thanks for inviting me to your wedding. I won't be able to come as I have a prior hairdressing appointment that day. I'm sure you understand.

I hope you have a lovely day and a joyful life.

Love,
Joy

She'd been happy with that – harsh without being bitchy, sharp without being unpleasant. She'd made her point.

Barbara had made herself busy today. She was seeing friends in Saffron Walden and wouldn't be back until late, and Joy had felt something pulling her irresistibly towards the loft since the day her father's wedding invitation had arrived. There was something in there calling to her. Yes, she wanted to find nice things for her new flat, but there was more to it than that. She wanted to find something, anything, to explain the calamity of her parents' marriage and within that, hopefully, possibly, an insight into her own inexplicable behaviour of the previous seven years.

She swung the torch around the loft, wondering where to start first. She could make out corners of picture frames and backs of chairs. There were some packing boxes to her left covered in freight stickers and a pile of cardboard boxes to her right. In front of her was something that she already knew would be coming with her when she moved into her new flat – a red silk lantern decorated with black satin tassels hanging from a 1960s-style curved chrome lamp stand. It was ugly and beautiful at the same time, and seemed to Joy to encapsulate the particular hybrid of time and place that her parents had inhabited at that point of their lives.

She also found a foot stool with black-lacquered splayed out legs and a pale blue satin seat, some garden lights shaped like Chinese lanterns and a full traditional Chinese tea set including a teapot with a bamboo handle.

She pulled her finds from the loft like trophies and

piled them up in her bedroom. Once she'd made some room, she started unpacking the freight containers.

The picture came to her hand almost immediately and the minute she saw it she knew exactly what it meant.

It was tucked away at the back of a recipe book called *Cooking the Hainanese Way*. It was small, about ten centimetres square and printed in bright 1960s Technicolor. It showed a young boy of about eighteen years old, dressed in loose-fitting canvas trousers and a knitted vest over a green shirt. He was posing in a highly manicured garden, standing in front of a palm tree and leaning against a rake. He had dark hair and high cheekbones, and smiled at the photographer with blatant affection, bordering on adoration.

His eyes were all the evidence she needed, but she turned the picture over anyway, just to be sure.

The date had been stamped on the back by the photo lab.

August 1968. Two months before she was born.

And there, in neat, navy ink, was written underneath;

To my Barbara, I will never forget you. Charles.

A strange noise escaped from between her lips then, a rush of air expelled from the very deepest corners of her soul. She held the picture up again and angled it towards the light. There was no doubt about it. This beautiful young man with the slanted eyes, the high cheekbones and the shiny black hair had been her mother's lover – and *her* father.

*

Joy's certainty about this matter was hard to explain. Yes, the boy looked like her, but there was more to it than that. Joy had always felt displaced, *distanced*, from her parents. She'd entertained fantasies over the years that maybe she had been the result of an affair between her father and some exotic Singaporean beauty, but the birth certificate bearing her mother's name had poured cold water over that line of thought.

She'd also entertained fantasies about her mother, about the person she might have been if she hadn't married Alan, about a girlish, flirtatious butterfly, homely but sexy, plain but alluring. But it had never before occurred to her to put the two fantasies together.

Joy walked down to the off-licence later that day, the photograph of her father tucked firmly in her purse. She bought a bottle of Veuve Clicquot and when she got home she put it in the freezer. Then she had a bath, put on a new dress and nice shoes, and waited for her mother to get home.

'He was the garden boy,' said Barbara, handling the photograph tenderly. 'There were four of them; they tended the grounds of our apartment block.'

'How old was he?'

'Seventeen.' Barbara shrugged, and let out a small groan of embarrassment.

'No!'

'Yes. Well, seventeen when it . . . started. Eighteen by the time it finished.'

'And how did it actually, you know . . . *start?*'

Barbara shrugged again, and rested the photo on the

coffee table. 'Oh, there was an awful lot of it going on. I'd heard about other wives seducing these boys. Not just the garden boys, but the bell hops, the delivery boys, all that kind of thing. It was rife. These women – they were in a strange country and their husbands were out all day, all night, working, entertaining. They got lonely. And so did I.'

'So did you . . . *seduce* him?' she said, pointing at the photo.

'Oh, no. I wouldn't say that. It was more of a flirtation, really. He used to smile at me every time I saw him. And then we started saying good morning to each other. Eventually it turned into a friendship. I'd make him fresh lemonade and bring it down for him when I saw him toiling in the heat. He would pick me tropical flowers and give them to me as a gift. He called me his English rose,' she smiled wistfully. '"Good morning, my lovely English rose," he'd say when he saw me. I thought he was teasing me at first, playing with me.'

'Could he speak good English, then?'

'Oh, yes. He was a student, business studies. He was pretty much fluent.'

'So,' Joy urged, clasping her champagne glass between her hands, 'what happened next?'

'Well,' Barbara blanched slightly, 'I suppose it was around the time I found out about your father's affair with the Clarke woman.'

'Which Clarke woman?'

Barbara shuddered. 'Ginny Clarke,' she spat out the name as if it tasted bitter in her mouth. 'Your father's first affair. Her husband was a senior sales manager at

431

Jaguar and gone to seed . . . very fat, very florid, too much gin, I suspect. I also suspect that he may have been homosexual. But for whatever reasons, she made it very plain from the moment we arrived in Singapore that she wanted Alan and stopped at nothing to get him. It was a terrible time for me. Failing to conceive, feeling lonely, the heat, being so far from home. And when I found out that your father had succumbed to that horrible skinny woman – she had a *lisp*, you know, like an annoying little girl – ooh, I just got so angry. And there was Charles, smiling at me, giving me hibiscus blossoms, calling me his English rose. It was inevitable, I suppose . . .'

'So, did you invite him in? Did it happen your apartment? What happened?'

'Well, there was a downpour one afternoon and I came upon him taking shelter in the car park. He was all bedraggled. So I took a deep breath and I invited him in, to dry off,' she laughed wryly. 'We both knew what it meant. And that was that.'

'Was it lovely?'

Barbara blushed furiously and fiddled with the hem of her skirt. 'Oh,' she said, 'I don't know. Yes, I suppose. But it was such a terrible thing to do.'

'No, it wasn't,' said Joy. 'It was totally understandable.'

'No, you see, it wasn't. Because it wasn't just to get revenge. I didn't do it just to make myself feel better and I didn't just do it because I was lonely. The main reason why I did it . . .' she paused and took a deep breath, 'was to get pregnant.'

Joy stopped breathing for a second as she felt her romantic fantasies start to lose a little momentum.

'I had no idea whether it was me or your father who had the physical . . . *shortcoming* that was preventing us from getting pregnant. Your father refused to visit a specialist; it would have been too much for his ego to bear if he'd been told it was his fault. And I wanted a baby so so much, more than anything. I was thirty-nine years old and I knew my days were numbered. And this boy, this Charles – he was so young and vital. And I'm afraid I rather *used* him,' she bit her lip and looked at Joy for reassurance.

Joy gulped and blinked, not knowing what to say.

'We slept together at least three or four times a week for the next year.'

Joy nodded slowly, trying to make a mental correlation between the look of open adoration on the face of the boy in the photo and her mother's primal and clinical need to be impregnated. 'Didn't you love him, even a tiny bit?'

'Oh, yes,' she said forcefully, 'I was ever so fond of him. He was the kindest, sweetest most charming boy, the sort you'd be proud to call your son. We had a very gentle, *affectionate* relationship. Please don't think it was purely about what I could get out of him . . .'

'And then, once you got pregnant, what happened then?'

'Well, I told him immediately. And your father. And as chance would have it, it was a month during which either one of them might have been the father. Your father wouldn't have suspected a thing . . .'

'But did Charles think it was his?'

'He knew it *might* be his.'

433

'And he didn't mind?'

'No. Not at all. He wasn't ready to be a father. He was so young, had so much he wanted to do. He was perfectly happy for Alan to raise his child. He felt it was his gift to us.'

Joy swallowed another mouthful of nameless disappointment.

'I'd been hoping to come back to England before you were born, but I suffered from pre-eclampsia in the last few weeks, had to have total bed rest. So you were born in Changi General Hospital. Alan knew immediately. The minute he saw you, he knew you weren't his. It was the eyes, you see.' She cupped Joy's face with her hand. 'Your eyes. And you had all this thick, black hair. He –' she stopped as her voice caught on the words and put her hand over her mouth. 'He took one look at you and left the room.' A tear fell from her left eye and ran down her cheek. She wiped it away. 'I have never seen a man look so ... *destroyed* as your father did at that moment. It was as if he shrank in front of my very eyes, like a little wax man slowly melting in the sun –' She choked again on more tears. 'And he never said a word. Never mentioned it. Not once.'

Joy stared at the floor. Suddenly this wasn't just about her mother being exciting, having affairs, living up to her own sophomoric fantasies. It was about her father being cuckolded in the most hurtful way imaginable. It was about years of buried resentment and humiliation. It was about raising someone else's child for twenty-five years without complaint, and, for a man like her father, a man brought up to believe that man was king, a man whose ego was as fragile as a glass bauble, Joy could barely think of a more painful state of affairs.

Everything began to fall into place as the truth filtered through her consciousness drop by drop. Everything began to make sense. Her father's resentful attitude towards her, his manipulative control of his wife, the affairs, the deep-seated anger, her mother's subservience and refusal to stand up to Alan.

Joy was somebody else's child and he'd chosen to shut his mouth, grit his teeth and get on with the job of raising her. No wonder he was angry. No wonder he'd left. No wonder he'd married Toni Moran on a cliff top in Cornwall this very morning.

Joy drained her glass of champagne and topped it up. 'More?' she asked her mother. Barbara nodded stiffly, and Joy filled her glass. They sat and sipped their champagne in silence for a while. Joy had so many questions she wanted to ask and so many conflicting emotions swirling around inside her that she didn't know what to say first.

'Say something,' said Barbara, smiling wanly.

'I don't know what to say,' she mumbled. 'That's the problem.'

'Are you angry? . . .'

'No. I'm not angry. In some ways I'm pleased. In some ways everything makes so much more sense this way. But . . . I feel bad about Dad. I feel bad for hating him all these years, for not understanding what he was going through.'

Barbara nodded. 'I know,' she said. 'I tried my hardest to soften you up on him. But, obviously, I couldn't ever really make you understand.'

'Why didn't you tell me before? Would you ever have told me?'

'No,' she said sadly, 'I'd decided a long time ago that you would never know. I couldn't do that to your father …'

'Not even after he left you?'

'No, not even then. He sacrificed so much for us. And however poor a father he was, I couldn't bear for him to suffer the double humiliation of his daughter finding out that he wasn't man enough to sire his own child, that he'd had to raise somebody else's.'

'But what about me? What about how I felt, knowing that my father hated me, that I was the greatest disappointment of his life. Wouldn't it have been better for me to have known?'

Barbara sighed. 'Oh, Joy. I don't know. I really don't know. Either way I was going to let one of you down, either way we'd all have been miserable. I just thought it was for the best to let sleeping dogs lie.'

'And my father. Charles. Did he meet me? Does he know about me?'

'Yes. He met you. Once. The day before we left for England. The day he gave me that photo. He thought you were beautiful. He chose your name.'

Joy threw her a look of surprise.

'Yes. He said you should be called Joy because you would bring me so much happiness through the years. But that was it. We didn't stay in touch. We didn't swap addresses. He left the apartment that day and that was the last I saw of him.'

'And what was he? Was he Chinese? Malay? He looks

. . .' She picked up the photo and examined it. 'I don't know. He doesn't look like anyone else I've ever seen.'

'He was half-Tibetan, half-English. His father was a captain in the Royal Navy. His mother was a seamstress. He was brought up in Singapore by a Chinese couple who adopted him after his mother died when he was five.'

'Oh, my God.' Joy stood up slowly and walked to the mirror over the mantelpiece. She examined her face with her fingers, looking for the nuances of her newly discovered eclectic genetic make-up.

Tibet, she thought to herself. She didn't even know where it was.

'What was his surname?' she asked.

'Yung. Charles Yung. At least, that was his adopted surname. I don't know what his original surname was.'

'Charles Yung,' she repeated. 'Gosh. So. He'd be about, what . . . fifty-one now?'

'Yes, I suppose he would. It's hard to imagine . . . I always see him as a young man . . .'

'I wonder where he is. I wonder what he's doing. God, he's probably got other kids by now – maybe even grand-kids.'

'More than likely.'

'And I wonder if he got his business degree in the end. I wonder if he's successful.' Joy's head was starting to buzz with the myriad, infinite possibilities thrown up by the existence of this new person in her life.

'Oh, I'm sure he is. He was very ambitious. Very bright.'

'I want to meet him,' she said abruptly.

'Good,' said Barbara, 'that's fine.'

'You don't mind?'

437

'Of course I don't mind. Just as long as you're aware of the pitfalls. He might be dead, you know. Or impossible to track down. He might not want to know you . . .'

'I know,' said Joy, distractedly, 'I know all that. But I at least want to try.'

Joy took the photo of Charles Yung to bed with her that night. She propped it up against her table lamp and stared at it until she felt her eyelids begin to sag under the weight of a long and emotional day.

She tried to imagine what Charles Yung would be doing now. She imagined a slim, fit man in a luxurious apartment, maybe in Singapore, maybe in Hong Kong, maybe even in San Francisco or New York. She imagined his wife, maybe Asian, maybe blonde, but definitely reed-thin and beautiful. And she imagined three children, a few years younger than her, studying at Ivy League colleges in the States, practising law and medicine in Europe, professional, beautiful, successful people – her brothers and sisters.

And then she thought about her father. An elderly, unhappy man, living a lie for twenty-five years, finally finding happiness with a pretty, fun-loving woman who made him feel like a man again. She imagined her father and Toni Moran snuggled up together under the canopy of their four-poster bed in their twee Cornwall honeymoon suite and for the very first time in her life she felt happy for him. Good for him, she thought, to snatch a few years' happiness at the tail end of his existence. Good for him.

And with that novel and comforting thought, Joy let herself sink gently into a dream-filled slumber.

Fifty-Five

Jess and Vince got married at the Heavenly Bliss wedding chapel in Las Vegas on the anniversary of their first meeting. Chris was there as Vince's best man and Jon Gavin was there as Jess's. They all stayed at the Bellagio for three nights and didn't tell anyone they were getting married until they got back.

Kirsty was livid with Chris when he got home.

'You bastard,' she ranted, 'I can't believe you went away, left me to look after the kids and watched *my own son* getting married.'

Chris just shrugged defeatedly and grinned. 'What could I do?' he said. 'He invited me.'

Kirsty wasn't the only person to need appeasing. Jess's mother cried for half an hour when they arrived to collect Lara, flashing their wedding bands at her.

'But you're my only daughter,' she wailed, 'my only girl. I spent my whole life fantasizing about this moment . . .'

'Oh, get a grip, mother,' Jess teased. 'You got to see me pushing out your first grandchild, what more do you want?'

Their friends had been gutted, too, feeling robbed of yet another all-expenses-paid Saturday in a castle or stately home drinking free champagne in Karen Millen.

Jess had looked stunning in a long cream chiffon skirt,

cerise halterneck and glittery flip-flops, with a camellia in her hair, while Vince wore a cream linen suit from Paul Smith and a cerise Ted Baker shirt to match. And as much as the day had been everything a Las Vegas wedding should be, Vince couldn't help but feel a little cheated, too. Jon Gavin had managed to appropriate a gram of coke by some nefarious means or other, then managed to persuade both Vince and Chris to join in, even though neither of them particularly wanted to. Chris on coke was not something that Vince had ever seen before and, in retrospect, was not something he ever wished to see again.

They drank champagne from ten o'clock in the morning until three o'clock the following morning, and most of the day was a blur. They looked cool and the wedding was rock and roll, but there was something hollow at the very core of it that left Vince feeling like they hadn't really got married at all.

It felt to Vince as if Jess had viewed the whole event as an excuse to get away from Lara and get wasted for four days and, although he thoroughly approved of the sentiment – parenting may well have been its own reward, but you still deserved time off for good behaviour – he just wished that the party element hadn't overshadowed the actual wedding quite so heavily.

Nothing changed when they got back, either.

Vince knew he was probably being a little naive to imagine that being Mrs Jessica Mellon would really have any impact on her attitude or behaviour, but if anything it seemed to make her worse.

Ever since the day she'd gone AWOL and proposed

to him, it had become unofficially written into the rule book of their relationship that she went out every Saturday night. It had also, by extension, become written into the rule book of their relationship that, because she ended up staying out all night on Saturday night, Vince would remove Lara fully from her sphere of consciousness until late the following afternoon, while she recovered from whatever hangover or drug-induced comedown she'd inflicted upon herself the previous night.

Vince had no idea who she was with on these nights out, although they usually involved Jon Gavin and a random selection of people with names he recognized from her past – people called Simone, Rio, Dexy, Todd and Puss, for example, who sounded to Vince like members of a 1970s glam rock band and who he consequently always tended to envisage in skin-tight catsuits and thigh-high Lurex boots. They went out to clubs, the newer the better, and danced on podiums, then found people with flats where they could head on to afterwards to smoke spliffs, listen to chill-out music and phone taxis.

'I love being married,' she said one day, glancing fondly at her wedding ring. 'It's the perfect fob-off for creeps in clubs.'

This unwanted insight into Jess's mysterious social existence did nothing to alleviate Vince's discomfort about her nights out. As well as thinking about her writhing around on podiums in low-slung jeans, he could now envisage fat-tongued uglies following her around all night making lewd propositions.

Vince of course was never invited along on these nights

out. They were tightly packaged in a compartment far away from his own 'husband and baby' compartment and, besides, he wouldn't have wanted to go even if he was invited. Vince hated clubs, drugs and people who liked clubs and drugs in equal measure. And Vince didn't resent Jess's nights out. She worked hard all week and still did the bulk of the childcare when she collected Lara from her mother's at the end of the day. On her days off, she cooked Lara wonderful nutritious meals full of organic ingredients and took her to educational play-groups and petting zoos. She deserved her time off. Vince just wished she would do something different with it.

She came out to his friends' 'boring little dinner parties' under sufferance, claiming that she much preferred to see them during the day when they could all compare children and discuss teething and tantrums, then be home in time for a glass of wine and an early night. And Vince had the occasional night out with his mates, tame affairs involving a pub, a curry and being in bed by eleven.

But what really bugged him was that despite the fact that both Jess's mother and Vince's mother had made full and genuine offers to baby-sit at a moment's notice whenever they fancied a night out together, they never took them up on it. Jess was always too knackered.

'Oh, God, no,' she'd say in response to a gentle suggestion of an Italian round the corner or a trip to the local cinema. 'I really can't face it. Let's just get a take-away, eh?'

Vince could appreciate that she was tired. She had a tiring existence. But it galled him that however tough a week she'd had she still managed to find the energy to swan off into a narcotic oblivion every Saturday night. It galled him that, if someone was having leaving drinks on a Friday night, she managed to stay out drinking until closing time. It galled him that on the night before her thirty-third birthday, she went out partying with Jon and the gang, but on the day itself stayed in drinking champagne and eating king prawns in front of a DVD with Vince. It galled him that Jess chose to do all her socializing with other people and all her staying in with him. It galled him that he wasn't her friend . . .

But Vince could cope with all this because, even though it unsettled him and even though it upset him, it had become a part of the rhythm of their lives and he'd learned to accept it. If his wife wanted to go out clubbing with strangers every Saturday night, take drugs and drink gallons of Cristal paid for by dubious acquaintances, then spend the following day in bed looking wan and ignoring her daughter then that was fine because that was what she did. But when she'd come to him yesterday afternoon with a look on her face that suggested that she was about to up the ante and fluttered her eyelashes at him in that special way of hers, Vince knew he was in trouble.

'I have got *the* most incredible news!' she opened, and Vince knew immediately that it would be something that he would find exactly the opposite.

'Jon Gavin's been booked for Amnesia. In July.'

'Wow,' he said. 'That's a club, right?'

'Uh-huh – it's the biggest club in Ibiza. And they're giving him this big fuck-off villa in the hills. It's got a pool, a gym, a chef. He gets a convertible fucking Lexus, this, like, millionaire gangsta-mobile, a chauffeur if he wants it. The works. For a whole month.' Jess was bouncing up and down on the sofa with excitement as she spoke.

'Wow,' said Vince again. 'That sounds really cool.'

'It is,' she said, 'it's *so* cool. And what's even cooler is that he's invited me to stay with him . . .'

'Oh,' said Vince, feeling the bottom of his belly lurching upwards.

'And obviously I wouldn't stay for the whole month. Although, shit, I'd love to. But I definitely want to go for a week. That's OK, isn't it? You don't mind?'

'Er . . .'

'And he did say that it would be cool for all of us to come, you know, the three of us, but I just don't think that's a very suitable environment for Lara, you know, with the pool and the drugs and everything. Way too dangerous.'

Vince nodded his agreement.

'So I'd probably go the second week of July – Puss and Dex are going then, too, so it'll be even more of a laugh . . .'

Vince didn't know what to say. He knew what he *wanted* to say. He wanted to say: *For fuck's sake, Jess, you're a fucking thirty-three-year-old wife and mother, not a twenty-something beach bimbo.* And actually, he wanted to add, isn't Ibiza a bit passé, isn't taking pills and dancing until the sun comes up just a little bit *last millennium*, aren't you and Jon and your stupid friends with their stupid names just a little bit *old* to be carrying on like this?

444

Because it wasn't the fact that Jess wanted to go away without him for a week that rankled. If she was going on a hen weekend, for example, or on a city break with some girlfriends, he'd be all for it. It was the nature of the time she wanted to spend apart from him that bothered him. It was the people she wanted to go with and the way she was going to behave. It was the sheer breadth of the disparity between what he thought constituted a good time and what she thought constituted a good time.

But he didn't say any of this because a) he didn't want to spoil Jess's fun and b) it was pointless because Jess had already made up her mind that she was going, and there was nothing he could say to stop her.

'So,' said Charlene Okumbo, at the end of her forty-second lesson, 'how's married life?'

Vince turned to her and smiled wanly. 'Yeah,' he said, 'it's good.'

'Does it feel any different?'

He shrugged. 'Not really.'

'You don't sound that excited about it, considering,' she complained as she manhandled the gear stick into neutral.

'Considering what?'

'I dunno. All that eloping stuff. Sounded really romantic to me.'

'Yeah, well, you know. Weddings and marriages – two completely different things, aren't they?' He turned to Charlene and sighed. 'Supposing your boyfriend . . . what's his name again?'

'Tarif.'

'Tarif. Right. Supposing you and he were married . . .'

'Yeah, right, in his dreams . . .'

'Yeah, anyway. Just supposing. And supposing you had a baby.'

Charlene snorted disdainfully.

'How would you feel if Tarif said that his ex-girlfriend, who looked like . . .' – he scoured his memories of the latest edition of *heat* magazine, trying to find a suitable comparison – '. . . who looked like Beyoncé, was hiring a villa in Ibiza and she invited him and a load of their mates over for a holiday and they'd be clubbing every night and taking shitloads of drugs and stuff. And supposing Tarif said he was going and you weren't invited – what would you do?'

Charlene's eyes were bulging out of her head with the improbability of the imagined scenario. 'Dump him,' she squeaked, emphatically.

'Really?'

'Er, *yeah*. I mean, that, like, just *so* isn't acceptable behaviour.'

'Well, what am I going to do?'

'Shit. I don't know. It's a toughie. But if you're asking *me* what *I* would do, me personally, I wouldn't put up with that shit. Seriously.'

Vince nodded slowly.

'But, you know. It's different for you. You've got a kid and shit. You're married. You're *old*. Maybe you're gonna have to swallow it. Put up with it. The main thing is – do you trust her?'

Vince stopped for a second to consider the question. It was deeply fundamental, but failed to elicit an immediate answer. Did he trust Jess? Despite her tendency to keep the various elements of her life firmly separate, she was always up-front with him, gave him honest answers to open questions. He knew without a doubt that if he were to ask her if she'd ever been unfaithful to him, she would respond with the truth. She was secretive, but she wasn't a liar. But, he pondered, most people were put off following their natural adulterous instincts by the knowledge that they wouldn't be able to live with the guilt and the lies, that the aftermath would make it untenable. But Jess was different. She *would* be able to carry on living her normal existence with Vince and Lara at the same time as conducting an affair; she *would* be able to maintain her composure, to juggle two separate lives. And that was what scared him.

'It's not that I don't *trust* her,' he answered finally. 'It's that I don't really *know* her.'

Charlene's eyes boggled again. 'This is your *wife* we're talking about?'

'Uh-huh.'

'And the mother of your *child*?'

'Yeah. I know.'

'Jes-sus,' she said, rolling her eyes, 'that is *sad.*'

'I know,' said Vince, 'I know.'

'You know what it is?' she said, looking him directly in the eye. 'You're too nice, that's what it is with you. Too nice for your own good. You need to toughen up a bit.'

He shrugged. 'Not going to happen,' he said. 'This is me. This is the way I am. I don't do tough.'

'Well, then,' she sniffed and went to open her door,

447

'you're going to have to get yourself a nice girl, then. Because that one you're married to – if you don't stand up to her, then she's just going to chew you up and spit you out. And I tell you something, come next week, I'll be tearing up those L plates for good and you won't ever see me again, so you'd better hurry up and get this shit sorted out before I go.'

Vince smiled and nodded. 'I'll see what I can do,' he said.

'You do that,' she said. And then she got out of the car and sauntered up her garden path, his sweet little nineteen-year-old dispenser of wisdom and counsel, leaving Vince feeling more confused than ever.

Fifty-Six

Vince's approach to 'standing up' to Jess went something like this:

'Jess. I've been thinking. About you going to Ibiza . . . ?'

'Yes.'

'Well, I haven't actually got a problem with it in principle – with you going away. But I was just thinking, I don't know, maybe we could all go . . . ?'

'Vince. I told you. It's not the kind of place to take a baby.'

'Yes. That's why I thought we could hire a villa. The three of us. Near Jon's place. But somewhere a bit more baby friendly. That way you could still do all your clubbing and stuff, but we could spend the days together – as a family.'

'Oh, Vince, you are joking, aren't you?'

'No. Why – is that such a stupid idea?'

'It's not a *stupid* idea. It's just . . . it's not what it's about. The whole Ibiza thing – it's about staying up all night and chilling out all day. Not running round after a toddler every five minutes.'

'Yes, but that Jade Jagger – what about her?' countered Vince, who'd done comprehensive research into the subject and had all his bases covered. 'She's got two kids and she's always out clubbing all night.'

Jess raised her eyebrows. 'First,' she said, 'Jade Jagger's

449

kids are much older than Lara, and secondly she's probably got a full-time nanny.'

'Yes, but that's what I'm saying. *I'll* be there. *I'll* be your nanny. I won't be coming out with you at night, so I'll be fine during the day looking after Lara, and you can just lie around reading and sunbathing.'

'No,' she said, 'it's not going to work like that. Lara won't accept that Mummy's feeling ill for a whole week. She'll be demanding my attention. And I'll feel too guilty lying around while you do everything. And besides, I don't want to stay in some piddling little villa with you. I *want* to stay at Jon's villa.'

'Oh,' said Vince, feeling the familiar kick in the gut of one of Jess's classic blunt responses.

'That's the whole point. It's all about the villa. About the experience. It's more than just a holiday. It's a once-in-a-lifetime opportunity. It's a tick in a box. You know . . .'

And Vince did know. Of course he knew. But that still didn't stop him feeling mortally injured.

'Well, then,' he countered desperately, 'how about if Lara and I hire a villa, and you stay with Jon and we could just meet up for lunch and stuff?'

'Vince. What the fuck is the matter with you? Have you actually gone mad?'

'No,' he answered, unnecessarily.

'Then why the hell are you so desperate to crash this holiday?'

He shrugged. He didn't really know why. It was as close as he could get to refusing to let her go, he supposed. 'I don't know,' he said. 'We've never been on holiday as a family, and I just think it would be nice to go away somewhere.'

'And I agree with you. Let's book ourselves a holiday. Let's go to Italy in August. I'll ask my mum to come along. Or you could ask yours. We'll have a fantastic time. But for God's sake, just let me have this time in Ibiza being myself.' And with that she disappeared into the kitchen from where Vince could hear her frantically opening a bottle of wine.

He considered following her in, continuing the conversation, but knew that it was completely futile. He'd blown it. He couldn't reason with her now, not after that spectacular display of deranged desperation. 'We could meet you for lunch.' The words rang in his head. What was he thinking? What was he becoming? And more to the point, what had Jess turned him into?

He sighed and let his head drop into his hands.

He was a sap. A schmuck. A mug. And, quite possibly, a cuckold.

He wasn't cut out for a woman like Jess. He wasn't strong enough.

'Why did you marry me?' he asked, as Jess reappeared bearing a large glass of white wine.

'What?'

'I mean, you know so many men and they're all into the same things as you. You've got nothing in common with me. So why did you marry me?'

Jess frowned at him. 'Because you're the father of my child. Because I wanted us to be a family . . .'

'Yes, but we're not, are we? We're two single parents who happen to live together.'

'Oh, that's bollocks. We do loads of things together ...'

'Like what?'

'Like seeing your parents ...'

'And when was the last time we saw them?'

She shrugged. 'I don't know. A couple of weeks ago ...'

'It was last month. I take Lara there every Sunday while you're in bed. The last time you came with me was over a month ago.'

'And we see your friends.'

'No we don't. *I* see my friends. You haven't seen them since Christmas. And I can't remember the last time I saw your mother ...'

'I see her every day.'

'I know you do, but I don't. We haven't done anything together as family since Christmas Day. And you and I haven't done anything as a couple since ... since ... I can't actually remember the last time we went out together. I mean, what are we actually doing here? What is this?'

'Oh, Christ, Vince,' snapped Jess, 'is this because of Ibiza? Are you jealous or something?'

'No, Jess, I'm not jealous. I'm just ... *lonely*.' And it wasn't until the word left his mouth that he realized that that was exactly how he felt.

'Lonely?'

'Yes. I'm lonely.'

'Oh, Vince, don't be so wet.'

He shrugged and shook his head at her. 'But that's the truth. I feel as if I'm all alone.'

'Then why don't you make more of an effort? See your friends? Get out a bit?'

'That's not what I meant. I don't want to see my friends. They're always in couples anyway. I feel like a fucking gooseberry. I want to see *you*.'

'You see me every night, Vince.'

'Yes, but not properly. I see the dregs of you. The bits that are left over after work and Lara and your precious fucking friends . . .'

'Ah,' she snapped, slamming her wine glass down on the table, 'finally, we get to the crux of the matter. You *are* jealous. You're jealous of Jon and you're jealous of my friends and you resent me having a life outside this domestic fucking *prison* . . .'

'What?'

'You just want to me sit around with you playing the happy little housewife and seeing your prematurely middle-aged friends talking about nannies and organic fucking breadsticks. Well, I'm sorry, Vince, but that's not the woman you married and that's not the woman you will ever turn me into. Because I'm *better* than that.'

'Er – sorry. But you think hanging around in night-clubs designed for people ten years younger than you and filling your body with drugs and alcohol every Saturday night is something to be proud of?!'

'Yes, actually, I do.'

'Well, then, I feel sorry for you, Jess.'

'And I feel sorry for you, Vince. Because you think that this –' she gestured around the flat – 'is enough. You think playing mummies and daddies is the be-all and end-all of life. Because you never once stop to think about the big wide world out there, the possibilities, the panoramas.'

'Christ, Jess, I thought you'd seen everything you wanted to see of the "big wide world". I thought you'd been there, done that. I thought you were ready for parenthood.'

'I am ready for parenthood. I'm a fucking fantastic mother.'

'Yes, you are. You're incredible. I'm not disputing that. But, to me, having a baby is the greatest adventure you could ever have. To me, this –' he echoed her earlier gesture around the flat – 'is everything. This is what it's all about. You, me, Lara. I don't need anything else.'

'Well, I do. And if you don't let me have it, then . . .'

'Then what?'

'Well, I'll have to go.'

'Go?'

'Yes. Leave. Because this is who I am and, if you can't accept that, then there's no hope for us.'

'And you'd do that, would you? Just walk away? Because I wouldn't let you out to play?'

'Uh-huh.'

'Shit, Jess. Is that how little all this means to you?'

'No. It's not. But I can't be controlled, Vince. I *won't* be controlled. And the reason why you and I work so well together is because you're the only man I've ever been with who's let me be myself. That's why I love you. That's why I married you. That's why I wanted you to be the father of my baby.'

'Because I'm a *sap*, you mean?'

'No. Because you're an angel.'

Vince stopped and gulped. He didn't know how to respond to that. Was there actually any difference between a sap and an angel? And did the fact that he liked being referred to as an angel in fact *make* him a sap? Whatever, the comment had effectively defused the incendiary path that the conversation had been taking. He sighed.

'Look,' he said, 'all I'm saying is that I'd like a bit more of you. I'd like us to go out together occasionally.'

'OK,' she soothed, crawling on to his lap and looping her arms around his neck. 'We can do that. Let's ask my mum to baby-sit. Let's go out tomorrow.'

'OK. And I'd like to see Jon. Remember you said you'd get him over for lunch one weekend?'

'I remember.' She ran a fingertip around the contours of his ear.

'And you never did. And I haven't seen him since the wedding. He's such a big part of your life, I just think it would be really nice for us to see him more as family. You know . . .'

'Absolutely,' she purred, running her fingers through his hair, 'I couldn't agree with you more.'

'I really like Jon.'

'I know you do.' She landed a soft, plump kiss on the back of his neck. 'And I really like you.' She pulled up her T-shirt. She wasn't wearing a bra. 'Now shut up and get your clothes off.'

'Oh,' he said, 'right.'

Forty minutes later Vince had carpet burn on his knees, scratch marks on his back and a full, fresh and eager acceptance of his wife's wilful, wayward ways.

Fifty-Seven

Jess didn't come home at all the following Saturday.

Vince was accustomed to finding her on the sofa when he got up on Sunday mornings. She would groan as he opened the curtains, peel herself off the sofa, then stumble directly into the bed that Vince had just vacated.

He called her on her mobile when he realized that she wasn't there, but it went straight through to her voice-mail.

He then called Jon, whose phone was also switched off.

He tried calling every half an hour until lunchtime, when he finally started to worry.

He speed-fed Lara her lunch, strapped her into the back of his car still eating a custard cream and drove over to Jon's fancy apartment in a new canalside development in Walthamstow. They were buzzed in and directed to the fourth floor by someone with an American accent.

A man with a cropped Mohican answered the door to them. He was wearing a pair of combat shorts that hung so low that Vince could see the first few millimetres of his pubic hair, and had black tattoos all over the top half of his body. He stared at Vince and Lara questioningly.

'Hi. Is this Jon's place?'

'Uh-huh,' said the man with the pubic hair, scratching his chest.

'I'm looking for Jess. Do you know where she is?'

'Uh-huh,' he said again. 'She's here. You wanna come in?'

'Yes. Please.'

They followed the American in the shorts through a wide, white corridor to a large open-plan room at the end. He walked so slowly that Vince almost trod on his heels. The room had full-height plate-glass windows overlooking the canal that led on to a balcony. There were various people sitting on the balcony, swigging beer from bottles and smoking under a glowing chrome patio heater.

'Any of you guys know where Jessie is?' asked the American.

The people on the balcony turned and glanced at him, then did a double take when they saw Vince and Lara standing behind him.

'Oh, cute!' a girl with plaits and cut-off jeans said when she saw Lara, jumping to her feet and coming over to say hello. 'Hello, little girlie,' she squeaked, breathing fag breath all over them. 'Aren't you just a cutie, cutie little thing?'

Lara took one look at the girl with plaits and turned and buried her face into Vince's shoulder.

'Oh, bless,' said the girl, 'she's shy.'

Vince smiled grimly and looked at the other people. There were about six of them. They were all younger than him and none of them was Jon.

'I think she's in the bedroom,' said a posh bloke with long hair wearing a T-shirt and a *tie*. 'Are you Vince?'

'Yes,' he said, moving Lara on to his other hip when she started wriggling.

'Cool,' he said. 'Good to meet you. I'm Rio.'

'Right,' said Vince.

'And this is Todd,' he said, pointing at the American. 'That's Simone,' he added while indicating the girl in the plaits. 'And this is Dex and Puss.'

'Nice to meet you all,' said Vince, absorbing the reality of the people behind the stupid names and realizing that they were just a bunch of people he wouldn't give a second glance at if he passed them in the street.

Todd beckoned him with his head. 'Third door on the left,' he said, pointing at the corridor they'd just come through.

'Right,' said Vince, 'thanks.'

He put Lara down and she ran towards the bedroom. Lara seemed very confident in her surroundings, and Vince suddenly remembered that she'd spent a lot of time here since she was born. The thought made him feel prickly and uncomfortable.

'Mummy, Mummy!' She pushed open the door and ran in ahead of him.

Vince followed behind her and watched as she threw herself on to the enormous bed in the middle of the room.

He stopped in his tracks when he saw that Jess wasn't alone in the bed.

She was with Jon.

'Shit. Jesus.' Jess sat bolt upright as Lara threw herself at her. Her hair was matted, her mascara was smudged around her eyes and she wasn't wearing a top. 'Christ,' she looked at Vince, 'what are *you* doing here?'

Vince glanced from Jess to Jon and back again. Neither

of them had the decency to look guilty. 'I had no idea where you were. I was worried,' he said flatly.

'Jesus,' said Jess, 'what time is it?' She looked totally confused and disoriented.

'It's one o'clock,' he said.

'Shit. You're kidding?' She pulled the palms of her hands down her face and tried to shake herself back to life. 'I've been out cold. Shit.' She glanced at Jon. 'Why didn't you wake me?'

Jon shrugged. 'Didn't know what time it was, either.'

Lara snuggled herself between the two of them on the bed, showing not the slightest confusion at finding her mother naked in bed with another man. Vince stared at the three of them feeling a dark rage start to boil up in the pit of his belly. 'So,' he managed, 'what's going on?'

'What – you mean . . . ?' Jess looked at him, then looked at Jon. 'Nothing,' she said bluntly. 'Nothing's going on.'

Vince opened his mouth to say something, then looked at Lara, sitting innocently at the epicentre of this triangle of deceit, and decided to pursue a different line of questioning.

'Why are your phones switched off? Why didn't you come home?'

'Oh, God.' She let her head fall into her hands. 'Christ. Jon. You tell him. I haven't got the energy.'

Jon sighed. 'We were at this party last night. In Islington. We shouldn't have gone. It was all a bit heavy . . .'

'Heavy?'

'Yeah. You know. A lot of stuff going on that we didn't really want to be around.'

Vince's mind raced with possibilities. 'Like what?'

'Not stuff I'd want to talk about in front of ...' Jon glanced at Lara. 'You know.'

'What – sex?'

'No! Not sex. Just people jacking up, crack, that kind of thing.'

Vince shook his head in disbelief.

'It really wasn't our scene and we knew that the minute we walked in. But we just kind of felt we should hang around for a while. And then this bloke started getting ... a bit *full-on* with Jessie ...'

'What d'you mean, "full-on"?' Vince could feel the veins on both temples standing proud of his skull.

'I mean, trying to, you know ... *get off with her*,' he whispered.

'Christ – and where were you?'

'I was there. Keeping an eye on it. But then it got a bit out of hand and he started getting a bit aggressive.'

'Shit. Jess. Did he hurt you?'

'No ... no,' she shook her head, and pulled Lara on to her lap.

'I didn't want to get involved in a scene. It was too dangerous. So we just made a run for it. Slipped out the front door and legged it to the nearest cab office.'

'And that was when I realized that I'd left my bag there. At the flat.'

'Your *bag*? What. With all your stuff in it? Your front-door keys? Your wallet?'

'Yes,' she sighed, and scraped her hair back from her face. 'And my mobile phone.'

'You left a handbag in a crack den with our front-door keys in it?'

'Yup. And pictures of Lara. And all my credit cards. And fifty quid. And my driving licence. And my digital camera.'

'Crack addicts have pictures of Lara?'

'Uh-huh.'

'And our address? Shit – Jess, what about our address?'

'Well,' she said, 'it's on my driving licence. So, yes – they've got our address.'

'And you didn't think to let me know? You didn't think that maybe I'd like to know that a bunch of crack addicts have our front-door keys and our address. While I slept with our baby daughter . . .'

'Shit.' Jess dropped her head on to her hands again. 'Shit. Vince. I'm sorry. I didn't think. I was so busy cancelling my credit cards and my mobile phone, and I just thought that we could get the locks changed this morning. I didn't think they'd come that quickly, you know . . . then I overslept. I had no idea it was so late.'

'Christ, Jess, they're probably there *now*. Do you realize that? As we speak. Taking everything.'

'Shit. Vince. What are we going to do?'

Jon got out of bed, revealing himself to be wearing boxer shorts, a small detail which Vince, in his panic, was unable to take any comfort from. 'I'll come with you,' he said. 'The girls should stay here.'

'Yes,' said Vince. 'You're right. Stay here. We'll be back in an hour.'

They called an emergency locksmith as they drove.

'I'm really fucking sorry, mate,' said Jon.

'It's not your fault,' said Vince, tersely.

'No, I know, but I should have thought. I should have got Jessie to phone you. We were so wasted and so wired by the time we got home ...'

'Not a problem,' he muttered. 'Not your responsibility.'

'It was. You're my friends. I should have thought.'

'Yeah. Well. You're not a parent. You think differently when you've got a kid.' He said this knowing that it was a verbal kick in the balls, especially in the light of Jess's abortion, but not caring.

'I hope you don't think –' Jon paused.

'What?'

'Jessie. I hope you don't blame me for her veering off the rails again. I know she was pretty together when you met her. It must be a bit *weird*.'

'Just a bit,' he sniffed.

'It's the bus thing again. You know. She's taken the bus off course. She's driving too fast. You can ask her to slow down, but she won't hear you. If you want to get off the bus, you're gonna have to jump.'

'Yes, but I'm not the only passenger on the bus any more, am I? There's Lara now, too. She has to slow down, for all our sakes. And maybe after what's happened today, I don't know, maybe it'll be like a wake-up call.'

Jon smiled wryly and shook his head. 'I wouldn't count on it.'

The locksmith was waiting outside the flat when they got back. There were no marauding crack addicts in the vicinity of the flat and everything was quiet. Vince breathed a sigh of relief. But it wasn't until he'd handed fifty quid to the locksmith and watched him pull away in his van that Vince started to relax. And as he started to relax, a few pertinent questions popped into his head, rudely demanding answers.

What was Jess doing in Jon's bed?

Why hadn't she phoned him?

Why was Jon's phone switched off?

How had they ended up in a crack den?

He bit his tongue and waited. He wanted Jess to be there. He wanted to see the whites of her eyes when she answered them.

Apparently, Jess had slept in Jon's bed the previous night because she was feeling 'freaked'. She'd been wearing knickers and they hadn't so much as shared a hug under the duvet. Apparently it wasn't any big deal because they'd done it loads of times before. She hadn't phoned home because she didn't want to wake Vince and Lara, and she hadn't come home because she didn't have her front-door keys. Jon's phone was switched off because it had run out of juice (he showed him the dead phone by way of evidence) and the reason they'd ended up in a crack den (which wasn't apparently an *actual* crack den – just a flat full of people *taking* crack) was because they'd met a nice middle-class bloke at a club and he'd invited them back to a party being held by a graffiti artist in Islington. Being, on the whole, nice middle-class boys and girls, this had conjured up images of a groovy lateral conversion in a Georgian town house with a roof terrace and over-sized canvasses on the walls, not the eighth floor of a tower block off the City Road.

And although these answers were, in and of them-selves, wholly satisfactory, not one of them went even a quarter of the way to mollifying Vince. Because, however innocent the night had been (and Vince believed that it probably had), nothing could take away from the fact that Jess had gone to sleep last night knowing that potentially dangerous people had her front-door keys and her address, that she'd fallen into a naked, impenetrable slumber in her ex-boyfriend's bed, leaving her daughter as open prey.

And even as he drove his wife and child home from Jon's flat, even as they discussed plans for tea in the park and a visit to his mother's, Vince was mentally filing away the details of his wife's shocking negligence to use as future ammunition to fire from his position on the moral high ground.

Fifty-Eight

Joy pushed down hard on the lid of her suitcase in an attempt to get the two locks to meet.

She was only going away for two weeks, but because she had absolutely no idea what to expect from her trip she'd felt obliged to pack almost everything she owned.

She checked her handbag again for her passport, tickets and purse. And then she sat and waited for her mother to collect her. It was a straight journey on the Piccadilly Line from Southgate to Heathrow, but Joy couldn't face the prospect of an hour on the Tube, trying not to look at people, trying not to think about what she was about to do. So Barbara was going to drive her there. She'd offered to fly with her, too, but Joy knew the offer was born more out of maternal anxiety than a desire to share the experience with her. And besides, Joy wanted to go to America on her own.

Because that's where her father lived.

Not quite in a San Francisco penthouse or an LA mansion, but in a house with a big number in Columbus, Ohio, with his second wife and their ten-year-old son.

She'd found him on the Internet, like a second-hand wedding dress or a hotel room in Bristol. It took a total of three hours to find her father. It felt too easy.

She'd had to sift through dozens of Charles Yungs to get to the right one. Porn stars, film agents, university professors, dead musicians, electrical engineers. And then she'd found him on a website for a small chain of super-markets in the Mid West called Reisens. He was regional CEO for Columbus and Dayton, in charge of ten stores. She knew it was him because there was a picture of him on a page called 'Meet the Management!'. He still had a full head of dark hair, but had developed a quite pro-nounced grey stripe at the front, like a racoon. He wore wire-framed glasses and was very slightly jowly, but there was still no doubt that it was him. It was the eyes. *Her* eyes.

She sent him an e-mail the very same afternoon:

Dear Charles,
My name is Joy and my mother's name is Barbara. I believe you are my father. I would love to talk to you if this is the case, but appreciate that this might be difficult for you.
    I am thirty-three years old, single and living in London.
    I hope very much to hear from you.

There'd been a reply in her in-box the next day:

Dear Joy,
Yes, I am definitely your father! I am delighted that you have got in touch. I have thought about you many times, particularly on your birthday, and wondered what might have become of you. I am married to my second wife, Carrie, and we have a young son, Curtis, who is about to turn eleven.

466

I have two grown-up children from my first marriage – Deanna, who is twenty-three, and Debra, who is twenty-two. They live in Maryland with their mother, and I see them as much as I can.

There are so many things that you and I have to discuss. I would love for us to talk properly. Maybe we could speak on the phone?

Yours,
Charles

They did talk on the phone after that, a handful of times, and it quickly became clear that, although Charles Yung was not the most exciting person in the world, he was decent, polite and uncomplicated enough for a face-to-face meeting not to be out of the question.

Carrie wouldn't hear of Joy staying at a hotel and insisted that she stay with them, in their house with the big number.

In the run-up to her departure date, Joy received a flurry of e-mails from Carrie:

We have a small Jack Russell terrier called Barney. I do hope you don't suffer from any dog allergies or phobias?

I have made up your bed with a goose-down quilt. Please let me know if you have any feather allergies.

I was just planning your welcome dinner and wanted to be sure that you eat meat. In particular, beef and chicken.

467

Charles wanted to cook for you one night, some traditional Singaporean dishes. Some of it might be a tad spicy. Are you OK with this?

Curtis was wondering if he might interview you for the school magazine? (He is the editor-in-chief! Grand plans to be an international reporter!) Everyone in his class is very excited about his English 'sister'!

Please be sure to bring photos of you 'through the years'! Charles and I would love to see how you've changed and grown through the 'missing' years.

It was obvious to Joy that Carrie was thoroughly enjoying her role coordinating this exotic visitation. She had corralled cousins and second cousins and great-aunts and great-uncles from five different states to come to visit while Joy was with them and had, it seemed, planned a menu for the full two weeks of her stay.

In the days leading up to her trip, Joy started to feel nervous.

Would she find it suffocating?

Would it be too intense?

Would she end up spending more time with Carrie than with her father?

How would Curtis react to her?

Was she staying too long? Not long enough?

But she put these concerns to the back of her mind and focused on the positives.

Her father was alive.

He was normal and ordinary and wanted to see her.

He'd been incredibly easy to track down. It felt like destiny. It felt like perfect timing.

His family was going out of its way to make her feel welcome.

She had her mother's full support.

Everything was in place for a successful and constructive experience.

She looked round her flat. Her home. By the time she next sat and looked at these four walls, she'd be a different person. Stronger, maybe; weaker, possibly. But definitely different. Nothing would ever be the same again.

The doorbell buzzed and Joy got to her feet to let her mother in.

The adventure started here.

Fifty-Nine

Halfway through the third week of March, Jess's friend Clare sent her an e-mail announcing that she was coming back to London after five years in Australia.

Clare had just found out that Dave, her live-in lover and love of her life, was sleeping with three other women, including her best friend. Her heart was broken and she wanted her mum. So she was coming home. In two weeks.

This snippet of girlie gossip from across the globe would not normally have registered particularly with Vince. But this piece of gossip came attached to a bunch of major implications for himself. Because Clare was the owner of their flat. And she wanted it back.

It couldn't have come at a worse time. Vince and Jess had been hanging on to each other by a filament since the shocking night of the lost handbag. Jess could no longer claim that her hedonism and pleasure-seeking were fundamental rights to be defended, and the fact that she had lost her grip on the moral high ground made her moody and resentful. Equally, Vince could no longer justify his wife's shady secret life and long absences from the house with the fact that she deserved it because she was such a perfect, flawless mother, and he had become intolerant and short-tempered.

It wasn't a good combination of mind-sets and the atmosphere in their little flat had become tense, bordering on nasty. So the process of renegotiating their living arrangements (which had always been so tenuous anyway) was not something that either of them was prepared for.

The options open to them were:

1. Rent somewhere together.
2. Move in with Jess's mother while they found somewhere to buy.
3. Beg Clare to stay with *her* mother and let them stay in her flat while they found somewhere to buy.
4. Split up, get divorced, fight for custody of Lara.

They sat and discussed the first three options, but left the fourth option hovering silently in the background of their conversations like a bad smell they were both too polite to mention.

Four days after the e-mail from Clare, Vince did something he'd never done before. He cancelled all his morning lessons, claiming that he had to look after his daughter because she was ill. He then dropped a perfectly healthy Lara off at nursery, parked his car at the station and got the first train into Euston. He didn't really know what he was planning to do once he got into town – he was simply responding to an instinctive and overwhelming need to get out of his immediate environment and put some space between himself and his dilemmas.

The first building he stumbled upon as he wandered aimlessly in the brightness of a crisp March morning was the British Library. Something about the clean, graphic lines of the building pulled him in. It looked so new and fresh, full of light and air and space to breathe.

He wandered aimlessly for a while, up and down escalators and corridors, glancing idly at framed ancient manuscripts and works of modern art. A group of schoolchildren was being led around by a very enthusiastic woman in a tight red dress, whose bare legs were festooned with varicose veins that looked like earthworms crawling across her skin. Vince sat down on a bench and watched the children for a while. They were about fourteen. Some looked old for their age, some looked young, but they all that air of self-conscious desperation that Vince remembered so well from his own adolescence.

His peers had seemed so mysterious to him when he was fourteen. He couldn't have imagined what any of them were really thinking or feeling, what they really dreamed about or what they really wanted. They were each hermetically sealed against the world, hungry to taste it yet terrified to let it in in case it revealed their inherent childishness, unworldliness, *uncoolness*.

But now, more than twenty years on, he could look at these half-formed people and read them like books. That one there, wearing too much hair gel, with the crescent of acne around his jawline – he was his mother's favourite. He liked her cooking and wanted to marry someone just like her one day. The boy standing next to him with the hint of patchy stubble and the angry blue eyes – his mum shouted at him from the minute he woke up to the minute he went to bed, and he just wanted to get out of here so he could have a fag. That one was a virgin; that one wasn't. That one had an eating disorder; that one was the school slag. That one cried herself to sleep every night; that one practised her Oscars' acceptance speech.

And then he saw the boy who was him – the Melonhead of his year. He was standing slightly to the left of the group with his hands buried deeply into the pockets of voluminous black combats. A pair of earphones dangled from the breast pocket of his blazer. He was slightly overweight in an unkempt, middle-aged way, and his hair was dyed black and grown long in an attempt to cover a face that God appeared to have had no hand whatsoever in the creation of. Vince stared at him. He could tell he wasn't listening to the enthusiastic woman with the varicose veins. He was either listening to music in his head or just praying and hoping that no one would look at him. He just wanted to be left alone.

Vince wanted to talk to him. He wanted to tell him that everything would be all right, that one day beautiful girls would talk to him and that everything would make sense. Because if someone had tapped him on the shoulder in the British Library when he was fourteen years old and said that one day he'd be thirty-five years old and married to a beautiful woman who loved sex and that they'd have a gorgeous daughter together and live in a cool flat in Enfield he would never have believed them. And he certainly wouldn't have asked questions about the quality of the relationship or whether or not the foxy wife went out too much or took too many drugs or played Russian roulette with their daughter's security. He'd just have smiled and said, 'Cool!'

But then, he thought, what if that same man had told him that one day he'd be thirty-five years old and losing his hair, that he'd be teaching people to drive for a living and was about to be evicted from the cool flat with nowhere else to go? He wouldn't have been quite so pleased with his prognosis, then.

And that was when it dawned on Vince – he'd been looking in all the wrong places for an explanation for the collapse of his marriage to Jess. He'd been so busy blaming her for everything that he'd forgotten to look at himself. And really, who could blame Jess? Who could blame an exciting, passionate, spontaneous woman for looking outside of her dull, safe relationship for stimulation, to find *herself*? What did he really have to offer someone like her? Yes, he was a good father, but that wasn't enough for Jess. She needed more than security and safety. She needed a man she could feel proud of – a man she wanted to spend time with.

And Vince needed more from himself, too. He was thirty-five. He should be able to afford a house for his family. He should have put money aside for this sort of eventuality. He should be in a position to be planning for the future instead of sitting stalled at this junction like a clapped-out old motor.

He looked at the boy in the combats and smiled to himself. He was going to make him proud. He was going to get a job that stimulated him, that took him around the world, that paid for a house for Jess and Lara with a garden and a playroom and a spare bedroom for another baby. He was going to take his family on Mediterranean holidays and take up a hobby. Maybe he'd learn to ride a motorbike. Or start playing football on a Sunday. Maybe they'd all go skiing or sailing together. Maybe he'd learn to cook or play the guitar. Join a band. Write a novel. Learn massage. Take up yoga. Study a foreign language. Evening classes. Painting. Theatre. Salsa. Tae kwan do.

His head began to race with all the possibilities, with all the things he'd forgotten to think about since he gave up on London and moved back to Enfield. He wasn't a *driving instructor*. He was a *man*. There was a whole world out there and Jess was right – he'd forgotten to look at it. He'd become embedded in his little corner of Enfield and set in his ways. He'd become middle-aged. And he was only thirty-five.

He jumped to his feet. He wanted to see Jess now. He wanted to apologize for dragging her down, for thinking that decency and reliability were acceptable substitutes for passion and life. He wanted to pick her up and swing her around and tell her she was beautiful and amazing. He wanted to start making plans with her. He wanted another baby. He wanted three. Four. He wanted her to enjoy her life *with* him as much as she enjoyed her life *without* him. He wanted her to see him the same way she saw Jon. He wanted *her*. He loved her.

He headed for the foyer, stopping as he passed the boy in the combats. He looked at him and opened his mouth to say something. The boy looked back at him, lifeless eyes appraising him slowly. There was no spark there, no opening. Vince closed his mouth and smiled at him instead.

And then he walked triumphantly outdoors, the tender spring sunshine touching his face as he walked as fast as he could back to Euston Station.

*

Jess was eating a noodle salad from a clear plastic bowl when Vince arrived at the radio station an hour later.

'Vince!' she spluttered, dropping her plastic fork into the bowl and looking up at him in surprise. 'What are you doing here?'

'I've been thinking,' he said, not wanting to pause for breath, even for a second, in case he lost his momentum, 'about everything. About us. I love you, Jess. I always have and I always will. I don't want to lose you. And I've got to accept some responsibility for what's been happening between us these past few months. I haven't been living up to my potential. I haven't been making an effort. And I want us to make a fresh start.'

'Vince, I –'

'I'm prepared to do whatever it takes, to make you happy, to make this work . . .'

'Oh, God, Vince . . .'

'We could go and live in Ibiza! Or maybe take a year off and sail around the Med. The three of us. I don't want to be a driving instructor any more. I don't want to be this dull, middle-aged man. I want to change. I want to be the man of your dreams –'

'Vince. I've got to tell you something.' She pulled his hand towards her across the table.

'What?'

She cast her eyes downwards and took a deep breath. 'I'm pregnant,' she said.

Vince stopped for a moment and absorbed this new and unexpected fact. His face broke into a huge smile. 'But, Jess – that's fantastic! That's amazing! This is just what we need! A fresh start. A new baby. Oh, God, this is perfect — you're perfect. Come here!' He stood and opened up his arms to her, but she just stayed exactly where she was.

'No, Vince,' she said softly. 'It's not perfect because the baby . . . it's not yours.'

Al & Emma's Kitchen, 1.58 a.m.

Natalie unpeeled her hand from over her mouth. 'Jess is pregnant – and it's *not yours*?' she exhaled.

'Yup,' Vince shrugged, and picked up his wine glass.

'Fuck,' said Emma.

'Shit,' said Natalie.

'Whose is it, then?' said Claire. 'Is it Jon Gavin's?'

Vince shook his head.

The girls gasped again. 'Then who?' said Claire.

Vince smiled. He was almost enjoying the impact his shocking news was having on his friends – it made him feel strangely useful to be able to inject a little high drama into their unexceptional lives. 'It's Bobby's. The ex before me,' he said. 'The old one who wouldn't leave his girlfriend for her. The one she went into therapy over. The married one. The *ugly* one.'

'Nooo,' said Natalie.

'Uh-huh. All that time I spent feeling insecure about Jon Gavin, it never occurred to me that she might still have feelings for the old ugly one . . .'

'See,' slurred Emma, 'that's the problem with men. You *assume* women are as shallow as you. That we're as obsessed with looks as you are.'

'Yes,' agreed Claire, 'because the old one might have been

ugly – but he was the One Who Got Away, wasn't he? The one who fucked her head up. The one she couldn't have. And Jon Gavin might have looked like Matthew McConaughey, but he wasn't a challenge. She could have clicked her fingers and had him.'

The girls all nodded sagely.

'So how far gone is she?' asked Natalie.

'Eight months. It's due next month.'

'And was she having an affair with him?' said Emma.

Vince nodded. 'Pretty much for the whole time since Lara was born. They met up at the same hotel once a fortnight, had dinner, went upstairs, had sex, went home. I thought she was at yoga . . .'

'Oh, God,' she said, 'how tacky.'

'I know,' said Vince. 'I know.'

'So, what's she going to do? Has she told him?'

'Yes. She told him. He wanted her to get rid of it. But she didn't. She's going to keep it. Live at her mother's. Bring it up alone.' Vince stopped and swallowed, feeling a wave of emotion threatening to engulf him.

'But what about Lara?' said Claire, looking horrified. 'What's happening about Lara?'

'She'll spend four nights a week with me and three nights a week with Jess.'

'Oh, my God. And how do you feel about that? About not living with Lara any more?'

He shrugged again. 'I'm trying not think about it, really. The whole thing's just . . .' He stopped briefly to control another sudden surge of emotion. 'It's all my fault,' he said. 'I should never have got involved with Jess. I knew from the outset that she was all wrong for me, but I was so flattered and so desperate to settle down and start a family, and she was so fucking good in bed.' He smiled wryly. 'I loved her more than she loved me, that was the problem. A basic imbalance. Relationships like that never last, however hard you try. And now she's pregnant and in love with a man who'll never love her the way she loves him. It's a series of vicious circles, and the only way to stop it is to find someone who loves you the same. Like you love Al, and like you love Simon. You know. No power struggle. No insecurities. Just friendship. Because you can never be friends with someone if you love them too much . . .'

'Can I just say something?' said the increasingly drunken Emma. 'I've wanted to say this for years. And I probably shouldn't be saying it now. But I'm drunk, so fuck it, but I *never* liked that Jess. From the first moment I met her, I thought – *I don't like you.*'

'Me neither,' said Natalie, raising her hand sheepishly. 'Nowhere near good enough for you.'

'Can I third that?' said Claire, much to Vince's surprise, as he'd never heard Claire say a bad word against anyone in all the years he'd known her.

'Really?' he said.

'Yeah. She's not horrible or anything. I just thought she was a bit . . . *self-centred*. A bit wrapped up in herself. That's all.'

Vince gulped and nodded. He'd always suspected that Jess wasn't the type of woman other women warmed to, but it was still a bit startling to hear it stated so bluntly.

'But anyway,' Claire conciliated, 'she's the mother of your child and we shouldn't slag her off. It's not respectful.'

'Also,' said Vince, 'it's not always that cut and dried, is it? Jess isn't actually a *bad* person as such. She was just the wrong girl for me.'

'And what about you? What are you going to do?'

'That's a very good question,' he replied grimly. Because he could just about cope with the fact that his wife was pregnant by another man and that his daughter was only going to be living with him for half the week, but living back at his mum's, sharing a bedroom with Kyle and still teaching people to drive every day was more than he could bear. 'I'm going away for a while,' he said, 'on holiday. I need a couple of weeks by myself, on a beach, somewhere quiet. I need to decide what happens next.'

'Oh,' said Emma, 'that's a fantastic idea. And you never know,' she winked, 'you might meet someone while you're out there.'

Vince smiled wryly. 'I don't think so,' he said. 'I'm not sure that's really what I need in my life right now.'

Simon walked into the kitchen and sat on his wife's lap. 'What are you girls gossiping about?' he said, as Natalie promptly pushed him off her lap good-humouredly.

'Life, love, destiny and everything in between,' she replied.

'Fuck,' he said, 'we've been talking about fucking pensions for the past half an hour. I should have stayed in here.'

The other men wandered in one by one, and the conversation splintered. Cabs were called and coats were collected and the evening drew to a gentle halt.

Emma and Al saw Vince off at the door. Emma drew Vince towards her for a hug as he left. 'Hang on in there,' she said into his ear. 'You are the nicest bloke I know. You'll get your happy ending. I know you will.'

Vince nodded and headed towards his taxi, turning to wave before he got in.

'Oh,' Emma shouted into the still night air. 'And don't forget – keep your eyes peeled for cats!'

He smiled at her and waved. And then he got into the cab and headed back to his mum's and a sleeping bag on Kyle's bedroom floor.

October 2003

Happy Ending

Sixty

Cass never usually bought glossy magazines. Cass despised glossy magazines. As far as Cass was concerned, glossy magazines were the root cause of every case of anorexia, bulimia and body dysmorphic disorder in the entire western world, so the fact that she picked up a copy of *Company* on the platform at Northampton station for her journey back to London was entirely out of character.

It was one of the cover strap lines that had caught her attention:

THE INTERNET CHANGED MY LIFE!

It caught her attention because the Internet had indeed changed her life. She'd met Hayden on the Internet. Hayden Moyses. Twenty-six years old, a landscape gardener, beautiful inside and out. They'd chatted for weeks in a chatroom for amateur psychics. He stood out from the rest because he was sane while everyone else was mad. They had so much in common – tarot, gardening, veganism, the occult, a love of cats – and eventually they'd arranged to meet up. And now here they were, eighteen months down the line, insanely in love, deliriously happy and about to move in together. They'd just bought a cottage, in the Northamptonshire countryside. It had two bedrooms, a chicken coop and a genuine Victorian pet cemetery at the bottom of the garden. It was beautiful. They'd exchanged contracts two days ago and now Cass was on her way back to London to pack up her stuff and say goodbye to city life for ever.

She opened up a packet of pumpkin seeds and flicked through twenty pages of adverts full of seventeen-year-old girls with eating disorders wearing dresses that cost as much as holidays until she finally found the article she was looking for.

The first story was about a secretary from Kent who'd found love with a Palestinian car mechanic in an Internet chatroom for fans of Michael Jackson. It was a sweet story and they were obviously genuinely in love, but, try as she might, Cass couldn't see a happy ending for them.

The second story was about a lesbian from Dundee who'd found the courage to come out of her closet at the age of thirty-two after joining a chatroom for Scottish lesbians and was now a successful stand-up comedian.

But it was the third story that really caught Cass's attention. A story about a thirty-four-year-old Internet MD from London – a story about a girl called *Joy Downer*.

It had to be her. It was an unusual name, the age was about right and the photograph of a petite, stylish, dark-haired girl with slightly oriental features perfectly matched the mental image that Vince's description had left her with.

Cass tipped a handful of pumpkin seeds into her mouth and started to read:

I found my father – then I found myself

*Joy Downer, 34, was a thirty-something divorcée,
living at home with her mother and working in a photo lab
when a chance find in her parents' loft changed the course of her life
for ever. She now runs* Whateverhappenedto.com, *the UK's most
successful search and reunion website for friends, families and lovers.*

'My marriage was a disaster,' says Joy, thirty-four. 'I'd married in haste, barely giving a thought to the consequences, and of course it went horribly wrong very quickly. My parents had had a difficult marriage, too. They eventually divorced and, on the day that my father remarried, I found myself rooting around in the loft in my parents' house. Within minutes I'd found a photo that I believed held the key to all the confusion in my life. It was a picture of a handsome young half-Tibetan boy, and I knew for certain the moment I saw the photograph that he was my real father. My mother later told me that he was a gardener in the apartment block where they lived in Singapore, that they'd had a passionate affair and that he was indeed my father. For some reason I didn't feel all that surprised by the discovery. I'd always felt displaced, as if I didn't quite belong in my environment. I was like a human chameleon – always trying to fit in with what other people expected of me, never being true to myself. I really didn't know who I was, and my immediate and overwhelming reaction on hearing about my father was that I wanted to meet him.

'My mother encouraged me and the very next day I went on-line to see if I could track him down. All I knew about him was his name and age, but in less than three hours I'd found him. I sent him an e-mail immediately, which he replied to the very next day. He sounded warm and friendly, and very soon I was organizing a trip to stay with him and his family in Columbus, Ohio.

'I had no idea what to expect as I set off for America, but the minute I walked through customs at Columbus and saw my father standing there, I knew I'd done the right thing. He was everything I could have hoped for – sweet-natured, gentle, clever and family-minded. His wife made me feel incredibly welcome and, even though it felt a bit strange at first, being in a foreign country, living in a stranger's house, I soon came to feel as if I was one of the family. I extended my trip from two weeks to two months so that I could spend as much time as possible with my father. I found that we had so much in common – it was little things, such as the fact that we both love people watching, we both pick our toenails and we both hate the smell of Scotch. We shared mannerisms, too, and his feet were exactly the same shape as mine!

'When I eventually came home I felt like a different person, like I finally made sense. So instead of finding another job in a photo lab I decided to try something different with my new-found confidence. My experience of looking for my father on the Internet had inspired me. I'd been lucky – it had only taken me three hours to find my father. But it could have taken me much, much longer, or I might not have found him at all. It occurred to me that instead of trawling randomly through search engine results for a missing person, wouldn't it be great if there was a website that did all the hard work for you. I mentioned the idea to my father in America and he loved it – so much so that he offered to lend me the money to start it up! Eight months later, the website finally went live. We now get over ten thousand hits a day and have been responsible for reuniting hundreds of people, from ex-colleagues and first loves to old mates and adopted children. If we can't find the person you're looking for, you don't pay a penny. I employ ten people and we have just won an industry award.

'It's so great going to work every day knowing that what I do makes a difference to people's lives. I feel professionally fulfilled for the first time in my life and, on a personal level, reuniting people for a living made me realize how wasteful it is to let important people fall through your fingers. About two years ago I tracked down the man I originally thought was my father, the man who brought me up. I'll never have a proper relationship with him, but it was reassuring to see him after so many years and to know that he is happy and content.

'The Internet is an incredible thing. Every day I feel amazed and overwhelmed by its ability to impact on people in such tiny, personal ways and such huge, impersonal ways. I wouldn't be where I am today without it – in fact, I would say that I owe my happiness to the World Wide Web.'

Cass sighed. She didn't have a great deal of fondness for much that the modern world had to offer – she often felt that she'd have been happier in a more medieval setting, in a world with fewer flashing lights and more handicrafts (but possibly a touch more personal hygiene). But she made an exception for the Internet. It was a truly remarkable thing – so inherently human and touchingly old-fashioned.

She flicked back to the photograph of Joy Downer and stared at it for a while. She really was an incredibly pretty girl in an ethereal, slightly indie kid kind of a way.

And now she'd seen her she could totally see why Vince had been infatuated with her. They would have been perfect together. A dream couple. Just like her and Hayden. She gulped at the thought of ending up apart from your soul mate. Poor Vince. Poor Joy. Everyone should have what she and Hayden had.

As she stared at the picture of the girl with the pretty eyes, Cass thought back to ten years ago, to her life as a carefree single girl in a flat share in Finsbury Park, before she'd got all grown-up and wrinkly, when Madeleine was still alive and she'd been convinced she was going to drop dead on her thirtieth birthday. She thought about Vince and his sweet smile and the way he'd carried on going out with that Magda girl for about six months longer than he'd meant to because he was too nice to dump her. She thought about the passage of time and how you really knew you were getting old when you had to start chucking out old memories to make room for the new ones, and she wondered how Vince was now, what he was up to, if he'd ever found a girl who truly appreciated him.

And then, as the train rushed through a tunnel and deafened her to the chatter of her fellow passengers, she closed her eyes, clasped her hands together and said a prayer to Carlos, her 150-year-old spirit guide, that Vince would read the October issue of *Company* magazine, that he'd send Joy an e-mail and that Vince and Joy would finally be reunited.

Sixty-One

Vince hated coming home. He could feel the Portuguese sunshine falling off him like flakes of dead skin as he headed towards passport control at Gatwick. With every step down the carpeted walkway he felt more and more of the mellow warmth and relaxation of his holiday being left behind. His bag weighed heavily on his shoulder, and the thought of what he was coming home to left him feeling sick with despondency. He wanted to turn around and start walking in the opposite direction, get back on the plane and be back at Faro airport in time for a nice dinner overlooking the sea.

His two weeks away had changed nothing. He was still living at his mum's, still getting divorced and still a driving instructor. In a couple of weeks his tan would have faded to nothing, and it would be as if he'd never gone away.

He'd had plenty of time to think in Portugal.

He'd thought of all sorts of things he'd like to do with his life, but they were exactly the same things he'd thought about doing after being made redundant from Coalford Swann. Stupid, teenage fantasies about being both creatively fulfilled and ludicrously rich. But he was too old for teenage fantasies. He had a child. He had nowhere to live. He needed to do something that would earn him money, and quickly.

He flashed his passport at a dreary, disinterested British

person and sighed heavily. The only good thing about coming home, he mused, was seeing Lara. He'd missed her like he'd miss an eyeball or a thumb. The ache of missing her had been physically painful.

He stopped with the rest of his flight mates under the luggage screens, waiting for his flight number to come up. He stared around him at the same faces he'd been staring at three hours ago at Faro airport, faces that had looked playful and cosmopolitan in the Portuguese light, faces that had started to fade as the minutes ticked by in the air, faces that now looked cheated and dampened as they waited resignedly to collect their luggage and head home. Coming back from holidays made Cinderellas out of everyone, he thought.

And then he caught the eye of a girl he hadn't seen at Faro. A small, slim girl with straight brown hair cut into a feathery bob. She was dressed in a denim miniskirt and blue cotton halterneck and was laden down with duty-free vodka. She looked about thirty and was wearing slightly too much make-up. There was something vaguely familiar about her, but Vince couldn't put his finger on it.

She looked at him quizzically. He looked away. When he looked at her again she was still staring at him in that probing way. He blushed. Suddenly she walked towards him.

'I've just worked it out,' she said, smiling at him. 'You're Vince, aren't you? Vince-with-the-funny-surname?'

Vince looked round him, checking that no one was watching this slightly embarrassing exchange. 'Er, yes,' he said.

'I knew it!' she said, 'I've got a memory for faces. It's a talent. A skill.' She beamed up at him. Her teeth were crooked and tinged yellow.

He smiled at her politely. There was something unsettling about her, something not quite right. 'I'm sorry,' he said, 'I don't really, quite . . .'

'No, no, no,' she said, patting his arm reassuringly, 'you're not supposed to remember me. It's all right. I've changed quite a bit since we last met.' She beamed at him again. 'Do you remember, about, God, must be about ten years ago now – do you remember a cat? A big orange cat called . . .' The girl clicked her tongue against the roof of her mouth, trying to recall.

'Madeleine?' he offered.

'That's right!' she pounced on his offering. 'That's right, Madeleine. Except *we* called her Mou-Shou and thought she was a he.' She laughed and looked at him expectantly, and something began to rise, vapour-like, from the reservoirs of his memory. 'Were you . . . ?' he began, tentatively.

'That's right. Bella. I'm *Bella*. The new and improved version,' she said as she flicked her hair.

'Oh, my God,' he said, 'you look so . . .'

'I know. I know. It's fab, isn't it? I had the op last year,' she whispered. '*Finally*. Thank God. It only took, like, *twenty years*. So now I'm me. At last. Bugger of it is that no one ever recognizes me any more.' She laughed nervously and took a breath. 'So,' she said, 'what are you up to these days?'

Vince was still reeling from the shock of Bella's transformation, not to mention his first ever face-to-face conversation with a post-operative transsexual. 'Er . . . just in the middle of a divorce, actually,' he said.

'Oh, dear. Is it a nasty one?'

'Not too bad. But then, you know, no divorce is good, is it?'

'Ooh, I don't know. That Joy's divorce was good,' she stopped momentarily. 'Did you know?' she said. 'Did you know that Joy and that weird bloke got divorced?'

'Yes,' he said, 'that was the last time I spoke to her, actually. She was just about to get divorced.'

'Thank God. That was such a relief, I tell you. I don't know what she was thinking of. He was so wrong for her.' She shook her head incredulously. 'But getting divorced from him – the best thing she ever did. And that George has already remarried and got a kid. It was best for both of them; it really was. She's just *blossomed* since they split up. Bought a flat. Got a proper job. Found her real dad.'

'Her real dad . . . ?'

'Oh, yes – the drama of it. She found a photo in her mum's loft. Some handsome young fellow with a fruity message written on the back. Turns out that old dumpling of a mother of hers had had a torrid affair with a boy young enough to be her son. Turns out that he was Joy's real dad.'

'Shit. You're kidding.'

'No. And Joy found him on the Internet and went and met him last year in the States. And she's just been like this *new* person ever since. So confident. So go-getty.'

'Go-getty?'

'Yeah. Leaving George, then finding her dad. She

494

knows who she is now. She's got an *identity*. And, boy, do I know how she feels.' She stopped and smiled.

'So, you're still in touch with her, then?'

'Oh, yes,' she said. 'It's funny because I really didn't like her when I first met her. I don't know why. I didn't warm to her. But over the years she's become one of my closest friends. She's just the loveliest person I've ever known. And I'm fussy about people, I really am.' She stopped and glanced up at the luggage announcement screens. 'Fucking hate this,' she said, 'I mean, what are they actually *doing* with our bags, for God's sake?' She tutted and looked at her watch. 'I'm seeing her tonight.'

'Who – Joy?'

'Uh-huh. Going round to hers for dinner, with Jules. D'you remember Jules?'

'Is that the, er . . . *large* woman?'

'Yes. Julia. With the boobs. That's right. And Julia's boyfriend – I mean, *fiancé*. She's getting married in July.' She smiled.

Vince smiled back. He didn't know what to say. He couldn't quite get his head around the concept of Joy still existing, of her still knowing these people who seemed like such a distant and dream-like part of his existence. He couldn't believe that once upon a time all he'd had to worry about was weird flatmates, ex-girlfriends and missing cats. He couldn't believe he'd lived in a flat share in Finsbury Park, that he'd worked as a copywriter, that he'd been twenty-six years old without a care in the world. It all seemed so petty and foolish.

'So,' he said, eventually, 'what's Joy up to these days?'

'Well, she's living in Southgate. She's working for

herself, running a website. Got her own little offices in Palmers Green, employs a few people. She's doing really well . . .'

'Wow,' Vince nodded appreciatively. 'And is she, you know, *with* anyone?'

Bella shook her head. 'Nope. All alone and single. Why, are you still interested?'

Vince blanched. 'God, no. Well, not in that way. I mean . . .'

'God, that was weird, wasn't it, that business with the cat? Spooky. And I tried to tell Joy that you were after her then, but she didn't believe me. Said she'd seen you with some stunning woman and a kid, that I was winding her up. And then she went and married that weird man and that was that. Didn't really see her again for years.'

'I saw her,' said Vince, 'just before they split up. I saw Joy in Covent Garden. We had a chat. She left him the next day.'

'God,' said Bella, 'you two. You've got some kind of weird *connection*, haven't you?' She wiggled her fingers. 'And now here we are again. Another spooky coincidence. Do you think maybe fate's trying to tell you something?'

Vince shrugged. 'Maybe,' he said.

'Ooh, I tell you what. Why don't you come along tonight? For dinner?'

'What!'

'I'm serious. It would be so incredible to see her face when you turned up at the door.'

'But I can't. I'm not invited.'

'Oh, sod that. What are you – a vampire? Joy always cooks way too much anyway. And she's been single for long enough. She's in danger of turning into a weird old spinster. Come along. It'll be amazing.'

'Oh, God,' Vince began to fluster, 'I don't know. I mean I've only just got back from holiday. I need to unpack. I want to see my daughter . . .'

'Your daughter goes to bed, doesn't she?'

'Yes.'

'Well, then, put her to bed, then jump in a cab. You'll be there in time for the main course.'

'I'm very tired . . .'

'*Tired?*' she complained. 'Joy Downer, the loveliest girl in all the world, the girl you lost your virginity to, a beautiful *single* girl who makes the best mushroom risotto in north London is waiting for you in Southgate and you're *tired?* You're just going to go home to an empty flat and *sleep?*'

Vince stopped and licked his lips. Because he wasn't just going home to an empty flat, was he? He was going to visit his daughter for half an hour before she went to bed, engage in a few minutes of mealy-mouthed questions and answers with Jess, then head back to his mum's to sleep in a thirteen-year-old boy's bedroom.

Suddenly the thought of a plate of home-made risotto and a bottle of wine in convivial surroundings struck him as just the cure for the post-holiday blues. And the idea of seeing Joy again, well, he wasn't quite sure how he felt about that. He brought her face to mind, tried to remember what she'd looked like at seventeen, a moody teenager in army surplus, at twenty-five, a radiant bride in cream linen, and the last time he'd seen her, a chic girl about town in jeans and sunglasses, about to leave her husband and reclaim her independence. He remembered that strange feeling he'd had after he spoke to her for the last time, that feeling of wanting to share her journey. Before life had started piling up on top of him like the contents of an over-full cupboard and he'd forgotten all about her again.

But here she was again. The third time she'd come back into his life since Hunstanton. Maybe it was too much of a coincidence to be purely a coincidence. Maybe Cass had been right all those years ago. Maybe the girls had been right at dinner a few weeks earlier. Maybe he did deserve to end up alone and unloved if he didn't 'do the right thing'.

'Here, look.' Bella started ferreting around in her handbag and brought out a notepad with a pony-skin cover and a ballpoint pen. 'I'll give you her address. Eight o'clock, but don't worry if you're late.' She tore a page from the pad and handed it to Vince. 'Ooh, look, finally,' she said as she glanced up at the monitors, 'my bags have arrived. Anyway. You go home and think about it. But for what it's worth, I really really think you should come. Seriously.' She squeezed his fist with her hand and adjusted her shoulder bag. 'See you later!' She waved and trotted off towards the baggage reclaim hall.

Vince stood and watched her go.

He still didn't know what to do.

He folded the piece of paper into a square and slid it into his jacket pocket.

He'd wait until he got home. And then he'd decide.

Sixty-Two

'Red or white?' Joy shouted into the living room.

'White, please,' Bella called back.

'Jules?'

'Whatever's easiest for you.'

'Mick?'

'I'm easy.'

Joy poured Pinot Grigio generously into three wine glasses and brought them through to her guests.

'Look at the bloody colour of you,' she said, pointing at Bella. 'Sickening.'

Bella smiled. 'And I *am* this colour *all over* – in case you were wondering. Every inch of me.'

'So, did you meet anyone?'

'No. Not really. Not in that way. But, I did meet *someone*. A man. At the airport ...'

'Oh, yes ...'

'No. Not a *man* man. A friend of yours,' she glanced at Joy. 'A blast from your past.'

'Oh, my God – who?'

'Someone tall and handsome. Someone who's just getting divorced from his wife. Someone who I gave your address to.'

'You gave my address to someone you met at the airport? Bella – that's terrible.'

'No. It's not. I invited him for dinner – and if he turns

up I can assure you you won't think it's terrible at all.'

'Oh, God, Bella – who is it? You have to tell me.'

'No. It's a surprise.'

'But what if he doesn't come?'

'Then we'll never mention it again.'

'Nooo!' Joy howled in protest, 'Bella. You can't do this to me!'

'Yes, I can,' she said, crossing her legs primly. 'But I wouldn't worry about it. Because he'll definitely turn up. I know he will.'

'Give me a clue.'

'No.'

'Oh, please.'

'No.'

'Oh. God. Do I look all right?' Joy bounced to her feet to examine herself in the mirror.

'You look stunning. Now sit down and relax.'

'Relax? How the hell do you expect me to relax after what you've just told me?'

Joy sat down, then jumped to her feet again as a terrible thought struck her. 'It's not George, is it?' Even now, three years after leaving George, Joy still had regular nightmares in which she found herself in a church or chapel, about to marry George again in the full, dreadful knowledge of the fate that awaited her.

'No, of course it's not *George*. Now just stop talking about it and get on with cooking our dinner.'

Joy scuttled obediently back into the kitchen and took a deep breath.

She pulled a packet of fresh sage from the fridge and tore it into pieces absent-mindedly.

She knew who was coming for dinner.

It was Vince.

It couldn't be anyone else.

She'd had an intense and vivid dream about him last week. She dreamed that they had a little girl and were living somewhere warm in a big, white house. She dreamed that they had long, intense conversations together across a big oak table and ate chocolate cake with marshmallows in it. She dreamed that she'd never felt happier in her life.

She'd felt an intense sadness when she woke up the next morning and realized that it was just a dream. It had felt so real and joyful. It had felt exactly how she wanted her real life to feel and ever since then she'd done nothing but think about Vince.

And the minute Bella had said that just now, about the blast from the past, the tall handsome man at the airport, she'd known it was him. And she also knew that he would come. Because he had to. Because everything else in her life had finally fallen into place. Because the time was right. Because she was ready. Because it was the only thing that made any sense.

She dropped the sage into the risotto and waited for the doorbell to ring.

Sixty-Three

Vince paid the cab driver and stood in front of Joy's house for a moment. The front window was framed with white fairy lights and hung with muslin curtains. He could see candlelight flickering within. It was the most welcoming house on the street. If he'd happened to be walking past, it would have caught his eye. He'd have wondered who lived there, what they were doing.

He wondered the same thing of himself.

Chris had persuaded him to come. Told him he'd be as stupid as he looked if he didn't. And once a man as pragmatic as Chris started rattling on about destiny and fate, Vince decided that maybe it was time for him to start believing, too.

And actually, as he'd ordered himself a minicab from Jess's mum's and said good night to Lara, Vince found that each of his actions started to take on a kind of significance, a resonance, like steps in dance. And as the minutes had ticked by in the cab and his destination had neared, Vince had started to get an overwhelming feeling in the pit of his belly that maybe this was right, that maybe this was exactly what he should be doing and exactly the time he should be doing it.

A man walked past him as he stood outside Joy's house. He was walking a small white dog with brown patches. A dog like the one that he and Joy had stooped to pet outside the Seavue Holiday Home Park all those years ago. He heard her voice, echoing in his mind. 'I like people who like dogs,' she'd said. 'Never trust a man who doesn't like dogs. That's my motto.'

Vince remembered looking down at Joy's hand where it had touched the dog's fur, and then he remembered the feeling that had completely taken him by surprise. The sudden, miraculous, magical realization that had totally overwhelmed him.

Do you believe in love at first sight?

He held that feeling tightly to his chest and rang the doorbell.

THE BEGINNING